# PROTECTING YOU

WRIGHT HEROES OF MAINE
BOOK 5

ROBIN PATCHEN

JDO PUBLISHING

Copyright © 2024 by Robin Patchen

All rights reserved.

No part of this book may be reproduced in any form or by any electronic or mechanical means, including information storage and retrieval systems, without written permission from the author, except for the use of brief quotations in a book review.

Published in Austin, TX.

Cover by Lynette Bonner

Paperback ISBN:

Large Print ISBN:

Hard Cover ISBN:

Library of Congress Control Number:

# NOTE TO ADVANCED READERS

Please overlook errors and the unfinished back matter. If you see an egregious error in the manuscript that you think the copyeditor might miss, don't hesitate to contact me at robin@robinpatchen.com.

One more thing... Please forgive the unfinished cover. If you would like a copy of the book after the full wraparound cover is created, email me, and I'll forward you one when the paperback publishes.

God bless!

Robin

# CHAPTER ONE

Alyssa Wright's client had insisted they meet here.

She'd never been to this restaurant. White tablecloths, sparkling silverware, fine china. The servers all wore crisp button-downs, black slacks, and black aprons. They displayed overpriced bottles of wine with the pride of new parents showing off a treasured child.

Classical music played over hidden speakers, the hush of private conversations interspersed by the clinking of glasses, the tinging of forks and knives on plates, and the occasional pop of a cork.

Despite the complete background check she'd done on her client, the man the maître d' sent her way wasn't what she'd expected. Alyssa had worked for Charles Sanders for months, and she'd formed an opinion of him based on their frequent phone conversations. She knew he'd attended Oxford. His aristocratic British accent confirmed what she'd learned about his wealthy parents. He was the kind of guy who never had to rent a tuxedo because he had one hanging in his closet, Armani labels intact.

She knew the type.

Wearing a perfectly tailored navy sports coat over a pale blue shirt, he was slight and unassuming with swarthy skin, black hair, and thick eyebrows. His cheeks were clean-shaven, though his soft jaw would look manlier with a little scruff. He was no taller than her own five-nine.

Her client skirted the nearest table, and she stood to greet him. "Charles?"

"It's a pleasure to meet you in person." His palm was cool, his voice smooth as silk.

She gestured to the chair opposite hers, and he settled and eyed the menus and water glasses between them.

"Help yourself." She slid her palm around her own so he'd know which glass she'd already sipped from.

A college-aged waitress approached, giving Charles a warm look that had Alyssa studying him more closely.

Though his features were bland and unassuming, there was something attractive about him she couldn't put her finger on. No, attractive wasn't the word. Inviting, maybe? Charming?

"May I get you a drink, sir?" the server asked.

Charles nodded to Alyssa, who said, "Water's fine for me."

"Surely, you'd like something stronger." He held her gaze as if he could convince her through telepathy. "Their wine list is quite extensive."

He hadn't looked at it, which meant he'd been here before. His earnest look made her consider ordering a glass.

For about one second.

She didn't drink alcohol often, and certainly not at business meetings with practical strangers. "I'm happy with water. Thank you."

Charles studied her a moment too long before ordering a glass of Sangiovese.

There was something about the way he watched her, as if he could read her thoughts. Their relationship had always been cordial on the phone, but in person, the man made her skin crawl.

He handed the server their menus. "And an appetizer or two, whatever's popular, but nothing with salsa." He gave a false shudder as if the idea of it horrified him.

Was his arrogance supposed to impress somebody?

Alyssa had perused the menu earlier. "I'd like to try the heirloom tomatoes and burrata. And bring something with lobster for our English friend. That'll be all." She turned to Charles. "If that's all right with you?"

His lips quirked at the corners as if he found her amusing. "Whatever you think."

He seemed accustomed to getting what he wanted, but nobody'd ever accused Alyssa of being accommodating.

However, he was her best-paying client, and she needed the money. Ever since she'd left her government job to start her own cyber-investigation company, she'd struggled to get enough work—and enough income—to justify her decision. One customer had refused to pay a bill, and she'd had a couple of lean months. If not for Charles's regular assignments, she might as well tear down her metaphorical shingle and get a real job.

And then what?

If the business failed, would she need to vacate the apartment her father paid for? Would she be forced to go home to her parents' house—and endure her father's I-told-you-so's?

Anything but that.

Most of her clients were private detectives who needed information available on the internet but didn't have the technical expertise to locate it themselves. Alyssa, given enough breadcrumbs, could dig up almost anything or anyone.

Except paying clients. They weren't so easy to find.

"Tell me about the job," she said.

Charles pulled a lighter from the inside pocket of his jacket.

It wasn't a plastic throwaway but tarnished silver with a vintage patina. He flipped open the top, lit it, then snapped the lid closed, snuffing out the flame, repeating the action a few more times. "I seek a Russian," he finally said. "I have an IP address and the names of some of his business associates. I've heard rumors about his family, though I don't know how accurate the whispers are. The man lives in St. Petersburg, and I believe he traveled to Munich last fall."

The server delivered Charles's wine. He swirled and sniffed it, as only wine connoisseurs do, then took a tiny sip. He nodded to the server. "This will do."

"Very good, sir."

Alyssa did her best not to roll her eyes.

She waited for Charles to continue, but he said nothing else, just opened the lighter, lit the flame, and closed it again.

"That's it?" she asked. "That's all you have?"

"Surely, it is enough for you. You've proved yourself quite capable. I hired you because I was led to believe you could find anybody on the Internet."

"Who told you that?" He'd never told her how he got her name. She'd assumed he'd found her through her online ads.

Charles closed the lighter in his fist. "A man I had an interaction with in Germany last year. He was very tall with dark brown hair and a short beard. I believe he works for the CIA."

Michael? The description fit her cousin, and he'd been in Germany in the fall. Who else in the CIA would recommend her?

Nobody knew her skills like Michael did. Nobody asked her to use them more than he did either, usually for free.

Not that she minded, considering her work had helped save lives. And some of those people were now part of the family—Leila, Jasmine, Eliza, and little Levi.

If Michael trusted this guy enough to give him her name, then Charles must be a decent fellow.

"Are you saying you cannot help me?"

"It's not a lot to go on." But she'd found people with less. "It'll take time and, as is always the case, I won't break any laws."

"Certainly not. I wouldn't ask you to." By the way his lips tugged up on one side, he was saying the words but didn't mean them.

Whatever he expected, Alyssa wasn't going to prison for Charles Sanders or anybody else.

The appetizers were delivered, but Alyssa didn't look away from the man across the table.

Without asking, he served her a bit of the lobster appetizer, then took some for himself. He cut a piece off and swallowed it. "Excellent selection. Please, tell me your objections."

"I'm not sure I can do it."

"Of course you can, Alyssa." He pulled a square of paper from his jacket pocket and held it across the table. "Go ahead."

She unfolded the note and stared at the number he'd written down. All those zeroes. This one job would cover months of expenses. It would justify her existence. Justify her decision to quit her job.

It was more than he'd ever paid her before. Much more than she would have asked.

Which roused her suspicions, but she'd made her boundaries clear.

"I'll initiate the transfer into your account. You'll get the same when you deliver the man's name," Charles said. "If you get a name to me within two days, I'll double it."

"What happens if I can't do it?" She waved the paper between them. "I assume you'll want this back?"

"Certainly not." He flicked his hands toward her, brushing

away her question. "That is for your trouble. I know you'll do your best, and if you can't find him"—he shrugged—"no harm, no foul, as they say."

This was her chance to hang onto her dream—and prove to Dad she hadn't made the biggest mistake of her life when she'd quit her job.

So what if she didn't like Charles Sanders? She worked with a lot of arrogant clients. This one was no different. Just better paying.

She held out her hand. "We have a deal."

He slid his palm against hers, and despite all those zeroes, when she caught the brief but unmistakable triumph that crossed his expression, she had to stifle a shudder.

She pulled away. "I look forward to—"

"Darling!"

The voice twinged her memory, familiar enough that she couldn't help looking toward the person who'd spoken it, though she was certainly nobody's *darling*.

The man headed straight to their table. "Sorry to interrupt. I couldn't wait to see you and took a chance you'd be finished." He bent toward Alyssa, his back to Charles, and kissed her cheek.

Callan Templeton?

What was happening?

He whispered, "Trust me. Go with it." His words were more breathed than spoken, sending shivers of pleasure down her spine, which annoyed her as much as the interruption.

Callan straightened and turned to her client, sticking out his hand. "Caleb Thompson. Sorry to interrupt."

Wait. *Caleb?*

"Charles Sanders." He stood to shake his hand. "Please, join us."

"If it's okay." Callan shot a look toward Alyssa as if asking permission, which he obviously wasn't, all things considered.

He took an empty chair from an adjacent table and scooted it beside hers, and she didn't object, not because she wanted him there but because... Well, she knew Callan. She didn't *like* him, but she had no reason not to trust him.

Whereas Charles, despite his connection to Michael, gave her the creeps. She had no reason to trust this smooth-talking client of hers.

Callan, a.k.a. Caleb, knew something she didn't.

Of course he did. Because the CIA gave Callan access, all the access she'd craved.

Old bitterness infected her lungs and made her itch to clear her throat.

"I take it you two are together?" Charles gave Alyssa a pointed look.

"Actually—"

"I've been out of town for so long that it doesn't feel like it." Callan-slash-Caleb gripped her hand on the table, squeezing a little too hard. "How long has it been?"

"Feels like years." Was that her voice, all normal and flippant?

His smile was light. "I've missed you, too, darling." He scooted his chair closer and wrapped his arm around her shoulders. "She hates it when I travel, but work beckons. You understand."

He was talking about her as if she weren't there. Was this how he treated actual girlfriends? She was scanning the table for a knife. Why hadn't she ordered a steak? The butter knife would do minor damage, but a well-aimed fork—

"Too bad." Charles gave her a dark look that made her almost happy Callan's arm claimed her. Almost. "Perhaps that explains why she wouldn't have a drink with me."

"Loyal to a T. That's why I'm marrying her."

Whoa. *Marrying?*

Charles flicked a glance at the naked ring finger on her left hand.

"You gotta claim the good ones before they get away." Callan added a wink, like he and Charles were old and dear friends, then leaned in and lowered his voice. "We haven't told our families yet. We've been savoring it, you know?"

"Certainly." Something about his countenance told her he was unsettled by Callan's presence.

*Join the club, buddy.*

"What takes you away from your lovely fiancée for such long periods?"

"I sell computer hardware to small and midsize municipalities—cities, towns, and counties—all up and down the East Coast."

The lie slipped off Callan's tongue as if he spoke it regularly. Maybe he did.

"Sounds fascinating." By his smirk, Charles thought Callan's job—fake job—was anything but fascinating.

"Did you two get your business completed?" Callan/Caleb asked.

"We did." Charles pushed his chair back and stood, focusing on Alyssa. "It was a pleasure."

She would have stood as well, except Callan and the wall boxed her in. "I'll be in touch as soon as I know something."

"I look forward to hearing from you." He walked toward the door.

Callan called too loudly to his back, "Nice to meet you!"

As soon as her client was out of sight, Alyssa shifted to face the intruder. "What in the actual—?"

His lips met hers, soft but insistent. It was a shut-up kiss.

But...oh boy.

She needed to push him away. She should definitely not enjoy the kiss she'd dreamed about for four years during college, when Callan had been both her biggest rival and her biggest crush. He'd reveled in the first role and remained, thank heavens, ignorant of the second.

Too soon, he ended the kiss and backed away just far enough to meet her eyes. "Listen to me, Alyssa." His voice was low but insistent.

She managed a nod.

"I guarantee he has people here surveilling you—us, right now. And I know we have people here. Unless you want to land on the terrorist watch list, you'll play along."

What was he talking about?

"Don't look," he said, as if she were the biggest idiot in the world.

Had she? Well, how did you not look when somebody claimed you were being watched? "What is happening?"

"The man you just shared a meal with..."

Appetizers, not that she'd eaten any of them.

"Is a terrorist." Callan smiled like he was discussing a Red Sox game with his favorite person in the world, though his voice remained low. "He's wanted for kidnapping and arms smuggling—not to mention murder."

Callan's words and facial expression were so incongruous that she almost laughed, which would only add to the story he was trying to sell.

Wait. Murder?

"But he knows my cousin." She leaned back and looked at—really looked at—Callan's face for the first time since he'd sat down.

His blond hair was as trim as it'd been when he'd gotten out of the Army. He'd grown a matching beard that had unexpected hints of red. A few wrinkles fanned out from his pale blue eyes, which surprised her, considering he couldn't be much older than her thirty years. Those wrinkles didn't detract from his looks. If anything, they only made him more handsome.

Which was the last thing she needed to notice right now. Especially when his eyes narrowed in frustration. "You don't mean Michael."

"How do you know Michael?"

"It's a small community." He brushed off her question as if it were irrelevant. "You're sure that's what he said? That he knows Michael?"

"Not in so many words, but he described him. He said he got my name from him."

That had Callan's lips pressing closed for a second. Then he seemed to remember they were pretending to be on a date or something, and he grinned. "Ask Michael about Dariush Ghazi. I bet he's heard of him."

Dariush Ghazi.

Not Charles Sanders.

She would ask Michael, but he was on his honeymoon, and he and Leila were taking the whole "moon" part of it seriously, planning to be gone for a month.

This was ridiculous. Alyssa needed out of this restaurant. She'd stand if not for Callan's too-solid body blocking her exit. There was no room for her to push her chair back or swing her feet to the side. "Would you go away?"

"No." He laughed, though she wasn't joking. "Eat your dinner."

"I'm not hungry."

"Humor me."

The server came by, delivered him a fresh glass of water, and asked if he wanted anything. The woman regarded Callan as if he were on the menu.

"Just the check, please," he said.

"The other gentleman paid for it and whatever else you two might need."

"Perfect!" His false enthusiasm was giving Alyssa a headache. "For now, we'll just finish these."

She cleared Charles's place setting and left a fresh plate and silverware for Callan.

After she walked away, he turned his gaze to Alyssa again, his back to the rest of the room. "Eat. I'm serious. We have to sell it or he'll know you lied to him."

"You didn't give me much choice. Why didn't you just mind your own business?"

"He's my business, Alyssa." Callan whispered in her ear as if sharing an intimate secret. "He is my business, and now that you're involved with him, so are you."

"I'm not involved with him." She pushed back, but Callan snaked his arm around her shoulders, holding her in place.

With a smile on his face, he said, "It's not my fault you decided to do business with a terrorist."

"I'll just back out. If you'd told me—"

"There's no backing out with this guy." Callan's words were low and hot against her skin. "I'm sorry, but as soon as you accepted his check, you ran out of choices. Probably before that, back when you took the first job. I assume there have been a few before this one?"

She hated that he had guessed that.

"Get used to pretending to like me." Callan backed away enough to smile at her. "Until this is over, I'm not leaving your side. Now, eat your food."

Eat? Was he kidding?

She pushed her plate away. "Tell me what's going on."

He pushed it back. "Later, darling."

Alyssa wanted to know now. She wanted to insist she didn't need Callan's protection or anything else from him.

And she wanted him on the other side of the table—or the country—so she could think straight.

But since none of those was going to happen right now, she took one of the tomato slices onto her small plate, added some of the cheese, and slid a bite into her mouth.

The tomato tasted like it was fresh from the garden. The cheese was smooth and creamy, and the tangy balsamic glaze brought the flavors together perfectly.

It was almost good enough to make her forget this crazy situation.

Callan dug into the lobster, uttering a low moan. "Holy cow. This is amazing. Have you tried it?"

"Lobster is lobster. It's not my favorite."

Callan finished his glass of water. Before he had a chance to look for a server, one was there to refill it.

Callan thanked him. "I could get used to this."

Between bites, he talked about nothing—inflation, traffic, weather—keeping up a steady stream of conversation.

She responded at the appropriate times, barely paying attention to what he was saying, forcing occasional nibbles of the tomatoes and cheese.

What had she gotten herself into?

AS SOON AS Charles was out of sight, Alyssa shifted to face the intruder. "What in the actual—?"

His lips met hers, soft but insistent. It was a shut-up kiss, she knew that.

But...*oh boy.*

She needed to push him away. She should definitely *not* enjoy the kiss she'd dreamed about for four years, when Callan had been both her biggest rival and her biggest crush. He'd reveled in the first role and remained, thank heavens, ignorant of the second.

Too soon, he ended the kiss and shifted just far enough away to meet her eyes. "Listen to me, Alyssa." His voice was low but insistent. "Are you listening?"

She managed a nod.

"I guarantee he has people here surveilling you—us, right now. And I *know* we have people here. Unless you want to land on the terrorist watch list, you'll play along."

What was he talking about?

"Don't look," he said, as if she were the biggest idiot in the world.

Had she? Well, how did you *not* look when somebody claimed you were being watched? "What is happening?"

"The man you just shared a meal with..."

Appetizers, not that she'd eaten any.

"...is a terrorist." Callan smiled like he was discussing a Red Sox game with his favorite person in the world, though his voice remained low. "He's wanted for kidnapping and arms smuggling —not to mention murder."

Callan's words and facial expression were so incongruous that she almost laughed, which would only add to the story he was trying to sell.

Wait. *Murder?*

She stifled the urge to look around again, as if an ax-wielding crazy might be sneaking up behind her at that very moment.

It didn't make sense, though. "He knows my cousin." She backed up and looked at—really looked at—Callan's face for the first time since he'd barged in.

His blond hair was as trim as it'd been last time she saw him. He'd grown a matching beard—trimmed very short—that had unexpected hints of red. A few wrinkles fanned out from his pale blue eyes, which surprised her, considering he couldn't be much older than her thirty years. Those wrinkles didn't detract from his good looks.

That was the last thing she needed to notice right now. Especially when his eyes narrowed in frustration. "You don't mean Michael."

"How do you know my cousin?"

"It's a small community." He brushed off her question as if it were irrelevant. "You're sure that's what he said? That he knows Michael?"

"Not in so many words, but he described him. He said he got my name from him."

That had Callan's lips pressing closed for a second. Then, he seemed to remember they were pretending to be on a date or something, and he grinned. "Ask Michael about Dariush Ghazi. I bet he's heard of him."

Dariush Ghazi.

Not Charles Sanders.

She would ask Michael, but he was on his honeymoon, and he and Leila were taking the whole "moon" part of it seriously, planning to be gone for a month.

This was ridiculous. Alyssa needed out of this restaurant. She'd stand if not for Callan's too solid body blocking her exit. There was no room for her to push her chair back or swing her feet to the side. "Would you go away?"

"No." He laughed, though she wasn't joking. "Eat your dinner."

"I'm not hungry."

"Humor me."

The server came by, delivered Callan a fresh glass of water, and asked if him wanted anything, all the while regarding him as if he were on the menu.

"Just the check," he said.

"The other gentleman paid for it and whatever else you two might need."

"Perfect!" His false enthusiasm was giving Alyssa a headache. "For now, we'll finish these."

The woman cleared Charles's dishes and left a fresh plate for Callan.

After she walked away, he turned his gaze to Alyssa again, his back to the rest of the room. "Eat. I'm serious. We have to sell it or he'll know you lied to him."

Alyssa didn't like being dictated to, certainly not by this guy.

But a few of the words he'd said resonated still. *Terrorist. Murderer.*

She forced a bite of tomato salad into her churning stomach. She'd gotten herself into something. Maybe Callan was trying to help her get out.

But he was a CIA agent whose plans were much grander than one cyber-investigator.

So maybe not.

## CHAPTER TWO

Fine.

Maybe the kiss hadn't been completely necessary.

Callan Templeton could've found an equally effective—and much less distracting—way to keep Alyssa quiet. Besides, didn't a guy need some kind of signed permission slip to kiss a woman these days? He could probably be sued or imprisoned for that move.

No way would Alyssa ever give him permission to kiss her.

His college roommate had once called her the ice queen. She wore a veneer of toughness, but Callan had always suspected that warmth and passion hovered beneath her brittle surface.

He'd been right. He'd tasted both in her kiss.

And *that* was why he shouldn't have done it. Because when he was surrounded by enemies, he definitely shouldn't be thinking about her lips.

Alyssa was glaring at him with that familiar mixture of irritation and confusion. She'd pushed her blond hair behind her ears. Her large, honey-brown eyes were narrowed, her lips pinched, which made her high cheekbones even more pronounced.

It was an expression he knew well. At Boston College, they had the same major and often competed with each other—who had the better design, the better grades, the higher class rank? Whenever she lost, she'd wear that same look.

Irritation that he'd bested her (again). Confusion as to how she could possibly have lost. Determination not to let it happen again.

He'd lived his life to get that look.

He finished the melt-in-your-mouth, tastes-so-good-it-should-be-illegal lobster. If he ordered another, the restaurant would add it to Ghazi's tab. Callan certainly couldn't afford it, especially not now that he had Peri to worry about.

He put thoughts of her away. He didn't want his daughter anywhere near this job, this life he'd built.

And there was a problem he hadn't figured out how to solve.

Maybe a problem he should've considered before he'd hopped to do the bidding of a disembodied voice on the phone. But the voice had told him that Ghazi would be here. And that *somebody* would be in danger.

The *somebody* hadn't been named, but surely whoever had tipped him off had meant Alyssa.

Callan hadn't worked out who the man behind the voice was yet, but he would. Meanwhile, he was glad he'd followed his instincts and come to the restaurant. Alyssa was involved in something way over her head, and if he knew her—and he *did*—she wouldn't ask for anyone's help.

"Do you mind?" He nodded to the tomato dish, which she somehow hadn't finished. Who couldn't manage to eat four tomato slices and some cheese?

"I've lost my appetite." She deadpanned the words, and he couldn't help the smile he knew must annoy her to pieces.

A couple of middle-aged women stepped out of a shop and turned toward them on the sidewalk. Alyssa angled toward him to let them pass.

He slid his arm around her, pulling her against his side.

"Charles is a client." She tugged away, but Callan held on. "An entrepreneur."

"Fine. Maybe I was jealous." Lowering his voice, he added, "There's no telling who's listening."

She made a show of watching traffic pass on the busy street. City noises were loud, but what kind of technology was being employed to eavesdrop on them?

"I've been working with Charles Sanders for months."

Callan slowed to look at her. "You've met him before?"

"This was the first time we met in person, but yeah, I've done jobs for him all year. He's never asked me to do anything suspicious or illegal. I've made those boundaries clear with all my clients, and I reiterated that tonight."

Funny that she'd felt the need to mention her boundaries to the so-called Charles Sanders—and to Callan. That told him she wasn't as certain as she was trying to make it sound that the man was aboveboard.

"You'll need to tell me all about those jobs."

"That's between me and my client."

Not for long, but he didn't argue. "What did he hire you to do tonight?" He made the question conversational, the kind of thing a fiancé would ask.

"He wants me to find a name for him."

"Who?"

"I haven't found it yet, and when I do, I certainly won't be telling you."

Callan laughed, though he felt no humor. He shifted close to whisper, "It's national security, darling."

She ducked away and shot a glare.

They reached Hereford Street and turned.

"When we get to your place, you can tell me all about him."

"I don't know what you think is going to happen..."

Callan kissed the top of her head. "He's a terrorist."

"And there's zero chance you're wrong? You're that confident?"

"Correct."

She bristled. If she were a porcupine, he'd be headed to the ER.

"Fine. I'll just return his money and—"

"It's too late."

"You don't know that."

"We'll see. My guess is it's too late for that. We're just going to have to wing it."

"I'm not exactly a *wing-it* kind of woman."

"You'll learn."

They crossed Commonwealth Avenue. Halfway down the block on the opposite side, Alyssa climbed the steps in front of an old brownstone.

He waited until she'd unlocked the exterior door, then followed her into the lobby. Small, octagonal black-and-white tiles stretched across the floor beneath gleaming woodwork and freshly painted cream-colored walls.

It wasn't fancy, certainly not compared with the five-star restaurant where they'd just eaten, but it was out of his price range.

It was also too quiet. He assumed there was at least one listening device.

He followed her up the winding staircase.

"I have an idea." His voice was bright and enthusiastic. "Let's get out of the city for a couple of days. Take a weekend away."

At the landing between the floors, she turned to glare. "I have a job to do."

He nodded forward, telling her to keep going. "You can bring your laptop, darling. I can share you, a little."

"No." Though the staircase wound upward three more flights, she stopped on the second story and headed to the apartment straight ahead. She pulled out her keys to unlock the door.

A thump came from inside.

He gripped her arm. "Do you have a roommate?"

She shook her head, eyes wide.

He urged her back toward the stairway. "Up," he hissed. "Go up."

Without watching to make sure she did, he focused on the apartment. He was about to go in when a man barreled out, straight into Callan.

He stumbled back and crashed into the stair rail. Pain shot through his shoulder, but he ignored it, gripping the railing to keep from tumbling down.

The man wore a face mask and aimed a fist at Callan's head.

He ducked to the side, then angled sideways and elbowed the guy in the gut.

An amateur would be stopped, at least momentarily, but this guy was no amateur.

He bent, spun, and jabbed flat fingers toward Callan's throat.

Callan protected himself but, thanks to the awkward railing and close wall, couldn't plant his feet. He gripped his attacker's jacket, and they both fell.

They were wrestling, each fighting for the upper hand, when another man ran out of the apartment.

Callan didn't get a look at his face but caught sight of a bag swinging from the guy's hand.

*Alyssa!* Where was she? Had she gone upstairs like he'd asked?

His attacker was trying to scramble back, but Callan grabbed his ankles and yanked, pulling him off balance.

By the pounding of the heavy footsteps, the second man was headed to the lobby.

Callan's attacker jerked away and bolted.

Callan popped to his feet. He wanted to chase, but...

*Alyssa.*

He waited until the heavy door downstairs slammed, then called, "Alyssa?"

She bent over the railing above, eyes wide. "Are you all right?"

"Yeah. You?"

"Sorry. I didn't know what to do."

She started down, but he stopped her with a palm. "Stay there until I get you. Scream if you need me."

Again not waiting for her answer, he moved into her apartment, cataloguing the space.

Small foyer with four doors, all open. One led to a living area/office, another to a bedroom. The one on the left opened to a tiny galley kitchen. The one behind led to the bathroom.

Pretty pale blue curtains. Sand-colored walls. White furniture. Stunning landscape photographs on the walls.

Dumped drawers. Gaping file cabinet. Papers scattered. Computer tower lying in the middle of the floor, disassembled.

A whoosh of air had him swiveling, preparing to fight.

Standing in the open doorway, Alyssa's eyes widened.

"What part of stay there—?"

"This is my apartment." She stepped past him and took in the chaos of her office. "What did they...? Why would anybody—?"

He closed and locked her apartment door. "Pack a bag."

She swiveled to face him. "What? No. I'm not—"

"You're not staying here, *darling*." He couldn't help the aggressive tone. Seriously, was she going to fight him on everything? He shifted close and lowered his voice, making it barely audible. "They could have planted a listening device."

She looked around as if the intruders might've left a cassette recorder in plain sight.

He inhaled a deep breath for patience and blew it out, then reached toward her. When her eyes widened like it was Callan she feared, he let his hand drop. "You're not safe here."

She seemed to be taking in the magnitude of what had happened.

"For all we know," he said, "they're gathering troops and preparing to return. Please, trust me."

She blinked and stared for seconds that felt like hours.

Then she swiveled and marched into her bedroom.

He stood in the threshold while she pulled a small suitcase from her closet. The intruders either hadn't had time to search this room or had been certain whatever they sought would be in the office.

She opened it on her bed, then looked at him. "How long do you think?"

"Grab clothes for a few days. Jeans, sweaters. You should bring some business attire, just in case."

"I know how to pack." But there was no vinegar in her tone.

"Sometime, it's hard to think these things through."

She didn't say anything as she pulled items from her closet and bureau and put them in the bag.

When she paused, seeming confused, he said, "Toiletries, hairbrush."

She slipped past him into the bathroom and returned with a fancy, feminine Dopp kit or makeup bag or whatever women called those things.

"Undergarments. Pajamas."

She grabbed the items as he listed them.

"Leisure stuff—sweatpants, sweatshirts."

By the time she added those, her suitcase was nearly full.

She paused as if waiting for more instructions. A look crossed her face that he'd never seen on his tough-as-nails rival. Vulnerability.

She blinked, and her expression shuttered.

"You have your laptop, right?" He nodded to where she'd dropped her purse on the nightstand. "In your bag?"

"Yeah."

"Charger? Planner? Tablet?"

"Oh." She slipped past him and into the office, where she yanked a cord from an outlet. While she wound it in her hands, she scanned the space, then toed things on the floor aside. "My iPad's..."

"Probably stolen."

"And my planner."

"I'm sorry." He itched to pull her close to offer comfort. But stayed planted where he was. "Can you think of anything else?"

She shook her head.

"You won't be back until...until we know what this was about."

Again, he waited for her to argue. Again, she seemed to consider it. Instead, she said, "Where are we going?"

He smiled. "Somewhere safe, darling." Getting back into character. "Somewhere nobody will find you until we can figure out who would do this."

"Why, though? They've already been here and gotten what they wanted. Can't I just stay?" She returned to her bedroom and dropped the charger cord into her oversized purse. Then faced him, waiting for him to explain himself.

"What if they didn't get what they wanted?" He gave her

laptop a pointed look. "What if what they really want is on that? Or in your head?"

"But why would—?"

"I don't know. What I *do* know is that you're in danger. What kind of fiancé would I be if I left you here alone?"

She pressed her lips closed, most likely barely keeping her argument inside. "Fine." She zipped up her suitcase and shouldered her bag.

He grabbed the luggage, then urged her into the hallway, where they stopped so she could lock the door. Not that the flimsy deadbolt would keep anyone out who wanted in.

Now what?

He'd promised to take her somewhere safe. But where? His apartment was secure, but if they went there, then Ghazi's people, who were no doubt still watching, would figure out who he really was.

The fictional Caleb Thompson's address was the size of a rented mailbox at a UPS store. Literally.

One step at a time.

Right now, he needed to get them away from here. And then away from whoever tailed them without letting on what he was doing. Because he was playing the part of a salesman, not a CIA agent, and the last thing he wanted was for Ghazi to figure out that anyone was onto him.

And Callan had to do it all with a beautiful blonde he'd claimed was his fiancée—while she questioned his every move.

Were they having fun yet?

## CHAPTER THREE

Alyssa trembled as if they'd stepped into an Alaska winter, not a mild Boston spring night.

Her teeth chattered.

She'd kept it together, so far. She'd kept it together while listening to the scuffle a floor below, though she was mortified that she'd run away. She, the woman who'd wanted nothing more than to be a spy like her father and her cousin Michael, had hidden like a mouse.

Shame heated her face.

But what had her choices been? No weapon, no training, no...clue. Callan told her to run, so she ran.

Stupid, obedient coward.

Or maybe that made her wise.

She'd kept it together as she'd packed, though she would surely have forgotten something important if not for Callan's gentle reminders.

She'd kept it together while they stood in her building's foyer, her watching out the window for enemies, him tapping on his phone.

Now, they walked along the sidewalk, exposed, and she still kept it together. As far as he could tell, anyway.

"Can you pull your suitcase?"

"What?" Then Callan's words registered. "Yeah, okay." She plopped her purse on top and then took the handle.

"Thanks." He kept his voice low. "I want to be ready, just in case."

She scanned their surroundings, certain that new enemies were going to pop out from an alley or drive up in a dark van. People were everywhere tonight, young professionals and students out to enjoy the spring temperature.

They crossed Comm Ave, a wide, divided road. The heavy traffic made it impossible to talk.

On the far side, she asked, "Where are we going?"

"South."

"That's really helpful. Thanks."

He shot her a smile. "You okay?"

"I'm fine." Not really, but he was kind enough not to call her on it. "Seriously." She stopped on the sidewalk, causing people to stream around her. "Where are you taking me?"

He gripped her arm and tugged. "Could you just trust me?"

Considering she was with him, she clearly trusted him. But why didn't he trust her enough to give her an answer?

He turned toward the Hynes Convention Center and snaked along walking paths that led around it.

"You're trying to lose them."

"Darling." His smile was tight. "Would you please shut up?"

"Why? Nobody can hear—"

"You don't know that."

"Fine."

They reached the Prudential Center, one of the tallest buildings in the city. The lower floors—all restaurants and shops—were open to pedestrians. They meandered to the entrance.

As soon as the doors closed behind them, he grabbed her arm and started running.

On the opposite side of the giant atrium, he pushed open a door, slowing as they exited the Huntington Avenue side. He led her down the steps and across the courtyard to a waiting car.

A man stepped out and popped the trunk. "Caleb?"

"That's us! Hop in, darling." He reached for the suitcase handle. "I'll get this."

She grabbed her purse and settled in the backseat while Callan plopped her luggage into the trunk.

It slammed, and he slid in beside her.

The driver settled behind the wheel. "South Station, yeah?"

"Thanks." Callan exhaled a long breath. Though his tone had been casual, tension tightened the skin around his lips.

"Are you all right?" she asked.

His gaze flicked to the driver. "Why wouldn't I be?"

For crying out loud. Did they have to keep up the stupid charade with an Uber driver?

Callan took her hand and squeezed. "Just trying to figure out where we should go. My place won't work because of the exterminator. And now your place won't work." He raised his voice. "Her apartment was broken into. Jerks made a mess of it."

"Frickin' thieves," the driver said. "Imagine if they used their powahs for good, not evil, eh? Got jobs like the rest of us."

"You're not kidding, man."

Seemed Callan was the kind of guy who made conversation with strangers.

She'd never been able to do that.

Callan leaned in and whispered. "I know a place. It's not exactly the Ritz, but they don't ask any questions."

There were places like that on both ends of the cost spectrum. Cheap by-the-hour dumps, and high-end boutique hotels.

At the second, the patrons paid very well to ensure their privacy would be honored above all.

Not that she was a snob, but if she had to choose between the two, she'd take the second, thank you very much.

"Why don't we go to—?"

Callan coughed, shaking his head.

Right. Discretion.

She tapped a note on her phone and showed it to him.

He read it, then looked up the place up she'd suggested on his cell. His eyes widened, and he shook his head.

"Why not?"

He rubbed his thumb against his fingers, telling her his objection was the cost.

She whispered back, "I got it."

Not that she could afford the price tag, but Dad had an account, and he'd told her she could use it anytime she needed. What he lacked in affection, he made up for in cash.

Callan didn't look happy, but he agreed. It was the first battle she'd won since this whole bizarre thing started.

It took two Ubers, a taxi ride, a quick stop at an office supply store, and a two-block trek. All the while, she worried, tried not to look over her shoulder, and told herself they were safe.

Finally, they reached the place she'd chosen, a five-story brick brownstone in Cambridge that, aside from the small sign outside that simply read *Rooming House*, looked like all the other brownstones on the block.

The door opened as they approached, and a uniformed bellman said, "Welcome back, Ms. Wright."

She felt Callan's surprise but didn't react to it. "Thank you."

The small lobby tucked into what used to be a sitting room consisted of a tall counter that was either antique or replicas. The fiftysomething man on the far side gave them a practiced smile. "Good evening, Ms. Wright."

"It's good to see you, Jonathan. Is the suite available?"

"It is." He tapped on a laptop. "Will your father be joining you?"

"Not this time. And we would appreciate your discretion."

"Certainly, Ms. Crenshaw." He shifted to the false name seamlessly as he tapped his keyboard. He handed a small folder containing their key-cards to Callan. "Enjoy your stay, Mr. Crenshaw."

They took the elevator to the fifth floor. Though the building looked narrow from the front, years before she was born the hotel had expanded into the brownstones on both sides. It was much larger—and more confusing—than anybody would guess from the street.

Alyssa led Callan along a maze of corridors that had them going through open doors, stepping up in one place, then stepping back down in another.

Callan asked, "Should we drop breadcrumbs?"

"Almost there." She led him down one more hallway and stopped in front of Dad's favorite suite.

Callan unlocked it, and she stepped inside and exhaled, blowing out her fear. Nobody would be able to find them here. They were safe. For now.

# CHAPTER FOUR

Callan followed Alyssa through a door labeled *The Library*. Rich people didn't need anything so banal as *numbers* to differentiate their hotel suites.

He didn't hate that. Even if Ghazi or his men figured out where they were staying, they'd never be able to locate their room.

"Crenshaw?" Callan asked.

The clerk had come up with the name so quickly, it was as if he made up aliases every day.

"We'll be in the system under that name." Alyssa continued into a living room.

Callan passed a bathroom on one side of a short hallway, a kitchenette on the other, then stopped in the living room's threshold.

This was a hotel room?

The dining table and chairs alone were worth more than his car.

Definitely not in Kansas anymore.

The overstuffed sofa and love seat faced a sixty-inch TV

that rested on a carved mahogany sideboard. That matched the end tables and coffee table, all of which probably dated to the nineteenth century. A desk perpendicular to the bay windows looked even older, though the wheeled chair pushed up to it was modern, and even that was out of his price range.

On the two walls facing the deck, antique bookshelves were filled with books. Maybe that was why they called this room the library.

The carpet was plush, the drapes lavish, the artwork expensive reproductions. Were the books first editions?

Everything about it was sturdy and masculine. Callan had never met Gavin Wright, but he'd heard stories. He'd seen the man on more than one occasion. The room suited him.

"Does your dad own this place or something?" Callan asked.

"He just comes to the city a lot." Alyssa had already settled on the sofa, toed off her shoes, and plopped her feet onto the coffee table. "This is his favorite suite. Once, it was taken—he was offended they would dare rent it to someone else—and they gave him a similar one on this floor. Similar in design, but the decor was all pink toile and lace." She grinned, shaking her head. "He was not impressed."

Callan still didn't move into the living room. He'd known Gavin Wright made a killing when he left government service. The private sector paid more, no question about it. But this much more? Crazy.

"What will he think about us being here? Are they going to put this on his bill? Because I want us to be safe, but I can't afford this place, and I don't like the idea of you paying—"

"Dad will cover it." She gathered her blond hair on top of her head, reclined, and let it drape over the couch.

A beautiful, graceful lioness, relaxing in her den.

"Don't worry about it." She flicked her hand toward him as

if to flick away the thousands of dollars per night this place must cost.

He didn't like it. He didn't like relying on someone else to pay his way. He didn't like knowing he could never set foot in this building, much less this room, if not for Alyssa.

Hopefully, Gavin Wright would forgive the expense if it meant his daughter was safe. If Callan took her elsewhere and she were to get hurt... *That* would be unforgivable.

Callan checked out the two bedrooms. One had a four-poster bed and an attached private bathroom. The other had two queens and a door that led to the same bathroom he'd seen from the hallway. He carried her suitcase into the master. "I'm going through this."

She pushed to her feet and followed. "What? Why?"

He'd already unzipped her luggage on the bed and opened it. "Your intruders weren't concerned about you knowing they'd been there. If *I* wanted to track your movements, I'd put a tracker in this." Still bent over her things, he turned her way. "Do you have other luggage?"

"Just that and a big one for longer trips."

"Okay, good." The suitcase had been in her closet, on a high shelf, so it was likely that, if they'd wanted to track her, they would've dropped something into one of the pockets. He'd check the clothes first. He pulled out a pair of yoga pants and ran his hands along the seams. Nothing out of the ordinary in the hems, and it had no pockets.

She watched him from the end of the bed. "If they put a tracker in it, then they could be on their way here right now." Her voice rose the slightest at the end, as if the idea terrified her and she was working to hide it.

"Unlikely." He added a reassuring smile to the word. "If you were their target, then what happened at your building would have gone down very differently." He worked his way through her clothes.

But she wasn't wrong. He should've done this before they reached the hotel. He'd been so focused on getting here, getting Alyssa out of danger, he hadn't been thinking.

He needed to do be, be better.

When he reached toward a bulging zipper pocket, she slapped her hand over it. "You're not sifting through my underwear."

"I'm not a pervert, Alyssa. I'm trying to—"

"Just tell me what you're looking for."

He stepped back. "Anything that's not clothes. Anything that doesn't belong. It'll be tiny, maybe no bigger than a fingernail."

She scooped all her personal items into her arms and carried them to the bureau. She picked up a pair of socks, checked each one, and then folded them again and set them in a drawer.

Confident she was being thorough, he focused on the suitcase itself, probing every pocket and fold with his fingertips.

"Nothing that doesn't belong." She closed the drawer and faced him. "You?"

"It's clean." He zipped the suitcase and slid it into her closet. "I think we're safe here."

"We *are* safe here." Alyssa grabbed the knob on the door that led to the living room.

This was the second time he'd gone into Alyssa's bedroom in a matter of hours. Mom would slap him upside the head for his rudeness.

Mom was so tiny that she'd need to climb a step stool first.

"The entrance is always locked," Alyssa explained, "and the bellhop doesn't let people in without Jonathan's say-so. Jonathan only opens to people he recognizes. Others have to buzz for entrance and explain who they are and why they're there before he'll allow them inside."

Callan had known, theoretically, that such places existed. His family vacations consisted of tent camping. They went fishing and hiking and cooked hot dogs over a fire. If they wanted to splurge, they'd rent a canoe.

Her life wasn't even in the same universe as his.

Tangible proof that he didn't belong with this woman. Not that she'd ever shown the slightest interest in him.

Knowing that had never kept him from wishing things could be different.

CONSIDERING the maze of hallways they'd navigated to get here, he was surprised when he looked out the window to find they faced the street and not an alley. He usually had a good sense of direction, but he'd gotten turned around.

He closed the drapes against the darkness and rolled the desk chair closer to the sofa where Alyssa had settled. Sitting with his back to the window, he propped his feet on the coffee table. He refused to be intimated by furniture. "Your father takes security seriously. Which makes sense, considering what he does for a living."

"The understatement of the century." Her eyes narrowed. "You know my father?"

"I know of him. I've never met him personally, but I've heard him speak. So, do you believe me now?"

"That something weird is going on? Sure, but what? Why would Charles break into my apartment minutes after I agreed to work with him? I still think you could be wrong about him."

"If I'm wrong about Ghazi, then so is the entire intelligence community."

"It wouldn't be the first time. But I'm saying maybe my client isn't this Ghazi person. I never work with anybody without doing a background check on them, and he checked out."

Callan opened his phone and navigated to a website. Then, he handed the phone to her.

She scrolled down, scanning all the fake information about the fictional Caleb Thompson.

"Go ahead and click the links," Callan said. "You'll find social media profiles and posts. You'll find old addresses, where Caleb went to college and high school. You'll learn that Caleb volunteers to feed the homeless occasionally—there are photos of that. He teaches Bible study at his church."

She handed him the phone back. "So everything I read about Charles Sanders was a lie."

"Sorry to prove to you, once again, that you're not infallible."

"I never said I was."

"You spent four years in college trying to prove you're better than me."

"I *am* better than you." She glared.

He grinned. "At a few things, maybe." His amusement faded. "Charles Sanders *is* Dariush Ghazi. And Dariush Ghazi is a very dangerous man."

He needed to convince her, sooner rather than later.

"Fine. Why would he break in when I agreed to work with him?"

"Maybe he got spooked when I showed up. Maybe he wanted to find something to use to blackmail you. Or maybe it wasn't him. Who else—?"

"Why couldn't it just be thieves, like you said to the Uber driver?"

"Think about it, Alyssa. Why *your* apartment? It wasn't

exactly a crime of convenience. Your building is secure. Even if someone gained access, there are lots of other apartments they could've chosen. Why yours?"

Her lips pressed together. "But why would Charles do it? There's nothing there he could use to blackmail me."

"His name is not Charles."

"You know what I mean."

Callan dropped his feet to the floor. "Let's go over what they took."

"My iPad. The hard drive from my desktop. Which reminds me..." She dug through her purse and pulled out the thumb drive she'd purchased on the way here.

"You think they could access the information on it?"

"Probably. Nothing is completely secure. You know that. Every code can be broken if given enough time and resources. That's why all my sensitive data is stored on a secure cloud server."

"Which can also be accessed."

"But they'd have to know where to look."

"Will the desktop tell them where to look?"

"Yes. Which is why I need to download everything off the server." She powered up her laptop.

"What else was taken?"

"My planner, which holds my calendar and to-do list."

Funny that she kept a paper planner, considering all the technology at her fingertips.

"That's all I know," she said, "but it's not like there was time to look around."

"Did you have anything of value?"

She shrugged, though it didn't come off as casual as she probably hoped. "Jewelry. Not super valuable, but sentimental. It's not like I keep bundles of cash hidden in the cookie jar."

"The thing is, I don't think your burglars were Ghazi's people."

"You don't?" She set the laptop aside. "I thought...why do you think that?"

"When they heard your keys in the lock, they were taken off guard, which tells me they didn't know you were home. So either Ghazi's men didn't follow us to your apartment, and I'm pretty sure they did, or the intruders weren't Ghazi's men."

"I see what you're saying. Ghazi's men would have warned the intruders that we were on the way." She seemed to consider that. "Then who were they?"

"It could've been his enemies."

That had her straightening. "What do you mean? What enemies?"

"People like him always have enemies. It's not like all bad guys are buddy-buddy."

"I know that. But why target me? What do I have to do with anything."

"Maybe they're after the information you've already found for him." He nodded at the thumb drive she'd inserted into the USB port of her laptop. "You need to secure it."

"Right." She returned to what she was doing.

"Or it could've been our guys. I don't see the FBI attacking the way they did, or being surprised. But if they wanted it to look like it wasn't them, then maybe."

"Could it have been someone working off-book?"

"Maybe."

"But that still begs the question, why me?"

"No matter who it was, the *why* isn't that confusing. You were dining with a terrorist. That tends to set off alarm bells."

"We weren't 'dining.'" She put air quotes around the word. "We were having a business meeting."

"The distinction is irrelevant."

"And anyway, whether it was FBI or Ghazi's enemies, they moved very quickly. Either that or they knew about my meeting beforehand. But how could they have?"

"The FBI is surveilling Ghazi. Chances are good someone else is as well. Maybe someone—whoever it was—realized he's been in contact with you. If they've bugged his comm—"

"Wait a minute." She stood and paced in front of the TV. "I'm confused. I thought *you* were the one watching him. Wasn't that why you were there tonight?"

"That's a long story."

She made a show of looking around. "I don't have anywhere else to be."

"Don't you need to"—he gestured to her computer—"finish that?"

"The files are downloading."

Should he tell her the truth? He considered the ramifications but couldn't think of any reason not to.

"I got a call from a person who said Ghazi was going to be at that restaurant and that *somebody* would be in danger."

She froze and crossed her arms. "Not *that* long a story. Who called?"

"I think it was a man."

"You *think*?" She propped her fists on her hips. "How do you not know?"

"The voice was distorted. The speech patterns made me believe it was a man, but of course a woman could alter her speech patterns, so..."

"Why would you follow an anonymous tip from a distorted voice? What if the person was setting you up? It could've been dangerous or—"

"I was curious. The person said Ghazi was meeting someone at a restaurant in town, a target."

"What target? What do you mean?"

It wasn't that complicated.

After a moment, color drained from her face. "Wait. You think *I'm* the target?"

"That's what the voice said, but of what? And why? And why you?" He lifted his hand in a show of *who knows?* "I've never been assigned to Ghazi, and now that he's in the US, the FBI is keeping tabs on him and his activities." Until the tip had come in, Callan hadn't thought about Dariush Ghazi in months. But he'd done his homework before leaving for the restaurant. "When did you and Ghazi set up the meeting?"

"Last night. He flew in yesterday."

"FYI, he's been in the country for months. But if the appointment was only set up yesterday—"

"Last night. He called about seven."

"Okay. So whoever called me didn't have a lot of notice. Maybe he would have been there in person if he'd had enough time. Or maybe he'd have gathered his own people."

Or maybe the caller didn't want his own people to know what he was up to. Also plausible.

"You're saying they didn't have time? That doesn't make sense. The entire intelligence apparatus couldn't get one person to the restaurant in time?"

"The FBI had people there."

She blinked. "I don't... How do you know that?"

"They're easy to pick out, if you know what to look for."

She perched on the end of the sofa. "I don't understand. Why call you?"

He shrugged. "I don't know. That was part of the reason I was curious. The powers-that-be have reason to believe Ghazi is up to something big, but they don't know what. I want to know why you were pulled into it."

"I wasn't pulled into it. Not until you showed up"

"You're working with the guy."

"I'm not working *with* him. He hires me to find things, and I find them."

"Right. But how did your small—and brand-new—investigation business get on his radar?"

"How do you know how old my business is? Or big it is?"

"I keep tabs on old classmates." Some of them, anyway.

A handful.

Okay, just Alyssa. But not for any nefarious reason. He just missed their rivalry. Their banter. He missed...her.

Which was ridiculous considering they'd never been more than acquaintances. And she could hardly stand him.

"There are more experienced investigators he could've hired," Callan said.

Her eyes narrowed, and he worked to hide his pleasure.

He'd successfully diverted her attention.

"I'm very good at what I do."

"Nobody knows that better than I do, Alyssa, because you were the only one who could best me—occasionally. The question is, how does Ghazi know?"

"He said he got my name from Michael."

"Which we know is a lie. Your cousin would never point a terrorist your direction. But..." He considered that, thinking out loud. "If he knows Michael, and he knows Michael is in the CIA, then...he must've figured out his real name. Which would have led him to you."

She was nodding. "Right. That makes sense." She spoke with a curious lack of concern.

"How does it make sense?"

"I don't know the details. But Michael's wife, Leila, and her sister, Jasmine—she's married to my youngest cousin, Derrick—are Iraqi. There was some trouble last winter at my aunt and uncle's vacation home. Something about how someone wanted Jasmine back in Iraq? Maybe this guy, Ghazi, was involved."

"We need to talk to Michael."

"He's on his honeymoon."

"He'll forgive the interruption. Call him." Or Callan would.

"Yeah, okay." She snatched her cell phone and tapped the screen. "I'll just text him, in case they're sleeping or...busy." Her cheeks turned pink at the implication.

That quick flash of embarrassment, the way she avoided looking up, only peeking at him through her eyelashes. He'd never thought of her as shy, but something in that expression...

Man. She was gorgeous. Too distracting.

"Michael will get back to me when he can." She sent the text and set her phone on the coffee table, then stepped into the kitchen. She returned with two bottles of water. "You need one?"

"Please."

He twisted the cap off.

"A question." She sipped from her own bottle. "Why the whole fake-fiancé thing?"

"I wanted to throw him off, make him think he missed something important."

She took that in. "But we have to pretend we're engaged."

"It's a good excuse for us to stay together until this is over."

By the way her eyebrows lowered, she didn't like that idea at all.

He'd try not to be offended.

That look...

That was the reason he'd never asked her out in college. No matter how much she appealed to him—and between her looks and her brains and her quick wit, she'd always appealed to him—he'd never had a single reason to believe she returned his feelings.

He'd been a coward back then, too afraid of rejection to risk it.

Today, he'd take the chance. Alyssa put on a tough front, but how much of that was a defense mechanism?

If things were different, he'd ask her out. He'd take the risk.

But now that he had Peri, it was too late.

He'd keep Alyssa safe and then let her go. No matter how much the idea twisted his gut.

# CHAPTER FIVE

Alyssa used to love coming to the Rooming House.

When she was a girl, she and her sisters would pretend they were in a castle filled with secret passageways and hidden treasures. They'd wander the hallways haphazardly and try to get lost—often successfully. Whoever designed this hotel must've been going for maximum confusion.

Maybe that was why Dad liked it so much. Intruders might get in, but how would they ever find who they were looking for?

Callan had brought her suitcase into the master bedroom, and she'd been too flustered to protest, but she preferred the other room. It was the one she and her sisters used to share when they were little. They'd hop from one bed to the other, seeing which of them could leap farthest or jump highest. Alyssa usually won the contests.

It helped to be the oldest.

That was back when she'd still been close to her sisters, when they were her very best friends.

But she'd gone off to college and drifted away. She wanted to fix that, but she had no idea how.

Not only that, but she'd lost touch with her one good

college friend, though she'd always believed there was time to reconnect with Megan. The time for friends and fun would come later, after she proved herself. After she achieved all her goals.

She was shocked when she learned about Megan's death—months after it happened. Too late to do much more than send a card and flowers to her parents.

Alyssa was thankful for the yoga pants Callan had reminded her to grab when she'd been packing. In the bathroom, she slipped into them and a sweatshirt, then put her hair in a ponytail as she returned to the living room.

She was ready to end this day.

Not just this day. She was ready for this whole crazy thing to be over, the sooner the better.

Callan hung up the hotel phone as she walked in. "I sent for a pizza. Thought I'd better let Jonathan know." He gave her a quick once over. "Comfortable?"

"More than I was. What are you going to do for clothes?"

"I'll figure it out. What do you know about the person Ghazi wants you to find?"

"He'll email the information he has."

"Can you see if he sent it to you?"

Settled on the sofa, she checked the progress of her download—the files were still transferring to the thumb drive—and opened her email.

There was one from Charles Sanders. She read it, shaking her head. "It's just an IP address and some names."

"You think it'll be enough to find who he's looking for?"

"It would be easier and faster with my desktop. I have programs on there and private bots and..." She'd been so focused on the intruders in her apartment, the strange journey through the city, and the very distracting man at her side that she hadn't yet processed what the break-in meant.

The enormity sank in in. Her desktop's hard drive was gone, and with it, most of the tools she used to do her job.

She could rebuild the bots and download the programs again, but it would take time.

Callan settled beside her on the sofa, his scent wafting toward her—some combination of mahogany and musk. He peered over her shoulder. "Huh." He tapped one of the names on her screen. "I know this guy. Of him, anyway. He used to be high up in Putin's government, but last I heard, he'd left his job."

"Do you know any of the others?"

"They're not familiar, but I can look into them." He sat back, and though he wasn't as close, he still took up way too much space on the small sofa.

Would it be rude to move to the loveseat?

"What else has Ghazi asked you to do for him?" Callan asked.

"Mostly things like this, though he usually has more information. He once wanted me to do a thorough background check on some French diplomat."

"Named?"

She told him, hoping he'd shift over, maybe grab a notepad and pen from the desk to write it down. But he just nodded. "What else?"

"Just, you know, stuff like this."

"I'll need to know everything. Did he ever asked you to do anything illegal?"

"I already told you, I won't do anything illegal." Well, maybe, *technically,* some of the stuff she did skirted laws. She'd hacked into private databases occasionally, but it wasn't like she was stealing credit card numbers.

Callan nodded, though the gesture seemed more contemplative than agreement. He tipped his chin toward her laptop. "Is the download almost done?"

"Close." She'd started with Charles's folder, so she deleted it from the cloud.

"If your intruders are interested in something you've saved, then you're just making yourself a target."

"Do you have a better suggestion?" She stood and moved to the loveseat so he wouldn't see the names of her other clients. Not that she didn't trust him, but...

Well, she didn't, not *that* much, anyway.

This whole story was bizarre, and he'd offered zero evidence that anything he was telling her was true.

From her quick glance his way, he looked more amused than offended.

She set her laptop on the coffee table.

"All the information you've collected for Ghazi is on the thumb drive?" At her nod, Callan said, "I'll need to see it."

"You have a warrant?"

"You're funny."

"I'm not trying to be funny, Callan. I've already told you more than I should have. I promise my clients confidentiality. You need to give me a good reason to break that."

His brows lowered. "Alyssa."

"Callan." She matched his tone and expression. "This is my business. My livelihood. I can't just betray my clients because you said pretty-please."

He blew out a breath. "Do the words 'national security' mean anything to you?"

"Does the word 'warrant' mean anything to you?"

"I'm not... I can't help you officially. I don't work for the FBI. I can't get a warrant."

"Then I can't tell you—"

"Oh, come on." He leaned forward and settled his forearms on his knees. "I'm trying to protect you."

"And I'm supposed to just believe that? Just believe everything you're telling me."

His eyes popped wide. "Seriously? Why would I lie?"

"I don't know. Why would you? You lied to Charles."

"You're being ridiculous."

"You've offered zero proof of all your claims."

"I don't need to..." He took a breath and started again. "Your apartment was broken into."

"Maybe those were your people." Now that it occurred to her, it all seemed so obvious. Callan had inserted himself into her meeting, then insisted on walking her home. He'd *saved* her from the intruders. But what if the intruders worked for him?

What if he was the one she should fear?

What if this was all some elaborate ruse?

"Are you serious?"

"I need proof—"

"For the love of all that's holy." He launched to his feet. "Call. Michael."

"He'll call me when—"

"Fine. I'll do it." He pulled his phone from his pocket. Surely, he didn't have her cousin's number on speed dial. A moment later, he spoke. "I need contact information for Michael Wright. It's an emergency." He waited moment then said, "I'll hold."

"Fine." Alyssa snatched her cell off the coffee table. "I'll call him."

Callan glared at her.

She turned away and dialed her cousin, hating that she was intruding on his honeymoon.

On the other hand, how many times had he called her, needing a favor? Surely, he would forgive her for interrupting.

The call rang four times and went to voicemail.

"It's Alyssa. Call me ASAP. It's an emergency." She hung

up and turned to find Callan still holding his phone to his ear. "He didn't answer."

"I heard."

"I'll give you his number. You don't have to—"

"Thanks." Callan lifted his hand, telling her to be quiet. He put the phone on speaker. "Go ahead."

A female voice recited Michael's number.

"Thanks." He ended the call. "Decided I'd better go through with getting it so you'd know I wasn't trying to pull a fast one."

"I never said—"

"Sure you did." He dialed, keeping the phone on speaker. It rang, and then Michael's voicemail picked up again.

"It's Callan Templeton. I'm here with your cousin, and we need to speak to you about Dariush Ghazi. Call her back ASAP." He hung up, then said, "Satisfied?"

As if she'd admit it at this point.

"Michael is going to confirm everything I've told you. I don't know what you suspect me of, but whatever it is—"

"Nothing. Not really. Just... It's strange, that's all. You're a spy. You could just be trying to get information on my client."

"You're an American. I'm a CIA agent. It would be illegal for me to—"

"I know the rules. I also know not everyone plays by them."

Callan paced to the window and peered out.

What should she say? She'd offended him, but did he really expect her to just accept his every word without question?

He turned and leaned against the desk. "I play by the rules. I'm not running an op here. I'm trying to protect you, that's all."

He'd called her cousin. Every word he said must be true.

It irritated her that he thought she needed his protection.

It irritated her even more that he was right.

She needed to think. To sleep. And to get out of Callan's very distracting presence.

THEIR ARGUMENT still hung between them a half hour later as they ate pizza.

She wouldn't apologize for her doubts. If word got out to her clients that she couldn't be trusted, then the business she was barely keeping afloat would be sunk for good.

Couldn't he understand that?

Callan worked for Uncle Sam. His pay would be deposited into his bank account no matter what he did. Sometimes, she missed the security of her government job.

But she didn't miss the mundane routine. She didn't miss that she could've left her brain at home. She definitely didn't miss knowing she'd been passed over for the job she really wanted.

Passed over in favor of Callan.

She doubted he knew that they'd been up for the same job. The only reason she knew was that she'd seen him going into the interview after she left. And then heard through the alumni grapevine that he'd been hired.

Whatever he was up to, she wouldn't risk her career to help him. Sanders wasn't her only client, but he was her best-paying one. If she was going to lose him, then she needed to work harder to promote her business. Which meant she didn't have time for whatever it was Callan was up to.

She needed to get back to business ASAP.

She'd accepted Sanders's job, and it seemed innocent enough to her. She'd find the name of this Russian guy, pass it along, and then be done with the man for good.

She finished her slice—she'd barely tasted it—and pushed

back from the table to check on the download. The rest of her files had transferred onto her thumb drive, so she deleted them from the cloud, then deleted her account altogether.

Whoever had stolen her desktop wouldn't be able to access any sensitive information now.

With that done, she closed her laptop and faced Callan. "I'm going to bed."

"Okay." He wiped his hands on a napkin. "We'll talk in the morning and make a plan."

She snatched her water bottle to take with her into the bedroom. She'd be awake for a few more hours, but she didn't need to spend another minute with him. "I have a plan."

He pushed his plate aside. "Can you share it? Or is that top secret too?"

She ignored his sarcasm. "I'm going to get the name of the Russian and pass it along. Then, I'll be done, and you can go on with whatever it is you think you need to do."

"First, you can't pass along anything until we talk about it. Second, it's not going to be so easy to sever our ties with him"

"Sure it is. I'm not required to work for Charles. He can't force me to. I'll just make up some excuse and—"

"His name is not Charles." Callan seemed to be working hard to keep his frustration in check. "And I guarantee it's not going to work."

His arrogance had her heart rate spiking. "You *guarantee* it? There's zero chance you might be the tiniest bit wrong about anything."

He smiled. "You're finally figuring that out."

"We'll see." She swiveled and headed to her bedroom.

"Hey, Alyssa?"

She turned at the door. "What?"

"I'm sorry you're caught up in this." He wasn't smiling now. "You need to remember two things. One." He lifted his pointer finger. "I didn't get you involved. You were already working with the guy when I showed up."

True. And if Sanders was Ghazi, and Ghazi was who Callan thought he was, then the man was dangerous.

"And two"—his next finger popped in the air—"I have nothing to gain by lying to you. I stepped in because you're an old friend, and I don't want you to get hurt. I am not your enemy."

Her irritation dissolved.

It was true that Callan was arrogant. But also, he was probably right.

She nodded.

"Please, don't reach out to him until we talk, okay?"

"Okay."

"I need to go to my apartment and pick up some things. Don't go anywhere while I'm gone."

The thought of Callan leaving spiked her anxiety, but she wasn't about to admit that.

"If for some reason I'm not here when you wake up in the morning, then call your dad, tell him what's going on, and ask him to get you out of town."

The last thing she wanted was to run to her father for help. "Be careful." She swiveled and went to her bedroom.

It was after midnight, three hours later, when she finally closed her laptop, her eyes as gritty as beach sand. But she'd found the name of the Russian. Once she passed it along, she'd be done with all this craziness.

Despite Callan's so-called guarantee.

# CHAPTER SIX

Callan was almost positive nobody had followed him.

Almost wasn't good enough, though.

After he'd arrived at his Charlestown apartment, he'd taken his time packing a bag. He'd meandered to the bus stop and waited for ten minutes before the bus finally arrived. After a short ride to North Station, he'd hopped on the Green Line T into Boston.

All that time, he picked up no tail.

He exited at Park Street, aimed for the exit, then shifted to the underground corridor that led to Downtown Crossing.

It was late on a Wednesday night, and nobody else traversed the tunnel.

If there had been somebody watching, surely he'd have seen them behind him. Unless they monitored every T-stop in the city.

His own people could do that, if they had enough advance notice, but he was fairly certain Ghazi couldn't.

He caught what was probably the last train headed north on the Red Line. He didn't take it all the way to the Harvard stop, though, which was the nearest T-station to the hotel. Instead, he hopped off just north of the Charles River at MIT and met an Uber he'd ordered on the way.

If people had followed him on the subway—and he didn't think anybody had—the car certainly would have thrown them off.

Altogether, it'd taken him an hour and a half to return to the fancy-shmancy hotel from his apartment, which was, as the crow flies, about two miles away.

But he'd gotten the things he'd need for a few days and confirmed that nobody was watching his apartment.

The door to the Rooming House opened as he approached.

"Good evening, Mr. Crenshaw," the bellhop said.

"Good evening, Jeeves."

The man's lip quirked at the corner. "It's William, sir." He lowered his voice. "But you can call me Jeeves if you want."

Callan stepped inside, giving the man a quick smile. "I was afraid you'd gone to bed, William."

"There'll always be someone here to let you in." He flicked his gaze to Callan's suitcase. "And collect anything you might need."

"I appreciate that. Good night." Callan headed for the elevator.

It only took him six minutes and two wrong turns to find his way back to the room.

Inside, everything was as he'd left it. No light shone beneath Alyssa's door, so she'd finally gone to sleep.

Though her light had remained on for hours after she'd fled into the bedroom, probably still not convinced he wasn't lying to her about everything.

Exasperating woman.

Callan closed his bedroom door and left a voicemail for his

boss, giving him a quick rundown on what was going on. He didn't know Malcolm Springer well enough to predict how he'd take the news.

He might be furious.

He might be impressed.

Callan had left the field a few months earlier, instead working support from the Boston office. He didn't hate using his field skills again. He missed it.

Which was probably why he'd followed a tip from a disembodied, garbled voice on the phone. Was he so desperate for action that he'd walk heedlessly into danger?

No, it wasn't that.

It was just that he knew what he was doing when he was running an op. He knew what he was doing at the office, of course, but it was dull, definitely not what he'd signed up for when he'd applied for the CIA.

With Peri, he was in way over his head.

For the first time since he'd discovered his daughter's existence, he'd gone hours without thinking about her.

Guilt squeezed his midsection. What kind of a father was he, anyway?

It wasn't as if she could escape what had happened. It wasn't as if any of it was Peri's fault.

And now he had a new female to worry about, and just like Peri, no matter how hard he tried, Alyssa wanted nothing to do with him.

So.

This would be fun.

Some reprieve he'd signed up for.

Unlike his fake fiancée, Callan didn't unpack all his things and fold them neatly in the drawers. Instead, he opened his suitcase on one of the queen-sized beds, grabbed a pair of pajama pants—because he couldn't exactly sleep in his boxers with a woman in the suite—and tapped the thermostat to reduce the temperature.

The A/C kicked on immediately.

He felt like someone had dumped two hundred puzzle pieces in front of him—from a thousand-piece puzzle—and demanded he solve it. Without giving him a clue what the final picture was going to look like.

The more he tried to manipulate the pieces, the messier the image got.

Maybe morning would bring clarity.

Maybe God would bring clarity.

If he'd learned nothing else in the months since Peri had come into his life, he'd learned he needed to rely on God.

Heaven knew, Callan didn't have a clue.

He paraphrased his new favorite Psalm. *Lord, give me counsel, and instruct me as I sleep.*

Because he needed sleep. And he needed to wake up with a hint as to how all these pieces fit together.

He took a warm shower to wash off the day and all the questions assaulting him, then brushed his teeth and climbed onto a mattress about ten times as comfortable as his own.

And trusted he'd wake up with a plan.

CALLAN'S PHONE WAS RINGING.

He grabbed it off the nightstand and checked the caller ID, fearing bad news.

But it wasn't his parents. It wasn't about Peri. It was his boss, calling from his cell. Probably not a good sign, considering it was just past six o'clock.

Callan let the call go to voicemail. He needed coffee before he dealt with Malcolm.

He headed through the living room, flicking lights on along the way, into the kitchen. A pot of coffee had already been brewed.

Alyssa must be awake.

He poured himself a cup, added half-and-half from the mini-fridge—not the cheap little peel-off-the-top deals, either, but a pint-sized container. From a basket of different types of sweetener on the counter, he grabbed two sugars, dumped them into the hot liquid, and stirred.

These were definitely nicer accommodations than a campsite.

He stepped out of the kitchenette just as Alyssa's bedroom door opened.

"Oh, hey." She froze in the threshold. "I didn't realize you were up." Pink crept into her cheeks.

He probably should've put on a T-shirt.

Where he was barefoot and wearing nothing but pajama pants, Alyssa wore jeans and a pink T-shirt. Her hair was wet, a little wavy, hanging below her shoulders.

She was far more attractive than anyone had a right to be so early in the morning.

"Thanks for this." He lifted his mug. "Exactly what I needed."

"I'm glad you made it back last night."

Was that relief in her voice? "Nobody followed me. As far as I could tell, nobody was watching my apartment."

"I found the name of the Russian."

"Already? Is that why your light was on so late last night?"

"I thought it would take longer, to tell you the truth."

Was it Callan's sleep-addled mind, or did Alyssa seem nervous?

Interesting.

He sipped his coffee, enjoying the sweet warmth. And the fact that his confident rival seemed anything but at the moment.

"I thought I'd send him the name," she continued, "and tell him I'm taking a break for a while."

"You can't send him the name."

She leaned against the doorjamb and crossed her arms, the frustration she'd worn the night before flashing in her eyes. "Look, Michael called me an hour ago. He confirmed that Dariush Ghazi is in Boston. He seemed furious that the guy hasn't been picked up and incarcerated. He said if you thought Charles Sanders is Ghazi, then you're probably right. Michael thinks I should get out of the city. Not just out but...he wants me to go into hiding."

"Huh." Callan set the coffee mug on the table and slid into a chair, nodding to one on the other side, an invitation for her to join him. "That's not a bad idea. Did he say where?"

Alyssa didn't move. "Dad's got a few places that are off the radar. A cabin in West Virginia. A chalet in the Alps. A house on Kauai. I don't want to go that far away, but I guess Uncle Roger's vacation house off the coast of Maine is a bad idea. That's where all the craziness went down last winter, and Michael says Ghazi was there."

"Is that all the choices you have? No yacht with a crew on stand-by? No..." He struggled to think of another option. "Paris penthouse?"

"That's a good idea. I wouldn't hate hiding out at the apartment..." Her eyes narrowed. "You were kidding."

"I thought I was."

"Doesn't matter. Mom is having it renovated, and the work isn't finished yet."

"I guess you could just stay here in this dump."

She scowled. "They're not *my* properties."

"Whatever you say, Paris."

Her scowl turned to a glare. "And I don't want to run away. I can't. I've got a business to run. I promised I'd talk to you before I reached out to Char... Ghazi, so that's what I'm doing. Unless you have an objection, I'm going to send him the name this morning."

"Who is it?"

She disappeared into her bedroom and returned with her laptop, which she set on the table in front of Callan.

On her screen was a photo of a man called Yefim Lavrentiy.

"Guy's name really rolls off the tongue, doesn't it?"

She didn't smile.

"I've never heard of him." Callan peered at the image. "He doesn't look familiar."

"Michael doesn't know him either. He's going to have his team look into him."

"What does he think about your plan?"

Alyssa's lips pressed together. She shrugged.

"He doesn't think it'll work, either, does he?"

"You could both be wrong."

"Possible." Unlikely, but it seemed rude to say so. "I'm going to jump in the shower and then make a call. Hold off until I get out before you call him, okay?"

"All right, but I want to do it soon." She closed her laptop.

"While you wait, could you order us some breakfast?"

Irritation crossed her features, and he braced himself for accusations of misogyny or chauvinism. But she forced her mouth into a smile he didn't believe for a second. "What do you want?"

"Whatever, Paris. You choose."

"Don't call me that."

He grinned, enjoying her ire. "Why not? It fits."

"It absolutely does not—"

"Breakfast, *Alyssa*. Please."

At her curt nod, he returned to his bedroom. It was too early in the morning to navigate the minefield that was conversation with Alyssa Wright.

His phone rang before he'd made it to the bathroom.

He snatched it up and saw his boss's number again.

Might as well get another unpleasant conversation under his belt. Or...elastic waistband, as it were. He swiped to answer. "Callan Templeton."

"What the blazes are you doing?"

"Good morning, Malcolm."

"Who is Alyssa Wright to you?"

Why did Malcolm's question sound like an accusation?

Callan flicked on the light and pulled back a corner of the curtain. The sun was working its way up, the black-and-gray world starting to tinge with color.

"She's an old friend," Callan said.

"That's all? Just a friend?"

Callan chose not to respond to the implication.

"How do you know her?"

"We went to college together." Callan had left in his message that he'd seen Alyssa dining with Dariush Ghazi—though he hadn't used the man's real name—and stepped in. He'd assumed this conversation would be about the terrorist, not the attractive cyber investigator. "Alyssa was at the restaurant with—"

"I listened to your message. What were you doing there? How did you know she was going to be there?"

"I got a tip Ghazi would be there and somebody would be—"

"In danger. You told me that too."

Callan clamped his lips shut. Malcolm was angry, and until

Callan understood why, he figured the more he talked, the less good he could do himself.

"Why did you follow the tip?" Malcolm asked.

"Curiosity."

"That's a stupid reason to insert yourself into someone else's op."

Since it wasn't a question, Callan didn't say anything.

"Spill it, Templeton. What's the real reason you were there?"

Malcolm thought he was lying, but why? "I got a tip. I had nothing else to do."

"We both know *that's* not true. You have a a kid. You had other places to be. *Better* places to be, or at least most people would think so."

The words were aimed with precision, and Callan felt them like a knife to the gut.

On this point, Malcolm wasn't wrong. The problem was that Callan felt competent walking into an unknown situation to observe, or even to insert himself, into danger.

But where his eight-year-old daughter was concerned, he felt utterly incompetent.

He'd been a successful agent. As a father, he was a complete failure.

"You're not in the field anymore," Malcolm added, "and for good reason."

Still not a question, so Callan remained silent.

"You should have told me immediately."

"I'm not in the habit of running my dinner plans by you. Sir."

"I don't need your sarcasm."

"I'd like to know what I'm being accused of. I got a tip. I followed it. I didn't plan to *insert myself* into anything, certainly not an op I knew nothing about. I went to observe, nothing else."

"You should've stuck to that plan."

Maybe. But it was Alyssa. Callan hadn't thought twice about interrupting her conversation with a murderer.

"She had no idea who her client was," Callan said. "He hired her to find a name. Which she did, last night."

"Which is?"

"Yefim Lavrentiy."

"Without our say-so, she's just going to give the guy what he wants?"

"Of course not. She'll do what we ask. She gave the information to a CIA agent assigned to the White House. That team is looking into it. I'll forward everything I learn. If you don't want her to give Ghazi the name, then—"

"Whether she does or doesn't, she's involved with this guy. You really think she can just walk away?" Scorn filled the man's voice.

What was happening? Callan had had a cordial relationship with Malcolm prior to this conversation. The man had respected him, or so he'd thought.

Now, Callan was being treated like an enemy—or a fool, at the very least. But why?

"I do not think it'll work. I was just informing you of her plan. Alyssa hasn't told me everything she's done for Ghazi prior to this job, but—"

"There's a shock."

"—I'm sure she will now that she's confirmed her client's identity. I assume Ghazi has a bigger plan at work here, and Alyssa is part of that plan. He's not about to let her go. What he'll use to manipulate her, I don't know—threats of some kind, I'm sure. The point is, after she realizes one doesn't walk away from men like Ghazi, I'm going to get her out of the city until this is all over."

"That's not how this is going down," Malcolm said. "Now

that she understands she's under surveillance, she's going to gather intel for us. She'll continue to work for Ghazi and pass along—"

"No." Callan's hands curled into fists.

"I hate to break this to you, Templeton, but you're not the boss."

"You might be *my* boss, but you're not *hers*. You have no right to expect an innocent civilian to put herself in danger. It's not safe."

"*Innocent?* Is that how you see a woman who works with a terrorist?"

"She didn't know who he is." He hadn't meant to shout and worked for a calmer tone. "She's not an operative. She's not..." He paused to think, then tried a different tack. "Do you know who she is? Do you know who her father is?"

"Do you?" The words were a challenge.

Uh-oh. What was he missing? "Gavin Wright was next in line to run our agency."

"Yeah. And then he retired."

"There's no law against that." What did Alyssa's father have to do with anything?

"I guess that depends on where you think his money came from. Do you really think he got as rich as he did by building a legitimate business?"

Seemed reasonable to Callan. Except...

A West Virginia cabin. A Swiss chalet. A Hawaiian house. A Paris apartment.

A standing account at this high-priced boutique hotel, a hotel known for discretion?

"Do you know how much Gavin Wright is worth?" Malcolm asked.

"Not off the top of my head." He deadpanned the words as if he didn't care. As if it didn't matter.

"Estimates say somewhere between fifty and seventy-five million dollars. I wouldn't be surprised if there's more stowed in off-shore bank accounts, hidden all over the world. A guy like Wright, with contacts on every continent, would know how to make—and hide—large sums of money."

Callan turned to face the closed door between himself and Alyssa.

Was her father into something illegal?

Was she involved?

No. Of course not.

"What does Alyssa have to do with any of that?"

"His daughter just happens to have contracts with terrorists. You really think that's an accident?"

"More likely, Ghazi targeted her because of her relationship with her father. Or her cousins. Michael Wright has had run-ins with Ghazi. That doesn't make Alyssa guilty."

"Doesn't make her innocent, either. And whatever her status, she's in it now. If she refuses to help... Well, we'll know where her loyalties lie."

Callan already knew where her loyalties lay. Didn't he?

He replayed all the conversations he'd had with her in the last twelve hours. There was nothing in her words or her tone that led him to believe she'd known who Ghazi was.

No, whatever her father was into, assuming he was involved at all, Alyssa was innocent.

And Malcolm wanted to turn her into a pawn.

"And we'll know where *your* loyalties lie too." Malcolm's voice was smug as he added the threat.

"I have nothing to do with anything."

"You impeded a federal investigation."

"I understand Ghazi's being surveilled, but I wasn't impeding anything. I joined an old friend at dinner because I was concerned for her safety.."

"Maybe. But if you want to keep your job—and your freedom to take care of your daughter—you'd better get Alyssa to work with us. Your future is at stake here."

Malcolm ended the call, leaving Callan to stare at the blank screen.

What in the world was going on?

More importantly...what was he supposed to do now?

# CHAPTER SEVEN

Alyssa was being irrational.

She set down the dryer too hard in the hotel bathroom and yanked her brush through her hair.

Wasn't identifying the problem the first step toward reaching a solution?

She couldn't help her irrationality, though.

It irritated her that Callan was right about Charles—the terrorist, Dariush Ghazi.

It irritated her that Michael had agreed with every one of Callan's pronouncements.

It irritated her that Callan knew more about Ghazi than she did, considering that the man had attacked her family.

When Michael called at just after five that morning, he'd apologized for not getting back to her sooner. He and Leila had been sailing off the coast of some remote Indonesian island. He hadn't checked his phone in hours because, you know.

Newlyweds.

He'd filled her on how Ghazi had played a part in the attack on his family's Maine vacation home the previous Christmas.

Alyssa still didn't know much about what had happened,

though she'd seen the house after the fact. Bullet holes and shattered glass. Second-floor rooms had caught fire, thanks to a Molotov cocktail lobbed through a window.

The beautiful home her uncle's family had built, one nail at a time, had been a mess, but between Uncle Roger, Aunt Peggy, the six Wright brothers and their wives and girlfriends and kids, plus Alyssa and her sisters and Mom and Dad, they'd had the downstairs cleaned up and the upstairs mostly rebuilt in time for Christmas.

No easy feat, that.

She'd known, theoretically, that terrorists had been behind the attack.

But now she had a face to go with the story, a man who'd affected a very believable British accent. A man who'd hired her, been friendly with her.

Targeted her.

"It's no coincidence, Alyssa." Worry had infused Michael's voice. "Ghazi is smart, and he knows our family."

"How? How could you let that happen?" She'd allowed all her fear and frustration to seep into her voice. Shouldn't a CIA agent be better at hiding his identity?

Michael hadn't appreciated the implication. He'd told her a story about old friends of Jasmine who'd needed help, and Derrick jumping in, and Iraqi nationals who snuck across the border and...

"I'm not getting into the details," Michael had said. "And I'm not blaming anyone. The point is, whatever Ghazi's plotting, you're involved. I'm going to book us a flight out of here—"

"Absolutely not. You're on your honeymoon."

"You're in danger, and it's my fault."

"You just said it's not your fault. It was Derrick and Jasmine who led them to us."

"Because of—"

"It doesn't matter, Michael. You're not coming back. I'm safe right now. I'm with Callan Templeton."

"He's a good guy. Trust him."

She'd managed to stifle her groan enough that Michael didn't hear it over the phone. But she could put up with Callan if it meant not ruining Michael and Leila's honeymoon.

"And anyway, if worse comes to worse, I could call Dad."

"Yeah, well..." Michael's hesitation had her heart thumping.

"What?"

"I'm not sure Uncle Gavin can help you with this one, even if he wants to. I'm not saying don't call him, but I'd rather you stick with Callan and reach out to me if you need help."

What did that mean? Dad knew everybody in the intelligence community. He had money and contacts.

She knew it wasn't true, but in her head, her father could do anything.

"Call me if you need me," Michael had said. "I can get on the first flight, but it'll take some time. Maybe we should just head—"

"Don't you dare. I'm safe. I'll let you know if anything changes. If you cut your honeymoon short because of this, I'll never help you with anything again."

"So you *want* me to come home," he'd joked, "to give you an excuse."

She'd forced a laugh, trying to sound more confident than she felt. But his words resonated even now.

*"Whatever Ghazi's plotting, you're involved."*

She finished drying her hair and added some makeup because... Well, not because of Callan. Just because she didn't know what else to do.

All she wanted was to be *un*involved in Ghazi's schemes.

As long as she could remember, she'd wanted entrance into her father's world of intrigue and spies, a world he'd willingly helped Michael become a part of. But she'd been denied again and again. And now, against her will, she'd been sucked in, not as an agent. Not even as an analyst, like she had been before she'd quit the NSA.

Nope.

Alyssa had somehow become a victim.

The whole thing irritated like an itch she couldn't scratch.

A knock sounded, and she hurried out of the bedroom and through the living room to answer it. Of course it was a hotel employee delivering breakfast. But fear had her pausing, hand on the knob. "Who is it?"

"It's your breakfast," a woman answered.

Could be true.

But Alyssa's heartbeat raced.

Could be a trick. Could be killers or terrorists or...

She was being ridiculous.

Nobody knew where they were staying, and even if Ghazi had located her, he didn't know she'd figured out who he really was. Why would he come after her?

And the intruders at her apartment? They couldn't possibly know where she was. Even if they had followed her and Callan, they wouldn't make it into the front door.

Tamping down her fear, she swung the door open to a familiar gray-haired woman on the other side.

"Good morning, Ms. Crenshaw." The woman winked as she pushed a cart into the short hallway, carrying with it the scents of bacon and pancakes.

"Good to see you, Aline." Alyssa had known the Brazilian housekeeper since she was a girl.

"Your father is with you?" Aline transferred the covered dishes from the cart onto the dining table.

"Not this time."

Callan's bedroom door opened, and he stepped out. "Something smells good out here."

Aline nodded to him, then shot a look at Alyssa, mouthing *aye-aye-aye*.

The look on her face, and the implication of her reaction, had Alyssa's cheeks burning.

At least Callan had put on a shirt. She couldn't imagine the housekeeper's reaction if she'd caught the man in his pajama pants, that flat abdomen, those defined muscles.

Alyssa managed not to fan her face at the memory.

"Enjoy your breakfast, Mr. Crenshaw." Aline turned her back on him and waggled her eyebrows at Alyssa as she walked out.

Alyssa locked the door behind her.

"I think she's scandalized." Callan didn't seem all that upset at the notion.

"You could've stayed in the bedroom until she left."

"I needed to know who you'd willingly let into our suite. I'd prefer you let me open the door from now on, please. We need to be careful." He rounded the table and pulled out a chair for her. "Milady."

"I need another cup of coffee."

She escaped into the kitchen and refilled her mug, not that she needed more. She was hiding until her stupid blush was under control.

Why did that man have such an effect on her? She didn't even like him.

That wasn't strictly true.

Callan had always been a competitor, but he'd never been cruel or petty.

She opened the refrigerator, calling, "You want a bottle of water?"

"Sure."

She startled and spun.

Callan was right behind her, taking up way too much space. And grinning, the jerk. "I didn't mean to scare you."

Sure he did, but she wouldn't say so.

He was still chuckling as he reached past her into the fridge and grabbed two bottles of water. "Come on. We need to talk."

She returned to the dining table and lifted the lids off the plates of food. Scrambled eggs with bacon and toast, pancakes with sides of butter and maple syrup, and a yogurt parfait. There were two glasses of orange juice and a bowl of cut-up fruit.

He peered over her shoulder, much closer than necessary, his breath fanning the skin behind her ear.

She shivered, praying he didn't notice how his nearness affected her.

"Which is whose?" Worry tinged his words.

She was tempted to tell him it was all for her, just to mess with him.

"I wasn't sure what you'd want, so I got a few options. I'd like the yogurt, but I can eat the toast instead."

He plopped the lid back on the pancakes, slid the yogurt in front of the chair he'd pulled out for her, and then gripped the back of it. "After you."

"I can seat myself."

"Can you? I wasn't sure." Annoyance infused his words. He waited until she'd settled in the chair, then rounded the table, sat across from her, and dragged the eggs closer. "You're going to have to get used to having me around, not stiffen whenever I touch you." He sipped from one of the glasses of juice, and his eyes widened. "Wow. This is good."

She nodded to the juice. "It's freshly squeezed. Why?"

"Why do they squeeze oranges when the juice comes in

cartons?" He shrugged. "Before today, I would've guessed snobbery, but—"

"You know what I mean. Why do I have to get used to you?"

"Because I'm not going anywhere. Because engaged people don't cringe when they're together. They *like* being together. They *like* to touch."

"You know this because you've been engaged?"

"I know this because I've been in love. And because, you know, I live on the planet and have eyes." He forked a bite of breakfast.

She focused on stirring her parfait, mixing the granola and berries into the yogurt, not thinking about Callan's being in love. Or having been, it sounded like. Which meant he wasn't now.

Not that it was any of her business. Not that she should care.

She dug into her yogurt, then swallowed a bite. "I'm not playing this game with you."

His wiped his mouth with the cloth napkin. "Which game is that?"

"The we're-engaged-and-in-love game. I've got better things to do than play pretend."

His close-lipped smile was anything but happy.

"What?" She didn't temper the demanding tone.

"Okay." He ate a slice of bacon, then worked on his eggs.

Okay? That was all he had? *Okay?*

What did that mean?

Callan finished the first plate of food, then uncovered the pancakes. "You want some of these?"

"Go ahead."

He traded his empty plate for the full one, buttered the stack, then covered the whole thing in maple syrup.

Apparently, the thought of terrorists didn't affect his appetite.

A low buzzing had her pushing back in her chair. She found her phone, which was vibrating with a call, and read the caller ID.

"It's him. It's Ghazi." Her pitch was too high. She took a breath. "Charles."

If she was going to talk to the man, she needed to think of him as Charles Sanders, British entrepreneur, not Dariush Ghazi, international terrorist and murderer.

She turned to find Callan, once again, right behind her.

"We need to make some decisions before you answer that."

She wanted to get the conversation over with, but Callan, for all his silence and stuffing his mouth with food, clearly had more to say.

Carrying the ringing phone, she scooted past Callan—the man had no sense of personal space—and returned to the table.

"I talked to my boss this morning." He sat across from her. "He's not happy with me. He didn't say so outright, but he implied that Ghazi wasn't the only one at your dinner last night who was being watched."

The phone finally stopped ringing. "Someone else was there? One of Ghazi's people, or...?" Too late, she realized what he meant. "Me? They're watching me? Your people?"

"Not the Agency, Alyssa. I assume FBI, but Malcolm didn't spell it out."

"But why—?"

"Your client is a terrorist. You're a hacker. They can't assume you're innocent or unaware. My boss wants you to use your connection with Ghazi to get information. He implied that if you don't, it'll look bad for you."

"I haven't done anything wrong."

"You haven't *knowingly* done anything wrong."

She thought back over the information she'd gotten for Charles Sanders. Maybe it was *technically* illegal, but it wasn't as if she'd get caught. And after the fact, there was no way to prove she'd done it.

Maybe no way for your run-of-the-mill law enforcement agencies, but the NSA, the CIA, the FBI...

They could figure it out.

But how was she supposed to do her job if she couldn't occasionally access private systems?

Yeah, that excuse was really going to fly.

What a pickle she'd gotten herself into. Even when she tried to do the right thing, she managed to mess it up.

Dad was right about her. She was a useless, worthless fool.

Callan was watching her, eyes narrowed as if he were trying to read her thoughts.

"What am I supposed to do?"

"I don't think Ghazi is going to let you back out of your relationship."

"Relationship? It's not—"

"Bad choice of words." He lifted his hand to silence her. "The point is, I don't think it's going to work. For one thing, Malcolm doesn't want you to pass the name along."

"Why? Who is this guy?"

"I don't think he knows. Maybe Michael and his team will have more information for us. The point is, you're going to have to tell Ghazi you haven't gotten it yet, and that you can't get it."

"He's not going to like that." She pushed back in her chair.

Why, why, why had she started working with him?

She needed the money to keep her business alive, but it wasn't as if she were starving. She'd rather have a failed business than...than all of this.

She'd done her homework on Charles Sanders, same as she did her homework on all her clients. Sometimes people had good reasons for hiding, and she wasn't about to expose somebody who'd risked life and limb to get away from an abusive spouse or a vengeful criminal.

Everything she'd learned about Charles Sanders had confirmed the story he'd told her. Obviously, she'd failed to detect his lies.

"You'll tell him you won't be able to find the name, and you're taking a break from work. Use me as an excuse. Tell him your fiancé is back in town, sooner than you expected. We're planning a wedding, and there's just no time for work. You've enjoyed working with him. Whatever you would normally do in this situation, do that."

"But your boss wants me to get information. How can I do that if—?"

"Get out of it if you can. I'll deal with Malcolm. If you need to get an attorney, then so be it. Legal troubles won't hurt you, but Ghazi...might."

"You really know how to make a girl feel safe."

"I wish you were safe, Alyssa. I wish I could..." His words faded.

"You don't think he's going to let me off the hook."

"I do not. I think he'll coerce you, somehow, to work with him. If he does that, then you could go into hiding. But this guy has a pretty extensive network. I don't know if that'll make you safe."

"I can't hide for the rest of my life."

"Better to hide than end up..." Callan pressed his lips closed and looked away.

"He knows who I am," Alyssa said. "He knows my family. How do I know he won't target them?"

"You don't. He could do that."

"So going into hiding won't work. Tell me you have a Plan C."

"You're going to have to work with him, do what Malcolm

wants. Get information for him, and hopefully *from* him. And then pass that along to the Agency."

"If he finds out I'm working against him?"

"You can't let that happen."

" I don't know how to do this." Fear had her volume rising. "What if I mess it up?"

"This is why we need to stay together. I a field agent—*was,* anyway."

"What do you mean, was? Did you leave the CIA? Then who's—"

"I'm out of the field."

"Oh. Why?"

"Try to focus," he snapped. "The point is, I'll do my best to keep you safe."

"I was just..." She took a breath. Their conversations felt like a contact sport. "What do I say to him?"

"If he refuses to let you off the hook, feel free to show your annoyance. You need to demonstrate that you don't know Charles Sanders is anybody but who he claims to be. Unless he threatens you, you shouldn't let on that you're afraid. Just end the call, and we'll figure it out. Okay?"

At her nod—she couldn't seem to make herself speak—he lifted her phone from the end of the table and held it out to her.

"Now?" Fear had her voice pitching too high. "Shouldn't we...come up with a script or something?"

"The last thing you want is to sound scripted. You'll have to wing it. The longer you make him wait, the worse it'll be."

She took her cell, inhaling a deep breath. This was just a conversation with Charles Sanders, mild-mannered businessman.

Not a terrorist. Not a killer.

Somehow, the lies she told herself didn't make her feel better.

# CHAPTER EIGHT

Callan followed Alyssa into the living area, pulling his phone from his pocket, and settled on the desk chair.

Alyssa sat catty-corner to him. Her cheeks, pink with embarrassment earlier, had paled. Her eyes were wide and fearful.

He'd do anything, anything to get her out of this. But how?

"Go ahead." He nodded to the cell in her hand. "Put it on speaker."

She bent over her phone.

"Wait."

She looked up, eyebrows lifted.

"I don't know what you believe." Was he really going to do this? Now that he'd stopped her, he could see no way out without looking moronic. And anyway, the idea had occurred to him—and probably hadn't come from him. "Would it offend you if I prayed about it real quick?"

Surprised jolted her back straight. "Uh. No. That would be... Go ahead."

Callan held his hand out, and she slipped hers into it.

He wasn't in the habit of praying with people, certainly not at work. Certainly not in situations like this. To be fair, it wasn't as if he had ever been in a situation like this—staying in a fancy boutique hotel with the one woman he'd never been able to get out of his head.

Her hand felt just right, nestled in his grip.

He prayed for Alyssa, asking Go to give her wisdom and words and safety and guidance.

After he said, "Amen," Alyssa's head stayed bowed. So he kept his mouth shut, figuring she was asking for something she hadn't wanted to say aloud.

He liked that.

Was she a Christian? He hadn't known her well enough to ask before, but the way she prayed now made him wonder.

*Just keep her safe, Lord. And me. And...and help me keep my head on straight.*

Because as much as Alyssa meant to him, he had Peri to think about now. His daughter needed to be his top priority.

Alyssa looked up. "I'm ready."

He released her hand and turned on his voice recorder before setting his phone on the coffee table. "Go ahead."

She dialed.

The phone rang twice before Ghazi said, "Charles Sanders."

"Charles, it's Alyssa." Her voice shook the slightest bit, and she cleared her throat, shifting away from Callan a little. "Sorry I missed your call."

"It is early in the day. I realize it's quite soon after giving you the assignment, but I'd hoped you might have a name for me."

"Not yet, I'm sorry to say. I wanted to get that done ASAP," Alyssa continued, "but it's proving as difficult as I feared it would be. And now that Caleb is in town, I want to spend time with him. His job has him traveling so often."

"I wasn't aware of your engagement. And I noticed no ring last night."

A ring! Why hadn't Callan thought of a ring?

"We haven't told our families yet." Alyssa was good at thinking on her feet, which shouldn't surprise him. "I'm not going to wear the ring until we do."

"I'm sure they'll be very happy." The terrorist sounded perfectly pleasant and at ease. He was good at the deception game.

"I hope so. The point is, I'm not going to be able to complete this project for you. I'm taking some time off to spend with Caleb. It's been a pleasure—"

"Ah, well, that *is* a problem. I'll need you to complete the task you've been paid for."

Alyssa's gaze flicked to Callan. "I'm sorry, but I really can't take on anything right now."

"I'm afraid I need that name. And I need your help with another project. Therefore, you will keep the money I've already transferred into your account, and I will pay you more—"

"Even if I wanted to, Charles, I really can't. I didn't want to bring this up because...well, it's not your problem. It has nothing to do with you at all. But my apartment was broken into last night. When Caleb and I got home from dinner, there were thieves there. They got away with some of my equipment, including the hard drive from my desktop, which stores my programs and private bots. I need those things to find—"

"What are you saying?" For the first time in the conversation, Ghazi sounded rattled.

The man's reaction confirmed Callan's hunch that Ghazi's men hadn't been behind the break-in.

"Is the information you've gathered for me secure?" he

asked. "Or has it been compromised?" Warning hummed in his words like power on a wire.

"I keep all my clients' information on a cloud server. I did worry that there might be a trail on my desktop that led to the server, so I downloaded all the data—yours and that belonging to other clients—last night and deleted my account. It's safe."

There was a long pause.

Alyssa met Callan's eyes, fear clouding her expression.

He nodded to tell her she was doing great.

"I appreciate how seriously you take security," Ghazi said. "That tells me you're the right person for my next job."

"Thank you, but like I said—"

"I like you," Ghazi said. "I like working with you. I trust you. So you're going to need to do this job for me."

"Even if I wanted to, without my equipment—"

"Whatever you need, I'll provide for you. I have an office that I've filled with state-of-the-art equipment. Anything not already here, I'll have delivered for you immediately. You can stay on site until you've completed the assignment. You'll find this house quite comfortable."

"I'm going to have to decline. But thank you so much for—"

"Perhaps you're not hearing me, Alyssa." That warning tone was back, more overt than undercurrent this time. "I can't take no for an answer."

She pushed to her feet. "You cannot force me—"

"Alyssa, let's not throw around words like *force*. You've procured much information for me. If anybody were to look too closely into how you got that information, I assume they would discover that you've broken a few laws. And they might even discover that *I've* broken a few laws. By helping me, you would be considered an accomplice in those crimes. Since I'm not a citizen of this country, I would be able to relocate to a more hospitable nation. I suspect that would be harder for you, what with a family and a fiancé. But if you do one more job for me—"

"One more," she snapped. "And then one more, and then one more after that. Is that how this works? Are you blackmailing me?" The shock and outrage in her voice sounded legitimate.

"I'm encouraging you to act in your own best interests."

Callan gripped her arm. When she looked at him, he mouthed, "Hang up. Hang up now."

But she wrenched away. "And what am I supposed to tell Caleb? We have plans. I'm supposed to just back out, tell him… what? I'm being forced to work against my will?"

"You'll come up with something. It will only take a few days."

Callan reached for her phone, but she angled back, shooting a look.

Though she didn't speak, he got the message.

*Trust me.*

The problem was, though Alyssa was quick on her feet, she wasn't an agent. She didn't know what she was doing.

He shook his head, hard. *Stop talking.*

She turned away, taking her phone with her.

What was she thinking?

"What do you want me to do?" she asked.

"We'll discuss it in person."

"Fine." The word sounded as if it had been spoken through gritted teeth, but her anger made sense. "I'll replace my equipment. Just let me know—"

"I think not," Ghazi said. "That will take too long, and since your apartment was compromised, I'd prefer you somewhere safe. I promise to protect you."

Protect her? Ghazi was the dangerous one.

"Besides, knowing you," the terrorist continued, "you'll have the information we need by the end of the day."

"I don't like being dictated to."

"I assure you, Alyssa, when you finish this task, I'll be out of your life. I'll pay you well for your work, and nobody ever need know what *interesting* tactics you've used to get my information. We both get what we want."

She huffed. "You're not giving me any choice. What's the job?"

"I'll tell you when I see you."

She said nothing. And Ghazi didn't, either.

Callan moved around the coffee table to get in front of her. He was nearly there when she spoke again.

"I'll do it."

He shook his head, mouthing, *Stop. Stop!*

But she added, "Caleb's coming with me."

Callan froze. What was she saying?

On the phone, Ghazi said, "It is not *take your boyfriend to work* day."

"He changed his schedule to be home with me this week. We have things we need to manage. I'm not going to blow him off. Look, Mr. Sanders...Charles." She softened her voice with his name. "I don't know anything about...anything you're doing, and I don't want to know. But when Caleb saw us together last night, he got the wrong idea. I'd told him I had a business meeting, but when he came in and saw me sitting with an attractive, charming man... It's stupid. There's nothing between you and me, but anyway." She uttered a nervous laugh. "I'm embarrassed to say all this, but how am I supposed to tell Caleb I'm blowing him off to be with you?"

Callan's heart was thumping hard.

She was selling a story, and she was doing it well. But would Ghazi buy it?

"You have a job to do," Ghazi said. "A man who travels for work as much as your fiancé does should understand that."

"Well, yeah. Probably." She paced in front of the coffee table. Even when she walked toward Callan, she didn't make eye contact. She was in the zone. "I get that you need me to do this thing for you, and I get that you probably even think you could...blackmail me or whatever." A hint of humor laced her words now. "I'm sure whatever it is you've done, it's not that bad. You're a nice guy."

Alyssa managed to acknowledge that Ghazi was a criminal and, in the next breath, blow that fact off as irrelevant.

She was eerily impressive.

Callan would need to stay on her good side. Well, if he could *get* on her good side.

"Caleb comes off as super confident," she said, "but he can be insecure. And, I have to admit, if he told me he needed to go to some gorgeous woman's home for a few days to do a job, I wouldn't like it either."

And there was a roundabout compliment, comparing Ghazi to the male equivalent of a gorgeous woman.

Masterful.

"It would be one thing," Alyssa said, "if I could do this job at my apartment. Then Caleb could come over. He could do his thing, I could do mine, and we could be together. But after last night, my apartment doesn't feel safe. I never get this personal with clients, but I don't know what else to do. Either you let me rebuild my setup at Caleb's place, which I can probably do in a few days, or you let Caleb come with me to yours."

Only the sound of breathing came from Ghazi's end of the phone.

Callan considered what this would mean for himself and his family. He'd promised his parents and Peri that he wouldn't go into the field again, which was why he'd transferred to work in the Boston office. Now he'd be going back on that promise, taking on a field assignment that might be innocuous.

It probably wouldn't be dangerous.

But, it could be more dangerous than anything he'd ever done.

His parents had agreed to keep Peri until he could figure out his life, how to be a single father. But Dad hadn't been feeling well the day before.

Maybe Hannah could take her for a few days. Not that his sister didn't have anything better to do, but if she could handle the overnights, then Mom and Dad could keep Peri during the day.

They'd figure it out. Peri loved his parents and his sister, and they adored her.

Callan was the one who didn't belong.

Alyssa lifted her gaze and met Callan's. She still looked nervous, but she'd managed to turn that to her benefit.

Callan nodded, trying to tell her silently, that she'd done well, no matter what happened next.

"All right," Ghazi finally said. "Your fiancé can come. But I take security very seriously. Please, make it clear to him that he's not to tell anybody where we are, and he'll be limited to certain areas of the house."

"I'll tell him. He's got work to do, so as long as he can bring his laptop—"

"Fine, fine."

"Good. Give me an address and—"

"I will have somebody pick you both up. Can you be ready in an hour?"

Callan lifted two fingers, already snatching his phone.

"Can you make it two hours?" she asked.

"Two hours. And the address?"

"We're at a hotel. Let me just look..."

Callan turned his screen for her to see. He'd found a nearby hotel, and she read the address.

"My driver will meet you there." The phone beeped.

She checked the screen, then checked it again before tossing her cell onto the coffee table.

She collapsed onto the sofa.

"That was perfect."

Studying him through squinted eyes, she asked, "But?"

But worry churned inside him. "I don't love that we're going to walk into the man's lair."

Her eyebrows hiked. "Lair? This isn't a comic book."

"You're right. It's not. And he's no fictional villain. He's a terrorist, and we're about to let him take both of us." Maybe for the reasons the man had said. But maybe not. "There's nothing about this that feels good to me."

"Should I have refused? I don't know how I could have."

"He didn't give you a choice. And now we're going to have to go through with it. And pray the Lord brings us out the other side."

## CHAPTER NINE

Ten minutes after she'd ended the call with Ghazi, Alyssa dragged her suitcase out of her bedroom to the door.

It was taking all her energy not to let her fear show. But this was terrifying enough that she was tempted to call her father.

Dad would never let her walk into danger. He'd find a way to get her out of this, whatever *this* was.

But Callan hadn't suggested bringing her dad in, and Michael had warned against it, which she still didn't understand.

And frankly, Dad had never seen her as anything but a nuisance. The last thing she wanted was to reinforce his negative impression of her. Not only was she in trouble, it was trouble of her own making, working for a terrorist.

What kind of fool got herself into a situation like this?

If she didn't tell her father and he found out, he'd be furious with her. But how would he find out?

If things got out of hand, if she started to feel like she was in over her head, then she'd reach out to her father. Until then, she'd go along with Callan's plan. Not that she knew much about it. Get information for his boss at the CIA. Malcolm, he'd said. What information, and how she was supposed to get it, she had zero idea.

Just like she didn't know what information Ghazi wanted from her.

She felt like she was walking through a gray mist. Nothing was clear. Nothing was certain. And when she tried to understand, the mist just slipped through her fingers.

She hated this.

When she neared Callan's closed door, she heard his voice, but his words were low and muffled.

She moved to the living area and perched on a chair, opening her phone to check her email.

"I'm doing my best."

That came through loud and clear, sounding both angry and defensive.

His door swung open. He rolled out a suitcase he must've gotten from his apartment the night before and left it next to hers. When he turned and saw Alyssa, he attempted a smile, but it was tight. Still talking into his phone, he said, "Listen—" And then was quiet as he stepped into his room. He didn't close the door this time. "I hear what you're saying, and if I could..." Silence, then, "Yes, I would. I'm trying."

Alyssa moved into the kitchen and grabbed a bottle of water, mostly to give Callan his space.

The rest of his conversation was muffled. A moment later, he appeared in the doorway. "Sorry about that."

"Everything okay?"

"Yup. You ready?"

So...no explanation for the phone call, not that it was any of her business. She twisted the cap back onto her water bottle. "Let's go."

She put on her jacket then stepped out, heading to the elevator.

She felt safe here at the Rooming House. Out there, she'd be exposed and vulnerable. If not for Callan's presence beside her, she wouldn't have the courage to leave.

She stopped at the counter in the lobby, thanked Jonathan and returned their keys, then joined Callan at the door.

His eyebrows lowered. "You okay?"

"Sure. Great."

His smirk told her he wasn't buying it. They stepped past the doorman and into the cool April air. Though the sun was out this morning, the buildings blocked its light.

They met an Uber, despite the fact that the hotel where they'd told Ghazi to pick them up was just a few blocks away and the walk across Harvard Square would be lovely.

Callan didn't want anyone—by that, he meant Ghazi and his men—to see them on the street with their suitcases.

The Uber driver aimed for the hotel's front door, but Callan insisted he take them into the parking garage beneath the building. The bill he slipped the guy convinced him to go to the extra trouble.

They took the elevator up to the fourth floor, then got off, walked away, waited around the corner, and then returned to the elevator.

Inside, Callan pressed the Down button.

This whole thing was weird, but she understood. He wanted them to be seen getting off the elevator from above floors. Maybe there were floor numbers above the first-floor elevator doors that would show where the car had come from.

Seemed a little paranoid, considering they still had an hour and a half before Ghazi's man was supposed to pick them up, but Callan knew what he was doing.

The lobby was spacious and grand with high ceilings, dark

woodwork, and multiple little seating areas. It teemed with people coming and going, some working at desks along one edge, others sipping coffee in a little café on the opposite side.

Callan marched across the room like he knew exactly where he was going. He left his suitcase against the wall outside the coffee shop. "What do you want?"

"Uh...I'm not—"

He leaned in and whispered in her ear. "We're putting on a show, Alyssa. Could you play along?"

It would be a lot easier if he'd give her a script or at least a hint as to what her lines were supposed to be. "Whatever you think, dear."

He grinned. "Stay with our stuff. Be right back."

She leaned against the wall and scanned the space, looking for...she wasn't sure what. Enemies. Terrorists. Spies.

All she saw were families and businesspeople and probably parents whose kids attended Harvard or MIT.

Feeling exposed and off balance, she took out her phone and scanned her emails again. One message had come in from a client asking her to do a job for him. She replied and asked him to send her the details, that she'd be back in her office by Monday.

Was that wishful thinking?

Would she still be alive in four days? Would she be out of this...whatever it was?

Warmth beside her, then Callan's voice in her ear. "You ready, Paris?"

There was that nickname again. But she didn't hate how it sounded on his lips. Or how his breath felt against her neck.

She had no idea how she was going to pull this off. Pretend to work for Ghazi while gathering information, and all of that while faking an engagement to this man, who somehow made her skin tingle and her insides tremble. And infuriated her at the same time.

It was too much.

How had she ever wanted to be a spy? This was insane. Like taking the stage in front of a roomful of critics and knowing that if you forgot your lines, you'd probably end up dead.

What in the world was she doing?

"I CAN PULL YOUR SUITCASE." Alyssa stopped Callan from trying to carry two coffee cups and a sack in one hand. When he gave her a go-ahead nod, she gripped the handle. "Where are we going?"

"Is that coat warm enough?"

"For what?"

He started across the lobby, and she walked beside him down a corridor that led to meeting rooms on one side.

He stopped at a glass door leading to a little courtyard with a large window between it and the lobby. The other three sides were brick. Planters overflowed with spring flowers and greenery, and a little fountain bubbled into a small pond in the center.

His eyebrows hiked, a question.

"It's fine."

The door closed behind them, silencing a low hum of the building that she hadn't noticed until it was gone. Aside from the occasional rumble of a particularly loud vehicle on the street behind the walls, it was quiet out here. Peaceful. "This is nice."

"Will you be warm enough?"

"I'll survive."

"Good." He moved deeper into the space, passing the pond filled with bright orange fish swimming in circles around their tiny home. "I wanted us to be like kids in the fifties." She was still trying to figure out what he meant, when he added, "You know, seen but not heard." He stopped near a loveseat in front of the lobby windows. "This okay?"

She sat, her back to the glass.

He settled beside her—a little too close. She started to get up and move to an adjacent chair, but he gripped her hand, holding her in place. "We're in love, Paris. Don't leave me."

"Ghazi isn't even here yet."

"How do you know?"

Oh. Right.

For all they knew, he'd sent men to stake the place out, which explained the elevator dance and the food she certainly didn't need.

He set the coffee cups on the table, sliding one in front of her, then tore the sack and laid it flat. He'd bought an everything bagel with cream cheese and a giant cinnamon roll. "Help yourself."

"I'm not hungry."

"Humor me." Grinning, he bit a huge hunk of the pastry as if he hadn't just scarfed down two entire breakfasts a couple of hours before.

She separated the top half of the bagel and tore off a tiny portion. "Now what?"

"We talk until Ghazi gets here. We need to be prepared for questions."

"I thought you liked to wing it."

"I thought you didn't."

Fair point.

"My name is Caleb Thompson. I sell computer hardware."

"Sounds fascinating."

He must've picked up her sarcasm because he smiled. "If you're asked, say you don't know much about my work because I don't talk about it, but it takes me away a lot, and I do well financially. You should also know I have one sister, and my parents are still alive and married."

"Have I met your parents?"

"Stick as close to the truth as you can. You haven't met them yet, but we're planning to tell both our families about our engagement this weekend. That gives us a hard deadline. We'll need to leave Charles's place by tomorrow night."

It was Thursday, so that made sense. But… "Can't we make it tonight, since it's all fiction?"

"Malcolm wants us to gather as much intel as we can, and we want to have time to compare notes, which we might not while you're working."

He set the cinnamon roll down—he'd managed to eat half of it already—and sipped his coffee. He was the picture of casual. "I'll need to know what he's asking you to do before you can complete the task. Then, I'll communicate with Malcolm, and we can make a plan about how to handle it."

"You think Ghazi will let you make calls? I mean, what do you think this is going to be like?" She tried to imagine what they'd be walking into, but it was all too nebulous. She'd insisted Callan come with her, but now she wasn't so sure this was a great idea. What if Ghazi hurt him? Or killed him?

What if she was walking into a trap that would destroy them both?

Callan's arm slid around her shoulders, and he urged her against his side. "It's okay, Paris. Don't worry."

How did he read her mind like that? It was eerie. And irritating.

"I have no idea what it's going to look like," he said, "but I'm prepared. I've got it under control."

"How, how do you—?"

"You need to trust me." He backed away enough to peer

down at her. His nearness was disconcerting, making her feel both protected and uncomfortable.

Her emotions were all over the place. How could she possibly do this?

"What's important right now," he continued, "is that we get our story straight."

Right. Of course. She flipped back through the conversation and remembered... "My grandparents' anniversary party is Saturday afternoon. Sixty-five years. Their anniversary isn't until Monday, but I guess Dad has to be in DC that day." Typical, Dad putting work before family. "Everyone will attend, and of course I'm expected to be there. We could announce the engagement there. Theoretically."

"In Shadow Cove?"

She was surprised he remembered where she was from. "Right. The party is at Dad's country club."

"Okay, perfect. So we have to leave Charles's house Friday afternoon. We're going to my parents' house first to tell them the news, then driving to Shadow Cove Saturday for the party, where we'll make an announcement. That's the plan, and we can't get out of it."

"Okay. And where do your parents live?"

"They still live in the house I grew up in. You've never been there, but I've told you about it. It's an old property on a pond in central Maine. I don't want you to share any more details than that."

She should've remembered Callan was from Maine. There hadn't been a lot of students from Maine in their class at Boston College.

"Is that all fiction? Where do they really live?"

"We're sticking close to the truth. That's where my parents really live, and my sister lives nearby."

"Aren't you worried Ghazi will be able to find your family, though?"

"Charles Sanders. That's his name."

"I know that. I'm just saying... That information is pretty detailed. It's not like central Maine is densely populated."

"Thompson is one of the most common last names in the state. I chose my alias carefully. Don't worry about any of that."

"Oh. I see. And your sister?"

"Hannah. She's two years younger than I am, and she lives in Augusta. You've never met her, but you will this weekend. You're going to like her."

Hannah. Two years younger. "Got it. What do your parents do?"

"They're both retired, and they like to travel. You shouldn't need to know any more than that. I doubt any of this will come up but, just in case, it's good to know enough to make conversation. How about your family?"

"I'm the oldest of five, all girls. The first four of us are all a little over a year apart. So it's me, then Brooklynn, Cecelia—we call her Cici—and Delaney. Kenzie is the baby."

His eyebrows hiked. "Wait. Alyssa, Brooklynn, Cecelia, Delaney. ABCD, and then...Kenzie?"

Alyssa couldn't help her surprise, or the strange wave of pleasure she figured showed in her smile. "Nobody notices that."

He shrugged. "I'm observant. Why the pattern change?"

"I don't know. I think it bothers Kenzie, though. Cici used to tell her it was because she was adopted, the brat."

He chuckled. "I bet it was fun growing up with all those sisters."

"You can say that because you only had one. Four sisters are...a lot."

"Are you close to them?"

"Used to be. I loved taking care of them. I miss being around kids."

He seemed to take that in, an unreadable expression on his face, which he schooled before she could examine it further . "Why aren't you close to your sisters anymore?"

She shrugged. "I went off to college and then moved to DC. We just grew apart. Brooklynn, Cici, and Delaney are best friends. Kenzie and I are on the outside of their little...clique, and have been for years."

"Are you and Kenzie close?"

"We don't have a lot in common, and we're so far apart in age."

Callan worked on his cinnamon roll, and she took another bite of the bagel and sipped her coffee, which warmed her on the inside. With her jacket on, it wasn't that cold out—maybe low fifties—but she was getting chilled sitting on the hard bench.

He finished the pastry and wiped his hands on a napkin. "What do we do for fun?"

"You probably need to tell me. I don't have a lot of hobbies."

"Why not?"

"I don't know. I just...don't. I work a lot. When I'm not working, I'm usually thinking about work. I like to read, sometimes. But that's not exactly a couple's activity."

"Do you exercise? Play racquetball or pickleball?"

"I'll take up pickleball when I turn fifty."

"It's actually really fun." He chuckled. "I know this because my parents play."

"Of course they do." Though she had no idea what his parents looked like, she imagined a happy couple, laughing together, playing doubles pickleball—was that a thing?—and beating all the competition.

So different from her own parents.

Dad golfed. Mom decorated and shopped and had lunch with her daughters.

Dad consulted with government agencies and defense contractors.

Mom volunteered on committees and planned galas.

Rarely did they do anything together. When they did, usually one of them had to talk the other into doing it.

Not exactly a marriage made in heaven. Nothing like her aunt and uncle. Peggy and Roger made marriage look easy.

"You must do something for fun," Callan prompted. "What do you love? Or what did you love as a kid?"

"I used to volunteer in the children's ministry at church. I should probably do that again."

He shuddered. "That's not something we do together. Kids hate me."

"I'm sure that's not true."

An expression crossed his features, almost...wounded, though that didn't make sense.

She groped for a subject change, not wanting to cause him pain.

And there was a new experience. She'd imagined causing him pain for four years of college. She'd also imagined kissing him.

She needed to get both of those ideas out of her head.

"I walk every morning before work," she said, "and sometimes after work, too, just to get me out of the apartment. What are your hobbies?"

"Rock climbing, hiking, fishing, skiing, boating."

"Oh, gosh. You're one of those people who love the outdoors."

"You mean planet Earth? Guilty. As your fiancé, I'll need to get you interested in the things I love. We can do them together."

"Thank God this is all fake."

He bumped her shoulder. "Aw, Paris, you're gonna love rock climbing."

"I think you should lose the nickname."

By the utter delight in his eyes, he was about to come up with some excuse as to why he couldn't or wouldn't, but the door to their private oasis opened, and a woman stepped out. Her hair was in a ponytail, and her makeup was overdone, from the too-thick eyeliner to the too-red lipstick. She wore jeans and a sweatshirt and a jacket. And a wide smile.

What were the chances?

Alyssa stifled a groan as the woman homed in on her.

"I thought that was you!" She hurried across the space, arms open wide. "I saw you through the window, and even from behind, I could tell."

Alyssa stood and stepped around the coffee table to hug her former schoolmate, wanting to pull away long before the intruder let her go.

Finally, she did, stepping back. "It's so good to see you." She glanced at Callan. "I'm in town for a conference. Don't you live nearby? What are you doing at a hotel?"

"It's a long story." Alyssa said. "Frannie, this is—"

"Caleb," he supplied, sticking out his hand.

They were keeping up their ruse. "Frannie and I went to school together," Alyssa explained. "She and Brooklyn were in the same class."

He shook her hand, then slipped his arm around Alyssa's waist. "Nice to meet you, Frannie. I've hardly met any of Alyssa's friends from Shadow Cove. It's a pleasure."

The woman's eyes popped wide. "Uh... Okay. Are you two, um...?" Her gaze flicked between them.

"We're engaged." He winked. "But it's a secret. We haven't told our families yet."

What was he doing? They couldn't tell Frannie their story.

Telephone, telegraph—tell Frannie.

Her eyes widened as she focused on Alyssa. "Brooklynn didn't tell me you were seeing anyone."

"I didn't realize you and my sister kept in touch."

"Oh, yeah. We talk a lot."

Great. Seemed Frannie kept in better contact with Brooklynn than Alyssa did. "I haven't told her or anyone about Caleb yet."

"We've kept it on the down low," Callan added. "I travel so much, and she's always busy and I guess"—he squeezed her closer to him—"we just haven't wanted to share each other."

Frannie's expression morphed from concerned to smitten. "Aw, that's so sweet. I'm just positive Brooklynn will be thrilled when she hears."

Callan leaned in. "Keep our secret for us, would you? I'm guessing she wouldn't be thrilled to hear about it from you instead of from her own sister." He shot Alyssa a thin smile. "I probably should've kept my mouth shut, but I'm so ready to start telling people. Aren't you, Paris?"

"Yeah. Of course."

"*Paris?*" The woman repeated the stupid nickname, looking between them. "Is that where you met?"

He laughed. "Just a little private joke."

"Ooh, my favorite kind." Frannie eyed one of the chairs in their seating area, clearly waiting to be invited to join them.

Alyssa was trying to figure out how to get rid of her when her phone rang.

She pulled it from her coat pocket. She didn't recognize the number but figured she'd better answer anyway. Maybe Frannie would get the hint. "Alyssa Wright."

"This is your driver," a man said. "I am in the lobby whenever you're ready."

She gripped Callan's arm and squeezed. "We're on our way."

His pleased expression faded.

Alyssa ended the call. "That's our ride, Frannie. But it was good to see you." She gave her quick hug while Callan tossed their trash in a can near the door.

Frannie was talking, all *let's get together* and *it was so good to catch up*.

Not that Alyssa was eager to walk into a terrorist's lair, but at least she could escape this torture.

Finally, Callan pulled their suitcases back into the corridor, and she walked side by side with him toward the lobby.

"He's early," Alyssa said.

Callan nodded.

"We didn't cover how we met or—"

"Shh." He wrapped the same arm around her waist again, whispering. "Your friend is ten paces behind us."

Alyssa stifled the urge to look. How did he know? He hadn't turned around.

"We met at a business event in the city," Callan whispered. "Caleb went to community college. If they start to ask questions, get annoyed. Our past is none of Charles's business. Tell him you're busy. Tell him you don't have time to chitchat, that you're on a deadline."

She could do that.

They turned the corner and crossed the lobby toward the registrations and concierge desks.

A man stood near the window that looked out at the courtyard, hands fisted, eyes tracking them. He'd been watching, and he didn't mind them knowing it.

He had blond hair and hazel eyes and a protruding jaw. His biceps looked thicker than her thighs. He wore an ill-fitting suit that didn't suit him at all.

The man looked nothing like his slight and unassuming boss. Of course, Ghazi—Charles—wasn't what he seemed. Not even close.

The driver stepped toward them. "Ms. Wright?"

"That's me."

The man sent a glare at Callan.

*Caleb. Not Callan.*

"This way." He turned and led them to the doors and outside.

It was happening too fast, and she wasn't ready.

Before she could protest or panic, the driver had stowed their bags and was demanding their phones. "Mr. Sanders insisted. He would prefer that his location remain secret."

Callan protested, but when the man told him his choices—give me your phone or stay here—he relented.

Alyssa was too afraid to refuse, handing her cell over without a word of complaint.

They slid into the backseat of a black Mercedes parked at the curb.

And then, the driver pulled away from the hotel.

And they left all safety behind.

# CHAPTER TEN

The back seat of the car Ghazi had sent was spacious enough for Callan to stretch his legs out, but that didn't mean he was comfortable, not with the tension wafting off Alyssa beside him and the fear in her eyes whenever she looked his way.

Nor was he comfortable with the driver, who hadn't spoken a word since they'd left the hotel.

They crossed the Charles into Boston, went east on Soldiers Field Road adjacent to the river, then turned west on Comm. Ave. to St. Paul Street. The driver continued past the Episcopal church for which the road was named and then started snaking through neighborhoods, seemingly willy-nilly, though perhaps this was the most direct route.

Callan knew Boston well enough, but they were outside the city now in an area he'd never been before. Based on the fancy homes, the wide and perfectly manicured lawns, and the expensive cars in the driveways, they'd reached Brookline.

It irked him that he didn't have his phone, but he'd anticipated that. This wasn't his first field assignment, after all. On the other hand, this wasn't a run-of-the-mill op. Normally, he went into the field with trained agents, not beautiful computer hackers who had no clue what they were doing.

The driver had powered down both their phones, but that wouldn't keep Malcolm from tracking Callan's. Of course, the Agency knowing where they were would do Callan and Alyssa no good if they didn't have a way to call for help if they needed it. Callan had his laptop, though. Hopefully, Ghazi wouldn't take that away when they got to the house.

If he did, Callan would figure it out. This was what he did, and he was good at it.

It was trouble on the home front he didn't know how to deal with.

*"You promised us, Callan."* His mother's words played on repeat in his head, the tone not accusatory but disappointed—which was so much worse. *"You have a child to take care of now."*

Did she think he'd forgotten about Peri? Did Mom really think his eight-year-old daughter was ever far from his mind? Since he'd discovered her existence the previous fall, he'd thought of little else. He'd given up his dream job for Peri. He'd changed his life for her.

Not that he resented it. Not that he shouldn't have done those things. Of course he should have. He was her father.

But he had a career, and his work was not just time-consuming. It could be *all*-consuming. Which was why it made sense for Peri to stay with Mom and Dad when Callan had to be in Boston.

They were retired. They had time for her. They had help, with Hannah living so close, and Callan's sister adored Peri.

And they knew what the heck they were doing.

Whereas Callan was clueless.

Peri was better off with his parents than she'd ever be with him. She knew it, his parents knew it. Hannah knew it.

Everybody knew it, even if they were too kind to say so.

Finally, the car turned into a narrow driveway, giving Callan something to think about besides the daughter he was failing in every way.

The driver stopped at a wrought iron gate. Interesting, considering the other houses on this road had no such security—just normal driveways for normal families.

Well, normal *rich* families.

The other houses they'd passed on this street had expansive lawns, but not this house. A tall, thick hedge made it almost impossible to see a white structure beyond.

The driver entered a code on a keypad, the gate swung open, and they moved slowly forward and around a bend.

The house came into view.

Three stories tall, it resembled buildings he'd seen in Italy, where he'd been on assignment. Romanesque with grayish-white stucco siding, a Spanish-tile roof, and dark green shutters, it was surrounded by trees and bushes and flowers everywhere he looked.

He squeezed Alyssa's hand. Since they were supposed to be in love, and they weren't supposed to be nervous, he smiled at her. "Nice digs, right? Of course, this is probably old hat to you." Her family's money wasn't exactly a state secret, so there was no reason for him not to mention it.

"It's an impressive building." She focused on the driver. "Any idea when it was built?"

Saying nothing, the man climbed out of the car and slammed the door.

Alyssa's fake smile faded, and her eyes widened with terror. She held his hand in a death grip as if she saw him as her protector.

He didn't hate that.

Callan was trying to sell a story, which was the only reason he leaned in and pressed a quick kiss to her lips.

That was exactly the kind of thing a fiancé might do.

The fact that the kiss felt so natural...

He didn't hate that either.

"It's going to be okay," he whispered. "If we get separated and you need me, just scream. Wherever you are, I'll find you."

Before she could answer, the driver opened her door.

She held Callan's eye contact another moment, then let go of his hand, shouldered her giant purse, and climbed out.

Callan exited from his side, reached back in for his laptop bag, then stood and stretched, relaxed as could be. "Wow, this place is beautiful, isn't it?" He headed to the trunk, where they'd stowed their suitcases. The driver had already unloaded them both.

"I got these. Go on." The guy nodded toward the front door.

Callan took Alyssa's hand, and they walked along paving stones set in a bed of ground cover. The garden was thick and wild and smelled of sweet flowers, fertile soil, and springtime. He was no gardener himself, but the scent brought him back to his childhood, to playing hide-and-seek in the woods and racing his sister and the neighbor kids to the boulder at the edge of the pond.

Would Peri have any happy childhood memories? Or was the joy of childhood behind her now that she was stuck with her dad?

That was a question he preferred not to ponder.

The front door opened, and Dariush Ghazi stood in the threshold. He wore jeans and a short-sleeved button-down that looked brand new, as if it'd come straight from the store. As if he'd purchased the clothes for exactly this occasion, in order to create an impression. "Welcome, friends. Please, come in."

Alyssa preceded Callan up the steps. "Hello, Charles." Her

tone was formal, a stark contrast to the man's exuberant greeting.

"Nice place you got here." Callan climbed the steps, noting the placard inlaid in the stucco wall that dated the building to 1916. He stuck out his hand, grabbing Ghazi's in a firm grip. "You lived here long?"

"It's only temporary while I conduct my business in the States."

His British accent was a little like his clothes—too perfect. Too practiced.

He stepped back, and Callan joined Alyssa in a modest foyer that had doors off both sides and a hallway that led toward the back of the house. The hardwood floors looked original. Light paint on the walls. The antique furnishings must have come with the place. A staircase that led both up and down wasn't grand but simple and utilitarian.

"Would you like a tour?" Ghazi asked.

"I'd love one." Callan infused enthusiasm into his voice. He angled to face Alyssa, hoping she read his mind. *Say yes.* "Wouldn't you?"

"I'd like to get started, to tell you the truth."

She wasn't so great with unspoken communication.

Ghazi seemed amused, a smile playing at his too thin lips. "I'll have my housekeeper show you around, Caleb, while Alyssa and I get started."

A woman materialized in the hallway as if she'd been conjured by the man's words. She was about five-five, not slender but more solid than fat with the look of a woman who spent as much time in the gym as Callan did. She had short spiked blond hair with purple tips and wore black jeans, sensible black shoes, and a long-sleeved black button-down shirt.

Nothing about her said *housekeeper*.

Ghazi waved her forward. "Ah, here she is now. Molly, take their coats, and then show Mr. Thompson around."

They slipped out of their jackets.

She took them. "I'll give him the grand tour." Her Boston accent was more North End than Southie.

Callan took Alyssa's hand and tucked it in his elbow. "We'd prefer to stay together."

"I'm afraid that's not going to work." Ghazi managed a regretful tone. "Alyssa and I have some business to discuss."

Callan scowled. "I'm not a corporate spy, man. I'm not here to learn all your secrets."

"It's all right." Alyssa jumped in, just like a good fiancée should. "You go ahead and have a look around while Charles and I talk. You can join us after." She focused on Ghazi. "Right?"

"Certainly." He didn't look away from Callan. "I only ask that you remain on the far side of the room while Alyssa works, so as not to accidentally see something you ought not to see." He smiled, adding, "Not that I suspect you of anything."

Callan had the strongest impression that he did, in fact, suspect Callan of something.

"I guess that's okay"—turning to Alyssa—"as long as you're sure you'll be okay without me for a little bit."

"Of course. Go on." She sounded cool and confident.

"Not that I'd have a clue what you were doing." Callan gave her a warm smile, then looked at Ghazi again. "I work with hardware. All that software stuff is"—he passed his hand a few inches above his scalp—"way over my head."

Alyssa rose to her tiptoes and kissed his cheek. "See you in a few." She turned to Ghazi. "Lead the way."

Ghazi gestured towards the staircase, and the two walked to the second floor, side by side.

Callan stared after her a few beats too long. Had she really just kissed him? Like it was nothing?

She would have made a great agent. She was good at pretending.

Even so, the thought of her stepping into dangerous situations made him feel ill.

The fact that she was in *this* dangerous situation made him want to follow her and not let her out of his sight.

"This way, Mr. Thompson."

He smiled at the guard playing the part of housekeeper—seemed everybody was playing a fictional role here. "This place is amazing. Have you worked here long? Did you like, come with the building, or did Mr. Sanders hire you? You must love it."

He'd keep up a steady stream of ridiculous conversation. His goal was to act like he had no clue anything unusual was going on.

To convince Ghazi and his people that he wasn't a threat.

Right up until the moment when he took them down.

# CHAPTER ELEVEN

On the second floor, *Charles* led her to an office. The room was wider than it was deep with floor-to-ceiling windows along the back wall interrupted only by glass French doors in the center that led out to a narrow balcony overlooking a rear garden.

Bookshelves lined the wall to her right adjacent to the windows.

On one side of the room, an antique desk faced the door, a leather rolling chair behind it. The desk held three screens, angled toward the chair, which would block the view of whomever worked there from the rest of the room. Perhaps that was why the two nearby chairs were situated in front of the windows to the side of the desk instead of across from it.

On the opposite wall, a redbrick fireplace rose to the ceiling with built-in shelves on either side. A cozy-looking couch and two club chairs were arranged in a little seating area in front of it. There were a couple of tufted footrests and side tables that held vintage lamps. She could picture a tabby cat curled on the rag rug in front of the hearth, flames dancing merrily inside.

Under different circumstances, this library would be the perfect place to relax and read a book.

Sadly, Alyssa wouldn't be doing much relaxing.

There was nothing personal, though. No photographs, though that made sense. This was a rental house, after all. But also, no opened books. No pens or notepads. She imagined it looked exactly as it had when the decorator had drawn it up.

"This is a lovely space."

"Indeed. I hoped you'd like it." Charles closed the door. "The computer equipment is ready for you. I wasn't sure what you'd need." He gave her a self-effacing smile. "I should have asked. We had a few things lying around, and I sent my driver to the computer store to get what I didn't already have. So the iMac is brand new. I hope we haven't missed anything."

She walked around the desk and settled in the rolling chair, scanning the equipment. To go with the three state-of-the-art screens were a desktop PC, an iMac, and a laptop.

He settled into the chair by the window that was nearest the computer. "I trust this will be suitable?"

"I won't know for sure until I power everything up—and until I know what you want me to do."

"If you find you need something, simply let me know and I'll have it delivered immediately."

"Okay." She pressed power buttons to get the systems running, then checked the different systems' specs. These were better than anything she had at home.

Or *had* had at home, considering the break-in the night before.

It felt like a week had passed since then, not a less than a day.

She swiveled to face Charles. "What is it you want me to do?"

"Straight to business. I like that."

"Caleb and I have plans, so I don't have a lot of time. The sooner I get started—"

"I understand." He pulled something from his breast pocket and held it out.

She took the small piece of paper and studied it. It was an embossed business card with Charles's name, a cell phone number she recognized, a website, and a logo bearing the letters SJSS.

"What's this?"

"Among my many businesses, I own and operate a security company. We provide protection for high-value and well-known individuals—A-list actors, owners of multimillion-dollar businesses, politicians, and the like."

"You must meet some interesting people."

He brushed off her remark as if it weren't relevant. "Some people hire us because they're paranoid. More people hire us because they want to *seem* important, though there is little true threat. But sometimes, we are tasked with protecting people who are legitimately targets. We have one such assignment coming up next week."

He paused, perhaps expecting her to ask who the client was. And then he'd tell her he couldn't say. She wasn't one to follow a script. "Okay."

"We have reason to believe there's a vulnerability in our system. As you can imagine, it's very important that no bad actors gain access to our schedules and plans. It's even more important that they don't gain access to our drone system. We always use drones for overwatch. If somebody were to hack their way into those drones, they could redirect them or even upload bogus video to hide behind."

"You want me to check your system and make sure it's secure." Seemed like a simple enough job. She'd done similar work for corporations in the past.

Footsteps sounded on the hardwood, then voices carried down the hallway. Callan asked a question about the house's owners. He sounded fine, which meant he hadn't been taken to a back room and roughed up or threatened.

Alyssa missed the housekeeper's response, but she felt better knowing he was all right.

Charles waited until their voices faded. "When you find a glitch, it's very important that you identify each step you used to get there. We need to know about every vulnerability."

A sick feeling churned in her stomach.

Why had she thought this might be a legitimate job? The man was a terrorist. He wasn't looking for problems so he could fix them.

He was looking for vulnerabilities so he could exploit them.

She turned her attention to the screens, hoping her epiphany didn't show in her expression, and navigated to the website on the card.

It led to a typical corporate homepage. There was nothing that identified what SJSS stood for, but that didn't matter.

If she didn't know who Charles Sanders really was, what would she do now?

She'd never made it a big habit of praying when she working. After all, why ask for God's help when you could do the job all by yourself?

She didn't stop to consider the arrogance of that thought.

*Father, help me know how to handle this. I need words and wisdom now so I don't give away that I know who he is.*

She found a dropdown menu, clicked to the About page, and read a short history of the security business and the names of its founders.

A quick perusal told her what she'd already guessed. "I don't see your name here."

"I like to keep a low profile. Those are the people who run the company. I am an owner."

"Hmm. The thing is"—she turned to face him—"for all I know, you're asking me to hack into a rival's company in order to do damage or glean proprietary information."

She wasn't sure what she expected. Feigned shock or insult? Defensiveness? Anger?

She definitely didn't expect the way he settled back against the chair, comfortable as could be. "It seems to me that your best course of action right now would be to trust me. We both know you're going to do this job for me—you've already agreed. And I've already transferred a sizable amount of money into your bank account."

What did he mean by *sizable*? She reached for her phone to check her bank balance, but the driver hadn't given it back.

"We hadn't come to terms on this job yet."

"You won't be disappointed."

"I already told you"—she gestured to the center screen—"I won't do anything illegal."

He smiled. "Of course not, Alyssa. I would never ask you to. This is a standard job. You look for open doors and show me where you found them so my team can close them up."

He was lying. She knew he was lying. He knew she knew he was lying. And yet...

And yet, he was convinced he had her. He'd put money into her account. She was here—and her fiancé was too. From his perspective, she was trapped.

She could refuse, find Callan, and walk away. Theoretically, she could contact the authorities and tell them everything.

He would deny it, of course.

Leave the country.

And disappear, which he'd done often enough, according to Michael.

But would he do that before exacting revenge on her? Doubtful.

More to the point, would he let her leave before she completed the task? Certainly not.

He was betting she would do as he demanded.

She looked past him, out the leaded windows that distorted the world beyond. "He can never know." She met Charles's eyes. "Caleb wouldn't understand. And my family... You would have no way of knowing this, but my father spent years in intelligence. It's critical that nobody ever find out."

"You have no reason to fear me, Alyssa. You will keep quiet about what you did, and I will certainly never tell a soul."

"That means you have to let Caleb do whatever he needs to do. He brought his laptop, and he needs to work. You'll let him work, right? Otherwise, he's going to get suspicious."

"My security people will look at his laptop. As long as they find nothing concerning, he'll be free to work."

"And our phones?"

"Yes, yes." He brushed off her question. "When you're finished with this—and when you've found the name of the Russian. How long do you think it will take?"

"Too soon to tell. I'll let you know if I need anything."

His lips quirked at the corners as if he found her dismissal amusing.

She focused on the website and got to work, ignoring Charles's presence beside her.

She had no idea how to play this. She couldn't give him what he wanted. And she couldn't *not* give him what he wanted.

Despite the ergonomic chair, the cozy space, and the cheerful spring garden outside, there was nothing comfortable about this.

# CHAPTER TWELVE

Pretending to be normal could be exhausting.

Callan was running out of questions, and Molly the pretend housekeeper wasn't exactly a riveting conversationalist.

He'd been directed to leave his laptop and suitcase downstairs and figured somebody was going through it right now. Unless they had Alyssa's hacking skills, they wouldn't find anything Callan didn't want them to find. And they wouldn't have hired Alyssa if they had her skills.

Meanwhile, he catalogued the house as they moved through it. They'd already toured the first floor—updated kitchen, dining room, living room, family room, and sunroom. He'd taken note of multiple phone chargers plugged into outlets and at least three sets of car keys hanging from a set of hooks near a side door. Glasses and dirty dishes in the kitchen sink confirmed that Molly was no housekeeper.

On the second floor, she showed him to a bedroom that faced the rear. It had a queen-sized bed so high off the floor that a little step stool had been left against one side. White linens, pale green paint on the walls. Heavy antiques everywhere.

"This is your room," Molly said.

He stepped in and looked around. "Where're our suitcases?"

"I'll have Benson bring them up right away."

Benson—whoever the was—was likely searching them first.

"This way." She continued down the hallway, and he followed her, peeking into other rooms on the same end of the house—two more bedrooms with four-poster beds, fancy wallpaper, and multicolored Persian rugs. There were a couple of closed doors she didn't explain. He guessed they were bedrooms being occupied by Ghazi and his people.

Between the doorways, the walls were covered in artwork with thick, heavy frames. He stopped to study one, spying a tiny camera on the top corner.

One camera meant many cameras, just as he'd suspected.

Though they'd only seen half that floor, she didn't take him to the other end but up to the third story, where there were still more bedrooms and more closed doors.

All the spaces were perfectly decorated.

The bathrooms had updated fixtures and original clawfoot tubs.

They didn't see anyone else during the tour. Where where all the people were who belonged to those cell phone chargers and car keys?

Aside from the size of the place, the property had likely been chosen because of its proximity to Boston, the secured gate at the driveway, and the thick hedge that shielded the house from view.

He paused at the doorway to the largest third-floor bedroom he could see. Wood panels, bookshelves, fancy bed with a navy-blue comforter. He'd swear the wallpaper wasn't actually paper but some kind of fabric.

Ostentatious to the point of ridiculous.

But he grinned. "This is the one I'd choose."

"Except there's only one bathroom on this floor," she said. "I think this floor was originally built for the staff. Either they remodeled to make the room bigger or they knocked down walls."

"Makes sensc. Is one of these rooms is yours?"

"I don't live here."

"Oh, really? I just assumed. Which room would you choose, then, if you could have any of them?"

The question garnered her first real smile. "None. Can you imagine having to clean this place?"

"Isn't that what you do, as the housekeeper?"

Her smile faded. "He has staff for that. I manage them."

"Oh, I see. That's the problem. You get a property like this, how much does it cost to keep up? I'm happy with my little two-bedroom apartment, though after Alyssa and I get married, we'll probably buy a house. She comes from money."

Molly led him back down the hallway toward the stairs. "Unlike you?"

"My family aspired to middle class."

She gave him a long look, eyes narrowing. "You seem to do okay."

"Good education and a lot of hard work." He looked around the space. "I always wonder about people like Sanders. I guess it's easy to assume they're all greedy and demanding. He a good guy to work for?"

Instantly, her guard went back up. The smile faded, the interest disappeared. "He's a fair boss. I would give you a tour of the gardens, but I think the sprinkler is running."

"Maybe Alyssa and I can poke around outside later when she takes a break. You think she and Charles are done? I'd like to find her now."

Molly gave a curt nod and started downstairs. When they

reached the second-floor landing, she said, "Wait here," and marched in the direction she hadn't taken Callan before. She knocked on a door, then stepped inside.

He stood near the stairs dutifully, despite his desire to peek past closed doors into the rooms she hadn't shown him. Maybe bedrooms for guards—yet, where were they? Or maybe something else. Offices? Some kind of security command center with banks of monitors watching the perimeter?

Callan was more interested in what he'd find in the basement. Was Ghazi running an operation out of this house? And if so, was he running it from the bottom floor? The floor with no windows, no way for anybody to peek inside or listen in?

Probably.

The door opened down the hall, and Molly walked toward him. "You're welcome to join your friend now."

"Great. I'm just going to run back to the kitchen and get my laptop bag so I can get some work done."

"I'll have Benson bring it to you."

Benson—whoever that was—was still searching it.

Callan didn't hide his frustration. "I'd rather just—"

"Follow me." She swiveled and strode away, leaving him little choice but to follow.

They entered a long, narrow space. Straight ahead were windows and doors that opened to a balcony. One end held a fireplace and shelves.

On the other, Alyssa stood from behind a desk and a bank of screens. "There you are. This place must be huge, considering how long it took you to see it all."

Ghazi was seated in a chair against the windows where he could watch what she was doing.

When Callan headed toward her, the man stood. "You need to stay over there."

Callan glared at him. "I was just going to greet *my* fiancée."

Playing the role of the jealous partner.

The man's grin was a little smug.

Alyssa stepped past Ghazi. She'd pulled her blond hair into a low ponytail, which somehow made her look younger and more serious. She gave Callan a quick kiss on the cheek. "Nice place?"

"Want me to find out if it's on the market? We could move right in." He nodded toward Ghazi. "After he's finished with it, of course."

She laughed. "This place is right in line with our budget."

So much stupid banter, as if all were well. But by the tightness around her mouth, she wasn't feeling as lighthearted as she was pretending.

Callan backed away and turned toward the other end of the room. "I guess I'll just sit over there?"

"That would be best," Ghazi said.

Callan asked Molly, "Could you please retrieve our phones and my laptop? I have work to do."

She looked at Ghazi for permission. At his nod, she disappeared out the door.

He wanted Alyssa to have a good reason to come to his end of the room every once in a while. He studied the fireplace. "This gas?" It was—he could tell by the little silver key and keyhole. "Mind if I fire it up?"

"Be my guest." Ghazi flicked his hand Callan's way as if to brush off a fly.

Arrogant jerk.

But Callan said, "Great!" with so much enthusiasm, he feared he'd oversold it. "You got a lighter?"

Ghazi pulled one from his pocket, and Callan turned the key to turn on the gas.

Ghazi leaned down beside him, flicked open an antique lighter, and lit the flame.

Oh, it was *the* lighter. Callan had heard about it and figured there was a story behind it. Everyone who'd ever had dealings with Ghazi had mentioned that lighter.

He pocketed it. "Anything else you need?"

"Nope. This is fine. Thanks." He settled in a cushy chair and propped his feet on a blue velvet—and way too fancy for dirty shoes—footstool. "I could get used to this."

Ghazi's smile was tight, and Callan figured he was trying to decide if keeping Alyssa in line was worth putting up with Callan.

He laced his hands behind his head. "So what are you working on, Paris?" He tossed the words across the room.

Alyssa peeked around the screens and gave him a look—eyebrows lifted, amusement on her lips.

"Not even a hint? I'm bored to death over here."

"I have every confidence you'll survive your boredom, Mr. Thompson."

"Caleb. Just Caleb." He closed his mouth, and Alyssa returned to her task, fingers racing over the keyboard he could see beneath the screens that hid her face.

Ghazi settled in his chair again, as if she required supervision.

Callan needed his laptop and his cell phone. And until he got those things, he needed to make a nuisance of himself so Ghazi would hurry up and get them for him.

He stood and thumped—maybe making his footsteps louder than strictly necessary—to the French doors leading to a narrow balcony. He opened one, then the other, and stepped outside. The gardens really were beautiful, an explosion of color and scents. Birds sang in the trees that towered over the house, a few twittering around the feeders hanging here and there. Squirrels raced across limbs, hopping from one to another. Bees buzzed among the cottony catkins on a pussy willow bush.

The yard was so deep, he couldn't see a house behind it.

"Whoa, Paris. You gotta see this."

"I'm a little busy," she called

He looked at her over his shoulder. "One minute won't kill you."

"Caleb. I'm trying to work."

"I've got work to do too." He allowed annoyance to color his tone.

"Perhaps you should've gone to your own office," Ghazi said.

Callan glared at the man. "You'd like that, wouldn't you?"

"Caleb." Alyssa's tone was appropriately irritated. "Please, stop it."

He shook his head. "You're right. I'm just restless." He crossed to the double doors that led to the hallway. "I'll just go check on—"

"Stay here, please." Ghazi tapped on his phone screen. "I'll ask them to deliver your things immediately."

"All right, then. Thanks."

He'd hoped the guy would go away, but no. He stayed right where he was, leaving Callan no opportunity to find out what Alyssa was working on.

Callan could wait. And meanwhile, he'd work on a way to get out of this situation. Because he seriously doubted that, once Alyssa finished this job, the man planned to let them walk away.

# CHAPTER THIRTEEN

Alyssa was trying to concentrate, but it was no easy task with Charles watching her every keystroke and Callan's refusal to settle down.

All an act, of course. He'd shown none of this manic restlessness the night before, nor during their years in college together. He was going for maximum irritation. She didn't know how it was affecting Charles, but Callan was certainly irritating her.

Finally, the driver who'd picked them up stepped into the room holding Callan's laptop bag.

Callan launched himself off the chair—which he'd settled into about thirty seconds prior. "Thank you."

The man didn't hand it over, though.

"Please, Caleb, sit down." Charles stood and walked toward the men. "Benson needs your help with something."

Alyssa tried to focus on her work, but she couldn't help listening.

"With what?"

She heard movement, but nobody spoke, so she levered up to peek over the screens.

The driver—Benson—opened Callan's bag and slid his laptop out while Charles pushed a small table in front of Callan.

Benson set the laptop on the table. "Unlock it."

Callan launched up from his chair so fast that Benson took a step back. "I must've misunderstood." Warning hummed in Callan's tone.

Benson was about six feet—slightly shorter than Callan—but he was plenty built. He nodded to the laptop between them. "You heard me."

Uh-oh. What did Callan have on that? Would they be able to find anything that indicated who he really was?

Surely not. But Callan wasn't backing down.

Callan turned his back on Benson to face Charles—effectively discounting the guard entirely.

By the rage that filled the driver's expression, he'd picked up on that.

"Look, this is my work computer," Callan said. "I can't let your guy here look at it. Sorry."

"Ah. Then I think we have a problem," Charles said. "You see, I can't let you work on it unless we examine it."

"Why? What are you...?" He spluttered as if utterly shocked. "My work has nothing to do with you or Alyssa or anything. This is... You can't be serious."

Callan was very convincing.

"I'm afraid I am quite serious." Charles shifted sideways, his back to the windows, and nodded toward Alyssa before addressing Callan again. "You see, until last night, I didn't know you existed."

"So what? Who she spends time with is none of your business. Do you expect her to give you a rundown on her life? All of this is already"—he gestured to the room and the house and the grounds—"paranoid beyond comprehension. But demanding to look at my laptop? You have no right."

"I'm sorry you feel that way." Charles flicked his gaze to Benson. "Please, drive our guest wherever he would like to go."

Alyssa's anxiety spiked. She needed Callan here, with her. How could she do this without him?

She pushed to her feet. "Caleb, just let him—"

"You'd like that, wouldn't you?" Ignoring her, Callan was focused on Charles. "To get rid of me." He strode forward, stopping one pace too close to the terrorist.

She rounded the desk. "Don't do that, Caleb. Just let them look at your computer. It's not like you've got state secrets on there."

He glared at her, and the look was so authentic that she froze a few feet away.

"*Company* secrets. Maybe that means nothing to this guy, but our client database is on there. I could lose my job."

"Charles doesn't care what you do for work. I promise. He's not going to steal anything."

"If it makes you that uncomfortable," Charles said, "feel free to leave the laptop with Benson and find a book to read. As you can see, there are plenty." He gestured to the wall of shelves.

"I need to work."

"It's a simple choice. You will let Benson have a look at your system to confirm it is what you say it is, that there's nothing questionable on there, or you will not use it on my property."

Callan's mouth set in a firm line. He looked from Charles to Benson and back.

Tension buzzed like a swarm of angry bees.

Then Callan sat, turned the laptop so none of them could see the screen, and typed. "There. It's open. But you're not taking it. I'm watching everything you do."

Satisfaction in Benson's expression, he sat opposite Callan's chair and turned the laptop toward him.

Callan leaned against the wall beside him and watched over his shoulder, arms crossed.

She guessed Benson took his time poking around, just to annoy him.

Charles resumed his seat and nodded for her to do the same, but she pretended not to notice. She wanted to be ready in case Benson discovered something that gave away who Callan really was.

If that happened, what would Benson do? Would he say something? Or take out a gun and shoot him?

More likely, he'd take Callan away, maybe try to get information out of him.

What would Alyssa do? Make a run for it? Try to help?

Her heart pounded with fear.

Nobody spoke, the only sounds coming from the man's thick fingers on the keyboard. The tension in the room mixed with the heat from the gas fireplace. What had felt drafty before was now stuffy.

Stifling.

She shouldn't be worried. If Benson had any hacking skills, he'd be behind this desk, and Charles wouldn't need her. She assumed Callan's security was tight enough that this guy wouldn't get past it.

After minutes that felt like hours, he set the laptop on one of the footrests. "It's what he says. A client database, a portal to a computer company."

"Thank you, Benson." Charles smiled at Callan. "Sorry we had to do that."

"You didn't *have* to do it." He snatched his laptop.

Dismissed, Benson stepped out.

Callan, still acting angry, gave her an unhappy stare.

"Please, get back to work," Charles said to her.

She sat and focused on her screens. She'd found the gateway to the private server. Now, to find a way in.

And a way to fix this company's system so that, no matter what Charles did, he wouldn't be able to follow the bread-crumbs she'd dropped.

# CHAPTER FOURTEEN

Callan didn't know what to think about Benson. He might look like a thug, but he'd sure known how to navigate the laptop.

There'd been a second there when Callan had worried the guy would get past his computer's defenses.

But the guy hadn't found the hidden profile. Nor had he discovered the built-in hotspot, which came in handy when Ghazi refused to share the Wi-Fi password and refused to return their phones.

"You can't be serious!" Callan had launched himself out of the chair. "If I can't have the password, and I can't get on my hotspot, how am I supposed to work?"

"I suppose you could go home." Ghazi's words had been polite, his expression smug.

"Fat chance." He'd huffed and settled back down, thankful they'd bought his little act. "I'll work on reports. It'll take me all weekend to catch up."

Ghazi hadn't even bothered to apologize.

When he was focused on Alyssa and those screens again,

Gideon navigated to his laptop's built-in hotspot, connected to the Internet, and sent Malcolm an update.

Molly delivered lunch a little after one o'clock—sandwiches and little bags of chips. Alyssa took hers back to the desk, giving Callan no opportunity to talk to her. Not that he could have with Ghazi in the room.

When the man walked out for a few minutes here and there during the afternoon, Benson or Molly came in.

His laptop screen was nearly impossible to read unless a person were right in front of it, so even if there were cameras, the image would be nothing but gray if picked up by a camera. With his back to the wall of windows, he investigated Dariush Ghazi and the people he did business with.

According to the Agency's dossier, he didn't hold to any religious beliefs at all. He became in each situation whatever was necessary for him to achieve his goals. When he was with Muslims, he adhered to Islam. When he was in Israel, he'd gone so far as to don a skull cap.

When he posed as Charles Sanders, he spoke with an aristocratic British accent, the picture of a businessman and entrepreneur.

In Germany the previous fall, he'd been known as Dariush Shahin, a Christian convert, and using that persona, he'd infiltrated a refugee mission. Back then, he'd worked with an Iraqi terrorist named Hasan Mahmoud.

Mahmoud was in custody, but Ghazi had escaped.

Another interesting tidbit... Hasan Mahmoud was uncle to Leila and Jasmine Fayed, who were now married to Michael and Derrick Wright.

That explained how Alyssa had ended up on Ghazi's radar.

Digging deeper into the operation in Munich, Callan learned Mahmoud had been after WMDs squirreled out of Iraq in the days following the invasion. Had Mahmoud, the head of that operation, intended to use those weapons, or sell them?

Callan sent a private text message to Alyssa's cousin, asking the question. Michael answered immediately.

*According to Mahmoud, they planned to release some at the Xmas market in Munich. The rest, they wanted to sell. He hasn't given us a name, though we heard the buyer was Russian. Maybe the one whose name Alyssa found? Interrogators will question Mahmoud and get back to us. Maybe Ghazi's reason for aligning with Mahmoud was to find that name.*

Lots of maybes.

Was what happened in Germany last fall related to whatever he had Alyssa doing now?

She tapped on the system across the room, diligently working to get whatever Ghazi had asked for, while the man watched from his chair against the windows.

It was after six o'clock when Molly knocked and then opened the door. "Dinner will be served in ten minutes."

"Excellent." Ghazi waited until the so-called housekeeper stepped out and closed the door again before focusing on Callan. "Alyssa and I need to speak privately for a few minutes. Please, make your way to the sunroom. Molly will get you a drink."

Callan closed his laptop and slid it into the bag, then crossed to the opposite side of Alyssa's desk. "You must be ready for a break."

She finished typing something. "Yup."

Her lips wore a smile that was tight at the corners, and that plus the flash of worry in her eyes had his stomach tightening.

There was nothing to do but play along. "See you downstairs." He nodded to Ghazi, then, against his will and every ounce of good judgment, left them alone together.

Molly was waiting for him in the hallway. "This way please."

"I'll be right down. I'm going to drop this off in our room." He lifted his laptop bag, then walked to the room she'd indicated.

She stayed at his side. "I'll wait."

Of course she would.

He stepped inside and closed the door, then took a quick look around. No thugs were hiding under the bed.

Callan found both his suitcase and Alyssa's in the closet, empty. Someone had unpacked their things. Ghazi and his people were playing off searching their belongings as if it were an act of hospitality.

He left his leather laptop bag on his bed, easily spied from the hallway, hoping that would indicate that he had nothing to hide. He could squirrel it away somewhere, but if they wanted to find it, they would. And hiding it would only raise suspicions.

He used the bathroom, combed his hair, and washed his face, taking his time and hoping Molly would tire of waiting for him. But five minutes later when he opened the door, the pretend housekeeper pushed off the wall. "This way."

"I could probably find it by myself."

She didn't bother to respond.

The glassed-in sunroom must have been added onto the original property. Wicker furniture with floral upholstery filled the space, along with potted plants overflowing with vines and flowers. Beyond the windows, the garden sparkled in the twilight beneath strings of cafe lighting that fanned out toward the sunroom to surrounding trees.

Low classical music played over speakers installed overhead. The room held a floral scent that mingled with a hint of rain, the perfect springtime fragrance, courtesy of a scented candle flickering on a side table.

Like everything else in this house, the veneer was just thick enough to prove more lay beneath.

A metal-and-glass cart held a decanter of red wine and a bottle of white, along with various liquors. On the far side, a round cafe table was set for two. A pair of cream-colored pillar candles had been lit.

It would be romantic, if any of it were real.

But at least this meant he and Alyssa would be given privacy. Or the *appearance* of privacy.

"What would you like to drink?" Molly asked.

"Red wine." Which he didn't care for, but he was playing along.

She poured him a glass, and he sipped it, then smiled. "I think I'm supposed to swirl it and sniff it or something, right?"

Her lips twitched at the corners, though she didn't give in to the smile. "I won't tell. Is it all right?"

"Tastes good to me. I can't tell French from boxed, though, so..." He'd never been a big fan of alcoholic grape juice.

"Your fiancée should be down in a minute." She gestured to a charcuterie board on a side table. "Help yourself."

"Thanks."

After Molly left, Callan grabbed a cracker and a slice of cheese, then perused the room as if fascinated by the plants and decorations. His search for cameras and microphones turned up nothing, though that didn't mean they weren't there. He had to be careful not to give away that he suspected their so-called private dinner was being surveilled.

He'd eaten a handful of olives, at least as many grapes, and half of the cheese and crackers by the time Alyssa stepped into the room.

She'd pulled her hair out of its ponytail, and it fanned around her shoulders and halfway down her back. If he wasn't mistaken, she'd freshened up her makeup. Not for him, he was sure, but to sell the story.

Story or not, she was gorgeous.

Molly poured her a glass of white wine.

Alyssa took it, swirled it, smelled it, and sipped.

Molly gave Callan a furtive look, and he winked, enjoying the private joke. Or wanting her to think so, anyway.

"Excellent. Thank you." Alyssa gave quick nod—a dismissal.

"Dinner will be served in a few minutes," Molly said. "Help yourself to the cheese board while you wait."

Alyssa waited until she'd left, then turned to Callan.

"It feels like I haven't seen you in hours." He crossed the room and pulled her into a hug, whispering, "We have to assume they're watching."

She leaned away to face him, eyes wide. "It's been a day." Her voice didn't betray her worry.

Holding her hand, he led her to a loveseat. "I know you can't tell me what you're doing, but how's it going?"

"I think I'll have what he needs by tomorrow."

They set the drinks on a low table and sat.

Callan wrapped his arm around her. "In time to get to my parents' house for dinner?"

"Shouldn't be a problem." She tucked in close to his side, fitting perfectly. Not that he needed to be thinking about that, or about how good she smelled, or about how much he liked her right there, beside him. "How about you? Did you get some work done? I know it's frustrating that you can't get online."

"Hmm." He allowed frustration into his tone. "Your client is a piece of work. Paranoid beyond belief."

"I assume he has reason to be." Alyssa patted Callan's knee as if to calm him.

The innocent touch did just the opposite, sending his heartbeat into overdrive.

"It's just for one more day." She gestured to the room, the romantic table, the lights beyond the windows. "At least we have the evening together. This is nice."

"Finally." He kissed the top of her head like a real fiancé would do, picking up hints of vanilla and jasmine.

He reminded himself that this was all fake. Pretend. Not real, despite the way her nearness made his body go haywire and his thoughts drift far from the operation.

He whispered in her ear, "You need to use the rest room."

She leaned back, eyebrows high. Her mouth opened—a protest, he guessed, but she said. "I'll be right back." She pushed up and walked into the living room. Her voice carried through the sunroom door. "I need a bathroom. Should I go upstairs or—?"

"I'll take you." Benson peeked his head in. "Stay here."

Callan lifted his glass of wine in a sort of salute, then wandered to the doorway and watched as Alyssa and the guard turned down a hallway toward the kitchen.

After counting to ten, Callan meandered through the living room and toward the front of the house, moving slowly, looking around as if were bored, not searching.

In the foyer, noises drifted up the stairs from the basement. Men's voices, at least two, maybe three. One of them was Ghazi.

They were speaking English, some accented with Arabic, he thought. Not talking about anything important.

Even though he was probably being watched, he moved up the stairs quickly and silently. The hallway lights were off, the space dim as he turned away from the office where they'd spent the afternoon. He opened his own bedroom door. He stepped inside, then, keeping it open, ducked as low as his six-foot-something body would allow and crept to the end of the hallway.

If the camera he'd seen earlier was a fisheye, then he wasn't fooling anybody. But he was betting it wasn't.

He guessed the master bedroom was on the back corner of the house. When he reached that door, he opened it and slipped inside before flicking the light on.

Fancy room, like all the others. King-sized bed, poorly made, probably not by the fake housekeeper but the room's occupant.

Personal items on the bureau—a handful of coins, a couple of envelopes. Nothing unusual.

Except for one photograph.

It was a little faded in a cheap, thin frame that showed wear on the edges. It displayed a young couple grinning at the photographer. The woman was beautiful with dark skin and fashionably curled silky black hair.

The man had his arm slung around her shoulders. In his other hand, he displayed a lighter, the same lighter Callan had seen earlier. On the table, an open box.

Had it been a gift?

Dariush Ghazi, at least twenty years younger, looked both casual and content.

The were seated at an outdoor café. The buildings on the far side of the road behind them were a stark contrast to the bright blue sky overhead. Based on the shape and design of the buildings, the dusty landscape, and the people in the background—many of whom wore thobes and hijabs—the photo had been taken somewhere in the Middle East, probably Iraq, since Ghazi had grown up there.

Cursing his lack of a camera, Callan committed the image to memory.

Footsteps sounded on the stairs down the hall.

Callan flicked off the light, crouched low, and slipped out of the room.

Two men reached the top of the staircase just as Callan made it to his own bedroom door. He slid inside, rounded the bed in the dark space, and entered the bathroom, where he flushed the toilet.

Just to be on the safe side.

Then washed his hands, taking his time. Hoping the men moved along.

He returned to the hallway, closing the door behind him, then turned toward the stairs.

And froze. "Oh, hey. You startled me."

The men were standing ten feet away. They each wore casual clothes, one significantly taller than the other. It was too hard to tell their age in the dim light.

Had they seen him creep into his bedroom? Did they know he'd been snooping?

If so, he was in for a world of hurt. Literally.

He doubted it, though. If they'd seen him, they wouldn't have waited politely in the hall outside his room before confronting him.

"What are you doing up here?" The shorter of the two spoke, his voice low—a warning tone. And also...low in volume, as if he feared Callan's getting caught even more than Callan did.

"Uh, Alyssa went to the bathroom, so I figured I would, too, since we're still waiting on dinner."

"You are not to wander around unaccompanied."

The other man whispered in Arabic, though loudly enough for Callan to hear and translate.

*"He lies."*

Callan did his best to look confused. "Sorry, guys. I'm not used to needing an escort everywhere I go. Your boss is wicked paranoid."

The shorter man spoke to the taller, again in Arabic.

*"Take him."*

Looking between them, Callan said, "What is that? Farsi? I used to have a friend—"

*"Now."*

The taller one moved forward, and Callan braced himself. Though there was nothing he could do. If this guy decided to hurt him, he'd have to take it.

Computer hardware salesmen weren't known for being adept at self-defense, and he didn't want to blow his cover.

"Look, I didn't mean to cause trouble." He lifted his hands and backed up. "I'm just trying to—"

"Silence." The tall one grabbed his arm and tugged. "Try to shut up for two minutes."

The shorter man continued up to the third floor as the taller one practically dragged Callan downstairs.

When they reached the landing, he was certain they'd continue to the basement.

Bad things happened in basements.

But he was manhandled toward the living room.

"Ooh." Alyssa's voice carried from the hallway where she and the guard had disappeared. "This is lovely. Have you ever seen the original?"

"No." Benson wasn't exactly a stellar conversationalist.

Alyssa responded, but Callan didn't pick up her words as the guard dragged Callan across the living room and shoved him toward the sunroom, hissing, "Stay there. Tell no one you left."

"Okay, okay."

"Do not wander again or you will be sorry." The man swiveled and hurried back to the staircase.

He settled on the loveseat again, his heartbeat racing. He'd gotten lucky. Had one or both of those guys been assigned to watch the video feed? Or to watch him specifically? They were afraid enough of Ghazi to not admit their failure.

His snooping had paid off.

Though Ghazi's dossier indicated no wife or girlfriend, there was a woman in his past he cared about enough to carry her photograph—and the lighter she'd given him—wherever he went.

## CHAPTER FIFTEEN

This all felt too real.

Alyssa had taken as much time in the bathroom as she could without raising suspicions, then studied every knickknack and painting she and Benson passed on their way back to the sunroom, praying like crazy that, whatever Callan had done, he was finished.

When she stepped into the sunroom, he stood from the loveseat as if he hadn't moved.

Only when she sat beside him did she feel the heat and tension wafting off his body.

"You all right?" she asked.

"Yeah, I'm great." He lowered his voice. "This place is super weird. I went back to our room for like, thirty seconds, and I thought these goons were gonna beat the crap out of me. What does this guy do, anyway?"

Oh, boy. He'd been up to something, and he'd nearly gotten caught. Someone who didn't think they were being watched—or at least heard—would tell his fiancée what happened.

"He owns multiple companies. I assume they've dealt with their share of corporate espionage."

"Like I care about...whatever it is your English friend does. Give me a break."

She gripped his wrist. His pulse raced beneath her fingertips. "I appreciate you for coming with me. I'd hate to be here alone."

He shifted to face her. "Weird as your Sanders guy is, I wouldn't want to be anywhere else."

Though she knew Callan's words were for the sake of the cameras and microphones, he sounded so sincere that she almost believed him.

A few minutes later, Molly brought their meals—steak, salmon, potatoes, asparagus, and a crisp salad. Based on the lack of scents coming from the kitchen when she'd walked through the house, the food had been delivered from a restaurant.

They sat across from each other and ate the delicious meal and talked about nothing. They laughed, they joked, they flirted.

Both playing their parts.

But the more time Alyssa spent with Callan, the harder it was to remember he was pretending. She'd spent four years in college scowling at Callan as if she felt nothing but scorn for him, all the while tamping down her attraction and denying her crush. Megan had never bought it. She'd questioned Alyssa more than once about her feelings for Callan, but Alyssa had never admitted anything.

She'd barely wanted to admit it to herself.

It was impossible to deny now, though, as the man who'd barged into both her dreams and her nightmares since she was eighteen years old held a spoon filled with tiramisu over the candlelit table, eyes twinkling.

"You know you want to."

This might be all pretend, but he knew her too well. "I'm so full already."

"One little bite. That's all I'm asking."

In pretty much any other situation, she'd clamp her lips shut. If she wanted to taste the tiramisu, she could use her own spoon, thank you very much. But he was going for maximum romance here, a little tiramisu-version of *Lady and the Tramp sharing spaghetti* scene.

Ridiculous.

Were they laying it on too thick? Was this how people in love behaved? She didn't have a clue.

She opened her mouth, and he slid the spoon inside. She took the creamy, mocha confection onto her tongue.

Oh, my.

She couldn't help a little moan of pleasure.

"Right?" Though he was smiling, his Adam's apple bobbed like he'd swallowed what he'd really wanted to say—or maybe whatever thought had come into his head. Since she'd refused dessert, he pushed his plate closer to her on the café table. "Have some more."

But he didn't offer to feed her again, and by the way his skin reddened, that was a good idea.

She took a tiny portion into her own spoon. Somehow, it didn't taste nearly as good as when he'd fed her. Then she sipped her decaf coffee. They'd both been served wine, but neither had finished a single glass. She'd barely touched hers, preferring the water they refilled from a carafe on the beverage cart.

They needed to stay alert tonight.

"We should ask who delivered the food." They needed a new topic of conversation. "We could take dessert to dinner tomorrow."

"Mom loves to bake."

"We have to take something. It would be rude to show up empty-handed."

*To a fake dinner, Alyssa? Really?*

She was getting far too deep into her role.

Callan smiled as if he'd read her mind. "Trust me."

Yeah. He kept saying that. And it wasn't that she didn't trust him. But she wasn't sure she trusted herself tonight, not with this man, not in these circumstances. She needed space between them, a lot more space than this tiny round table.

He finished the layered confection, then stood and held out his hand for her. "Join me?"

She did, and he pulled her away from the table and into an embrace. "I've missed you." He leaned down and whispered in his ear. "We have to argue."

She wanted to ask why but figured he'd explain as he tightened his arm around her back and took her other hand in his. He started swaying gently to the music being piped.

*Fake.*

*All fake.*

But being in his arms was even better than she'd dreamed.

And then he trailed kisses on her neck, and all coherent thoughts fled.

His breath was warm, fanning her hair, and tingles fluttered over her skin.

"I assume there are microphones." The words were so low, she almost missed them. "If not cameras. In our bedroom."

Our *bedroom?* Wait.

*Our* bedroom?

They'd be sharing?

She hadn't thought what the night would look like, too focused on getting through the day.

Of course Charles assumed they'd share a bedroom.

Callan led their gentle dance, staying close as he turned them in the small space.

"I thought about asking for separate rooms," he whispered,

"but I didn't want to raise suspicions. And I didn't want us to be apart."

"Okay." She tried to match his volume.

"Which is why we have to argue. It'll be a reason as to why they won't see or hear more...interesting activity in our room tonight, considering the story that we've been apart for months."

Would Charles really bug their bedroom? How creepy.

Not *Charles*, though. Ghazi. Why would she expect a liar, terrorist, and murderer to respect her privacy?

"Argue with me." Callan's whisper was barely audible. He stopped dancing and straightened. "Let's get an Uber to my apartment." Now his words were low but loud enough to be picked up by anybody listening. "I'll drive you back here tomorrow so you can finish"—he waved toward the house—" whatever it is you're doing."

"I wish we could, but Charles—"

"Who cares what *Charles* thinks?" The name dripped with scorn. "He's not even your boss. He's just a client. You've indulged his paranoia enough. We both have."

"I can't, Caleb. I have to stay."

He dropped her hand and stepped back "Seriously? You really want to stay here?"

"It's not that I *want* to, but it's important to him. This isn't bad, right?" She waved toward the table. "Dinner and dessert. It's romantic."

"Because we're together, but..." He lowered his voice. "I don't think that housekeeper chick actually cleans. And it's weird, right? I mean, why have a place this big for just a couple of people? And that Benson guy searching my laptop? And two of the guys got all threatening when I went to the room. This whole situation is creeping me out."

"Charles is security-conscious, no question. But he's also doing his best to make us comfortable."

"Don't defend him. What is he, some kind of gangster or something?"

"He's a businessman."

"Sure he is. Because renting a place like this is good business."

"Don't *you* start getting paranoid on me."

"Me? He's the paranoid one."

"You didn't have to come."

Callan crossed his arms and glared at her. "*You* didn't have to come, Alyssa. You should have just turned him down. You don't need his money."

"Actually, I do need his money. I'm trying to get a business off the ground."

"Oh, come on. I can support us both. And anyway, you can always run home to Daddy."

"That's not fair!"

People always assumed that since her parents were wealthy, she didn't have money problems. Sure, she could ask her father for money, but she didn't. Ever. Because Dad's money always came with strings. And lectures. And that disapproving look of his.

"Life isn't fair, *Paris.* Never has been. I'm sorry you feel like you need to work for creepy British guys in order to prove to Daddy you're not a failure, but some of us have real problems."

Fury clawed its way up her throat. "You have no idea what you're talking about."

Callan's eyes widened. He'd been putting on a show, but those last barbs had hit too close to home. "I'm sorry," he said quickly. "I shouldn't have said that. It's just my—"

"Jealousy," she snapped, getting back into character. "And I'm sick of it."

"I know. You're right. I'm..." He ran a hand over his short hair. "I don't want to fight with you." He lowered his voice. "I don't like it here. I don't like that guy. And I want to go home. I haven't been at my apartment in weeks. And we're going to Mom and Dad's tomorrow. It's not too much to ask that I get to spend one night in my own bed."

Now it was her turn to cross her arms. "Go ahead. I'll call you tomorrow when I'm ready to go."

"Don't do that."

"I made a commitment, and I'm keeping it. Just like you keep yours. We both know your work is more important to you than I am. More important than your family is."

He flinched as if she'd slapped him.

Whoops. Apparently, her words had hit a nerve.

This fake argument had turned painful, fast.

He clamped his lips shut.

Should she try to make it right? Or stick to her guns?

She wasn't sure what her next line should be.

"I'm not leaving you here with him," Callan said.

"Fine."

"Fine."

They stared each other down another few seconds, and then Alyssa swiveled and headed for the door.

The housekeeper was sitting in the dim living room. She stood when Alyssa stepped in. She must've heard everything, but she plastered on a smile. "Do you need something?"

"We're going up."

"I'll escort you, then."

Of course she would. Because they wouldn't actually get a moment of privacy in this house.

Not even in the bedroom they were about to share.

"ALYSSA."

Her name on Callan's lips was a whisper against her hair, a breath in her ear.

A dream. No more than a dream. And this one was vivid. Dinner by candlelight. Dancing.

His warmth against her felt more real than the sheets beneath her.

She snuggled in, wanting more than anything to go back to sleep and pick up where she and dream-Callan had left off. His presence was more delicious than the dream tiramisu lingering on her tongue.

"Alyssa."

This whisper was vehement, as if he were just on the other side of consciousness, drawing her back to him.

"Don't move." Pressure on her arm had her tensing.

What was happening?

"Don't react."

This wasn't a dream. She was in a guest room at Charles Sanders's house somewhere in Brookline.

In a bed. With Callan.

A bed they shared. She'd climbed beneath the sheets, and he'd slept between the top sheet and the comforter, so there was never any contact between them. Even so, she'd have preferred a king-sized bed. Because of his overlarge and over-warm presence, and the strange circumstances, she'd struggled to fall asleep.

And now he was pressed against her back, and the thin sheet between them was not nearly thick enough to keep her body from reacting as he wrapped his arm around her middle and gripped her hand. "If you can hear me, squeeze my hand."

His words were barely audible, but she heard and squeezed.

"We're just a couple in love, snuggling in our sleep. Okay?"

What was she supposed to say to that? There was nothing *okay* about this.

"I don't know about this room, but I've searched the bathroom and found no cameras or microphones. So we're going out the window."

"No." Was he kidding? They were on the second floor.

"It's going to be okay. Here's what we're going to do." He outlined the plan, then slipped out of bed in the darkness and into the bathroom. He gave her no opportunity to argue.

The vent fan went on.

A few minutes later, the bathroom door opened.

She counted to a thousand, just like he'd told her to do, then climbed out of bed and went into the bathroom, closing the door behind her.

Callan stood beside the window, tall and broad and somehow perfectly confident.

He'd changed from his pajamas into black pants and sweatshirt.

He nodded to the counter, where he'd left a piece of paper and a pen beside a stack of folded clothes.

While she'd slept, he'd gone through her things and found a dark pair of jeans, a navy-blue sweatshirt, and black socks. On top of it all were her white sneakers, except they weren't white anymore.

"What did you do?"

"Shoe polish. I keep it in my Dopp kit."

Of course he did.

They'd left their jackets downstairs, so there'd be no getting those back. And Charles had taken their phones.

Callan already had the window open, and cold air spilled into the small space. "Go ahead and change."

Even though he looked out into the dark night, she stepped into the claw-foot tub and pulled the shower curtain between them before changing out of her pajamas.

When she emerged, he said, "You decent?"

"As ever."

Turning her way, he smiled, though the expression didn't hold.

She didn't like this. Not at all.

"Write Charles a note." Callan indicated the paper and pen. "Apologize for sneaking out. Tell him you'll be back tomorrow. Don't try to explain. Just keep it simple."

"But we aren't coming back?"

Callan gave her a *what do you think?* look. Which she deserved. One didn't sneak out of places in the middle of the night to pick up donuts.

But then, why bother?

Rather than argue or question him, she wrote the note and left it beside the sink as if she really planned to go through with this.

She wasn't exactly a *jump out the window* kind of girl.

But Callan hadn't asked her opinion.

Now, he held out a black piece of clothing. "Tie this around your head."

"What is it?" She took it and shook it out. "A T-shirt? You want me to put a T-shirt over my head?"

"Not over it like you're a prisoner on camera. Just, you know"—he twirled his finger over the top of his head—"wrap it around there like a kerchief or whatever. To hide your hair."

"What about your hair?"

He pulled something from his back pocket. A black knit cap.

"Why don't I wear that, and you wrap the T-shirt around your head?"

"I don't want to look stupid, and you'll make it look good."

"Ha." She attempted to do what he said. Wasn't easy, but after a couple of tries, she managed to tie it tight enough to hold for a little while.

"Perfect," he said. "You first."

Good idea. If he went before her, she might not have the courage to follow.

The bathroom window was high on the wall barely wide enough to fit through. How was she going manage this? How was Gideon?

"I'll give you a boost when it's time. Go out feet-first, on your belly, then drop and dangle by your fingertips. Don't wait for long, just let go."

Easy for him to say. He was inches taller than she was and had those long arms.

But wait. What else had he said? "Seen by whom? Who's out there?"

"One guard." Callan didn't seem overly concerned. "One of the guys I ran into earlier. He patrols the perimeter regularly." Callan nodded through the trees. "See him there against the fence?"

She looked, but all she saw was fence and trees and bushes everywhere.

"In about thirty seconds," Callan said, "he's going to move. When he's out of sight around the edge of the house, that's your cue. Okay?"

"If I break my ankle—"

"You're not going to break anything. You're going to land with bent knees, then scramble behind those bushes." He pointed to a hedge that angled between the house and the outside of the sunroom, which jutted out from back of the first floor. "I'll be right behind you."

"I need my laptop."

He indicated his bulging bag at his feet—a backpack, though she'd never seen him carry it that way. "I've got both of ours."

"But all my stuff—"

"Isn't worth the cost of trying to escape with it. Or staying here."

Right. Of course he was right. This was all happening so fast, and she felt off-guard and off-kilter.

Like she always felt around this man. And not in a good way.

Callan watched out the window. A few tense minutes passed. "Guard's on the move. Remember what to do?"

"Climb, fall, and hide."

"She takes direction well." Callan laced his fingers together, but she didn't need his help. She levered up to the window, sat with her feet out, then turned onto her belly.

*Don't think about it. Just do it.*

Right.

She slid down to dangle, the rough wood scraping her stomach where her sweatshirt rode up.

Deep breath.

*Catch me, Lord. Don't let me break anything.*

She let go—

And landed on soft ground and scrambled behind the bushes, where she watched as Callan did the same. Despite his taller and broader body, he looked graceful as he climbed, dangled, and dropped.

He landed silently and joined her. "There's a rock wall at the back of the property." He pointed to indicate the direction they'd run. "Better quiet than fast, unless we're seen. In which case, sprint. Don't wait for me. On the other side of the rock wall, you'll be in a back yard. Get to the street and turn left. There'll be a car idling near the corner. Knock on the window. He should know your name."

"What's his—?"

"Doesn't matter. He'll know yours. Get in, tell him what happened, and do what he says. Got it?"

"I'm just supposed to leave you?"

"It won't come to that. That's a worst-case scenario. Tell me you understand."

She understood perfectly. If a guard caught them running, Callan was going to slow him down so she could escape.

She didn't like that one bit.

"Promise me you'll do as I say. Otherwise, this isn't going to work. You're the one they need to accomplish their purpose, not me."

Right. Which meant they'd have no reason to keep Callan alive.

"Trust me, Paris." His words were low. "I know what I'm doing, but if I have to worry about you, I won't do it. Promise me you'll do what I say."

"I promise."

He pressed a kiss to her lips, the movement so quick that she nearly missed it.

Her surprise must've shown because he shook his head. "Sorry. I shouldn't have..." Something flashed in his eyes, there and gone so fast, she wasn't sure if it'd been real. More than worry. More than determination.

It was affection, real and true.

He'd kissed her for no good reason except that he wanted to kiss her.

Or maybe the darkness and the situation were playing tricks on her.

"Be safe, Paris. Please."

"I will. But Callan?"

His eyebrows lowered. "What?"

"Don't get caught."

## CHAPTER SIXTEEN

That afternoon while Alyssa worked, Callan had studied satellite images that showed the layout of the property. The house was relatively close to the street, which gave the impression that the lot was small.

Not even close.

According to city records, the structure sat on a little over two acres. The lot was about a hundred feet wide but very deep. An eight-foot fence bordered the backyard on two sides.

Callan could easily scale an eight-foot fence, but could Alyssa? Probably, considering how tall and fit she was, but *probably* wasn't good enough.

He'd discounted going over the fences.

He and Alyssa wouldn't get ten feet from the house if they tried to escape down the driveway.

Which left one option. They would have to take the longest route—across the expansive backyard, through the garden, and then into the forest.

It was close to three hundred yards, but according to satellite images—and Malcolm's reconnaissance—the only thing separating this property from the one behind it was a low rock wall. No doubt if Ghazi had owned this property, he'd have extended the fence along the back edge, but he didn't.

The escape should be easy peasy.

As long as they weren't spotted leaving the house. And as long as there weren't cameras he and the team hadn't seen. And as long as nobody noticed they weren't in their room.

*Don't get caught.*

Alyssa's words were still resonating when he pointed to bushes that marked the far edge of the garden. Between here and there were nothing but grass and a long, narrow mulched flower bed, where spring bulbs poked out of the ground.

Once they made it beyond the bushes and into the cover of the old forest, they should be safe.

"Run straight over the flowerbed to the bushes and into the woods. I'll be right behind you."

She nodded, her eyes wide, not with fear but focus.

"Go."

She bolted, and he followed.

Alyssa stopped behind a couple of trees about fifteen yards into the forest. She was breathing hard.

He caught up with her. "Fast but quiet, emphasis on quiet. I didn't see any guards this deep, but that doesn't mean they're not here."

At her nod, Callan started forward. The ground had been cleared of brush, making it easier to move through—and easier to see through. He jogged carefully, not willing to risk being seen or getting injured. He did his best to keep trees between them and the house.

It was easier than he'd expected. Ghazi had bought their little act—

A shout carried from behind. Arabic words that shook him to very core. *"They've escaped!"*

Another man responded. *"Find them!"*

Lights came on—landscape lights high in the trees that he hadn't seen from the bathroom window.

They might as well have been spotlights.

"Go!" He urged Alyssa in front and stayed on her heels.

They were deep enough into the woods that they shouldn't be seen, shouldn't be caught.

But below the squishing of leaves, the snapping of twigs, the whooshing of branches pushed aside as they ran past, he picked up another sound. A low buzz, growing louder.

He had a bad feeling about that buzz.

A figure bolted toward them from the right, a guard who must've been posted deep in the woods.

Alyssa gasped, shifting away. But the guy had the angle on her. She wouldn't get away.

"Take this!" He shoved his bag forward, and she grabbed it. "Remember your promise!" Not waiting for an answer, Callan ran straight for the guard.

The man shouted. "Over here!" It was Benson.

Callan barreled into him, and they both tumbled onto to the soft, damp earth.

Benson landed on top.

Callan tried to add momentum to their roll to gain the upper hand, but Benson saw the move coming and stuck out his leg, bracing them both. He straddled Callan and reared his fist back for a punch.

Callan landed a sharp jab to his chin, which knocked his head back. He attempted to buck him off, but Benson was trained and prepared, clamping his knees tightly against Callan's sides.

A punch came out of nowhere, landing on the side of his head.

He saw the second coming through blurred vision.

He fought back, fought hard, but this guy was strong and capable.

Callan landed punches of his own. But more enemies would be coming. Regardless how hard he fought, he would eventually lose. He could beat Benson, but not in time to escape.

Didn't matter.

All Callan needed to do was keep him busy until Alyssa made it to the rock wall.

She'd be safe.

He wouldn't worry about himself. If he didn't survive this...?

*Peri.*

His daughter's image floated across his mind. Long brown hair that perpetually needed to be brushed. Big brown eyes always filled with sadness and worry. Peri had already endured so much heartache.

She didn't need to bury another parent.

Regret landed heavier than any punch Benson could throw.

Too late, Callan realized that for all his trying to protect others, he'd failed to protect himself.

And therefore, failed to protect his daughter.

*I'm sorry, sweetheart. I'm so sorry.*

## CHAPTER SEVENTEEN

*God, help me!*

Alyssa dropped the laptop bag and searched for something, anything she could use.

Precious seconds ticked past. Seconds filled with the sounds of battle. Of landed punches and gasps.

And then she kicked something hard.

A thick branch poked from beneath dead leaves and pine needles. She freed it from the wet ground, ignoring the dirt and bugs. It was as longer and thicker than a baseball bat, a little unwieldy, but she'd wield it anyway.

Hurrying toward Callan and the guard, she glanced into the woods. Flashlights bounced in their direction, men calling to each other, some in English, some not.

*Ignore them. One thing at a time.*

She choked up on the stick like she used to playing softball with her cousins, aimed for Benson's head, and swung.

The man toppled to the side. He wasn't unconscious, but he was down, for now.

"Get up!" She spoke to Callan, who was moving too slowly. "Come on, *come on!*"

She dropped the stick, found Callan's bag, then grabbed his hand and yanked.

He seemed to come back to himself, blinking as he looked around. "Which way?"

She kept ahold of him and ran.

He stumbled at first but seemed to gain energy as they moved. They still had so far to go.

Shouts behind them told her the guards were close.

"They found Benson," Callan said between huffs.

He understood Arabic?

She understood enough to know they needed to get out of here, fast. Her lungs were on fire by the time a low rock wall came into view. Beyond it, a house.

A nice, normal house, so incongruent with the situation.

Almost there.

*Almost there.*

A shout came from the side.

A gasp stole her breath.

She craned her neck and spied a woman running toward them. The housekeeper who wasn't.

A little behind, but not far enough.

She had no energy, no ability to push faster or harder.

Callan overtook her and propelled her forward. But they weren't going to make it, and even if they did, that rock wall wasn't going to stop this guy.

He was getting closer. She could hear him breathing behind her.

A warm hand grazed her shoulder.

She yelped, stumbled. If not for Callan's firm hold, she'd have fallen.

But the woman gripped her upper arm and yanked her around. She was falling, flailing.

Callan's hand slipped away.

Her knees hit the ground.

The not-housekeeper shouted for her compatriots.

Callan was fighting the woman, but she was trained. And he was injured.

Alyssa had no breath, no energy to fight.

Suddenly, something dove over her. A blur that took both Callan and the woman out. Another guard. They were overpowered. Overcome.

She levered to her hands and knees, tried to get to her feet, amazed when nobody stopped her.

She was turning, hoping she'd be able to help Callan as she had before, when an arm hooked beneath her armpits.

A scream crawled up her throat, but a hand clamped over her mouth.

"I'm a friend." The man's voice was deep and unfamiliar. "Come on."

*What? Who in the world...?*

"Where's Callan?" She spoke through heaving breaths.

"Right here, Paris." He took her other hand, and together, the three of them ran.

They'd gone too far before she remembered Callan's bag, which she'd dropped. "Your laptop!"

"I got it," the stranger said. "Hurry."

They scrambled over the rock wall, bolted across a backyard that held a swing set and a toddler slide.

Children inside, terrorists out.

She ran around the side of the house, still flanked by Callan and the unknown man. And then they were on the street and aiming for a sedan.

Callan scrambled into the backseat. "Hurry!"

She climbed in the front and slammed the door.

The other man settled into the driver's seat and hit the gas. She studied him in the low dashboard lights. He was black, clean-shaven, with close-cropped hair. A few wrinkles fanned from his eyes. He gripped the wheel with pale knuckles.

She turned to peer behind, where guards streamed out from beside the two-story suburban Colonial, watching them drive away.

They were free, for now.

How she wished she could believe this was over. But she knew better.

Dariush Ghazi had given her a glimpse of his plans. And he wasn't about to let her go.

# CHAPTER EIGHTEEN

What could Callan have done differently?

He replayed the events on a continual loop and came up with nothing, but there had to have been a way out. He should've anticipated the lights. He should've known they'd be caught, should've planned better.

If not for Malcolm, Alyssa would be back in Dariush's custody.

If not for Alyssa, Callan would be dead.

He squeezed his eyes closed. He wasn't afraid to die, but he had a child now. He'd left field work to care for her. And then he'd dived right back in at the first opportunity.

Idiot. *Idiot!*

He'd messed everything up, but he couldn't figure out what he should've done differently. Left Alyssa to fend for herself?

No.

Maybe he should've.

He didn't want to consider why it had never occurred to him. He'd seen her, inserted himself, and gotten them both into this mess.

The whole thing had spun out of Callan's control.

There was nothing, nothing he needed more than to stay in control. Especially now that he had a daughter to consider.

"You okay back there?" Malcolm met his eyes in the rearview mirror.

"How'd you know we were in trouble?"

"Saw the lights go on in the trees. Figured you could use a hand."

Callan hated that he'd needed help. He liked working alone. He was *good* working alone.

But not good enough.

"Thanks."

Malcolm nodded.

Callan reached between the seats and slid his hand around Alyssa's arm. "Are you all right?"

"I'm fine." She twisted to face him. "I'm not the one who got beaten up."

"I told you to run."

Her lips twisted into a smirk. "I can't believe you really thought I was going to leave you."

"You should have. If they'd caught you—"

"We're safe now."

"Hmm." He didn't hide his displeasure, though mixed with that was something else—admiration for her bravery and ingenuity.

Alyssa kept surprising him. He'd always found her beautiful. He'd never questioned her above-average intelligence. Maybe he'd underestimated her because she came from wealth, but the one he named Paris was a lot more than just intelligent and beautiful and rich.

The more he knew her, the more he liked her. Which was exactly the opposite of what he ought to be thinking about.

Callan's boss had driven too fast along the narrow Brookline streets, ensuring nobody followed, but now that they were on a main road, he slowed to a reasonable pace, glancing at his passenger. "I'm Malcolm Springer."

"Alyssa Wright. Thank you so much for helping us out."

"My pleasure. To help you, that is." He tipped his head back toward Callan. "That guy, on the other hand, is a pain in my rear."

Alyssa turned toward Callan, and he attempted a smile, though his head was pounding, and nausea churned in his gut.

Mild concussion. That big blond guard had packed a punch.

"There's water in here." Malcolm moved his elbow off the armrest between the front seats, and Alyssa opened it. She handed a bottle back to Callan.

"Thanks."

"You seemed a little off after the fight." She still wore the T-shirt on her head.

He could've reminded her, but he'd been right—she did make it look good.

"Does your head hurt? Should we go to the hospital?"

"I'm fine." He twisted off the cap and sipped. He was tempted to gulp the whole thing, but he knew better. Small sips until the nausea passed.

"Don't worry." Malcolm's voice was flat, his gaze flicking in the rearview. "He's got a thick skull."

Callan ignored him, speaking to Alyssa. "I'm okay."

She smirked, disbelieving, then faced forward again as they drove into Boston.

"Check the floor back there," Malcolm said. "Figured you'd need a few things."

Callan found a black nylon bag and pulled out two phones and chargers. A Glock and holster.

And, thank God, a bottle of ibuprofen. He swallowed four, then removed his sweatshirt, suddenly sweltering despite the cold air. He attached the holster over his T-shirt.

Alyssa turned to see what he was doing.

He winked. "Eyes forward, Paris. Though I know it's a sight to behold."

"I'm sure you think so." She turned forward again.

"You have your wallet, right?" Malcolm asked.

"Caleb's wallet, yeah. And I stuck Alyssa's into my bag before we left."

"Oh, thanks," she said.

He nodded. "My real creds are at my apartment."

"Which is secure," Malcolm said. "No indication anybody knows who you really are, but we're keeping an eye on it." To Alyssa, he said, "And your place too. We still don't know who broke in, but I've got a theory. I've reached out to sister agencies."

"You don't think it was Charles's people? I mean, Ghazi's?"

"I don't." Malcolm didn't expound or explain, and for once, Alyssa didn't ask.

Callan powered up one of the cell phones. He connected to his accounts and saw no missed messages from his family. All was well there, it seemed.

Guilt and shame pressed in, but he shook them off. He'd survived. Nobody would have to tell his daughter that her father had gone and gotten himself killed.

They crossed the Charles River into Cambridge, and Malcolm stopped on a side street a couple of blocks from the CIA field office. He shifted into Park. "Leave this car near your apartment. I have another set of keys." He climbed out.

When Callan joined him outside, the cold air bit against his damp skin, and he shivered.

Malcolm's eyes narrowed. "You okay to drive? You don't look so good."

"I'll drive," Alyssa said. "Where are we going?"

"You two are getting out of Dodge." To Callan, he said, "I expect a full report ASAP. As in, within the hour."

Callan shook his hand. "Thank you, sir." He wasn't one to give much deference to his superiors, but for all Malcolm's anger earlier, the man had saved their hides tonight.

He nodded, said goodbye to Alyssa, then hurried through the chilly April air and turned at the corner.

"If we're leaving this car, what are we driving?"

"Mine. You sure you're okay to drive?"

She moved close, right into Callan's space, and looked from one of his eyes to the other. "Your pupils aren't dilated, and they're the same size."

Her breath fanned his cheek, her nearness making his body react in a way that had nothing to do with his concussion. "Thank you, doctor." He worked hard for a lighthearted tone. "Did you get your MD while I was in the service?"

"My uncle's a physician. My cousins were always getting knocked in the head or spraining ankles or breaking bones." A slight smile graced her lips as if her cousins' injuries brought fond memories. "I was curious, and Uncle Roger was always patient, explaining what he was doing and why." She blinked and stepped back. "Anyway, for all I know, you could be dying."

"I'm fine. Well enough to drive, if you don't want to."

Grinning, she slid into the driver's seat and slammed the door.

He could argue, but Malcolm wanted a report, and the sooner, the better.

When he settled beside her, she asked, "Where to?"

He directed her the couple of miles to the garage near his apartment, where they left the Agency sedan, then headed for his cherry red Mustang.

The poor man's sports car. Maybe it wasn't a Porsche, but when he hit the gas, it flew.

"This is your car? It's a little ostentatious for a CIA agent, isn't it?"

"I'm not an agent, anymore. I'm an analyst."

Her eyebrows hiked. Whoops. He hadn't told her that.

"Long story. Anyway, Caleb-the-salesman can be as ostentatious as he wants."

They climbed in, and while she headed for the expressway, he pulled up directions to Portland on his phone, then connected it to Bluetooth so they showed on the navigation screen.

He sat back and closed his eyes, breathing in, blowing out.

They were safe, thank God. Much as he hated to need help...

*Thank You for sending it.*

*Thank You that Alyssa wasn't captured again tonight.*

*Thank You that my daughter isn't an orphan.*

Not that Peri needed him, or even wanted him.

He'd fallen in love with her the moment he'd laid eyes on her.

But that first day, she'd regarded him through squinted eyes, seeing him as a father who'd never cared about her enough to be in her life. A father who'd abandoned her and her mother to fend for themselves.

Lies. All lies.

But how did one defend himself against the accusations of a dead woman?

It had made sense for Callan to pass off Peri's care to his parents. They were competent to raise her, whereas he didn't have a clue. He'd still been in the field then, working overseas. His higher-ups had not been pleased when he'd asked for a transfer to Boston. And out of field work. They'd spent a lot of money training him, and he was throwing it away. His career, his future. To sit at a desk.

But he'd done it, for Peri. Thinking he'd figure out how to be a father. But by the time he'd moved back, Peri had gotten comfortable with his parents. She liked living in that old house in Maine, and he couldn't blame her. It had been the perfect place to grow up.

How could he take her away from that? Especially when he had no idea how to be father to a grief-stricken eight-year-old who didn't trust him?

With Peri, Callan was so far out of his depth he needed scuba gear.

At work, Callan knew what he was doing. As long as he could control everything, nothing would go wrong.

Or so he'd always told himself.

Tonight had shown him he was wrong about that, too. If not for Malcolm, Peri would be an orphan.

In those moments during his fight with Benson, one thing had become very clear.

He did not want to die. He did not want to leave his daughter fatherless.

He wanted her to know him, and someday, to love him.

If he'd died tonight, he would never have had the opportunity to prove his love to her.

Of course, he'd always planned to do that, someday. Somehow.

He'd thought he had all the time in the world. Wrong about that too.

He could be taken from Peri.

Or she could be taken from him.

Car accidents. Cancer.

Terrorists.

Nobody was promised tomorrow.

From now on, he'd fight for his daughter, even if it was the hardest fight he'd ever known.

# CHAPTER NINETEEN

Alyssa needed caffeine, or at least conversation, but Callan remained silent beside her.

Giving her way too much time to replay everything.

Callan's fight with the guard. Almost getting caught. The certainty that she *was* caught, and then Malcolm's firm grip.

Callan's kiss in the garden.

She should definitely not be thinking about that. Or reading into it. Or thinking he meant anything by it. Except there'd been no reason for him to kiss her in that moment. No cameras to pretend for. No witnesses who might see or hear.

Just her and Callan and a connection between them that she was having a hard time denying.

It was nearly two in the morning by the time they reached the expressway and headed out of the city.

He sat up and stretched his neck and shoulders.

She glanced at him in the darkness. "You all right?"

"I'm fine. Were you hurt?"

She touched her damp jeans and rubbed her tender knee

where it'd hit when she fell. She'd probably have a bruise by morning. "Nothing to worry about."

"I'm sorry that happened. I really thought we could escape without being caught."

"What went wrong?"

"My guess, the backyard guard saw the open window and had someone check our room." Callan took a breath. "I know it's late, but the sooner Malcolm knows what Ghazi wants, the better."

"He claimed to own a security company called SJSS Enterprises. He tasked me with searching for vulnerabilities, ostensibly because they've been hired to protect a well-known client they fear is being targeted."

"But...?" Callan prompted.

"But he doesn't own the company." She moved to push her hair behind her ears and bumped into the T-shirt still wrapped around her head. Yanking it off, she said, "You could've told me."

"But you look so cute."

She threw it at him. "Anyway, if he did own SJSS, then he wouldn't pay me to only *find* the vulnerabilities but to *fix* them. And he was very clear that he needed me to record my steps so he could recreate them. He's looking for a—"

"Zero-day exploit."

So named because it would exploit what programmers called a zero-day vulnerability, a flaw in a software's programming unknown to developers but discovered by criminals seeking to steal or corrupt files. A vulnerability that wouldn't be found until there were zero days to fix it.

Smart business owners hired hackers to find those vulnerabilities and fix them. Alyssa took those jobs sometimes. If she'd been hired by the true owners of SJSS, her job would have been to repair any weaknesses she located. What Ghazi wanted was for her to show him a way in.

"Did you?"

"Find one?" She flicked a gaze to the man at her side. "I found two, but I didn't pursue them. I didn't make note of them."

"In case he was recording your work."

"I'm sure he was." There were few cars on the road at this hour. She settled into the middle lane and set the cruise control. "Not just with a laptop camera, which I wasn't supposed to know was on. I'm sure Charles was recording my every keystroke as well."

"Do you think he can follow the breadcrumbs?"

"Maybe. Or someone else can."

"Could you find them again? And if so—?"

"Of course, and much faster than I did today. I figured Charles had no idea what I was doing, despite watching me all afternoon. I wasted a lot of time just poking around here and there."

"So we just have to figure out what SJSS is—"

"I know what it is."

"You do? I figured you didn't have any opportunity to look it up with him breathing down your neck all day."

"It's just a guess, but when Charles was explaining why he wanted me to dig into the code, he mentioned drones and how the company used them to provide overwatch. And then, right before Benson came at us—"

"I heard it too. A drone. That's how they found us."

"Maybe they're practicing controlling them or something. If I had to guess, I'd say SJSS manufactures drones, and I'd bet they manufacture them for the US military."

"A defense contractor."

"Exactly."

"And you found not one but *two* exploits?" He sounded incredulous.

"Inexcusable. I don't know who designed the software, but they should be fired."

"And probably tried for treason." By Callan's serious tone, it wasn't hyperbole.

"Meaning?"

"Why SJSS? How did Ghazi know the vulnerability was there?"

She considered the questions. "You're saying you think someone left them there on purpose?"

"Seems logical. There are thousands of defense contractors. Sure, they don't all manufacture drones, but I know more than one does. I think someone at SJSS left a couple of open doors. Maybe Ghazi paid the person to do it. Maybe he or she did it and then sold the information to the highest bidder. Either way, I'm betting someone made a big chunk of change."

It would be easy, really. As long as the programmer didn't tell the buyer where the vulnerabilities were, he could ignorance and incompetence, which were bad, but not *go-to-prison-for-treason* bad.

Whoever used those vulnerabilities would have to find them, and the finding of them would leave a trace, lending credence to the programmer's claims.

Brilliant.

"The question is," Callan said, "does SJSS design and build surveillance drones, or armed drones?"

"That's above my pay grade." But she had a guess.

She didn't know much about weapons technology, but like anyone who watched the news, she'd seen the damage a drone strike could do.

Drones had been used to take out enemies for years. But always *over there.*

What would happen if those drones were deployed in the US? Against American citizens?

Nobody would be safe.

# CHAPTER TWENTY

Callan focused on his surroundings.

A sheet and blanket over him.

A soft pillow beneath his head.

Far away, a door slammed. Voices carried, getting louder at first, then fading.

Nearby, it was quiet. A heater hummed, which explained his desire to throw off the covers.

He didn't, though. Not yet.

Not until he remembered where he was.

Though he didn't open his eyes, light shined against his lids. Sunshine? Lamplight?

Another sound, fainter. Breathing. And tapping on a keyboard.

He inhaled through his nose, picking up the subtle scents of jasmine and vanilla.

Which brought it all back.

The escape. The long drive to Portland. The hotel that had no adjoining rooms and no suites.

His irrational fear of being separated from Alyssa.

Her telling the clerk that they both needed two keys.

She'd taken one of his, he'd taken one of hers. He'd walked her to her door, and when she was inside, stumbled into his own room across the hall, head pounding, stomach roiling.

Though he hadn't moved, Alyssa said, "You're awake."

His breathing must have changed. He didn't think he snored, but then, he didn't generally sleep in the presence of others, so how would he know?

He opened his eyes.

The curtains were closed, but sunlight glowed around the edges. In front of the windows, Alyssa sat at her laptop at a little square table. She wore jeans, a pale pink blouse, and a navy-blue cardigan. Her hair fell in natural waves over her shoulders. Despite everything they'd gone through the night before, she looked gorgeous.

He imagined he looked—and smelled—far worse.

She was squinting at him.

"There's this thing we humans enjoy," he said. "Some of us even think we're entitled to it." His voice was scratchy, but he pressed on. "It's called privacy."

He expected a smile, but her brows lowered. "I thought you might be dead."

"Just sleeping, another thing we humans enjoy."

She made a show of checking her phone screen. "Most humans don't sleep for ten straight hours."

He sat up too fast, the movement making him lightheaded, which he did his best to conceal as he reached for his phone.

He found it plugged into the charger, though he hadn't done that the night before. He'd managed little besides peeling out of his clothes and brushing his teeth. He'd been pretty proud of himself for thinking to grab their toothbrushes and toothpaste from the bathroom the night before and shoving the items into his bag.

He was still melting—had to be seventy-five degrees in the

room—but he couldn't exactly throw off the covers, considering he wore nothing but boxers. "Why are you here?"

"You had a concussion. When you didn't answer my knock, I got worried. My uncle told me to check on you, so—"

"Your uncle?"

Her head tilted to one side. "I know I told you—"

"Right, right." He brushed her off. "Uncle Roger, the doctor. You called him?"

"Like I said, I was worried. He told me you were probably fine but it wouldn't hurt to make sure, so I let myself in and checked your pulse."

She'd checked his pulse, and he'd slept right through it?

*Disconcerting* didn't begin to cover how that felt. "And you're still here because...?"

"Because checkout was hours ago." She snapped her laptop closed. "Who knew you'd sleep until two o'clock."

Right.

Too much information before coffee.

She pushed to her feet. "I assume you'd like that privacy now. Why don't I get us something to eat? Anything sound good?"

Now that she mentioned it, he was starving. "Anything, and a Coke. I need caffeine."

"Would you rather have coffee? There's a Dunkin' Donuts—"

"No. It's a thousand degrees in this room."

Her eyes narrowed. "It's not warm." She stepped closer and laid a palm on his forehead.

Her hand was cool, her touch soft and tender.

"You don't feel feverish." She slid her hand to his cheeks. "Do you have a headache? Are you—?"

"I'm fine. It's just these blankets." He hadn't meant to snap, but sheesh. He needed her out of his bedroom. He tempered his tone. "Sorry. I'm cranky when I'm hungry."

*And when I wake up to find uninvited guests in my bedroom. Even gorgeous ones who smell like springtime and make my stupid heart go haywire.*

"Right." She backed away. "If you're sure, I'll be back soon." She snatched the car keys off the bureau and headed for the door. "I left a note for you earlier with the number to the cell-phone Malcolm gave me. Call or text if you think of anything. Oh, and I grabbed you some clean clothes. I wasn't sure what sizes you'd want, so I made my best guess."

Sure enough, a sack rested next to where she'd found his keys.

She walked out, leaving him alone. And as much as he told himself he was glad for it, he already looked forward to her return.

WHILE ALYSSA WAS OUT, Callan showered and dressed in the clothes she'd bought him—joggers and a T-shirt. She'd even grabbed a package of boxers. Awkward that she was buying his underwear, though they fit well enough.

Considering Benson-the-thug had hit him pretty hard the night before, most of his injuries weren't visible. His headache was better, thanks to the ibuprofen Alyssa had left on top of the sack. He had a slight bruise on his cheek, and his lip was swollen.

When he finished cleaning up, he texted Malcolm, who responded with,

Sit tight. We're formulating a plan.

Shouldn't Callan be a part of that? He and Alyssa were the ones who'd been at Ghazi's house.

If it were up to Callan, Ghazi and his people would be taken into custody and treated like the terrorists they were.

But it wasn't up to Callan.

He emailed Michael Wright, who knew more about Dariush Ghazi than anybody else in the Agency. Callan described the photograph he'd seen in the man's room and asking if he had any idea who she was.

Probably didn't matter, but more information was always better.

An hour later, Callan finished off the meal Alyssa had picked up from an upscale pub nearby.

He'd expected her to come in with fast-food bags, but she rarely did what was expected, not that he was complaining. He'd been wary when he'd first seen the topping, not ketchup or mustard but some kind of bacon chutney.

Bacon, anytime. But chutney?

It was beyond delicious.

She'd already finished her salad and sat on the chair opposite him at the square table, feet propped on the bed, glancing at the laptop resting on her thighs. Her brows lowered, and her lips dipped in a frown.

"Something wrong?"

"Brooklynn called."

Sister number two. "You gave her your number?"

"No. When I didn't answer, she texted. I get my texts on my laptop." She looked up. "Don't worry. I've already disconnected my cell phone. Even if they can get past my passcode, they can't track me."

"I wasn't worried. You know what you're doing." He pointed with his chin to her computer. "Something wrong?"

Alyssa read the screen. "She wants to talk to me about Grams and Pop's party and is wondering why I haven't answered her calls. I told her I lost my phone. I figure I shouldn't give her the number to the one Malcolm provided. I'll just text and tell her I'm not going to make the party."

"Don't do that until we hear back from Malcolm."

He had a bad feeling about what his boss might say, though he wasn't ready to let Alyssa in on his worries yet.

"I need to let them know. They're going to be mad, but it'll be so much worse if I cancel at the last minute—"

"Then you'll explain at the time. For now, don't say anything, please." He nodded to the hotel phone. "Call your sister from that, if you want."

"I'll just text her."

"She wants to talk to you. I can leave, if you want privacy."

"That's not it."

His face must've displayed his surprise because she said, "If I wanted to talk to her, I would."

Interesting. Callan didn't reject his sister's calls unless he legitimately couldn't talk, even though lately, Hannah mostly gave him a hard time about his life choices. Not that he didn't deserve it. Bossy as his little sister could be, he'd never avoided her calls. "I thought sisters were supposed to be close."

"They're close. I've always been an outsider."

"Why?"

She snatched his trash and shoved it in the can, ignoring his question.

"Are you close to your parents?" he asked.

"Mom and I are close, yeah."

He lifted his eyebrows, figuring his expression asked the question.

"I've always been a disappointment to my father. I don't even want to think about what he'd say if he knew the trouble I'm in now."

"It's not your fault. You did your homework on Sanders. You couldn't have—"

"It's fine." She lifted a hand to silence him. "His opinion of me is well deserved."

"What are you talking about? You're smart. You're successful. You're"—he almost said beautiful but managed to shift in time to—"capable. If your father doesn't see that, then he's blind."

Alyssa settled in the chair across from him again and grabbed her laptop. Focused on it.

He was about to try again when she sighed.

"Dad honors achievement. What have I achieved? All I ever wanted was to follow him into the CIA. I failed there." Her eyes narrowed in a glare. "Thanks to you."

"Me?" He sat back, surprised. "What did I do?"

"We both applied for the same job. Despite the fact that I'd been working for the NSA in intelligence for years, they gave it to you."

"I didn't know you were up for that job." He shouldn't be pleased he'd bested her, especially considering it'd been more important than class rank—she'd beat him by about a tenth of a percentage point—or the software development contest they'd both entered.

He'd won that one.

"I was qualified for it," she said. "More qualified than you were."

He laughed without amusement. "That's quite an assumption."

"Come on, Callan. I was already working in intelligence. You were off in the Army."

"I worked for INSCOM. Army intelligence."

"Oh." She blinked, then tilted her head to the side. "Really?"

"For the last three years of my service. What did you think, that they just...liked me more?"

"I thought...I thought you got the job because of your military experience. And because you're a man."

"It never crossed your mind that I might actually be more qualified."

She closed her laptop and tossed it onto the bed beside her. "I didn't think about it that way. I didn't realize you were... I should've gone into the service. I was going to, but Dad told me not to. He said I wouldn't need military experience. And then when I failed to get the job, he just acted like...like he wasn't surprised. Like he'd never believed for a minute I could do it."

"I'm sure it wasn't that."

"Trust me. It was."

"Does he act like that toward your sisters?"

Alyssa shrugged, gazing out the window. It was a rainy afternoon, typical for springtime in Maine.

Callan had turned on all the lights in the room to chase away the dreariness.

But darkness crossed Alyssa's face, her lips tightening as if she'd pressed them closed to keep whatever bothered her inside.

He should let it go. It was none of his business. But his whole life was about keeping—and exposing—secrets.

"Tell me the story."

"Who says there's a story?"

He raised his eyebrows, not letting her off the hook.

She snatched her cardigan from the top of the bureau and slipped it on. Enough time passed that he was sure she wasn't going to answer.

She settled on the bed across from him. "It was a long time ago. I shouldn't even..." Her voice trailed, and again, he kept silent.

"When I was twelve, my parents had to go to some event on the opposite side of Portland, about an hour away from our house. I'd taken a babysitting class, and they'd left me home with my sisters a couple of times. But this night, they hired a sitter. I was mad. I knew I could handle it."

Callan couldn't imagine leaving Peri home alone, ever. There was a big difference between eight and twelve, but even so, the thought of all the things that could go wrong had his pulse racing.

"Mom was the overprotective one," Alyssa said. "It was the only time Dad ever took my side. He told Mom I could handle it. 'You've got to trust your kids if you ever want them to be trustworthy.'" Alyssa had affected a man's voice. "I thought for sure Mom would relent, but she said they were going to be gone too long and were going too far to risk it.

"After they left, I decided to prove Mom wrong—and Dad right. I thought I'd make him proud."

By her smirk, things hadn't gone according to plan.

"That evening, while the babysitter played with my little sisters upstairs, I decided to cook dinner. Mom had gotten some take-and-bake pizzas. I preheated the oven, then slid the pizzas in and set the timer. Once they were cooking, I joined the game my sisters and the babysitter were playing, thinking about how surprised they'd be when the timer went off."

"What happened?"

"Before, when my mother had gotten take-home pizzas, they'd come on their own baking trays. But these didn't."

"Oh, no."

"Yeah. I put them in the oven on the cardboard, and the cardboard caught fire. It wouldn't have been a huge deal if I'd been watching them. I would have noticed and gotten the fire put out. But we were upstairs. I was just picking up the scent of smoke when the alarm went off.

"I thought the oven contained most of the damage, but the babysitter insisted we call the fire department anyway. Which... it's stupid in retrospect because obviously, I wasn't going to be able to hide the damage, but I didn't want my father to find out what I'd done. That was my biggest fear. Not the fact that I could've killed us all, but that I might get in trouble. That I might disappoint him."

Callan wasn't sure what to say, so he just nodded for her to continue.

"The fire department came. If I'd been in charge, the whole house would've burned down. Somehow, the fire had spread into the walls. We lost most of the kitchen, but it could've been so much worse."

"Aw, I'm sorry." He reached for her, but if she saw his hand outstretched, she pretended not to.

"I'll never forget the disappointment on my father's face that night. He could barely look at me."

"I'm sure it just scared him."

Alyssa met his eyes. "He called me a stupid, foolish little girl."

Anger sent Callan's heart pounding. "He said that? To your face?"

"He said it to my mother. I'm sure he didn't mean for me to hear."

"Your father sounds like a world-class jerk."

"He's not." Alyssa's lips slid into an almost-smile. "He was just angry and disappointed."

"You were a kid."

"I know that. He shouldn't have said those things, even if he believed them. Dad was never great at the whole fatherhood thing." Now that her story was over, she seemed to relax a little. "I think being a parent takes practice. It takes time, but Dad was always too busy, off on assignments or at work. I mean, we lived in Maine, but he worked in DC. He usually came home on weekends, but there were times when we'd go weeks without seeing him. Even after he retired from the Agency and went into the private sector, he was away as much as he was home. I don't think he ever really learned how to be a father."

Alyssa couldn't know how her words wounded him.

Here Callan was, judging Gavin Wright for being a lousy parent while he'd hardly spent any time with his own child.

Gavin had probably felt capable at work. He'd probably felt less capable at home.

He'd probably told himself that his daughters didn't need him. They had their mother, after all. But Alyssa had needed her father's love and approval.

The difference was that, no matter what Peri did, Callan adored her. But if his little girl didn't know that, what good would his love prove to be?

That was a question that required contemplation.

The answers would require he change his life and dedicate himself to his little girl.

Alyssa was watching him as though trying to read his thoughts.

"I'm sorry about what I said last night during our fake argument." He couldn't remember his exact words. Something about how she was working for Charles to prove to her father she wasn't a failure.

Maybe that wasn't really what drove her, but he guessed she had to fight that motivation a lot.

Alyssa waved off his apology. "You couldn't have known. And I shouldn't care." But she did.

"Your dad sounds like a hard man to please."

She propped her hands on the bed behind her, leaning back on them. "He was. Still is."

"Are you...?" He worked to figure out how to ask his question. "Does your father help you out, financially? Or are you cut off, or...?"

"He helps more than I want him to."

"Meaning?"

"Like with my apartment. When I quit the NSA, he was furious, even suggesting that he'd helped me get the job—as if I couldn't have done it without him. It was the first time in my adult life that I ever defied him, which is...pathetic, I know."

"You're an adult, Alyssa. The fact that your father issues orders and you feel like, in refusing to do them, you're defying him? That tells me more about him than it tells me about you. You get to make your own decisions."

"Yeah, well... The point is, I had a plan. My cousin Sam has a brilliant business mind, and he helped me draw it up and even loaned me the startup money. I decided to move to Boston instead of back to Shadow Cove in order to be close to potential clients. I rented an apartment and gave my two weeks' notice, and then I told my father.

"After Dad quit railing about what a stupid decision I'd made, he told me the area where I planned to live wasn't safe enough. He signed a lease and demanded I live in the Back Bay apartment instead."

"He demanded it, and you did it?"

She dipped her head side to side. "Probably the wrong choice of words. He strongly suggested it, and I would have refused if he hadn't gotten Mom on his side. She suggested I was being stubborn—which I was—and that my safety was more important than proving to my father I didn't need his help. I relented for her sake."

"He pays for it?" At her nod, Callan said, "It's a nice building."

"So much for it being safe, though." Alyssa's smile surprised him until he realized that the break-in proved her father wrong. She was enjoying that, anyway.

"So you're not still trying to please him?"

She shrugged. "Don't you want to please your parents?"

"My parents have always been encouraging. Growing up, I never felt like they were disappointed in me."

She tilted her head to the side. "Do you feel like they are now?"

"What?" He played back what he'd said, how he'd said it. *Growing up...* "No. They're...no."

He was lying. He didn't just guess his parents' disapproval. He knew it. They kept waiting for him to take on the role he'd been thrust into. And he kept...not doing it.

Any excuse to stay away, stay where he knew what he was doing.

He should tell Alyssa about Peri. She'd shared her story with him, after all. But the last thing he wanted was for Alyssa to realize what a terrible father he was. What a terrible person.

He liked this woman, far more than he should. Far more than he'd even admitted to himself.

But this relationship couldn't go beyond where it was right now. He and Alyssa needed to figure out what to do about Ghazi, and then Callan needed to focus on Peri.

He couldn't let himself be distracted by the beautiful blond who studied him as if she could see right through him.

His cell phone rang, and he was grateful for an excuse to end the conversation. Not that he wasn't happy to know Alyssa's secrets, but he wasn't ready to share any of his own.

# CHAPTER TWENTY-ONE

"It's Malcolm."

Alyssa half expected Callan to walk out of his hotel room or ask her to leave when the call came in. But he just swiped to answer it.

Considering she was no less involved in this Ghazi situation than Callan was, she stayed right where she was to hear to his end of the conversation.

It didn't yield much information. Callan was mostly listening as he tapped on his laptop's keyboard.

Leaving her too much time to think.

Why had she told him about the fire? It was far and away the most embarrassing, most shameful thing she'd ever done. If the fire in the walls hadn't been discovered, it could've smoldered for hours and set the entire house aflame.

Her whole family could have been killed because of her arrogance.

She would never forget the look on her father's face that day as he'd surveyed the damage she'd done. Utter disgust.

Eighteen years had passed, eighteen years of trying to be better, of striving to succeed. But sometimes she still caught that expression on Dad's face. No matter how hard she'd tried to make up for her shortcomings, she'd never been good enough.

When she'd graduated from Boston College summa cum laude, Dad had patted her shoulder and said, "Too bad you didn't get into an Ivy League school, where it would matter."

When she'd been hired by the NSA, Dad had said, "The CIA has high standards. The NSA is more your level."

When she'd failed a second time to join the Agency, Dad had suggested that maybe the rejection was "a sign to aim lower."

And when she'd quit her boring analyst job... She'd never forget his reaction.

"You want to own your own business? How will you ever make that work?"

As if the idea of her finding success was so far outside the realm of possibility that it didn't even occur to him.

In Dad's eyes, she was a failure and always would be.

"That makes sense," Callan said to Malcolm, pulling her back to the moment.

He met her eyes, wearing a scowl that wasn't meant for her. "No. That's not going to—" He stood and stared out the window. "That's the point," he said. "Which is why she needs to get out of—"

Well, this was frustrating.

She gripped his elbow. "Put it on speaker."

He shook his head and walked toward the door.

She followed, getting more annoyed by the second.

Callan spun to pace back, nearly crashing into her. He scooted past and kept walking. "I don't like it." And then, "Me? I didn't do any of—" And then, "Yeah, I see what you're..."

If he didn't finish a sentence soon, she would throw something at him.

"Fine." Callan didn't sound like he thought anything was

*fine*. "We'll get back to you." He ended the call and tossed his cell on the bed.

"What?"

"I had a feeling Malcolm was going to..." He ran a hand over his short hair. "I was hoping I could make him see reason, but...."

It took all her self-control not to stomp her foot. "Use nouns, please. And verbs. And full sentences so I know what the heck you're talking about."

He took a breath, then blew it out slowly. "I knew when Malcolm insisted we leave the note... They want you to try to smooth things over with Ghazi."

She dropped onto the bed. "You can't be serious. We went out the window. We *escaped*. They want me to walk right back in and—"

"No!" The word sounded almost angry. "You're not going back. You're not going anywhere he can get his hands on you."

Thank God. She didn't think she had the courage to return to Ghazi's presence, voluntarily or otherwise.

"They want you to call him. They want you to keep him on the hook so he doesn't realize he's been compromised. You need to convince him you're still loyal."

She started to state the obvious, that he wouldn't believe her.

But she didn't. Because this was what she'd always wanted, wasn't it? To be in the middle of the action. To have information nobody else had. To affect changes, to save lives.

To deceive enemies in order to gather information about them. To bring them down.

She wasn't trained. She wasn't prepared. But she *was* willing. She'd always been willing, even if the CIA hadn't wanted to take a chance on her.

"Okay. What's our story?"

Something flashed in Callan's eyes. Surprise and...respect?

Maybe he'd expected her to refuse or at least put up a fight.

"The thing is," Callan said, "even if he doesn't believe you, he'll try to convince you he does. He needs you to believe he's not a bad guy. You need him to believe you don't know he's a bad guy."

"We'll both be lying, and pretending the other doesn't know we're lying."

"That's one way it could go. But maybe he'll believe you. He'll want to believe you because he needs what you have. You're his best bet for gaining access to SJSS's systems. Because of that, he should be more inclined to take you at your word. It's the easier path for him, and people—even evil, homicidal people—tend to prefer the easier path. Does that make sense?" At her nod, Callan said, "But you're going to have to sell it."

"Okay." She pushed to her feet and paced from the window to the door. "We went out the window. Trustworthy people don't climb out the window." Her pitch rose at the end, betraying her fear.

A few feet from Callan, she turned to pace back to the window.

He caught her hand. "I know it feels that way." He tugged her around to face him. "It's okay, Paris. I'll be right here."

He was too close, his gaze too intense, as if everything they'd pretended for Ghazi's sake was real.

His Adam's apple bobbed, and he dropped her hand. "We'll come up with a plan."

Right.

She needed a way to deceive a homicidal terrorist.

She did *not* need to think about her one-sided attraction for Callan.

She took a few steps back. "What if he doesn't believe me?"

"No matter how well you sell it, he's going to be suspicious. But hopefully, not so suspicious that he gives up his plan."

"Isn't that what we want? For him to give up?"

Go away? Leave the country and never come back?

Seemed like a good strategy to her.

"Unfortunately," Callan said, "we need to figure out what he's up to—and what Lavrentiy has to do with it."

The Russian whose name she'd found but hadn't given to Ghazi.

"For that," Callan said, "we need time. And we need you to get as much information as possible from *Charles*"—he emphasized the name she'd need to remember to use—"without going near him again. You need to convince him you're still on his side, and that you'll do whatever he asks. You'll tell him that you'll do it, and then you'll show him you're not afraid of him by being where he expects you to be."

Realization washed over her

Callan didn't say anything, just gave her time to absorb the truth.

That Ghazi knew exactly who she was. He knew who her parents were. He probably knew her sisters' names and where they all lived.

Just like when she'd nearly burned the house down, her family was at risk, and just like that time, it was all her fault.

Only this time, there'd be no firemen showing up to save the day.

This time, it was up to her.

THIS WAS CRAZY.

Alyssa and Callan had talked through the plan, and it was simple enough.

Callan had settled back at the little table in the cramped hotel room, which seemed to be getting smaller and smaller the more time they spent in it.

Alyssa couldn't stop pacing. From the door to the windows, over and over.

She wanted out of the room. Out of the hotel. Out of this terrible situation. Just...out.

But *out* wasn't an option.

What if she couldn't convince Ghazi...*Charles*? What if... what if she blew it, and her entire family paid the price?

"Stop overthinking it, Paris."

She spun to face Callan, who'd somehow read her mind.

"I'm just thinking through what I'm going to say."

"Right. Overthinking it." He held out the hotel phone's handset. "It's time to practice winging it."

They'd decided she should make the call from the landline. Charles had her cellphone, and she didn't want to give him her new phone number.

It wouldn't matter if Charles traced the call. They were a hundred and sixty miles from Boston, and even if he happened to have people nearby, she and Callan planned to leave as soon as the call was made.

They'd done their best to work through every aspect of this.

Callan set the phone in its cradle again, then held out his hand to her. "Come sit with me, please."

She did, though she felt antsy and uncomfortable, like she needed to shed a too-tight sweater.

He took her hand, perfectly at ease touching her, as if it meant nothing to him, though she hadn't grown nearly as immune to him.

"I'm going to pray, okay?"

"Good idea." She should have thought of that. She believed

in God, had surrendered to Christ when she was a child, but He felt distant and distracted.

She needed His help, and maybe, since the situation was so dire, He'd get involved.

Callan prayed that God would give her the words to say and the peace and confidence to say them well. He prayed that Ghazi would believe her, and that God would show her and Callan a way out of this.

"Protect Alyssa and her parents. Protect Brooklynn, Cici, Delaney, Kenzie, and the entire Wright family."

She was impressed that he remembered her sisters' names.

"Let none of this touch her family." He squeezed Alyssa's hand. "We trust you, Father. Be with us."

At his amen, she looked up. "Thank you."

"You've got this, Paris. I'll be right here. If you start to feel panicky, find a way to end the call. Remember the plan."

She'd already found Charles's phone number on her laptop. Now, she took the landline's handset and dialed.

No answer.

"Try again," Callan said. "He just doesn't recognize the number."

She redialed. It rang four times, then went to voicemail.

Maybe this wasn't going to work. Maybe Charles had already decided she couldn't be trusted and had taken off, flown out of the country, never to be seen again.

Except Malcolm had sent a team to surveil the house, and according to the agents posted nearby, nobody had left.

She didn't look at Callan, not wanting him to see her hope that he wouldn't answer as she dialed again.

This time, the line connected. "Charles Sanders."

"Charles, it's Alyssa."

A beat of silence followed her words. "I didn't think I'd be hearing from you again."

"I'm so sorry. I never thought your guys would chase us the way they did. They probably thought we were intruders or something."

Which of course they hadn't, but she needed him to believe that she didn't believe the guards would've chased her and Callan if they had known who they were.

Charles didn't say anything, so she continued talking, not bothering to hide her nervousness.

"I have to say, Charles, I didn't appreciate the way they tried to keep us from leaving. Caleb thought you'd try to stop us, and I assured him you wouldn't. But even after the guards knew who we were, they still tried to detain us."

Still, Charles said nothing.

"Look, you have to understand." She blew out a breath. "Caleb swore he saw a camera in the hall. Like a small, hidden camera. It freaked him out, and he was so worried that, honestly, I started to think maybe he was right. You can hardly blame us. Your people were acting really weird, keeping watch on us all the time. And, I'm sorry to say this, Charles, but so were you. You asked me to come—no, you didn't ask." Her tone hardened a little. "You *demanded* that I come, and then you sat there and watched me work all day long as if you didn't trust me. During dinner, Caleb went back to our room to use the bathroom, and he was cornered by two guys who basically threatened him and told him not to wander off on his own again. The whole thing was...disconcerting to say the least."

"We are security-conscious, as we must be." Charles's tone was calm. "You can understand why my men were suspicious when your fiancé was wandering the house alone. And you can't blame them for wanting to detain you, considering you didn't exit the front door. They assumed you'd stolen from me."

"I would never do that. It was nothing like that. It was just that Caleb was freaked out."

"So you climbed out a second-story window? You left your phone and all your things and ran?"

"He thought we were in danger."

"Did you think that, Alyssa?"

"What would you think if the situation were reversed? I don't know what your family was like, but if my family invites someone home, we don't assign guards to escort them from the bedroom to dinner. That is not normal behavior."

"Perhaps your people are more trusting than mine."

She wasn't sure if he meant the words seriously or as a joke and decided not to respond.

"What does Caleb think about you calling me now?"

"Are you kidding? Do you think I told him? He'd be furious."

"Then why did you call, Alyssa? The truth now." He issued that last statement as a command.

She let a few beats pass before lowering her voice almost to a whisper. "You know why, Charles."

He said nothing, but she wasn't going to speak again, not until he did. She'd babbled enough and didn't want to lay the act on too thick. The goal was to make it clear to him that she knew she was trapped.

"Perhaps I do," he said. "Nevertheless, I'd like you to explain it to me so I know if we're on the same page."

"Yesterday, when you suggested I'd probably broken a couple of laws getting information for you, you weren't wrong. I'd assumed your lawbreaking was like mine," she said. "Small potatoes. No big deal. But now I think maybe..."

When she didn't finish her sentence, he said, "My potatoes aren't so small?" He sounded almost amused.

"Look, I don't want to know. I don't want to get caught up in whatever it is you're doing, okay? I can't. My father is sort of a bigwig in the government, and this could look very bad for him. Not that I know what *this* is. I'm just saying..."

She paused, hoping Charles would jump in.

He didn't.

"I just want your assurance that, when I'm finished searching for vulnerabilities at your company"—she was very careful to add the *your*—"then that'll be the end of our...partnership. After that, I'm going to take some time off and...and you know what I'm saying, right? I want out."

"I understand that, for a little while, you'll be focusing all your time and attention on your fiancé and wedding planning."

"Exactly. That's exactly right. This has nothing to do with you." And then she heard what he hadn't said and added, "But what I'm saying is not...temporary. After I complete this job for you, I will sever my ties with you, and that will be that. You understand?"

"You'll come back to my house today?"

"No!" The word came too fast. "I'm not...I can't. Sorry, but no. And I don't need to. I can do the searches on my laptop, and I won't have to tell Caleb or anyone else what I'm doing."

"Probably not the best way to treat the man you love, but alas, I've never been married. Perhaps a bit of deceit is necessary in a happy marriage."

"I don't want to deceive him. I just don't see another option. He doesn't trust you."

"What does he think I'm up to?"

"He has no idea. I haven't given him any details, and I don't plan to. Which is why I can't come back. I mean, we're in Portland, a long drive from Boston. There's no way I could come back without him knowing."

They'd decided her best bet was to be honest with Charles about her whereabouts. The more truth she could share, the more likely he would believe her. "We're going to his parents' house tonight and to my grandparents' anniversary party tomorrow. There's no way for me to come back there. I mean, unless it could wait until Monday."

Callan gripped her wrist to draw her attention, shaking his head vehemently.

She averted her gaze from the fear in his eyes.

The one thing he'd told her was not to agree to go back to Charles's house under any circumstances, and she didn't plan to.

But offering to felt right. She needed to sound as if she weren't afraid of Charles.

Though it wouldn't hurt to show a little fear, all things considered. It wasn't like she had to fake it. The thought of going back to that house with all those guards churned terror in her stomach.

"And, honestly," she said, "it wasn't just Caleb who was freaked out. I'd rather just work on my own, like we've done for months. You know you can trust me."

"Do I know that, Alyssa? After what you did last night, I'm not so sure."

"What *I* did? You blackmailed me. You insisted I come to your house even when I didn't want to. You watched over me as if you thought I was going to...I don't even know what you thought. You treated my fiancé like a criminal."

Charles said nothing. He was better at the silence thing than she was. But then, she wasn't trying to prove to him that she was as clever as he.

"Look," she said, "I don't want to argue with you or cast blame, but if I were having this conversation with one of my sisters, I'd say you started it."

She hated bringing up her sisters. But both Michael and Callan believed Charles knew all about her family. Mentioning her sisters would lend credence to the idea that she was being honest. That she had nothing to hide.

The last thing she wanted was to put her sisters on his radar. To make them into targets.

*Please, Father. Protect them. For their sake if not for mine.*

"Perhaps we were a little too protective," Charles said. "Though I disagree that your behavior was equal to mine—running away like you did was extreme."

She didn't say anything. She'd made her case.

After a moment, he continued. "I will make you a deal. If you get me the information I asked for regarding SJSS *and* the name of the Russian I seek, then we can part ways as friends."

She turned back to face Callan, who watched intently.

"You won't ask me to work for you again?" she clarified.

"I won't. But I need the information by the end of the day Sunday."

"Sunday?"

Callan mouthed, *more time.*

"I have plans all weekend, so I'm not sure—"

"Sunday, Alyssa. I trust you can make it work."

She shook head at Callan.

He held her eye contact a moment, then shrugged, telling her to say whatever she had to say.

"I'll do my best."

Callan lifted his phone and shook it, reminding her...

"Would you do me a favor, though? Would you have our phones and suitcases delivered to my fiancé's office?" She didn't know if Charles would do it, but under normal circumstances, a person would ask about their things. "I can reimburse you for the cost."

"The cost is minimal. I'll have your items delivered to where you are now, if you'd like."

"That's okay. We won't be here much longer, and we'll only be at his parents' house overnight. And then—"

"Tell me where you'll be tomorrow."

He probably already knew her parents' address, but she wasn't about to give it to him if he didn't. "We have everything we need for the weekend. Just have our stuff delivered to his office." She grabbed the paper where Callan had written the address of an office where Caleb Thompson rented space. "You can just have the driver leave the things with the receptionist in the lobby."

"I will have it done this afternoon. Meanwhile, you will work on your assignments. I look forward to hearing from you by Sunday night."

She hung up the phone and then plopped on the bed, exhausted.

They had two days to ferret out Ghazi's plan and bring him down.

She didn't want to think about what would happen if she failed.

# CHAPTER TWENTY-TWO

It was late afternoon by the time Callan and Alyssa reached the outskirts of Augusta. Callan aimed for a bookstore that had an attached coffee shop. The rain that followed them north had finally tapered off, and sunshine peeked through the thick clouds, sparkling against the wet pavement.

"You sure you don't want to come shopping with me?" Callan asked. "You could work later, whenever we get to the hotel." Alyssa had reserved adjoining rooms for them while he drove.

"Hmm... My choices are to use my strengths to try to protect my family or shop for boring men's clothes. What do you think?"

He shouldn't have bothered asking. Of course she wouldn't reconsider, even if the thought of leaving her on her own twisted something in his gut.

Callan was more impressed with this analyst-turned-cyber investigator all the time. She had zero field experience, yet she'd played Ghazi like a cello, using both fear and frustration to cover for the lies she told.

Whether Ghazi truly believed her remained to be seen, but if he didn't, that would be the result of a suspicious nature, not any shortcomings on Alyssa's part.

Her father had been a top-notch spook in his day, and though she looked nothing like the dark-haired man Callan had only seen in photos, in other ways, the apple hadn't rolled far from the tree.

He and Alyssa only had two days to figure out what Ghazi was up to before he'd expect information from her. And if she didn't provide it…

Malcolm was working on figuring out how the Russian played into Ghazi's plans.

Maybe the woman in the photo Callan had seen in Ghazi's room had nothing to do with anything, but it was another lead that needed following. Michael texted earlier saying he was still working on it.

When Callan told Alyssa about the photograph and her cousin's response, she'd been exasperated. "Why didn't you tell me sooner?" They'd been leaving the hotel room. "I could've been looking for her all morning."

"I didn't think of it last night," he'd said. "And we've been sort of busy today."

They'd decided that she could start searching while he bought some clothes. His least favorite chore—shopping. But he couldn't exactly wear dirty joggers to her grandparents' anniversary party the following day.

He stopped at the curb in front of the bookstore. "I don't feel comfortable leaving you."

"There's no way he can track me here."

"Your laptop—"

"I know how to hide my location, Callan. They won't find me."

"Okay. Fine. But... If anything happens, or if you feel the slightest bit worried or even get a bad feeling, call me. Don't text, don't email. Call."

"So I should call?" Her eyes widened in false confusion. "Is that what you're saying?"

"You want me to show you how it works?"

"Haha. Let me know when you're on your way so I can be looking for you." She opened the door.

He took her hand, which he'd done so many times in the last few days that it felt perfectly natural. It shouldn't, considering that before Wednesday, they hadn't seen each other in years. She shouldn't mean more to him than any coworker would.

She did, though. That was the problem. *One* of the problems.

Another problem was the terrorist trying to manipulate her into helping him pull off some unknown...something.

The biggest problem came in the form of a precious eight-year-old girl, thoughts of whom should push out any attraction or romantic feelings he had for the woman at his side.

Her eyebrows hiked. "Did you need something, or do you just like holding my hand?"

Yes to both?

"If you learn anything, email it to me and to your cousin, just in case."

Her amusement faded. "Will do."

Reluctantly, Callan released her, and she grabbed her laptop bag from the floorboard and walked inside.

She'd be fine. Of course she'd be fine.

Callan drove a few short blocks to a strip mall where he'd done his share of shopping over the years. Mom used to bring him and Hannah here every summer to buy new school clothes. Hannah would insist she had to try on every new style—in every single color. She couldn't make a single decision until she knew all the options in the entire mall.

Meanwhile, Callan would grab the cheapest jeans, T-shirts, and sweatshirts he could find. He'd only use the dressing room if his mother made him. And then he'd be finished shopping and bored, slumped in a chair—or on the floor, if that was all he could find—to wait for his slow-as-mud little sister.

But when they were loaded down with shopping bags filled with jeans and sweaters and underwear and jackets and shoes and all manner of things, Mom would take them to lunch. When Dad could get off work to meet them, he did. It didn't matter that it was cheap fast food. For his family, it was a rare treat.

These days, he didn't have to search for the least expensive items, but old habits weren't easy to break, no matter how his savings account grew.

He looked for sales and found a pair of trousers, a button-down shirt, and a sports coat, though Alyssa had said that last was optional. But they'd need to go forward with the whole fake engagement thing in front of her family, just in case Ghazi was watching. They had to assume he was, which meant Alyssa would need to deceive her entire family.

He hadn't broken that to her yet.

It was the reason that, even though they were within thirty minutes of his family, he didn't plan to take her there. If he got a chance to go home and visit Peri, he would take it, but he wouldn't be taking Alyssa with him.

Ghazi didn't know who Callan really was, but anytime they were in public together, they needed to keep up the ruse, just in case. And much as he'd insist she had to lie to her family, he would avoid lying to his own at all costs.

So, he chose clothes that fit the part of a fiancé who wanted to make a good impression.

His phone buzzed with a text, and he glanced at it on his way to the checkout counter. It was from Alyssa, an image. He clicked on it and froze.

It was the woman who'd been photographed with Ghazi.

Another text came through.

**Is this her?**

**Yes! How did you do that so fast?**

She added a little *haha* to his text, then responded with,

**I got skills, baby.**

A second later, she added...

**Michael helped. :) I'm looking into her.**

After he paid for the clothes, he headed to a discount department store, where he picked out a pair of black dress shoes that would probably last the duration of the party—though not much longer—socks, and a few more casual things to tide him over for the next few days.

Alyssa was going to borrow something from one of her sisters or from her mom. Or, if nothing else, she'd raid the clothes she'd left at her folks' house when she moved out.

Callan was at the cash register when his phone rang. The Agency had activated his old number on the new phone, so it could be anyone. Even so, the vibration in his pocket ticked his anxiety up.

He snatched it, relieved to see it wasn't Alyssa. It was Hannah.

He signed the credit card machine and took his things, thanking the clerk. On his way to the door, he answered the call. "Hey, sis."

"Thank God you answered."

He froze. "What's wrong? Is it Peri?"

"Not Peri. It's Dad. He had a heart attack."

~

CALLAN PUSHED through the door at the emergency room and rushed to the woman behind the desk. "My father was brought in. Hank...Henry Templeton."

"I think he's been moved already." She peered at a computer screen. "Yes, up to cardiology."

Callan had texted Alyssa from the car, sitting at a stoplight.

**My dad had a heart attack. On my way to the hospital. Get an Uber to the hotel and check in, and I'll meet you there.**

She'd texted back,

**Which hospital?**

**Just finish what you're doing and get some dinner. I'll see you soon.**

Not that Callan wouldn't love for her to be by his side, but that would cause too many problems.

She'd shared a lot of her life with him, but he'd kept the most important thing about himself a secret.

He needed to remedy that. Even if nothing but friendship came of his relationship with Alyssa, she deserved to know the truth about him.

Though he'd told very few people about Peri, he wanted to tell her everything about Peri and Megan and the whole terrible mess. Maybe Alyssa would judge him poorly—his family certainly did. But maybe she'd have good advice for him. She'd grown up with an often-absent father. Maybe she could help him find a way to connect with his daughter.

Not that he should continue being an absent father. He needed to remedy that. He just didn't know how.

He was heading toward the room a nurse had told him was his dad's when his sister stepped into the hallway.

Hannah took after their paternal grandmother with her curly brown hair and brown eyes. Like Nana, she was petite, a foot shorter than Callan. Despite having the same last name and living in a tiny town, people who knew both of them rarely guessed they were brother and sister.

Hannah wasn't exactly the put-together type. Her curls were usually unruly, and she rarely wore makeup. When she wasn't working, she preferred leggings to jeans or slacks and often paired them with oversized sweatshirts. Today, she wore one emblazoned with the name of his alma mater, Boston College. He'd bought the sweatshirt his freshman year—and been certain he'd lost it. The little thief.

He missed his sister.

She was, as a rule, a cheerful person. Fun to be around and one of his closest friends. Their easy friendship had become strained after Peri stepped into the picture. Not because of the child—Hannah adored her niece—but because of Callan's failures.

When Hannah saw him, she froze, a frown in place.

"Did something happen?"

She walked toward him, and he opened up to give her a hug, but she stopped short a few feet away. "How are you here?"

"What are you talking about?" He dropped his arms. "You called me."

"How are you *already* here?"

Oh. Right.

They'd left Portland because they didn't want Ghazi tracking them down.

They'd come to Augusta because he'd hoped that, if there was time and if it was safe, he'd be able to visit Peri. But he hadn't been sure, so he hadn't told his family he was coming. He hadn't wanted to make promises he couldn't keep.

"I just got to town a little while ago. How's Dad?"

"They took him for tests. When they're finished, they'll bring him to his room."

"Did you see him? Were you there?"

"How could I be?" She threw the words like missiles. "I have a job, too, you know. Which I left early so I could pick up Peri from school and take her back to my house."

Usually, Mom or Dad did that. Maybe his confusion showed on his face because Hannah blew out an exasperated breath.

"I told you on the phone the other night that Dad wasn't feeling well. Mom was exhausted from taking care of him and *your* kid—"

"Hey. Don't be..." He took a breath and exhaled his desire to defend himself. "Can we cover all my shortcomings later? Would you please tell me what you know about Dad?"

Her gaze flicked away. Her eyes were rimmed in red, her cheeks blotchy. His sweet, tenderhearted sister was always willing to jump in and help everyone. But sometimes, people took advantage.

Like he'd been doing for months. Not just taking advantage of her but of Mom and Dad too.

"I'm sorry." He gripped her arms and pulled her in for a hug. She didn't return it, but he deserved that.

He rubbed her back. "It's okay. They'll take good care of Dad. I'm sorry I wasn't here. I'm sorry I've asked so much of you lately."

She let him hold her for another moment, then pulled away.

"Where's Peri?" he asked. "Is she in the room?"

Again, her gaze flicked past him toward the elevator. "They told us it would be an hour at least before Dad's up here, so Mom took her for a walk. I'm sure they'll be here any minute."

He was itching to hold his daughter, hug his mother, and see his dad, even though all of them probably felt about Callan the way Hannah did.

"Were you even going to tell us you were in town?" Hannah asked.

"It was a last-minute decision."

She touched his swollen lip. "Those bruises have anything to do with that decision?"

"It's a long story. I was planning to call. I just wasn't sure of my plans, and I didn't want to disappoint—"

"You didn't want to commit. You wanted to keep your options open. That's what you do."

Not true. He was great at committing. To work. To his career. To school.

But where Peri was concerned...

It shamed him to admit it, but Hannah wasn't wrong.

Now wasn't the time to figure his life out. He pulled his phone from his pocket and tapped a text. "I'm going to let Mom know I'm here. Should we wait in the room, or—?"

"I can't sit in there anymore." She moved past him toward the nurses' station, and he fell into step beside her. "Mom hasn't told me much. He'd been nauseated for a couple of days. Then this afternoon he had heartburn, more symptoms of what he thought was a stomach bug." The hospital wasn't very big, so their circuit took them down another hall, where they retraced their steps. "She said his color was off, and then he started complaining of shoulder and arm pain, and she realized what was going on. She got him in the car and brought him here. She didn't call me until they'd confirmed it was a heart attack."

Hannah seemed annoyed by that, but Callan figured she ought not to complain.

Mom hadn't called him at all.

"They caught it early," Hannah said, "but still..."

"A heart attack is a heart attack."

"Yeah."

Callan had asked his parents for too much. He'd known that, but he'd done it anyway.

Now, Dad was in the hospital, literally fighting for his life.

And it was Callan's fault.

## CHAPTER TWENTY-THREE

Alyssa pressed the button to summon the elevator at the Augusta hospital. Callan's father hadn't been hard to find, considering there was only one hospital with an emergency room.

Right after Callan left her at the bookstore, she'd gotten a call from Ghazi, who'd told them where and when she was to meet him with the zero-day exploit.

Of course, Callan didn't plan for her to willingly surrender to the terrorist again. But sometimes things happened against a person's will. And since she also figured, if it came to that, she wouldn't be returned to the Brookline house, but taken somewhere else, somewhere nobody knew about, she'd called Michael.

They'd made a plan, just in case she had no choice but to meet Ghazi again. Hopefully, she wouldn't need to put it into play.

Now, she breathed deeply, shifting her focus from work to... this.

She wasn't great at social situations, but friends showed up for friends, right?

That was all this was with Callan. Friendship.

Her attraction to him didn't mean anything. Sure, he was kind and capable and protective in a way that made her heart go all wonky.

She liked him, more than she should, considering she knew her feelings weren't reciprocated.

Though, when she'd been in his arms the night before, when they'd danced, when they'd kissed... It had felt real.

What if it could *be* real? What if Callan kept taking her hand because he was seeing beyond friendship? What if the emotion in his kisses was more than just physical desire?

She'd never considered sharing a life with any of the men she'd dated. Brooklynn once accused her of only dating unsuitable men, men who either became too controlling—she wouldn't put up with that—or, as Brooklynn once said, "Twenty IQ points south of a century."

Alyssa would never be happy with a guy she could run intellectual circles around.

Callan liked to be in control, but he wasn't controlling. And he was sharp enough to keep her on her toes.

She had no idea what she was going to say when she saw him, how she'd react if he wasn't happy to see her. Or if he was.

She'd just have to wing it.

Not exactly her strong suit, but she'd been getting her share of practice the last couple of days.

An older woman and a girl who looked eight or nine joined her at the elevator doors just as they swished open. The three of them stepped inside, and the girl pressed the button for the second floor. She looked at Alyssa.

She smiled at the child. "That's where I'm going too."

Alyssa's palms were sweaty, her pulse thumping. Maybe she shouldn't do this. She could take the elevator right back down, and Callan would never know.

Did everybody second-guess themselves like she did? Probably not. Most people knew how to behave in situations involving humans. She'd always been better with computers and machines and books.

Sheesh. She'd walked into the lair of a terrorist, but she was afraid to visit her friend when his father was in the hospital?

If she sensed that she was in the way or that he didn't want her there, then she'd leave. It seemed better to offer the support and be turned down than not to offer it at all. At least this way, Callan would know she cared, that he wasn't alone.

"He might not be okay." The little girl's gaze had been on the floor when she said the words, but then she looked up at the woman Alyssa assumed was her grandmother. The child had medium-brown hair that hung halfway down her back and big brown eyes.

She reminded her of someone, but Alyssa couldn't put her finger on who.

"People die sometimes," the girl added.

The woman was short, maybe five-one or two. She bent to meet the girl's eyes. "Sometimes, people recover. I know it doesn't seem like it, but what happened today was a good thing. It could have been worse."

"That's true. He hasn't died yet." The girl's expression was solemn, as if she'd seen more of the bad than the good in her short life. As if death were as familiar as Christmas.

Alyssa's heart broke, and she lifted a prayer for her and whoever it was she loved who'd ended up in the hospital.

She added another prayer for Callan's father and his family.

The elevator car stopped, and the doors opened.

Alyssa let the others exit the elevator first. They hadn't gone far when the child stopped halfway to the nurse's station.

A tall man talking to a much shorter woman must've heard them approaching because he turned.

Oh. It was Callan.

Alyssa stepped off the elevator and was lifting her hand to greet him when he dropped to his haunches. "Hey, sweetheart."

The girl took a few steps in his direction. "Hi, Daddy."

*Daddy?*

He opened his arms, but she didn't rush into them. She inched forward tentatively, as if she feared he'd rescind the offer.

Callan closed the distance and scooped her off her feet, hugging her to his chest.

The little girl's shoulders shook, and he patted her back. "It's okay, sweetie. Papi's okay."

Her arms went around Callan's neck, and he closed his eyes and breathed her in as if she were his sun and moon and stars.

The older woman—she must be Callan's mother—touched his arm.

He smiled at her, but it turned tight at the corners when he saw Alyssa.

She should've turned around and jumped right back on the elevator. She should've run.

He looked at her a second too long before he greeted his mom with a side hug—not letting up on his daughter at all.

His *daughter*.

Shame and embarrassment burned Alyssa's cheeks. She'd told him the most horrible thing she'd ever done, while he hadn't shared the best part of himself with her.

She was a fool.

His mother reached up and brushed her fingertip over the bruise on his cheek. She must've asked him a question because he said, "I'll explain in a minute." He met Alyssa's eyes but the contact didn't hold. "Mom, I want you to meet someone." He gestured Alyssa forward.

"I can just..." She backed up a step. "I didn't mean to intrude."

"You're not intruding, darling."

*Darling?*

What?

"Come join us." To his mother, he said, "Mom, this is Alyssa Wright, my fi—"

"Friend." Alyssa hurried toward them, interrupting before he could force the word out. What was he doing?

His mother's head tilted to one side as if she'd suddenly been presented with puzzle, her shoulder-length wavy yellow-blond hair dipping to beneath her collarbone. Her eyes were the same blue as his, and just as sharp. She was comfortably plump and wore a short-sleeved blouse over a pair of flared jeans and flats. "You went to college together, right? Your name came up more than once."

Callan had talked about her? To his parents?

His laugh was nervous. "And here they say nobody remembers the person who took second place." He added a wink, going for casual.

"You wish." Alyssa tried for the same tone, but it came out forced. She stretched out her hand. "Mrs. Templeton. It's nice to meet you. I'm so sorry about the circumstances."

"I'm glad you're here." The woman cupped Alyssa's hand in both of hers. They were chilled and rough, but the welcome was warm. "I look forward to getting to know you."

As if that was a foregone conclusion. As if she were reading into... Well, not *reading into* anything. He'd called her darling.

"This is my sister." Callan nodded to the woman he'd been talking to. "Hannah, Alyssa."

Unlike her mother and brother, Hannah had dark brown curly hair, which she'd pushed back in a headband. She was petite, almost pixie-like. She flashed her brother an angry look, then seemed to try to temper that before nodding at Alyssa. "A friend, huh?"

"A little more than a friend," Callan said.

Alyssa shook his sister's hand. "It's nice to meet you. How's your dad?"

Her lips slipped into a smirk, and as she stepped back, she gave her brother another long look.

But he was focused on the little girl in his arms. Or maybe just trying to avoid everyone's eye contact.

"We're waiting to find out," Hannah said. "They've taken him for tests."

The child squirmed, and Callan set her on her feet. "Peri, this is my friend, Ms. Wright."

"Just Alyssa." She said quickly. "None of that *mzzz* stuff."

Peri rubbed her red-rimmed eyes with her fists. Though she was elementary-school age, the action mimicked that of a much younger child.

"Sorry about your Papi," Alyssa said. "I'm sure the doctors are taking great care of him."

Peri's gaze flicked not to her father but to her grandmother, who said nothing.

Silence stretched a little too long.

"Anyway, I just wanted to make sure..." Alyssa wasn't sure how to finish that. She met Callan's gaze. "I didn't mean to intrude. I'll just—"

"You're not intruding. Thank you for—"

"Excuse me?"

They all turned toward a nurse behind the counter a few feet away. "Is one of you Mrs. Templeton?"

"Yes." Callan's mom turned toward her. "Is my husband all right?"

"He was just taken to his room."

"Oh!" She hurried away without a backward glance.

"Come on, Peri." Hannah gripped the child's hand and followed her mother.

Callan didn't move, but his gaze darted toward his family as they left.

"Go," Alyssa said. "I can leave or wait here or—"

"If you don't mind waiting. I'm sorry. I should have... There's so much..." He leaned in. "We have to pretend."

Right. This was all pretend. "Just go, Callan. I'll be here."

He spun and followed his family with long strides, catching up with them outside a hospital room. They all disappeared inside.

Leaving Alyssa in the middle of the too-bright space, confused, feeling like an interloper.

And the biggest fool in New England.

# CHAPTER TWENTY-FOUR

Dad had opened his eyes a couple of times, but he hadn't come fully awake in the thirty minutes since he'd been rolled to his room.

He was connected to machines monitoring his blood pressure and pulse and other things Callan knew nothing about. A nurse who came in to check vitals told them the best thing for Dad was sleep, so Callan and his family had remained quiet. Funny how loud unspoken questions were, though.

Peri didn't seem to be picking up on the tension.

Mom had settled onto a fake-leather loveseat pushed against the wall, and Hannah was perched on a guest chair. Peri had done her homework, papers shoved in a folder in her purple backpack, then spun on the doctor's stool for a few minutes. When she tired of that, she settled in beside her grandmother. Nobody had thought to bring her anything to play with, but Mom handed over her cell phone so Peri could play games.

Callan didn't love that she was on a screen, but what was he going to say? He didn't have a better plan. The last thing his little girl needed was to be in this place. It had to be bringing back memories of her mother's death. Peri needed emotional support. She needed conversation and understanding. But Mom was overwrought. Hannah was too worried about Dad and angry with Callan.

And Callan had no idea what to do.

Dad would know. That was the thing about Dad. He always had wisdom to share, and the older Callan got, the more he marveled at it.

*Open your eyes, Dad. Be okay. I need you to be okay.*

Dad was the best man Callan had ever known. The biggest and strongest and healthiest. Despite the fact that Callan was all grown up and should have a more realistic perception of his father, in a way he still saw him through little-boy eyes.

But the man lying on the hospital bed did not match the one in his memory.

Dad's usually ruddy skin was pale and gray. His hair, also gray, was thinner than Callan remembered. The wrinkles Callan had thought made Dad look wise and distinguished had deepened and multiplied. The flimsy hospital gown revealed crepey skin interrupted by more gray, this in the form of chest hair.

Dad looked much older than his sixty-five years. He looked weak and vulnerable and sick, and it was terrifying.

Of course his parents wouldn't always be with him. But the idea of their deaths felt like something *out there,* like faraway galaxies and the South Pole.

How had this happened? How had he missed it?

"Are we gonna eat soon?"

Peri's question pulled his attention, but of course she hadn't directed the question at him.

"Yes. Of course you need to eat." Mom looked around as if a solution to the problem might present itself. None of them wanted to leave Dad's room. Aside from the fact that he could wake up at any minute, the nurse had said a doctor would come by soon, and they needed to hear the results of his tests.

Mom started to push to her feet. "I'll take you—"

"I got it, Mom. Sit down." He smiled at Peri, who regarded him suspiciously. "I'll take care of it."

Alyssa had texted once since Callan left her in the lobby by herself, letting him know she planned to stay and offering her help. Very kind considering how rude he'd been, especially after the whole *darling* thing. When they were in public together, they needed to keep up the ruse. He couldn't ask her to deceive her family and then refuse to do the same with his own.

Even so, dropping the *fiancée* word hadn't sat right. Thank God Alyssa had stopped him.

He didn't have the brain power to know what to do. And though it would be easier if she'd gone to the hotel like he'd asked, he was glad she'd come. She'd tracked them to the right hospital—not that there were many options in Augusta. She'd gotten a ride here. And even though she was sitting in the waiting room all by herself, she stayed.

It meant a lot to him.

As he tapped a text, he hoped her offer to help had been sincere. He got an immediate thumbs-up.

"Come on, sweetie." He held out his hand for his daughter, then waited patiently while she stared at it as if she didn't know what he meant for her to do. If Mom had offered, or Dad, or Hannah, she'd have immediately taken the hand. But then they'd earned her trust.

Finally, her small, smooth palm slid against his, ice cold in the chilly air conditioning.

He should've thought of that. He should've asked for a blanket for her. She was always cold, just like her mother used to be.

They headed down the hall, meeting Alyssa near where

they'd first seen each other. She was hiking her laptop bag over her shoulder. "Hey, you two. Any news?"

"Papi's asleep," Peri said.

"The doctor's supposed to come give us an update soon," Callan added.

"Then you need to stay." Alyssa focused on Peri. "But somebody needs to get dinner. I mean, come on! How are you supposed to survive without food? Am I right or am I right?"

Peri almost smiled. "I'm starving."

"I bet your whole family is. I know it's past my dinner time."

Callan hadn't thought about food since he'd gotten the call, but the sun was setting outside, and it had been hours since lunch.

Alyssa lifted her gaze to him. "What sounds good?"

He shrugged. "Probably anything."

"*You'll* eat anything. We know that." To Peri, she said, "You've seen your dad eat. He's like Pac-Man—a perfect eating machine. Are you like that too?"

Peri shrugged, the tiniest hint of a smile on her face.

"Just as I suspected." Alyssa looked back at him. "I'm guessing your mother and your sister have more discerning tastes, and all things considered, they might be craving comfort food. There are a lot of options around here. If it's okay with you, Peri and I will go find something awesome for us. Meanwhile, you let me know what you guys want, and we'll pick it up on our way back."

He'd only asked her to walk Peri down to the cafeteria to eat and take her mind off her grandfather for a minute. "Paris, you don't have to—"

"I don't have to do diddly," she said. "I want to have dinner with this cutie." She held her hand out, palm up. "Keys?"

"If you're sure." When her only answer was wiggling fingers, he gave them to her.

"Let's blow this popsicle stand." Alyssa waggled her eyebrows at Peri.

His daughter giggled. Actually giggled.

He lowered to get eye-level with her. "Are you okay going with Alyssa for a little while?"

Her laugh died. "Maybe I should stay with Papi."

"Papi's just sleeping. He'll wake up, be grouchy as a grizzly because he's in the hospital, and insist we take him right home. You let me worry about him, and you get some dinner. Okay?"

She shrugged, but her expression brightened. She wanted to leave, and he couldn't blame her.

"It's a plan, then. I'll call Alyssa if anything happens."

"Promise?"

He pressed his palms to her smooth cheeks and kissed her forehead. "I promise."

As they walked away, Alyssa called over her shoulder, "See ya later, crocodile!"

His daughter giggled. "That's not it."

"Whaddya mean?" Alyssa sounded perplexed, and amused, as they stepped onto the elevator.

He stared after them until the doors closed, amazed at how quickly Peri had warmed up to her.

Alyssa had already connected with her. As the oldest of five, she'd had plenty of experience with kids, but who knew that the woman who'd always seemed socially awkward could be such a natural with children?

His Paris kept surprising him.

HANNAH WAS WAITING for Callan outside the closed door to Dad's room, arms crossed. "What's going on?"

"It's a long story."

She stared at him, lips pressed closed. The fun, cheerful little sister who'd always been his biggest fan was none of the above today. "Not that long a story. It boils down to the fact that you have time for romance, but you don't have time for your daughter."

"It's not..." He couldn't tell her the truth, and he didn't want to lie. "It's not that."

"Explain."

"No offense, sis, but it's none of—"

"If you tell me it's not my business, I'll punch you in the nose."

He made a show of looking around, trying to lighten the mood. "How are you going to reach? I don't see any step stools around."

"Fine. I'll kick you in the shins." Despite the forced banter, Hannah wasn't kidding. "I've put my life on hold to help take care of your daughter. I deserve an answer."

He stepped closer and lowered his voice. "I'm sorry. I can't explain."

Far from mollifying her, his words stirred her ire. "Are you telling me—?"

"Shh."

A nurse walking by gave them a dirty look.

Hannah lowered her voice. "Are you on an op?"

"Not...not officially."

"What does that mean?"

"Alyssa was in trouble, and I stepped in. That's all. There are dangerous people—"

"Are they after you?" Fear flashed in her eyes, quickly replaced by the irritation he was getting used to.

"They don't know who I am. Alyssa needs help. I can't abandon her."

"You can't abandon a grown-up woman, but you can

abandon your daughter."

"I'm not... I didn't..."

The door beside them opened, and Mom stepped into the threshold, the room dim behind her. "If you two are done, your dad's waking up."

Hannah waited until Mom had swiveled and returned to Dad's side before muttering low, "We are not done."

He was grateful for the reprieve.

Callan hovered out of the way while Mom and Hannah fussed over Dad. He figured his strong, no-nonsense father would put up with them for about ten minutes. He didn't even last that long before he shot Callan a *save me* look.

"Why don't you two figure out what you want for dinner so I can let Alyssa know?" Callan stepped close to the bed. "Give Dad a little space."

Hannah looked like she wanted to argue, but Dad patted her hand resting on his chest. "I'm sorry I gave you a scare, Curlicue."

She smiled at his old nickname for her, though it only lasted until she turned and joined Callan in front of the wall opposite the bed.

He took her hand and gave it a little *I'm here* squeeze. Hers was stiff in his, and then she squeezed back. She was angry with him, but she loved him.

They'd be okay as soon as he could figure out the Peri situation.

When Mom leaned in and whispered to Dad, Callan tugged his sister down onto the love seat. Their parents needed a little privacy.

A few minutes later, Mom stepped away. "Any chance your friend could get me some soup?"

"Of course. Hannah?"

He got their orders—Dad asked for a burger, which Mom

didn't find the slightest bit funny—and Callan texted Alyssa, who promised to stop at a deli on her way back, then asked,

**It'll be another forty-five minutes to an hour. That okay?**

**Sure. That works.**

His task finished, he joined Dad near the head of the bed. Awake and sitting up, Dad looked marginally better. He had more color in his cheeks, and his eyes were clear and alert. His grip was strong in Callan's hand. "How did you get here so fast?"

"Good luck and coincidence." He tossed the words out like a soft pitch.

Dad's brows lowered. "No such thing."

"Yeah. I guess God knew I needed to be close." He should've been here all along, though.

Dad looked around the room. "Where's my granddaughter?"

"A friend of mine came. She took Peri to dinner."

"She?"

"It's a long story."

Hannah muttered a little *humph.*

Callan ignored her. "I'm sorry, Dad. For everything."

The weight of what had happened hit him. Dad could've *died.*

They could be discussing funeral arrangements.

They could be trying to figure out how to live lives without their family's rock. The cornerstone.

"I should never have asked so much of you and Mom." Callan's voice cracked, and he clamped his lips closed against the emotion.

Dad looked past Callan. "Why don't you two go for a walk."

Hannah said, "But we're waiting—"

"Do you need anything?" Mom asked.

"Just a kiss from my love."

She kissed him, then pressed a hand to his cheek. "You be good."

Dad grinned. "I'll try my best."

Mom looked at Callan. "If the doctor comes, you call me immediately."

"Yes, ma'am."

Mom hooked her arm around Hannah's back and urged her out, closing the door behind them.

"I love them both," Dad said, "but you'd think I was on death's door."

The words, spoken so flippantly, raised a flash of irritation. "Dad, you had a heart attack. They have a right to be worried."

"I just meant..." He looked toward the door for a moment. "You're right. I can't imagine if it was your mother."

"I asked too much of you. You shouldn't be raising a child. You should be resting. And now you're here because you took on my burden—"

"Don't say that." Dad pushed the button to raise the head of his bed until he was sitting almost straight up. "My granddaughter is not a burden. She's a blessing, an amazing blessing, and I'm not one bit sorry she's in our lives."

"I didn't mean..." Callan raked his hand over his head. "Only that you two shouldn't have to raise her."

"You're right, we shouldn't. But don't you go blaming her—"

"—not her, me."

"—or yourself for my heart attack. How much power do you think you have, anyway?"

Callan wasn't sure how to answer that.

"You listen now, son. You are not so powerful that you can clog a man's arteries. You are not so powerful that you can damage a man's heart. Maybe you should remember who's really in charge. Go look in the mirror in there"—he waved toward the bathroom—"and tell the man looking back at you the truth. That you're not in control, and you're not supposed to be."

Callan hadn't been scolded by his father in a long time. He tamped down on an adolescent desire to argue his point.

"Caring for Peri is taking a toll. That's all I'm saying."

"I've seen a lot of heart-healthy advice. I'm supposed to avoid donuts, not granddaughters."

"I know that, but you have to admit—"

"Don't take on guilt that's not yours to own. Don't take responsibility for what you can't control. Focus on what you can."

That was the problem. No matter how hard Callan tried, he couldn't control anything.

"Enough of that." Dad's tone shifted to playful. "Am I going to meet this girlfriend of yours?"

"She's not a girlfriend, she's—"

"A girl and a friend." He blew off Callan's correction.

"She's bringing dinner. You can meet her if you want."

Callan tried to make it sound as if he didn't care one way or the other, but he had a feeling his father would adore Alyssa. And Alyssa would adore him. Dad was everything a father should be, everything her father hadn't been.

He didn't hate the idea of them meeting.

"Is she special to you?"

Callan needed to tell his father that yes, she was special to him. They needed to stay in character.

The problem was, if he said Alyssa was special to him, it wouldn't be a lie.

But Hannah was right. Callan had no business starting up anything with a woman when he had a child he hadn't figured out how to take care of.

"I'm guessing, based on your silence, the answer is yes."

"It's just that..."

That he didn't know what he was doing. That he didn't know how he could pursue Alyssa and care for his daughter. That he hadn't realized until just this moment how badly he *wanted* to pursue Alyssa.

"She's an old friend from college. Until Wednesday, I hadn't seen her in years."

"So this hasn't been going on—?"

"There's nothing going on. And there's not going to be."

Dad's gaze pierced through Callan's armor. "Tell me about that."

Typical *Dad* question. When it came to little things—weekend plans, short-term problems—Dad barely paid attention to what was going on. But he had a weird sixth sense with the things that weren't so little.

"There's nothing to tell."

The slightest lifting of one eyebrow was the only indication Dad had picked up on Callan's lie.

"It doesn't matter what I think about Alyssa," he said. "She's in trouble, and I'm trying to help her out."

Dad said nothing.

"I probably should've just let her figure it out herself, but I was worried. She was having dinner with a guy... She didn't know who he was, and I thought... I shouldn't have gotten involved."

"Then why did you?"

"Because he's dangerous, this man. And I didn't want her to get hurt."

"If she'd been a stranger, would you have gotten involved?"

Again, typical Dad, cutting right through his crap.

"You're right. I have a child to take care of now. It was stupid."

Dad smiled. "I'm pretty sure I didn't say any of that. Unless I had a stroke nobody told me about."

"That's not funny."

"It's a little funny." Dad went quiet, giving Callan the opportunity to explain. But what was he supposed to say? After a moment, Dad continued. "I didn't say what you did was stupid. You were raised to protect the vulnerable. I have no idea what the circumstances were, so I can't say beyond that. But you're a protector. You can't stop being who you are."

"I should be protecting my daughter."

"Does it have to be one or the other?"

It did. Didn't it?

"You have room in your heart for Peri."

"She's in my heart, Dad." Did he really have to say it? Was he really so bad at showing it? "I love her."

Dad gripped his hand again. "I know that, son. And you're going to figure it out. Good men make good fathers."

Did they? Did that mean Callan wasn't a good man? Because he definitely wasn't a good father.

He'd been too proud to ask for help before, but knowing what could've happened, knowing his father wouldn't always be here, he realized how badly he needed Dad's counsel.

"I want that, to be a good father. More than anything. How should I...?"

His words trailed when the door pushed open and a white-coated doctor stepped inside, followed by Mom and Hannah, who must've been hovering just outside.

The doctor's hair was pulled back in a French twist, the elegant style contrasting with the fatigue that showed in bags beneath her eyes.

She introduced herself to everyone, then focused on Dad, explaining that he'd had a heart attack and would need to stay overnight in the hospital.

Predictably, Dad argued, but she just nodded patiently.

"I understand, Mr. Templeton. You seem like the kind of man who makes sacrifices for the sake of the people who love him." She gestured to Callan and his family. "So I know you'll do what's best for your health, even if you don't want to."

He wasn't the doctor's first stubborn patient.

Dad grumbled, but how could he argue with that?

She gave them test results and numbers and levels of this and that, along with the care Dad would need when he was released.

Callan struggled to hang onto the details.

The point was, if Mom hadn't realized what was happening and insisted he come to the hospital, Dad could have died.

If he had, Callan would have been crushed. But he would bury him knowing that Dad had loved him every minute of his life.

He thought of their narrow escape from Ghazi and his guards the night before.

If Callan had died, his daughter wouldn't have the same assurance.

No matter how much he cared about his job and his career, no matter how drawn he felt to Alyssa, proving his love to Peri was more important than anything else he could do.

## CHAPTER TWENTY-FIVE

After Alyssa and Peri ate dinner, they headed to the deli, where they waited near the pickup counter for the meals Callan had ordered for himself and his family.

Alyssa and Callan's daughter had bonded over a bucket of chicken and potato wedges, though it had taken a few minutes to break through the child's walls.

But Alyssa had years of experience relating to little girls. She was the oldest of five, after all, and despite the fire incident, she'd done a lot of caring for her sisters over the years. They knew how to relate to them, how to make them smile.

It was adults she'd always had trouble with.

By the time Peri had dipped her last potato wedge in ketchup, she'd been chattering like a magpie about everything from her favorite subject in school to her best friend Emma to her determination to become a cheerleader.

"Papi says of course I can do it, but Gigi told me I need to ask my daddy to pay for it."

"What did your dad say?"

Her enthusiasm visibly waned. "I haven't asked him yet."

"Why not?"

She shrugged but didn't answer.

The more Peri talked, the better understanding Alyssa had of the situation. Callan lived and worked in Boston while his daughter lived almost three hours away in central Maine.

What kind of a man abandoned his child to pursue a career? She knew the answer to that. She'd been raised—or *not* raised—by exactly that kind of man.

Alyssa didn't have the full picture, of course. Peri hadn't mentioned her mother, nor did she share any stories from more than a few months before.

Alyssa fought the temptation to pry. She could get the answers she wanted, if not from Peri then from the Internet. A quick search of birth records, family court records, death records... She could figure out Peri's past.

But that wasn't how true relationships were built.

Instead, she'd ask Callan and hope he told her the truth.

Not that she and Peri's father had a real relationship. If they did, she'd have already known about his daughter.

Her phone vibrated. She glanced at it, then handed it to Peri. "Good news."

She read it, then looked at Alyssa with those pretty brown eyes "Papi's okay?"

"Looks like he's going home tomorrow."

She expected Peri to smile or cheer, but her face fell.

"Oh, honey." Alyssa crouched to her level. "What's wrong?"

She shook her head and swiped eyes filled with so much emotion that Alyssa couldn't fathom what she was thinking. Rather than ask again, she opened her arms. Peri stepped into them, and Alyssa comforted her, knowing one hug wasn't about to heal all the child's wounds.

"Your Papi's going to be all right," she soothed "I'm sure they're ready for us to get back so we can all celebrate."

Peri didn't say anything, just stayed in Alyssa's arms until Alyssa's crouched legs shook.

A man called, "Wright?"

"That's us," Alyssa whispered.

Peri loosened her hold and backed up. Unlike an adult, who might be embarrassed by such a need for affection, the child just slipped her hand into Alyssa's as if it were the most natural thing in the world.

The action reminded her of Callan, who'd done the same thing countless times in the last few days. They were similar in that way—comfortable with physical contact.

Alyssa checked the bag to ensure everything she'd ordered was there, thanked the clerk, and headed to the door with Peri still holding on. "Let's get back to the hospital and see your Papi. I bet he misses you."

The girl practically skipped to the door, her mood right back to the joyful one Alyssa had finally coaxed out of her.

She'd needed to know her grandfather was okay. And she'd needed some affection.

Affection her father had failed to provide. Not that it was any of Alyssa's business, but Callan needed to get his priorities straight.

IF THEY WERE DRIVING in the daytime, Alyssa would have gotten a clearer picture of the little community where Callan's parents lived. Outside the windows of Callan's Mustang, all she saw was darkness, though streetlights hovered over a small part of town, illuminating a gas station, a local restaurant, and a strip mall containing a dollar store, a laundromat, and a veterinarian's office. Other shops and businesses were housed in old converted homes. The area reminded her of where Aunt Peggy and Uncle Roger lived a couple of hours away, barely a blip on the map halfway between Portland and the New Hampshire border.

This town was farther north, thirty minutes from Augusta, which was the largest city around, though to call it a city was being generous, considering she doubted twenty thousand people lived in Maine's capital.

"This is where you grew up?" She spoke over the soft rock playing a little too loudly.

Callan had been silent for most of the drive from the hospital. He'd wanted Peri to ride with them, but she'd opted to go with Hannah instead. He'd tried to hide his disappointment, but Alyssa hadn't missed it.

Now, he shot her a look that made her wonder if he'd forgotten she was there. "All my life."

"Seems like a nice place."

He turned down the stereo. "The house has been in my family for generations. It used to sit on a huge lot that ringed one side of a lake, but the land's been chopped up and sold off over the years." He tapped on the steering wheel. No streetlights here, just thick forest lining the two-lane road on both sides. "We almost lost it once."

"How?"

"Mom stayed home to raise us. She didn't work full-time outside the home until Hannah graduated from high school. Dad was in construction and decided to start his own business as a general contractor, but to do that, he had to leave his good-paying job. It should've been fine, but the local economy hit a snag. Dad had mortgaged the house to buy tools and equipment. He couldn't make the payments."

Alyssa couldn't imagine. Her parents had always had everything they needed and more. Even after she'd moved out, she'd known there was a financial safety net. Though she never wanted to ask her parents for money, she knew she could. And she knew they'd say yes. "How old were you?"

"I was nine. Hannah was seven. Mom and Dad didn't tell us, but I knew something was going on. One afternoon, I came home from playing with my friends and overheard my parents talking in the kitchen. Mom was crying and Dad was apologizing. I didn't want to interrupt."

"So you listened?" She imagined little-boy Callan, lurking at the door. "You were spying long before the CIA."

He grinned, but the expression didn't hold. "They were talking about moving out. Moving away from the only home I'd ever known. Dad was saying how it was all his fault, and Mom was trying to encourage him. I didn't understand the details at the time. I just remember feeling desperate to fix it, and utterly powerless to do anything."

"I'm sorry you even knew what was going on. You were far too young to take on that kind of responsibility."

"That's what my parents said when I asked how I could help. That it wasn't my problem. That they'd take care of it, but they weren't going to. Their way of taking care of it was to put the house on the market."

"Well, yeah, but—"

"There was another option. They needed to ask my grandparents for a loan. I guess... Looking back on it, I realize they had their reasons. Dad's parents had money, but his father could be controlling and manipulative. I didn't understand that at the time. I just thought they were both being stupid and stubborn. I was young enough that I thought he should just ask his mom and dad. That's what I'd do in a pickle, after all. It seemed simple enough to me."

"You had parents you could trust," Alyssa said, "parents who would help you without strings attached. So how could you have imagined another kind?"

He shrugged.

"And you didn't want to lose your home."

"Exactly." He slowed and turned onto a road so narrow that she'd have passed it without ever knowing it was there. "I decided to help Mom and Dad out. I called my grandparents myself and told them."

"Wow. That was—"

"Controlling and manipulative?" he suggested. "Not that they ever said so, but that's what they thought. Dad was furious that I'd shared their personal struggles outside the family. My defense was that they are family, but I knew what he meant. I knew he'd be angry, and I did it anyway."

"He forgave you." Alyssa had met Callan's father at the hospital. Despite the sick pallor, she'd seen Callan in Hank's features. His grip had been strong, his eyes bright and intelligent, his smile welcoming. Even though he hadn't felt well, he'd been warm, kind, and gentle, as different from her own father as light from shadow.

"Yeah."

When Callan didn't expound, she said, "I guess he figured out a way to save the house."

"My grandparents paid off the mortgage."

"Oh. So it worked?"

He nodded, but in the dim console lights, she saw how tightly his lips were pressed together.

"What?"

"I found out later, much later, that the deal was that they'd pay off the house if Dad made his father a partner in his business. Dad agreed because... Well, for our sake, so we wouldn't have to move."

"But it wasn't what he wanted."

"No."

"Do you think he regretted it?"

Callan's shoulder lifted and fell. "He'd never say so. He would never want to heap that guilt on me. I tried tp talk to him about it once, and he just told me he did what he did, he made choices, and none of that was any of my business. My father is the kindest man you'll ever meet, but he made no apology for his frustration with my behavior." After a full minute of near silence, the only sound the rumble of the asphalt beneath the tires, his fists tightened on the wheel. "The thing is, and this is terrible... I know it's terrible, but I'd do it again. The property means a lot to our family. I probably went about it the wrong way, but we didn't lose it. Dad was mad at me, but I got what I wanted. I've never been able to convince myself I didn't do the right thing."

She thought back to Callan's crazy behavior the night she'd met Charles-slash-Ghazi. The way he'd kissed her, pretended they were engaged.

He'd learned it was okay to manipulate situations in order to get the right outcome—according to him.

"I know it was hard for Dad," Callan continued. "He had to swallow his pride. But he did it, and ultimately, he built a successful business. Which was good. All of that was good."

That was one way to look at it.

"Maybe it would've been okay if you'd moved, though. Maybe your father's plan was also good."

"Maybe." His word held no conviction.

A few lights twinkled from deep in the woods, though the houses were too distant to make out their sizes or shapes through the thick forest. He rounded a bend, then slowed and turned into a narrow driveway. About fifty yards in, the woods cleared enough for her to see an old Victorian-style farmhouse complete with a circular turret at one corner and a porch that wrapped around two sides. Lit with pretty landscape lighting, it was two stories with a steeply pitched roof. An old oak tree stood at the far side of the house, a swing hanging from the lowest branch.

Beyond the house, the dark expanse must be the lake Callan had mentioned. "It's beautiful."

He parked. "I've always thought so."

She'd offered to stay at the hotel in Augusta, but Callan had insisted she cancel both rooms she'd reserved there, that there was plenty of space at the house.

This place was so far from everything, so remote and charming, so far removed from the terrorist that it might as well have been on another planet

They were very alone here. The lack of lights coming from within the house and the absence of cars in the driveway meant Hannah and Peri hadn't arrived yet.

Callan unlocked the front door with a key from his keychain, then pushed it open, flicked a switch inside, and stepped back to allow her to enter first.

She did, pausing at the threshold. The space had the scent of a house that'd seen a lot of life, a combination of vanilla and musk and old books that had her inhaling a deep breath.

Callan dropped their small bags on the stairs, and she did the same with her laptop bag. She kept her jacket on.

"It's chilly in here." He adjusted the thermostat, and the furnace kicked on. Then he moved from room to room, turning on lamps as he went. The shadowy spaces took form. A tidy foyer with a coatrack beside a narrow table that held a basket for keys and change and whatnot. Straight ahead, a narrow staircase rose a half flight before a landing, where the stairs rose in the opposite direction to the second floor.

The hardwood floors carried throughout the downstairs, the stain fading with age. The woodwork had been painted white, the walls of the foyer and attached rooms pale beige. The living room off one side had comfortable sofas oriented around a TV. Opposite that, the dining room—the turret room—had a round table with eight chairs that seemed designed for the space.

Had Callan's father made it?

"Come on back." Callan led the way to a kitchen with solid stone countertops, shiny pine cabinets, and an island in the center.

"Did your father do the updating?"

Callan opened one of the cabinets and took out two glasses. "He's always doing something." He filled them with ice water and handed her one.

"Thanks." She took a sip, enjoying the freshness. She was accustomed to city water, but there was nothing as delicious as cold Maine well water. She gazed through a window on a door that led to the back. The moon, peeking out between the clouds, sparkled off the still lake. "Did you guys do a lot of boating growing up?"

"We had a rowboat for a while. Hannah and I used to take it to a little cove and go fishing."

Her dad had never wanted to deal with maintenance of a boat, so whenever they went to the lake, he'd rent one, and sometimes a crew to drive it.

Callan gulped his entire drink, then set the empty glass on the counter. "Hannah and Peri should be here any minute."

"Does Hannah live here?"

"She lives in Augusta. She's going to grab some things for Mom and take them back to the hospital on her way home."

"Nice of her to drive all the way out here."

The door in the other room opened, and Callan headed down the hallway. "You made it." His voice sounded unnaturally enthusiastic.

Alyssa followed, grinning at Peri as the child stepped inside, a purple backpack in her hand. She seemed happy enough until she saw her father.

"Sweetheart." Hannah crouched at her side. "I'm going to talk to your dad for a minute and then go home. Why don't you give Miss Alyssa a tour."

"I'd love that," Alyssa said. "Would you show me your room?"

"Okay." She gave her aunt a hug, then took Alyssa's hand and climbed the stairs.

The house wasn't as big as it'd seemed from the outside. Upstairs, Peri stepped into her grandparents' room, which would have seemed larger if not for the king-sized bed that took up most of the space. The child was comfortable in here, insisting Alyssa come in—she felt like an intruder—to show her old family photos on the older couple's dresser.

Peri next pointed out a small room with a large table covered in fabric scraps and a sewing machine. A twin-sized bed covered in more random scraps of fabric took up one wall. "Gigi makes quits in here. She's making me one. Wanna see?"

"Sure."

Peri showed her the fabric squares the older woman would sew together. All bright pinks and yellows and blues, polka dots and stripes and graphic flowers. It was perfect for a little girl.

Peri tugged Alyssa to the next bedroom, but she didn't go inside this one, instead hovering at the door. "This is where Daddy stays when he comes," she explained.

The walls were blue, and a shelf unit on one wall held books and trophies probably from his high school years. It had a full-size bed that couldn't possibly be long enough for his tall frame..

After Peri pointed out the only second-floor bathroom—it had been updated and, she assumed based on the size of it, expanded from the original—they continued to the final bedroom on the floor. Peri pushed into this one and flicked on the light.

"This used to be Aunt Hannah's room, but now it's mine."

Alyssa stopped at the threshold, unsure if she was invited in. She didn't have to ask to know that this room had been updated since Hannah was a girl. Three of the walls had been painted bright yellow, and the fourth was covered in a yellow-and-white floral wallpaper. The pale wood twin bed had a canopy strung with fairy lights over a white blanket and bright pink pillows. More pink was scattered throughout the space—in the lampshade, in artwork, and in a giant P over the headboard.

The bed had been hastily made, the comforter hanging unevenly on one side. A pair of jeans draped over a small upholstered chair in a corner of the room. Peri dropped her backpack on a white dresser beside a framed photograph.

Alyssa gazed at the photograph, blinked. Confused at what she was seeing.

She bent closer to the picture.

Peri had been maybe four or five when it was taken. She wore a white satin dress, and her hair had been fixed in a beautiful updo that looked far too fancy for a little girl. The basket she held in one hand was filled with rose petals. A flower girl.

But it was the woman in the photo who caught Alyssa's attention. She was seated and leaning toward Peri, smiling for the photographer. Her hair was long and medium-brown with blond streaks. She had the same big, brown eyes, though they weren't nearly as innocent as her daughter's.

"That's my mommy," Peri said.

Alyssa hoped her press-on smile was believable. "She's beautiful." *Was* beautiful.

Megan had been killed in a car accident the previous autumn. After avoiding Alyssa's calls and cards for years.

Nine years, as a matter of fact.

Feeling suddenly too warm, Alyssa took off her jacket and draped it over her arm.

Peri unzipped her backpack and pulled out a folder. She opened it, tucking her long hair behind her ear, and Alyssa remembered the girl's mother doing the same thing a thousand times.

She and Megan had been college roommates, first in the dorm, then in an apartment. They'd been friends. Best friends, or so she'd thought.

In college, Megan had been convinced Alyssa had a thing for Callan. No matter how many times Alyssa tried to deny it, Megan had seen right through her.

And then...somehow, Megan had Callan's kid.

How long had it gone on? How had it happened?

Why hadn't Megan told her?

Peri held out a piece of paper, and Alyssa took it, all but shaking herself to return to the moment and focus on the little girl in front of her. It was a crayon drawing of a unicorn. "Wow. Did you do this yourself?"

"Uh-huh. In art class."

Alyssa traced the white body, the rainbow horn on its horsehead. "It's really good."

"Thanks." She pulled more artwork from the folder and showed Alyssa each one, chattering about what they were and how much she was learning and how she wanted to be an artist someday.

Artistic, like her mother, though Megan's talents had been literary. She'd taken every literature class offered at BC, along with every mythology and folklore class.

Like mother, like daughter. "You should show these to your daddy."

"Maybe." Peri returned her drawings to her folder.

Obviously, Alyssa had said the wrong thing. "They're very good. You've got a lot of talent."

That brightened her expression, but a yawn interrupted her smile. It was after nine, probably past her bedtime.

"I'm gonna ask Aunt Hannah for a snack."

"Is it okay if I use the bathroom?"

"Uh-huh." Peri stepped in and turned on the light. "See you downstairs."

"I'll find you. Thanks."

Alyssa used the restroom and washed her hands. Three towels hung from hooks near the porcelain tub. Two were pale blue and matched the decor. The other was smaller, pink-and-white striped.

How long had Peri lived here? Long enough to have her own bedroom. Long enough to fit right in as if this were home.

Megan's daughter. Megan and Callan's daughter.

She squelched a hot wave of jealousy. Stupid, considering her old friend was gone. Considering she'd spent four years pretending her Callan-crush didn't exist.

Had they been married? No, surely not. Callan had been in the service. But people in the service got married.

She obviously couldn't guess at what had happened. Maybe if she asked him, he'd tell her.

She made her way down, draping the jacket she'd bought that morning over a dining room chair, and was nearing the back of the house when Hannah's voice—low but angry—reached her. "I'm not doing it."

"I need your help," Callan said. "I can't—"

"You should've thought of that before you got involved in... in whatever this is."

Where was Peri? Surely they weren't arguing in front of the child.

"She was in trouble. I had to help."

"Right. It has nothing to do with the fact that she's gorgeous."

Alyssa cringed. Where was Peri?

"I'm doing my best." Callan's words came out hard. "I need you to take her. I can't have Peri anywhere—"

"Not my problem."

"Hannah, come on."

"I had to get someone to cover my classes today so I could take care of *your* daughter. Listen, I love her. I *adore* her. I'd love nothing more than to take care of her twenty-four-seven. But I have a job. Now, with everything going on with Dad, he's going to need help. Mom's going to need help. I can't risk my career because you refuse to risk yours."

Obviously, Peri wasn't with them. But where was she?

Hannah said something too low for Alyssa to hear as she tiptoed back toward the front door and peeked into the living room. Peri wasn't there.

"I know, I know." Callan sounded wrung out. "You're right. I know, it's just...I'm worried, that's all."

"If it's that dangerous, then *you* shouldn't be involved. You promised us, Callan."

"It's not. It's..."

Alyssa thought about their terrifying escape the night before and all the things that *could* have happened. It was dangerous, this thing they were involved in. And Callan shouldn't have anything to do with it. He'd stepped in to help her, and now look what had happened.

She peeked into the dining room and found Peri sitting against the wall between that room and the kitchen, her knees pulled up to her chest, her forehead pressed against them.

"You need to step up," Hannah said. "She's your daughter."

Alyssa scooped the child into her arms. "Come on upstairs, sweetie."

Peri didn't argue, just snaked her hands around Alyssa's neck.

They made it back to Peri's bedroom, where Alyssa settled on the edge, holding the girl in her arms.

She could feel little sobs against her chest.

"It's okay, baby. They'll figure it out."

"He doesn't want me." Her words were almost too faint to hear.

"He *does* want you. Of course he does." She backed up to see her face. "Who wouldn't? You're amazing."

She shook her head, her long hair falling across her cheek.

Alyssa brushed it back. "Your daddy wants to be with you more than anything." Alyssa hoped it was true. Prayed it was true. "He's just got a really hard job, and he's having trouble getting out of it. He's a hero. Did you know that?"

Peri swiped her fingers beneath her eyes. "Like Spider-Man?"

Alyssa smiled. "He's better than Spider-Man because he doesn't have to wear that silly outfit. Can you imagine your daddy in bright red tights?"

That elicited a smile.

"Your daddy saved me from a bad guy, and he's trying to keep me safe. He wants to be with you, though. More than anything."

The girl's smile faded. "Mommy said Daddy doesn't love me and doesn't want me."

Megan had said that? To a child?

Why?

Was it true? Or had she said it out of anger or jealousy? Alyssa had loved Megan, but not so much that she hadn't seen her friend's vindictive streak.

True or not, she shouldn't have said that to little Peri. Red-anger burned Alyssa's chest. How could any loving mother tell her little girl something like that?

How could Callan be such an inept father that he'd allow Peri to believe it?

"Your father loves you so much, and he wants to be with you." She hoped, anyway.

Thank God Hank and Fiona had taken Peri in. Thank God for Hannah, who was obviously doing everything she could for the child.

But Hannah was right. It was time for Callan to step up.

## CHAPTER TWENTY-SIX

Callan felt as wrung out as a used dishtowel.

"You can do this," Hannah whispered in his ear at the door. She'd already gathered Mom's things into her small suitcase. "You have to do it."

"I know. I know you're right. I will." He didn't add the *I promise* to the end of his statement. How many times had he said that and then failed?

Too many.

He closed the door behind his sister, then pressed his forehead to it.

Hannah was right about everything. Well, most things. Yes, he had to step up and act like Peri's father.

But he didn't share her confidence that he could do, certainly not well.

That was what nagged him. He didn't like to tackle things without a plan, without the confidence that he could not only manage but do great. Succeed. Overachieve.

He'd done all of the above in college, then in the Army, then with the Agency. He'd risen in the ranks. He'd been praised for his achievements.

How did one *achieve* with raising a little girl? How would he know if he was doing it right or failing miserably? What if he messed it up? He didn't care how it would make him look, though that had always been a huge motivator for him. He cared about Peri. If he messed it up, messed *her* up, he'd never forgive himself.

Even if he could, eventually, learn how to be the father Peri deserved, that wouldn't change the issues he was dealing with right now. He couldn't keep Peri with him until he'd extricated himself from the Alyssa-and-Ghazi situation.

He'd have to leave her here with Mom and Dad for the time being. It would be hard on them after Dad's heart attack, but Peri was incredibly self-sufficient for an eight-year-old. She'd had to be.

Megan hadn't given her much choice.

Familiar fury rose like bile, but he had no right to judge Megan for her choices when his own were so questionable. He grabbed the bags he'd left on the stairs and climbed to the second floor.

His daughter's bedroom door was open, and Peri and Alyssa were lying on their stomachs on the floor, coloring and chatting like old friends. They were facing away from him, both their legs swinging up and then plopping down on the area rug, casual as could be.

"And so then," Peri said, "she told me she was taller than me, but I was like, nuh-uh, because I'm like, way taller than her. So Nell said we should get back-to-back, and then everyone said I'm the tallest girl in the whole class."

"No way." Alyssa sounded duly impressed. "That's awesome."

"Uh-huh. And then the kids were mean to her, but I told them to be nice because it's hard to tell if you're taller than someone when you're looking at them, right?"

Alyssa rolled to her side, her back to Callan. She propped herself up on an elbow, her hand supporting her head. "You're a really cool kid, you know that?"

Peri shrugged. "I just know what it's like to not have friends. When I first moved here, I didn't have any. So I try to be nice. And now she's my friend."

"The girl who was mean to you?"

"Uh-huh. Emma. She's a cheerleader, and she thinks I'll be good, even though she says I'll be taller than all the other girls, she says it's okay, that I can be a base like her, so we can practice together, but we'll need shorter girls to climb on our shoulders and do tricks and stuff."

Cheerleading? Peri wanted to be a *cheerleader*?

Of course she wouldn't choose to play a sport he knew something about, softball or basketball or soccer or even field hockey. Something he could actually help with.

He had a flash of the cheerleaders from his high school days, those adorable girls with their big smiles and short skirts.

He'd need a way to signal all the high school boys that he wasn't a father to be trifled with. Casually mention his military and Agency history. Start carrying a sidearm. And billy club. Just in case.

"That makes sense." Alyssa rolled back to her stomach and resumed coloring. "You'll need to ask your daddy about cheerleading when you get a chance."

Right. She had to ask him. He could just say no.

Couldn't he?

No clue.

He cleared his throat. "Sorry to interrupt."

Though they'd sounded happy enough, when they turned to face him, neither looked happy to see him.

Great. He refused to let his smile falter. "You'd better get your jammies on, Sweet Pea."

"Aw," Alyssa said. "But I'm not tired!"

He laughed. "Not you." He shook his head, focusing on his daughter. "She's a goober."

Peri's hundred-watt smile dimmed to sixty when she aimed it at him.

He helped Alyssa to her feet. "You'll sleep in the sewing room."

"I figured, but there are fabric scraps—"

"Just pile them up and set them on the table. Mom won't care." He handed her the bag of things she'd bought that day. "Make yourself comfortable, then meet me in the kitchen so we can talk." She'd been researching Ghazi all day, but he'd yet to find out what she'd learned, too distracted by Dad's health and Peri's care. "I've got to tuck Sweet Pea back into her pod." He winked at Peri, who didn't get his joke at all.

"Sounds comfy." Alyssa kissed Peri on the head. "See you in the morning. Sleep well."

He tried not to get his feelings hurt at the forlorn look on Peri's face as she watched Alyssa leave.

Fifteen minutes later, teeth brushed and pajamas on, Peri picked out a book and climbed under the covers. "Gigi's been reading me this one."

It was *Sarah, Plain and Tall*, which he remembered from his own childhood. It had been one of Hannah's favorites. He settled beside Peri on the bed, found the bookmark, and started to read.

He was barely two paragraphs in when Peri said, "Daddy?"

"Yeah, sweetie?"

"Is Papi going to be okay?"

He used his finger to mark his page and lowered the paperback to his lap, turning to face his daughter. Her brown eyes never failed to melt his heart. Right now, they were filled with anxiety. She hadn't brushed her hair, and it was stringy and messy and absolutely adorable. She was everything a little girl should be.

Except happy.

"Now that we know there's something wrong with his heart, the doctors will take good care of him. They'll put him on medication. Thcy'll make sure he's healthy."

When she blinked, a tear slid down her cheek. "Okay."

"Do you believe me?"

She nodded, but said, "You don't know. Nobody can know."

Her words were heavy with more knowledge than any eight-year-old should have. "You're right, I don't know what the future is going to bring. I know I have a God who loves me, and He loves you, and He knows what He's doing, even if we don't."

He braced himself for a question about Megan, about how God could've taken Peri's mommy away. But she didn't ask it, not of him. Instead, she nodded for him to keep reading.

He finished two chapters, then sat with Peri while she said her prayers, which she ended with, "Please, don't let Papi die."

He added his own silent "Amen" to that. He shut off the light, kissed her forehead, and tucked her in. "I love you, Sweet Pea."

She didn't return the sentiment, never had, even though his mother had assured him that Peri did love him, that children naturally loved their parents.

She just didn't trust him enough to say it.

"Will you stay until I fall asleep?" She voiced the question with a small and tentative voice.

He loved that she'd asked. She needed to know she wasn't alone, and she needed to know he could be trusted.

As much as he was eager to get downstairs and talk to Alyssa, he lay down on top of the covers on the opposite side of her bed.

She snuggled up next to him, curling her back against his

chest, and he wrapped his free arm around her and held her close. And prayed.

*Lord, don't let me screw this up. She deserves so much more than I can give her. She deserves so much more than I can ever be.*

~

WHEN PERI'S BREATHING DEEPENED, when she'd been still for a solid five minutes, Callan eased off her bed and tiptoed out of her room.

He found Alyssa in front of her laptop at the kitchen table. He'd told her to get comfortable, but she still wore the jeans and pink blouse she'd bought that morning in Portland.

She looked up when he came in, so many questions in her eyes that he figured she was trying to decide which to start with.

He lifted his hand to hold her off. "You want a snack?"

"No." But then, she wagged her head side to side. "Depends."

He raided the pantry in search of...

Yes.

He snatched the bright red package, then poured them both glasses of milk and brought the treat do the table, along with two small plates and two napkins.

She pushed her laptop out of the way. "Milk and cookies?"

"The ultimate comfort food." He settled beside her and pulled back the top of the package to reveal perfectly arranged peanut-shaped sandwich cookies. His favorite, which Mom always kept on hand just in case he popped in unannounced.

Alyssa took one and broke it in half. "Peanut butter has protein."

"It's practically health food."

That earned a tiny grin, but it didn't last. "You and Megan?"

Whoa. Of all the questions, he hadn't expected that one. How had Alyssa figured out who Peri's mother was?

As if reading his mind, she said, "Peri has her photograph on her bureau."

"Oh, right. Yeah." He finished the cookie and sipped the milk, though he wasn't feeling all that comfortable despite the comfort food. "It was...uh..." Why did he feel guilty, as if he'd betrayed this woman who'd never felt anything for him but scorn?

"When did it happen?" she asked.

"Senior year, right after the holiday break."

She frowned. "I knew something was different that semester. She would never tell me..." Alyssa took another cookie, broke it in half, then in half again. "I'm sorry. I was shocked to hear about her death. I'm sure that was a terrible blow to both of you."

He wasn't sure what to say to that. He didn't grieve Megan the way he probably should. He grieved for Peri. He grieved the lost time. Mostly, he worked every hard not to resent a dead woman.

"I just don't understand why..." She shook her head. "It doesn't matter. With everything going on, it doesn't..."

But Callan wasn't buying her brave face. He saw hurt in her eyes, the tightness around her mouth. Her best friend had started a serious relationship, had fallen in love, or so Megan had claimed, and had never told her.

"She didn't want you to know," Callan said.

"But why? I don't understand why she wouldn't..." Alyssa swallowed and looked away. "It explains why she avoided me after graduation. I reached out to her so many times. She never responded to my calls or texts, just ghosted me. I even mailed a letter to her parents' house, thinking maybe she'd changed her number or something. But she never responded."

Alyssa brushed cookie crumbs off her fingers and slid her hand around the milk. She didn't sip, though, just spun it on the table. "I blamed myself. I thought I wasn't a good enough friend, that I should have tried harder." Alyssa met his eyes. "When I found out she'd died, I felt this weight of shame and guilt. I berated myself, trying to figure out what I could've done differently. What did I do to so offend her that she would keep your relationship secret? That she would hide...?"

Again, Alyssa looked away, but this time, tears shimmered in her eyes.

He slid his hand over hers on the kitchen table. "You didn't do anything wrong, Alyssa. It was Megan. She had this weird idea that you would be hurt if you knew we were together."

Alyssa looked at him again, eyes narrowed. He'd expected her to pull her hand away and was heartened when she didn't. "Did she say why?"

"I know it's nuts." He laughed, suddenly feeling stupid for even saying it aloud. "She thought you had a crush on me."

"Oh, right. She was always so sure." Alyssa didn't smile.

He guessed the reason. "I wondered sometimes why, if she thought you had a crush on me, she, uh..." Yeah. He probably shouldn't finish that sentence.

"Why she what?"

"She sort of came after me, you know, like she was super into me. I didn't know at the time that she thought you liked me. I didn't know any of that until later."

"What do you mean, she came after you?"

Callan remembered the night so well. A stupid party at the apartment he shared with five other guys. He hadn't planned the party, but he'd certainly indulged in it. He'd had way too much to drink when Megan hit on him. Shirt too low, jeans too tight. Music too loud, dancing too close.

Bedroom too near.

The next morning, he'd woken up with a heavy dose of shame. He wasn't a one-night-stand kind of guy, never had been, yet the evidence of his fall into debauchery was sleeping beside him. He'd barely known Megan, certainly not enough to know if he liked her or not. Certainly not well enough to take her to his bed.

Maybe it was a desire to redeem himself that had him suggesting they go on a date—a nice, innocent lunch date. When they did, Megan showed up looking not like the...well, he preferred not to think the word that he'd had used back then. She'd showed up looking like a normal girl. Long hair pulled back in a ponytail, big brown eyes, nerdy glasses. She'd sat across from him, cheeks red from embarrassment, and sworn she'd never done anything like that before.

"I don't know what got into me," she'd said. "I had a really rough time over Christmas with my family, and I just wanted to forget."

He'd apologized for taking advantage. She'd apologized for throwing herself at him. And then they'd dated.

She'd seemed the girl-next-door type who'd made one terrible decision and was trying to redeem it, just like he was.

He wouldn't learn the truth about her until it was way too late.

The longer he took to answer, the squintier Alyssa's eyes became. She'd gone back to her cookie, reducing it to a pile of crumbs on her plate, a shameful waste of Nutter Butters.

Callan gave Alyssa the Cliff's Notes version of events. If anything, her expression became more suspicious as he talked.

"She told you she had a rough holiday?" At his nod, Alyssa said, "She and her family went skiing at Chamonix that Christmas." He must've looked confused because Alyssa added, "In the French Alps. She told me it was the best vacation of her life."

So Megan had lied to him. That didn't surprise him at all.

"And the notion that she'd never done that before? She had a habit of sleeping with"—Alysa waved toward him—"random people. Not that you're random. You were targeted. I'm just saying..."

Again, Callan wasn't surprised. It seemed wrong to speak ill of the dead, but what he'd learned about Megan was that she was conniving and deceitful whenever it suited her—and sometimes just for fun.

Too late—way too late—he'd learned the depth of her depravity.

"You know how she was." Alyssa spoke as if Callan had broadcast his thoughts. "She wasn't exactly a paragon of righteousness. But why you? There were thousands of good-looking men on campus. Why did she go after you?"

He grinned, focusing on exactly the wrong thing. "You think I'm good looking?"

"Almost as handsome as you think you are."

He chuckled, but it sounded so out of place during the serious conversation that he clamped his lips shut.

"It was about me. I mean, no offense to you. You're a catch, and I'm sure she had a thing for you, but..." Alyssa stared beyond him. "She thought I had a crush on you, and...and she wanted to hurt me."

"Do you know why?"

"Do you?"

He shook his head. "She never talked about you. She never said anything except that you'd be hurt if you knew."

"Right. So the point wasn't to hurt me, or else she'd have told me."

He'd been over all these questions a million times in the last few months. "I think the point was to beat you."

"Oh." Alyssa nodded slowly. "Yeah. That tracks. I mean,

she was my friend, but she had some issues with... Well, she had some issues."

It wasn't as if Alyssa could tell Callan anything he hadn't already figured out about Megan.

"Anyway, if her goal was to hurt you, then it was all for naught," Callan said. "I tried to tell her that you didn't have a crush on me and wouldn't have cared..."

He lost his train of thought when Alyssa's cheeks pinked in the harsh kitchen light.

"Right? You didn't think about me that way."

She reached for the bright red package, but he plopped his hand on top of hers. "Let's not murder any more innocent cookies." He gave the one she'd pulverized a pointed look, trying to sound lighthearted, but his heartbeat thumped as if its continuing to beat was contingent on her answer.

She sighed. "I might have had the teeniest crush on you."

Far from making him smile, the words were a knife to his chest. He pulled away and settled his hands in his lap, staring at the table. He swallowed emotion crawling up his throat. Anger, frustration, and regret.

Alyssa sat unmoving across from him as if she sensed his turmoil.

He looked up. "I wish I'd known."

"Why? What difference would it have made?"

"I had a crush on you too."

She straightened, eyes widening. "What?"

"And it wasn't teeny. It was... If I'd had any idea you shared my feelings, I wouldn't have wasted one second with Megan."

"I had no idea. I thought you found me...annoying."

"Oh, I did. You were my only real competition. You think I want to be with a woman who can't keep up with me intellectually? You think I want to spend my life with..."

His words trailed as two things occurred to him.

First, he *had* spent a whole lot of time with a woman who couldn't keep up with him intellectually. Though, to her credit, Megan had run circles around him in other areas of life. Like deceit and trickery. She'd been much better at those things than he could ever hope to be.

And he'd been a CIA field agent.

Second, what was Callan doing, mentioning spending his life with Alyssa or anyone? Making it sound as if he'd been thinking of marriage—to Alyssa—way back in college?

He'd considered the idea that she'd make the perfect life partner. But he didn't need to say so. Not now, when it was too late.

"I found you annoying too." Alyssa infused humor into her words, though he got the feeling she was trying to lighten the mood. "And handsome, and funny. I always envied your ability to make friends, real friends. Everybody loved you. I figured you had your pick of women on campus. Why would you be interested in me?"

"Because you're gorgeous and brilliant."

Her smile was shy. She tugged her hand out from beneath his and snatched another cookie.

"You'd better eat that," he said. "There are kids in Africa who don't have peanut butter cookies."

"I'm sure it'll make a difference." She took a tiny bite and swallowed. "Did you and Megan get married?"

"What? No, no. We spent a couple of months together, but we broke up before graduation. I went into the Army, she went to grad school, and we lost touch."

Alyssa's eyebrows rose. "So you just left her to deal with the baby by herself?"

Anger flashed hot. He pushed away from the table and stood. "I knew nothing about Peri. Nothing." He snatched his glass of milk, downed the whole thing, then rinsed the glass and filled it with water. "You want some?"

"I'm fine."

After taking a long sip, he leaned against the kitchen counter.

"Megan didn't tell you she was pregnant?"

"We broke up. We graduated. I never talked to her again. I didn't know about the car accident. I didn't know anything."

"How did you find out?"

"October, I got a phone call from Megan's mother telling me about her death and asking to meet. I figured maybe she'd left something for me—a letter or... I didn't know, and frankly, I didn't care. But the woman had lost her daughter, so I figured I had to meet with her. I was out of the country but told her I'd reach out when I was back in Washington. I texted her, and an hour later, she and Megan's father were on my doorstep—with Peri. She believed—like Peri believed, like her whole family believed—that Megan had told me about the baby and I'd refused to step up. She brought Peri there to guilt me into taking her."

"You're kidding. She just dropped it on you like that? And used her granddaughter—?"

"Like mother, like daughter. I was furious and confused and probably handled it all very badly, but I instantly fell in love with my daughter. I set her up in my bedroom to watch a movie, then told Megan's parents the truth. Her mother called me a liar. Her father believed every word I said, which told me a lot. He loved Megan, but he also knew what she was capable of.

"They started talking about how I needed to provide enough money to send Peri to boarding school, and that was it. I told them I'd take her, and a couple of days later, she came home with me."

By home, he meant here, to his parents' house.

Callan didn't explain their reaction to finding out they had a seven-year-old granddaughter, equal parts joy and horror that he'd fathered a child out of wedlock, a child he'd known nothing about.

He didn't explain his sheer terror at the prospect of being a daddy to a grieving little girl.

He didn't explain how relieved he'd been when his parents had agreed to take her until he could transfer out of field work into something closer to home.

He didn't explain how he'd known the Boston job was too far away but had been dragging his feet about finding something closer, even if it meant leaving the CIA. Not because he didn't want to leave the Agency. His new job was dull as dirt. Not because he didn't want to be with Peri. He did, more than anything.

But because he was scared he was going to mess it up even worse than he already had.

He didn't tell Alyssa any of that.

"Your parents have had her all this time?"

He dipped his head in a nod and didn't lift it again, too ashamed to meet Alyssa's gaze.

"She's your daughter? You're sure?"

"The math works out, and I can see myself in her, a little. And..." He hated to admit this, but Alyssa was asking the question. And she knew Megan and what she was like. "I ran a DNA test, just to be certain, not that I told anybody."

"Your secret's safe."

He could trust Alyssa. Of that, he had no doubt.

"Can I just say one thing?" Alyssa stood and approached him, slowly, as if he might bolt.

Which, honestly, he was tempted to do.

But in her expression, he saw nothing but understanding. "I can't imagine how shocking it was to find out about Peri."

Alyssa's head dipped to the side. "Is her name...?" Alyssa smiled, shaking her head. "She actually named her daughter Persephone."

"How in the world did you guess that?"

"Megan always said she was going to name her daughter Persephone and her son Atlas."

"At least Atlas is a tough-guy name. Persephone lived in Hades with the dead. This is why children have two parents, so if one comes up with a ridiculous name, the other can talk her out of it."

"Among other reasons. But didn't the goddess Persephone bring springtime? Isn't that her myth?"

He loved that Alyssa knew that.

As if hearing his thoughts, she said, "Megan used to talk about mythology a lot. She loved the drama and intrigue of it."

Sounded like Megan. She loved drama enough that she'd created it all the time. "In that sense, the name fits. Peri is the epitome of sunshine and spring."

"I agree." Alyssa leaned against the counter opposite him. "Hey, Callan?"

Her serious tone had him tensing. "Hmm?"

"I overheard some of your conversation with your sister. And so did Peri."

He cringed, wiping his hand down his face as if he could wipe away the truth that, one more time, he'd injured his sweet little girl. "I thought you were with her." The words came out like an accusation. "I thought you two were upstairs."

"I went to the bathroom. I didn't realize you wanted me to keep her up there. The point is, Hannah is right. You need to figure out how to be a father."

"I know that." His volume was too high, and with effort, he lowered it. "You think I don't know that. It's not that simple."

"Sure it is. Move her to Boston with you."

"And put her in public school in the city? No way am I tossing my precious girl into that." He'd done just enough research to know it wasn't an option. He'd gone to rural country schools, safe schools. Not the kinds of schools that had metal detectors and uniformed cops roaming the hallways.

"Private school, then."

"Not all of us come from wealth, Paris." He was angry, and he was taking it out on Alyssa. It wasn't her fault, but he'd been hearing the same message in stereo for months. He didn't need to hear it tonight.

"Then quit your job and—"

"Some of us have bills to pay."

"I understand bills. I also understand you have a family that's willing to help you. You and I both know you could find another job or start your own business and do great at it. You don't need the Agency to be successful."

"It's not that simple." He realized he'd just said that. Was it true? Or was he just making excuses? "Raising a kid all by myself..."

"Megan did it, right? Or did her parents help her?"

Her parents hadn't helped her, not a bit. When she told them she was pregnant, they'd demanded she get an abortion. When she'd insisted on having the baby, they'd suggested she put her up for adoption.

When Megan refused, they'd told her she was on her own.

If nothing else, Callan was beyond grateful that Megan had at least gotten a few things right. His daughter was alive and well, and Callan was in her life now.

Megan had never told her parents who Peri's father was, but she'd added his name to Peri's birth certificate, which was how her parents had found him. Because of that, Peri hadn't ended up in foster care or boarding school.

It said something about the kind of people her parents were

that they'd told him all of that without the slightest hint of shame.

Alyssa must've read his expression because she said, "For seven years, Megan raised her, alone."

"She didn't have to. She could've asked me. I'd have supported her."

"Not my point."

Deflect. Change the subject. Anything to keep from having to face his own inadequacies.

"You claim you love her," Alyssa said, "but you don't."

"Watch it, Paris." His voice was low, humming with warning. "You have no idea how I feel."

"Love isn't something you *feel,* Callan. It's something you *do*. And you know what it looks like to children? It looks like care. It looks like breakfast every morning and story time every night and all the little things that happen in between. It looks like coloring books and bath time and Christmas trees and presents and cheerleading lessons, even if those lessons are all the way in Augusta. Love is listening to their stories and praying with them and putting princess bandages on their booboos. To children, love is *time*."

He wanted to close his eyes and cover his ears like a little boy. He didn't want to hear this, no matter how true it was.

"So don't tell me you love her." Alyssa's tone was gentle now. "Your feelings are irrelevant. Your actions matter."

Just like Mom and Dad and Hannah, Alyssa was right.

Callan wanted to love Peri. He planned to love her. He intended to love her. But how often did he actually show her he loved her? And if he didn't show her, then it didn't matter at all.

"You need to prove to Peri that she's worth any sacrifices you have to make or she's going to grow up believing all the lies Megan told her."

He knew the vitriol her mother had dripped into his innocent daughter's heart. That he didn't love her. That he didn't have time for her. That he couldn't even bother to send a check.

"I hate to say it, Callan." Alyssa stepped across the kitchen and gripped his arm. "Every day you don't prove Megan wrong, you're proving her right."

Despite the kindness in Alyssa's expression, her words were buckshot, piercing his skin.

His parents and his sister had been pestering him, nagging him, and guilting him for months, but none of them had ever put it like that.

It wasn't that Callan cared a whit about proving his vindictive ex-girlfriend right or wrong for his own sake. Megan was gone, killed in a senseless car accident.

But in proving Megan right, he was proving to be exactly the opposite man from who he wanted to be. He didn't want to be selfish. He wanted more than anything to be like his own father, generous and overflowing with love.

He would figure out a way to be Peri's father. He'd figure out a way to prove to his daughter how much he loved her.

Even if it cost him everything else in the world, Callan was going to become Peri's father. He was going to love her and take care of her.

As soon as Alyssa was safe.

## CHAPTER TWENTY-SEVEN

The anguish on Callan's face broke something inside Alyssa. She didn't think about what she was doing as she stepped closer and wrapped her arms around his waist. "You're going to figure it out."

He pulled her close and hung on as if her presence were his only hope. "I'm so glad you're here. I can't imagine having survived this day without you."

His words were a balm, calming her anxiety. She'd felt like a third wheel ever since she'd shown up at the hospital. She'd felt like she should have kept her distance.

But he hadn't seen it that way.

He hadn't told her about Peri, but as he'd talked, she'd realized that was more about him than about her. He was ashamed, not of his little girl, but of how she'd come to be, and how he was handling fatherhood.

She wondered how long he'd have waited to tell her if she hadn't gone to the hospital. She wanted to confront him, but he had enough of his plate. And really, he didn't own Alyssa anything. They were barely friends.

At least that was what she told herself as they hugged in the silent kitchen. Though it should have started to feel awkward, it didn't.

Until he hug went from comforting to friendly to something else, something she was afraid to define.

He loosened his hold, and she backed away and looked up.

He tucked a lock of her hair behind her ear, the slight touch sending prickles of awareness over her skin. His hand settled on her cheek, and he leaned closer, holding her eye contact as if waiting.

Her thoughts were too muddled to think straight, too muddled to catch up.

He pressed the lightest kiss to her lips.

It wasn't their first kiss, the shocking one at the restaurant with Charles as their audience.

It wasn't all the kisses between then and now, quick pecks designed to fool their observers.

It wasn't that quick peck he'd given her in the garden.

This wasn't Caleb, computer hardware salesman.

This was Callan, the man she'd secretly dreamed about for a decade.

She didn't think, just slid her hands behind his head and pulled him closer, wanting more of him.

The world narrowed to that house, that kitchen, that spot, until nothing else mattered but his lips touching hers, his fingers lacing into her hair. His hand on her back, holding her close.

His warmth. His breath. His scent. His everything.

This man who'd done so much to protect her. Who'd put himself in danger to keep her safe. Who'd confessed he'd had a crush on her before and, if his touch were to be believed, whose crush had morphed to something bigger and more powerful than she'd ever imagined.

Her attraction to him expanded, exploded. She cared about

Callan. More importantly, she *trusted* him. She'd never thought she could, but she did.

He ended the kiss, crushing her to his chest.

His racing heart thumped against her ear. A groan started low in his belly, escaping on an exhale.

She wasn't sure what to say. Of all the boyfriends in her past, none of them had ever made her feel anything close to this. Callan wasn't unsuitable. He wasn't controlling. He wasn't slow or inept. He was everything she'd ever wanted.

It was glorious.

It was...terrifying.

Because during the kiss, maybe over the previous few days, Callan had slowly pulled her heart nearer. Now it was his. He'd captured it. The question was, what was he going to do with it?

"Alyssa." His voice was low and rumbly, sending shivers over her.

"Hmm?"

"I'm sorry. I shouldn't have done that."

The shivers turned cold. She stepped back. "Okay."

"Don't. I don't... It's not that I didn't want to or didn't enjoy it." His arms dropped to his sides. "It's just...I have Peri. She has to be my priority. I can't get sidetracked until I figure things out with her."

"Right. No. I get it," she lied.

She didn't get it at all. Couldn't a man have a daughter and a girlfriend? Didn't people do that?

They did, and he could. He just didn't want to make the effort. Not with her.

She was a fool for thinking...anything.

This was why she chose unsuitable men. When they let her down—and they *always* let her down—it didn't hurt.

This hurt. This was excruciating.

She returned to the table and pulled her laptop close. "I have some updates."

"We should talk about—"

"Ghazi. We need to focus on him."

Anything besides the fact that she'd relinquished her heart. Callan had held it for approximately five seconds before crushing it to pieces.

That was her reward for letting it go.

She lifted her lips in what she hoped passed for a smile. "Don't you want to know what I've learned? We're running out of time."

"Alyssa."

She ignored the emotion in his voice. "Ghazi wants the zero-day exploit on a thumb drive by Sunday at noon, and he expects—"

"Please, let's... Wait. You talked to him?"

"He called to check on my progress. He moved up the timeline. I wasn't sure what to do, so I just told him I'd do my best."

"Why didn't you call me?"

"Your father had a heart attack. You were a little busy. The point is, he wants it Sunday, and he expects me to deliver it in person so he can make sure that it works. He told me he'd drive up here but didn't say exactly where he wanted to meet. I've worked out a plan, in case it comes to that. I'm going to build something that looks like it works but doesn't, just in case we need it."

Callan slid into the chair beside her. "It's not going to come to that. We can't let it. What did you learn about the woman in the photograph?"

"Michael figured out her name, which was good because I'd hit a dead-end. It's one thing to search for a person, but without a picture or a name, I was afraid we'd be relegated to searching through old yearbook photos. That didn't sound fun to me."

Alyssa was babbling. She needed to pull herself together. "Michael has a contact with Ghazi's family, a half-sister. He learned that Ghazi had a girlfriend when he was at university in Kirkuk. Her name was Fatemeh. There were only a couple people with that name who were at university when he was. I found one who sort of resembled the woman you'd described."

"You sent me her photo."

Right. She'd forgotten that. "Anyway, her name was Fatemeh Ebrahimi. She was a medical student at the University of Kirkuk. According to Michael's source, they dated for a couple of years and were talking about getting married."

Callan nodded for her to continue.

"Ebrahimi was killed in the bombing of a military outpost near her apartment."

"Collateral damage." Callan laced his fingers together on the table. "Anything else?"

"After her death, Ghazi quit school and disappeared. Nobody knows for sure where he went or what he did during that time. What we know is that when he was in school, he was a devout Muslim, or at least he did the things a devout Muslim would do. He was faithful to attend mosque and take part in the prayers, that sort of thing."

"And after her death?"

"It gets fuzzy. We have nothing on him for years. Then his face started popping up in photographs of other people being surveilled by the Agency. Once he was on the Agency's radar, they kept their eyes on him. He did go to the mosque and take part in the prayers. But Michael believes—and he's had interactions with him—that Ghazi lost his faith after college, though he'd never known why until now."

"We don't know for sure that the girlfriend's death means anything. Could be he was always exactly who he is now and just used her death as an excuse to become killer."

"Maybe." Born a psychopath? Wasn't that a pleasant thought. "The point is, whatever the catalyst, he lost his faith—if he ever had any—and became a chameleon. There are photos of him attending synagogue, kippah and all. In Germany last fall, he insinuated himself at a Christian mission."

"That tracks with the Agency's dossier."

"Until today, Michael said he'd thought Ghazi's only goal was money, a mercenary willing to betray anyone or anything to increase his own net worth. Michael never believed Ghazi cared about anybody. Not his family. Not friends. Not faith. That his only motivation has been amassing wealth."

Callan leaned toward her, eyebrows hiking. "Until today?"

"The photograph you saw paints a different picture, don't you think? Ghazi carries it with him, maybe looks at it every day. Because he loved her so much?"

"Or to remind himself of his motivation. Vengeance." Callan stood and disappeared into the other room, returning a moment later with his laptop.

He opened it and started typing. "If it's vengeance, then against whom? Who was responsible for that bombing?"

"I assumed us. The US."

"In the Iraq War, we were just one of the nations in the coalition of forces."

"The biggest, though. Far and away."

"True. Still, it could've been..." His voice trailed.

She slid her own laptop closer and searched. There weren't many details about bombing operations available on public websites. "Let me make a call."

He glanced over her head, and she twisted, catching sight of a clock mounted above the door behind her. It was after ten.

He said, "It's morning in Indonesia. They're probably—"

"I wasn't going to call Michael. My dad could get the information for us. I don't really want to tell him what's going on, but… What?"

Callan's brows had lowered. "I'm not sure that's a great idea."

"Why?"

"This is all classified. We shouldn't bring your father into it."

"My father could've run the Agency if he'd wanted to."

"I'm aware."

"Are you saying you don't trust him?"

"I'm not saying… I'm saying we have to keep the circle small. I can get the answer. I have other connections I can trust."

Meaning he didn't trust her father.

Good to know.

She supposed she was lucky he'd deigned to trust her.

She was being unfair, but whatever. He'd started it when he'd confessed to old feelings, then kissed her, then rejected her.

She didn't owe him squat.

"Fine." She pushed back in her chair and stood. "I'm going to bed."

"Wait!" He lurched to his feet. "I think we should talk."

"Nothing to talk about. I'll see you in the morning." She swiveled and headed for the door.

"Paris, please can we just—?"

"No." She turned to face him. "My name is not Paris. Good night."

# CHAPTER TWENTY-EIGHT

Usually, Callan crashed like a toddler after a sugar-binge when he stayed in his childhood home. There was something about being in his old bedroom, under his parents' roof, that made him feel secure.

But there was nothing *usual* about this visit. He'd wrestled with worry for his father, uncertainty regarding his relationship with Peri, and guilt about...all of it. Relying too heavily on his parents for their help with his daughter. Getting himself involved in danger because of Alyssa.

All of it he could justify. All of it.

Except that kiss.

There was zero justification for that. He'd hurt her. He'd rejected her when all he wanted was to hold her and make her his.

But how could he with Peri needing him so much? He already knew he was incapable of real love, the kind of love that mattered. He'd proved that with his daughter. Adding a second person to the mix wasn't going to improve anything.

That was the problem, wasn't it?

Alyssa'd had it right. Love meant time and care, neither of

which he'd shown to Peri. What made him think he could show them to Alyssa? And even if he could, he didn't deserve her love. He didn't deserve anything.

No shock those thoughts hadn't helped him sleep.

He finally fell asleep, waking up with the sunrise.

After texting Mom to confirm that he could leave Peri here for the weekend, he slipped onto the shower and tried to focus, though thoughts of Alyssa dogged him.

She wasn't vindictive. She wasn't Megan. She'd forgive him. She'd understand why he had to give Peri all of his attention. Ultimately, when he and Alyssa parted, they'd part as friends.

Assuming they survived the weekend.

If he wanted to do that—and he absolutely must make sure they both made it out of this unscathed—then he needed to think straight.

He dried off and dressed in yesterday's jeans and sweatshirt, not wanting to risk getting his new slacks and button-down dirty before they left for the party.

A few minutes later, he opened his bedroom door to find Peri sitting crossed-legged in the hallway, leaning against the opposite wall. She wore her pajamas and socks, which explained why he hadn't heard her approach.

"Good morning, Sweet Pea. Whatcha doing out here?"

She lifted one shoulder and let it drop. "Didn't want to wake you." She peered past him, looking confused.

"I was awake. Even if I hadn't been, you can knock on my door anytime." He scooped her into his arms. "You're looking chipper as a daisy this morning."

Which wasn't entirely true. She looked tired, her skin pale, dark smudges beneath her eyes.

"Did you sleep all right?"

She shrugged.

"Talkative in the mornings, aren't you, little one?"

She shrugged again, this time with the tiniest smile tugging her lips up.

"Hmm. What can I do to make you smile?" He carried her down the stairs, mulling the question.

He'd once tried tickling her, but she'd remained stone-faced. His mother told him later that people only responded with laughter to being tickled when the tickling was done by someone they trusted.

He decided not to face that disappointment again.

"When I was your age, food always woke me up. What do you think? Are you hungry?"

Again, she said nothing, but this time, he got the feeling she was being quiet because he'd said she wasn't talkative. Was she teasing him? Or punishing him?

The first, no doubt. She looked like her mother, but she hadn't inherited Megan's pettiness, thank God.

He carried her into the small walk-in pantry. "What do we have in here? Let's see. Do you want"—he gazed at the cans—"baked beans?"

She shook her head, horrified. She didn't seem to know if he was serious or kidding.

"How about spinach?"

She scrunched up her little face, but this time, she almost smiled.

"Hmm. Picky eater, I guess. Let's see... Ooh, I've got it." He grabbed a container. "Shortening."

That earned a grin. "Silly."

There were boxes of cereal, but when he lifted a box of bran-something, she shook her head. Smart kid.

Then, Callan spied pancake mix. He pulled it out, showed her the photo, and lifted his eyebrows. "Do you think your old man can pull off pancakes?" He read the directions. "All I have to do is add milk and eggs. What do you think? Can I do it?"

She took the question seriously, nodding after a moment of deliberation. "I'll help."

"You're the best." He carried her and the box back to the kitchen and plopped them both on the counter.

Callan kept up a stream of conversation, doing everything he could think of to draw Peri out, but she mostly sat silently while he started a pot of coffee, then measured the mix. He let her crack the eggs and add them and the milk, then set the bowl on her lap and gave her a spoon. "You stir that while I get the griddle hot."

"'Kay."

He stifled a sigh. She certainly wasn't making it easy for him.

"Tell me about your new friends," he said. "You were talking to Alyssa about someone named Emma, right?"

"Uh-huh."

He set the stovetop griddle on the gas stove, lit the fire, and then added a pat of butter.

"Is she nice?"

"I guess."

"Is she ugly? Does she have a huge wart on her nose?"

Peri giggled. "No."

"Good. Good. Little girls with wart-noses are twenty-seven percent more likely to be witches. You have to make sure they don't have brooms and black cats before you can be friends with them."

"Witches are just pretend, Daddy."

"Are you sure? I thought they were real."

She was smiling at him down.

"Hmm. Even if you're wrong, if Emma doesn't have a wart nose, then she's probably not a witch." Callan leaned against the counter across from his daughter in the U-shaped kitchen. "Tell me about other friends. I'm sure you've made a few."

She nodded but didn't elaborate.

She wasn't exactly loquacious. Not with him anyway.

Remaining quiet to give her the opportunity to talk, he took the batter and poured it into circles on the griddle, then set the table for three and added the crock of butter and maple syrup.

"I think they're ready to flip," Peri said.

He returned to the griddle and saw that, sure enough, the pancakes looked dry on top. He flipped the first and found it perfectly golden brown on the opposite side. "You're a chef!"

"Mommy used to let me help her."

"I bet your mom was good at pancakes." He worked hard to keep negativity about Megan out of his thoughts and words when he was in Peri's presence. She needed to remember her mother with fondness.

When they were finished, he stacked the pancakes on a plate, which he slid into a warm oven, then started the next batch.

He was flipping them over when footsteps sounded behind him.

"Alyssa!" Peri's voice was full of enthusiasm, a sea change from how she'd been talking to him.

He tried not to be too jealous.

"Hey, beautiful." Alyssa stepped up to the cooktop and peeked. "Ooh, my favorite. Did you help make these?"

"Uh-huh." She slid down from the counter and, while Alyssa poured herself a cup of coffee, chattered like they were old friends.

Callan focused on getting drinks, finding some fruit, and not letting his jealousy ruin their breakfast.

"Go ahead," Alyssa said. "Ask him."

He carried a glass of juice to the table, catching Peri's wary look. "Ask me what?"

When she said nothing, he turned to the oven to grab the stack.

Alyssa lowered her voice. "He's on your side. If he can say yes, he will."

He found a hot pad, set it on the table, and plopped the plate on top. Not asking. Not pushing.

"What am I missing?"

When neither of them said anything, he sat beside them, bowed his head and said a quick prayer, then transferred a pancake to Peri's plate. "Butter? Syrup? Both?"

"Both."

He was fixing it how she liked it when she blurted, "I wanna take cheerleading like my friend Emma but Gigi said I had to ask you. Can I?"

He smiled, pretending he didn't notice the fear in her expression. Did she think he'd be angry with her? Or say no?

Sort of, a little, he wanted to say no. Those short skirts. But his fears weren't a good enough reason to disappoint her. "I can't see why not. Do you know the name of the place where Emma takes lessons?"

Her expression brightened. "She wrote it down for me. I can get the paper. She said her mom and Gigi can carpool 'cause it's in Augusta." She slid down from her chair. "I'll go get it."

"It'll wait until after breakfast."

"Okay." But Peri seemed happy now. He had no idea how much cheerleading lessons cost, and he didn't care. He'd made his daughter smile, and that was worth any price.

His phone dinged with a text, and he pulled it from his pocket.

**You'll need to keep Peri with you for a few days until your father's feeling better.**

That wasn't going to work. He hated to do this, but he texted back,

**I'm sorry, Mom, but I can't. Hannah can't keep her, either. I know it's not ideal, but I need your help.**

Mom's response was immediate.

**No. You'll need to make other arrangements.**

No? Just...no?

Mom had never refused to help him.

Another text came through.

**They've told us Dad needs to rest, and he won't if Peri's there. She's your responsibility, Callan. It's time for you to step up.**

She was right, but...

**I need her to be safe.**

**She will be because you promised you'd stay out of danger.**

He had made that promise. And he'd intended to keep it. And then he'd broken it, but for good reason.

He could explain to Mom everything that'd happened to get him to this place. He could call her and justify his decisions.

But Mom's mind was made up.

And Dad's health mattered. How could Callan risk it?

He scrambled for another solution, but none came to mind. If he were in the city, he could ask a coworker to help, but they had to be in Shadow Cove in a couple of hours. There wasn't enough time to drive Peri to Boston, and even if there were, was he really going to foist his daughter off?

"You okay over there?" Alyssa asked.

He appreciated her kindness despite how he'd treated her the night before. All for Peri's sake, he knew, but even so, he appreciated it.

He settled back at the table. "Sure. I'm great."

Peri shoved a few bites of food into her mouth, then asked Alyssa, "How come you didn't sleep in Daddy's room?"

Callan nearly choked on his coffee.

Alyssa's fork froze halfway to her mouth. But the pause was short before she took her bite. She took her time chewing and swallowing, maybe waiting for him to jump in.

He had no idea what to say.

"I used to have sleepovers when I lived with Mommy," Peri said. "Gigi and Papi said I'm too young for sleepovers, but Mommy let me. My friends always slept in my bed."

"I bet that was fun." Alyssa's shoulders visibly relaxed. "You were with good friends. But grown-ups don't have sleepovers like that."

"Mommy said it was okay as long as he was a very good friend."

*Whoa*. What?

Callan stood abruptly. "I forgot the fruit. You want an apple? I'm going to cut one up." He grabbed a knife from the block and searched for a cutting board. He'd grown up here. He should know where they were. But he was having trouble concentrating.

"Hmm, that makes sense," Alyssa said. "Your daddy and I are friends, but maybe not that good of friends. Besides, I bet your daddy snores like a buzzsaw."

"Do not." He worked to keep his tone lighthearted as he found the cutting board and sliced through the apple, needing to do something with his hands.

"And he probably passes gas in his sleep." Alyssa waved her hand in front of her face. "Stinky."

Peri giggled. "Do you toot in your sleep, Daddy?"

"Probably, but I'm sleeping so..." He shrugged. "You girls are silly."

Alyssa must've made a face because Peri's laugh only grew louder.

"I wonder if Mommy's friends tooted in their sleep," Peri said.

"Did your mommy have a lot of sleepovers?" Alyssa asked.

"Uh-huh."

*Slice. Just slice the apple and don't think about what* friends *Megan had entertained while his daughter slept in the next room.*

Was it wrong to want to murder a woman who was already dead?

# CHAPTER TWENTY-NINE

After her shower, Alyssa slipped on a new T-shirt and yesterday's jeans, then added the cardigan to stave off the chill. Her hair was dry, her makeup applied, as she reclined on the twin bed where she'd slept the night before, checking her email. Nothing important, but she liked to clean it out every day, just in case.

The quilt covering the bed looked handmade—by Callan's mother, no doubt. The fabric squares she'd moved to the sewing table added splashes of color. The walls were decorated with old photographs of the Templeton family—Callan's parents on their wedding day, Callan and Hannah jumping off the dock into the lake.

It was cozy and safe, the perfect place to hide until it was time to leave. She was hiding, not trusting herself to have a conversation with Callan. Every time she thought of his rejection the night before, it stung. Yes, she understood he needed to focus on Peri. Of course he did. But that truth didn't heal the wound.

If he didn't want a relationship with her, then he shouldn't have given her that mind-blowing kiss. He shouldn't have led her to believe he cared about her. That there might be a future for them.

It didn't matter. She just needed to avoid him.

A knock sounded. Solid, forceful.

Callan.

She was tempted to tell him to go away, but the last thing she wanted was for him to know how hurt she felt. She swung the door open.

"Can we talk?"

His words had her defenses rising.

He must've seen something in her expression, because he added, "We need to go over the plan and figure out how to..." He turned his gaze toward Peri's room, lowering his voice. "She's going to have to come with us, so—"

"What? She's coming?"

"Shh." Again, his gaze flicked away. "I don't have another option." He ran his hand over his blond hair. "It's not ideal."

To put it mildly.

Alyssa wasn't about to invite him into the bedroom, so she shoved her feet into her shoes and then led the way past Peri's closed door and down the stairs. She snatched her jacket off a chair where she'd draped it the night before and stepped outside, where Peri wouldn't overhear.

It was supposed to warm into the seventies later, which would be perfect for her grandparents' anniversary party.

Now, it was in the low fifties. Sunshine dripped through the tall trees all around, sparkling on the puddles left over from yesterday's rain. New spring leaves were bright green against the darker pines. Birds chattered, squirrels hopped branch to branch.

Alyssa turned toward the side of the house, wanting to see the lake that had been nothing but a dark expanse the night before. Her bedroom was on the front side of the house, so the view from her window had shown only forest.

Through the woods, she glimpsed the neighboring house, which was probably a hundred yards' distant.

She zipped her jacket as Callan fell into step beside her.

"I'm trying to figure out how to do this," he said. "You and I have to sell the idea that we're engaged, but with Peri—"

"What?" She froze and faced him. "We're not telling my family we're engaged."

"Ghazi will be watching. Not personally—at least there's been no indication that he's left the Brookline house. But he'll have people there."

"This is my *family*. I'm not lying to them."

"We have no choice—"

"You didn't lie to your family." As the words left her mouth, she remembered that he almost had. She'd stopped him from introducing her as his fiancée.

"I would have," he said. "If not for Peri, if not for Dad's heart attack, I would have. We have to stay in character. But... I mean, you're right. I didn't. I thought they had enough to deal with, and since Ghazi doesn't know who I am..."

"Right. And who cares about my family?"

"That's not what I'm saying. I'm saying—"

"I thought you were a Christian." He'd prayed a couple of times for them. Didn't that mean something? "I don't know what church you go to, but at ours we're taught not to lie."

His expression hardened. "In my line of work—the line of work you wanted to be in—sometimes lying is part of the job."

She knew that. But this was different. This was her family.

"We have no choice, Alyssa." His words were softer now, gentle as the breeze. "I know it's awful. I get that it could do damage to your relationships. I get it." He ran a hand through his hair. "Do you think I want to do this? To let my daughter think I abandoned her so I could be off dating and falling in love?"

They both knew that part wasn't true.

"We told Ghazi we were going to announce our engagement at the party," Callan said. "We can't give him any reason to believe we lied."

"You shouldn't have told him we were engaged." All her emotions escaped in her voice and sounded like anger. "There had to be a better way."

The thought of facing her sisters, her mother, her father... The thought of telling them she was engaged when they hadn't even known she was dating somebody. They'd be furious.

No. They'd be hurt.

And her grandparents and cousins would be there, so her betrayal—and what else could she call it?—would be witnessed by everyone in her entire family.

She couldn't do it.

"You're probably right." Callan sounded defeated. "I just... It was instinct."

"To kiss me? That was instinct?"

He winced. "To pretend we were together. It seemed like the easiest way."

Right. Because her feelings were irrelevant. Her family was irrelevant.

"This is my *life* you're messing with."

His expression, kind and maybe even apologetic before, hardened. "I know that, Alyssa. That's what all of this has been about. *Your* life. Keeping *you* alive. I didn't have to get involved at all."

Now it was her turn to wince.

He'd insinuated himself at her dinner for *her* sake, not his. He was trying to protect her.

Didn't change anything. Didn't change that he'd made her

believe he had feelings for her and then rejected her. Didn't change that he was asking her to lie to her family. And then, what? Come back in a week and say, "Just kidding. Sorry I ruined Gram and Pop's anniversary party. It was all just an elaborate ruse"?

How could she do that? How could she do any of this?

"Can't we just pretend to be dating?"

"Sorry." He started walking again, so she did too.

They rounded the corner of the house, and the lake came into view.

The clear water was calm, the trees that ringed it reflecting off the surface like a mirror.

The grassy backyard led to a sandy beach bordered on both sides by trees that rimmed the lake like sentinels. On one edge of the property, a dock extended over the water, a fishing boat bobbing alongside.

The property was small and secluded and charming. It was perfect. It was so contrary to how she felt that she struggled to understand how this peace could exist in the same place and time as her own turmoil.

"I know it's not ideal."

Pretending to be engaged.

Lying to her family.

As if she hadn't already alienated herself from them enough.

"They'll understand," Callan continued. "When you explain, they'll forgive you."

Maybe. But it would only drive the wedge between her and them deeper. That wedge was her fault. She'd avoided them. Feeling like a failure, feeling like she had to succeed in order to matter, she'd kept her distance. Now, more of her failure would be evident. Her foolishness, getting involved with a terrorist.

"There's got to be a better—"

"Fine. You tell me what we should do." He halted in the

middle of the yard. Arms crossed. Scowl on his face. "Please, give me your plan B. Because I have zero ideas. I can tell Malcolm you're calling the whole thing off. You didn't want to go into hiding before. Are you willing to now?"

"I can't—"

"And even if you did, Ghazi knows who you are. He knows your family. Do you think he'll leave them alone? Do you think he's too *nice* to use your sisters to get what he wants? Or your mother?"

His words were darts, and she felt the sting of each one.

"This isn't a game of Scrabble, Alyssa. You can't just walk away. It's too late for that."

"I know that. Just...shut up and let me think." She started walking again. "Malcolm could just take Ghazi into custody. That's what Michael thinks he should do."

"I'll pass that along." Callan deadpanned the words. "I'm sure Malcolm will be very open to your cousin's advice."

"He knows what he's doing." Didn't he? Michael was a good agent, a great agent. As far as she knew, anyway. Not that she'd have any way to know.

"He's not unbiased." Callan softened his tone. "Not only does he love you and want you to be protected, he has a personal vendetta against Ghazi. He wants to stop the terrorist. Malcolm wants to know—needs to know—the bigger picture."

"Okay, then. You and Peri stay here. I'll go to the party myself, and—"

"I'm not leaving you alone. Forget it."

He would soon enough, though. When this was over, he'd leave her alone again. Which should be fine. She'd been alone before he'd barged into her life.

But the thought of it left her feeling bereft.

And admitting *that* made her feel like some frivolous heroine from a sappy British romance.

"I'll be with my family. I'll tell them all about my boyfriend and how he was going to come, but his father had a heart attack." Her feet squished into the damp grass, then sank in the sand until she reached the wooden dock. She hopped onto it, then marched to the end. "I'll be fine."

Callan followed, his footfalls heavy on the boards behind her.

All she wanted was out of this situation. She wanted to get back to where she'd been a week before. Safe and happy.

Well, safe, anyway. And lonely, though she hadn't realized it at the time.

She reached the end of the dock, and Callan stopped beside her, looking out at the water.

"Ghazi's men will be there. Anything we do outside what's expected puts you and your family at risk."

"I could call him and tell him..." Was she really going to call her terrorist employer and make up a story? What would that sound like? Maybe she could sell it, but that was a big maybe. And in calling, she'd indicate to him that she feared she was being watched, tipping her hand.

And if that wasn't bad enough, then Ghazi would have every reason to expect her back in Boston immediately. Then she'd have to make up another lie, and every conversation they had increased the possibility that he'd see right through her.

Callan stared out at the water, handsome and strong and beautiful in a way she couldn't articulate. This was a place he'd probably stood a thousand times. This dock, this lake. This property and all the peace that surrounded it.

He'd brought Alyssa here, to his sanctuary, to keep her safe. He was doing all of this to keep her safe.

His gaze flicked to her, catching her staring. He squinted the slightest, as if he was trying to figure her out. As if she were the confusing one. "I wish there was another way."

She looked away, knowing the truth. There wasn't another way, not one that didn't put her and her family in danger.

"Peri has to come with us? There's nobody else?"

"Mom doesn't want her here." He shook his head. "That's not fair. I shouldn't... Mom's done so much, and Hannah has some important event this weekend at the university."

"How will you explain to Peri the fake engagement?"

"Yeah. More importantly, how do we keep Ghazi's men from realizing she's my daughter? How do we keep her out of danger?"

Alyssa turned and faced the house where they'd left the innocent little girl.

"We're going to Brooklynn's house first so I can borrow a dress. We can all drive together. Maybe it'll look like Peri's with her."

"Okay." He pressed his lips together, seemed to have trouble holding Alyssa's eye contact. "I know it's unfair, but do you think there's a way Peri could be gone when we announce the engagement? I just...I don't want to lie to her."

Peri was only a child, a wounded, grieving child. She deserved their protection from all of this.

"I can tell Brooklynn the truth, and she—"

"No. We can't tell anybody."

Alyssa stifled a sigh. "Okay, then the truth. The *other* truth. We tell my family that we were going to tell your parents but your dad had a heart attack, so...so I'll tell Brooklynn about the engagement and ask her to take Peri for a walk while we make the announcement."

"Will she do it?"

"I don't see why not." Except for the obvious, that Brooklynn was going to be furious with her. Or disappointed, which would be even worse.

But this was the price Alyssa paid for doing business with a terrorist. This was the cost of keeping her family safe. It would be worth it, even if they never forgave her.

"IT'S JUST DOWN THE HILL," Alyssa said.

Callan rode the Mustang's brake, following the traffic toward the coast in downtown Shadow Cove.

"Ooh, it's so pretty!" Peri said from the backseat. "Look at the pink house!"

The "pink house" was actually an office building. The first floor contained a real estate company. Alyssa used to get her teeth cleaned on the second.

She'd grown up just a couple of miles from here, and when she'd been young, she hadn't thought there was anything special about her little town—all the old houses-turned-businesses. Back in the eighties, before she was born, somebody had started a revitalization effort in town, hoping to attract tourists. One of the woman's inspired ideas had been to paint all the downtown buildings bright colors. To hear old-timers tell it, there was a lot of pushback from locals, but their failing businesses had them grudgingly agreeing, with the caveat that they could paint everything white again if it flopped.

It didn't flop.

Shadow Cove was not only delightfully attractive and charming, as were most Maine towns on the coast—at least the ones tourists frequented. But it was unique. York and Kittery, Boothbay and Bar Harbor. They were lovely, but similar.

None of them had this. It was the best little town in Maine.

Maybe, she was the teeniest bit biased.

They passed souvenir shops, restaurants, coffee shops, and ice cream parlors. Some of the businesses were new, but most had been here as long as she could remember. The arcade, where they used to drop their weekly allowance in video game slots, back when they were a quarter. The pizza parlor, owned by third-generation Greek immigrants. The popular restaurant overlooking the coast, which served everything from local seafood to Canada's famed poutine.

"I wanna go there." Peri pointed at the new bookstore in an old building that had been completely remodeled. A bay window boasted a Winnie-the-Pooh display featuring the Hundred Acre Wood behind giant stuffed animals—Pooh-bear, Piglet, Tigger, and Eeyore.

"That building used to be the library," Alyssa said. "I borrowed every Nancy Drew mystery they had when I was little."

"I love Nancy Drew! Can we go, Daddy?"

"Maybe later."

As delighted as his daughter seemed, tension wafted off of Callan. And Alyssa got it. They were walking back into the lion's den. Callan was certain that Ghazi would have people at the country club, watching. The thought of getting themselves—and more than that, Peri—anywhere near the terrorist sent her anxiety spiking.

She wished he'd stayed home, stayed far away from this. Maybe it would put her in more danger, but better that than the sweet eight-year-old who'd already survived so much tragedy.

"Are we getting close?" he asked.

"Yeah. Just ahead." Alyssa pointed to the gallery Brooklynn had opened a few years back. The original rotting wooden siding had been replaced with teal-colored aluminum. Brooklynn had painted the shutters bright white and added a fancy sign in the front, making the place look cheerful and inviting, perfect reflection of her personality. "Take a left right after it."

Callan turned onto a street that was no more than an alley separating Brooklyn's shop from the attorney's office next door.

There was a parking lot, but it looked full, even though the summer season didn't officially start until after Memorial Day more than a month away.

"Park behind Brooklynn's truck." Alyssa indicated the spot, and Callan maneuvered the Mustang in the tiny space between the four-by-four and the crumbling asphalt that separated her driveway from the parking lot. An outdoor stairway rose to the third floor.

"Your sister *lives* here?" Peri asked.

Climbing out of the car, Alyssa said, "Above her store. She's a photographer, and she sells her pictures downstairs."

"That's so cool."

It was pretty cool, actually. Brooklynn had taken her lifelong love of photography and turned it into a business.

"Can we see it?"

"There's probably not enough time today," Alyssa said, "but another time. I know she'd love to show you around."

The second-floor door opened, and Brooklynn stepped onto the landing and leaned over the railing, waving. "Come on up."

They took the metal stairs and stepped into her apartment.

"Come in, come in." Brooklynn closed the door behind them, her cheerful smile wide. She was party-ready, with her curled dark brown hair falling in waves halfway down her back. She wore a bright pink dress with white polka dots and pink kitten heels with a white sparkly bow. If Alyssa had to guess, her sister would have a purse that matched the outfit perfectly.

Suddenly, it occurred to Alyssa that her sister would have a closet filled with bright-colored dresses covered with daisies and sunflowers.

Maybe she should've borrowed from Cici instead.

"Brooklynn, I'd like you meet Cal—"

"Caleb." He stuck out his hand to shake. "It's great to meet you. This is my daughter, Peri."

"Peri." Brooklynn's smile widened when she focused on the child. "That's a fabulous name."

Peri started to say something, then closed her mouth, looking confused.

"It's a nickname, right?" Alyssa said quickly. "Tell my sister your real name. She'll love it."

"Persephone," Peri said. "After the goddess of springtime."

Brooklynn gasped and slapped her hand to her chest. "That is literally the coolest name I've ever heard. You are so lucky!"

Peri's grin was shy but authentic.

"You guys need something to eat or drink?" Brooklynn asked. "Water, soda?"

Peri shot an eager look at Callan, *Caleb*, who said, "Water, if it's no trouble." To his daughter, he added, "I'm sure you'll get your fill of treats at the party."

"Oh, she will." Brooklynn winked at Peri. "I promise." She waved toward the living room to one side of the door. "Make yourselves at home." She hooked her arm through Alyssa's. "Come on, sis. You can help."

Not that Brooklynn needed help getting two whole glasses of water, but she followed her into the kitchen.

Brooklynn's photography adorned the walls, of course. One in the kitchen was new. Brooklynn had captured the sun glimmering peeking over the horizon, casting the waves in shades of red and bronze In the background, the rocky spit of land that edged the south end of the cove was snow-covered. "That's breathtaking."

Brooklynn smirked at the photo. "It's okay. It's not what I was going for. I'm trying to get a specific shot, and I just can't seem to get it right. It's frustrating."

Alyssa imagined her sister setting the shot up in the dark, waiting for the sun to rise. Waiting for the perfect wave. Snapping, snapping. Then trying again another day.

And then, she saw it differently. "You take someone with you, right? You don't go out by yourself in the dark."

"This is Shadow Cove, not Boston. It's not exactly the crime-capital of the world."

Facing Brooklynn, Alyssa crossed her arms. "Didn't you read about the college student who was raped and murdered? Evil people exist everywhere. You need to protect yourself."

Brooklynn started to argue, then grinned, eyes bright with curiosity. "Trying to distract me?"

"I'm serious. You need to—"

"Nothing's going to happen to me." Brooklynn's gaze flicked toward the living room. "Except maybe the vapors." Fanning her face, she affected a Southern accent. "Where'd you find that tall drink of water?"

"Ebay." Alyssa grabbed two glasses from the open shelves. "I need to talk to you about him."

"Ooh, what is it?" Brooklynn stepped closer. "I heard there was a secret?"

"You heard? From...?" She knew the answer.

Telephone, telegraph... "Frannie called you."

"She said she ran into you a couple of days ago—at a hotel with a hottie."

"We were talking in a courtyard." Sheesh. The gossipy woman had made it sound like they'd been caught in the act or something.

"I know." Brooklynn's smile froze in the corners. "She was just excited for you. So, tell me about him."

This was going to hurt. She hated it. Hated lying. Hated... all of it.

"He and I..." Didn't go to school together. She needed to remember the pretend story. "We met years ago, but we recently reconnected, and uh... This is going to be surprising, so try to temper your reaction."

Brooklynn's expression dimmed. "What?"

"We're engaged."

And now...Brooklynn's smile was gone. "You're *engaged.* To a total stranger?"

"He's not a stranger to—"

"You've never said a word about him to anyone. Except *Frannie,* I guess. Does she know?" She must've read Alyssa's expression, because she said, "Great. Frannie knew before me."

"Caleb didn't realize... He's excited to start telling people."

"Unlike you, I guess. We saw you last weekend. Could you really not... Wait. Did you at least tell Mom? Please tell me Mom knows."

"No, I—"

"Does Kenzie know?"

"Nobody knows." It said something about Alyssa's relationship with her sister that she didn't question the truth of it. She wasn't suspicious. She fully believed that Alyssa would start dating, fall in love, and get engaged, and never say a word. "It's brand new. You're the first to know. We haven't even told Peri."

Brooklynn's gaze dropped to Alyssa's left hand. No ring, of course.

"I'll start wearing it after everybody knows," Alyssa lied. So many lies. "Like I said, it happened really fast. We were going to tell his parents and Peri, but his dad had a heart attack yesterday. He's still in the hospital. It wasn't the right time."

"He's okay? His dad?"

"Yeah. But it was a scare."

"Hmm."

There was nothing to do but keep going. "We want to tell Mom and Dad and everyone else today, so I might need your help. We don't know what to do with Peri."

"I see." Brooklynn took the glasses and filled them with ice. After the rumble of the ice machine and the clinking, she faced

Alyssa again. "You're telling me now not because I'm your sister and you want to confide in me, but because you need my help."

"I mean, of course I want to confide—"

"It's fine. Congratulations, by the way. I'm happy for you. It's good to know there's somebody in your life you love enough to talk to."

"It's not... Brooklynn, I'm sorry. I'm not so good at—"

"It's fine."

It wasn't.

"It doesn't matter."

It did.

But Alyssa had no idea how to fix it, how to make it right.

Brooklynn added water to the glasses. "Eliza's bringing a babysitter to entertain Levi. Maybe you can ask if Peri can join them."

Eliza was their cousin Sam's wife. "How did you know—?"

"I see Eliza. We chat sometimes. We're family, you know. That's what families do. Talk. You should try it. Or at least, when people want to talk to you, maybe answer your phone."

Right. Brooklynn had called her...was it yesterday? She should've called her back. She could remind her that she'd lost her phone, but she had one now, but wouldn't be able to explain why she couldn't share her number.

It was all so convoluted. And frankly, even if Alyssa had had her phone, she wouldn't have called. "I'm sorry."

Brooklynn took a breath, then smiled, though nobody who knew her would buy it. "I am happy for you. I just wish things were different. But it doesn't—"

"It does matter." Alyssa took the glasses, set them on the counter, and pulled her sister into a hug. "It does matter, and you're right about all of it. You're right, and I'm sorry."

For being a terrible sister. For letting her relationships with them grow so distant.

For taking advantage of her kindness while lying to her.

Tears pricked her eyes. How could she do this? How could she hurt the only people in the world who loved her?

Brooklynn's return hug was reluctant at best.

Alyssa stepped back, taking her sister's hands. "There's a very long story here, and I want to tell you everything. I just can't today, okay? But I do want to confide in you. I miss you."

She realized as she said the words that they were true. That as much as she'd avoided her family in the last few years, she longed for them. She longed to have sisters who were best friends again.

Maybe Brooklynn read the emotion in her eyes because the hardness in her expression softened. "I forgive you. I look forward to hearing your story." She pulled her hands away, swiped her fingers beneath her eyes. "You're gonna make me ruin my makeup." The trademark smile filled her face as she swiveled and returned to the living room. "Here we go!" Her voice was perfectly chipper as she set the drinks on her coffee table in front of Callan. "Peri, you want to come help us pick out a dress for Alyssa?"

"Sure! Can I, Daddy?"

"If you want." He sat back and crossed an ankle on the opposite knee. "If you like all that frilly girl stuff."

Peri propped her fists on her hips. "I *am* a girl."

"Oh, yeah. I always forget."

"Silly."

"Come on, then." Brooklynn beckoned her toward the hallway and her bedroom, and Peri followed.

Callan gave Alyssa raised-eyebrows look.

She kept her voice low. "I've got it under control." She hoped, anyway. She'd text Eliza as soon as she got the chance.

~

A FEW MINUTES LATER, Alyssa stared at her image in her sister's full-length mirror.

"You're so pretty." Peri sounded awed.

"She's all right, I guess." Brooklynn added, "I'm only a little annoyed that you look better in my clothes than I do.

"Don't be ridiculous." Brooklynn's curves would fill out the dress better than Alyssa's stick-straight body.

As she'd feared, her sister didn't own a single little black dress. Nope. They were all colorful, many multi-colored. Stripes and polka dots and weird geometric designs. As she'd feared, there was even a bright yellow one covered with daisies.

Alyssa was not wearing a daisy dress.

Brooklynn had given her a choice of two solid-color options that would work with an outdoor afternoon event. One was royal blue—with sequins, an old bridesmaid gown nobody would wear in public on purpose unless they had no choice—meaning they'd made the mistake of becoming friends with a woman who had rotten taste.

The other choice was...this.

A sleek, one-shoulder number in pale lavender. It was meant to hit mid-calf, but Alyssa was taller than her sister, so it ended just below her knees. It might be considered modest if not for the slit that rose to mid-thigh.

"It's just a little... Maybe I should try the daisy one." How desperate was she? But this dress made her look like she was trying to stand out. To attract attention. To attract a man.

That was the very last thing she wanted anyone to think. Especially Callan.

"The purple one is way better than the daisies!" Peri said.

"I agree." Brooklynn propped her chin on her hand and tapped her lips as if seriously considering the problem. She walked around Alyssa, giving her assessing looks. "I don't think you'll look good in daisies. Now, if I had an orange dress with birds-of-paradise..."

Alyssa gave her a squinty-eyed *shut-it* look, which made Brooklynn laugh.

"I think you're right, Peri. This is as good as it gets. Ooh, and I have a little purse that matches it perfectly!"

Of course she did.

Before Alyssa could come up with a reason to change into something less...well, something else, Brooklyn and Peri practically shoved her into the bathroom.

"I'm going to grab a chair." Brooklynn focused on Peri. "You look through my top drawer and pick out a pretty eye shadow."

"Wait! I don't need..."

But Brooklyn wasn't listening to her.

Her punishment for not telling her sister she had a boyfriend was to be painted like a plastic doll.

Thirty minutes later, she was plastered with so much makeup she was afraid to smile.

Brooklynn had curled her blond hair and pinned it up at the back of her head, leaving pretty curled tendrils to float around her face.

And then, with Callan's permission, Brooklynn had curled Peri's hair while both sisters exclaimed about how lovely it was.

It was, too. Thick and luxurious, just like Megan's had been.

Peri wore a white dress with pink and purple flowers that she'd gotten from her grandmother for Easter. Brooklynn pulled the front of her hair back and tied it with a purple ribbon—of course she had a purple ribbon—on top of her head.

"You are gorgeous!" Alyssa said.

Peri's smile was as wide as Alyssa had ever seen it. "We match!"

Alyssa looked at their reflections in the mirror. Sure enough, their dresses were color-coordinated, as if they'd planned it.

"We're going to be late if we don't hustle." Brooklynn swept all of her makeup back into the drawer, a mishmash of tubes and cylinders and palettes with zero regard for organization or tidiness. Typical.

She and Peri hurried out of the bedroom while Alyssa took a deep breath, trying to summon her courage.

She wasn't ready for this, for any of it. But she was out of time.

# CHAPTER THIRTY

How long could it possibly take for one woman to change clothes?

By the little Callan heard coming from behind the closed bathroom door, he gathered Peri and Brooklynn were having a lot more fun dressing Alyssa up than she was having herself.

He'd spoken to Malcolm and left a message for Michael. It seemed that the information Alyssa had discovered about Ghazi's girlfriend's death and the bombing that had killed her, which he'd told his boss about immediately, should have led to something. But when he'd questioned Malcolm about fresh intel, he'd gotten nothing but an impatient, "I'm working on it."

They were the CIA, for crying out loud. How could they not find out who'd ordered the bombing? What its true purpose had been?

His guess was that the answers were hidden for a reason, and that bothered him. A lot.

They needed to know what Ghazi's endgame was before he demanded the zero-day exploit from Alyssa. If she had to turn it over—a flawed one that would infuriate him—then she'd have to go into hiding. She'd have to defy his demand that she give him the exploit in person.

That was absolutely not going to happen. Callan wouldn't let Ghazi within a hundred yards of her.

But what about her family?

Would they all have to hide until Ghazi was stopped? How would that work for Gavin and his wife? For Alyssa's four sisters, who had jobs and businesses and lives?

The other option was to bring Ghazi into custody and hope that whatever he was planning would be stopped when Ghazi was out of the picture.

There were too many holes in the emerging picture, and they were running out of time to place the rest of the puzzle pieces.

Callan was thankful Ghazi didn't know who he really was. His family should be safe. But Alyssa...Alyssa wasn't just an old college rival anymore. She wasn't just a crush he'd never quite gotten over. She mattered to him.

How could he retreat to safety if her life was in danger? But if he stayed with her—and he refused to acknowledge how much the idea appealed—then what about Peri? Could she stay with them, or would being with Callan and Alyssa put her in danger?

He wouldn't risk that.

*Lord...*

He didn't pray much. He'd always been more about asking God to bless his own plans than following God's lead.

But, despite all the danger he'd faced in the Army and in his work for the Agency, he'd never felt so out of his depth as he did now. Because the stakes had never been so high.

*Help me. Show me what I'm supposed to do. Please, lead me. I'm desperate for You.*

The prayer cracked something deep inside, a need for a

deeper relationship with the Eternal. A need to know that all his efforts mattered, that he was achieving not human praise, but the smile of God.

Could God ever smile on a man who'd messed up so badly?

*Can You forgive me, Lord?*

Of course Callan knew the answer. He'd only needed to ask, and forgiveness was there for him.

Ask, and repent.

Which meant his life was about to change in ways he wasn't ready to consider.

*Whatever You want, Father. I'll do it. Just please, please protect those I love.*

A door opened down the hall, and Peri stepped into the living room. She wore a wide grin, her eyes wide and expectant.

They'd curled her hair and added a ribbon, making his already beautiful little girl look perfectly adorable.

"Where's Peri?" he asked her. "Have you seen my daughter?"

"You're silly."

He crossed the room and swept her into his arms. "You look so grown up! I'll need a club to beat off the..."

Alyssa emerged from the hallway.

Oh, boy.

His mouth went dry. His thoughts fled.

He was in trouble. Serious trouble.

She wore a tentative smile, but it faded. Even with that worried look—which made no sense at all—she was gorgeous. Absolutely stunning.

Her hair was curled. She wore makeup that made her already high cheekbones even higher, her large eyes even larger.

And that dress... Those legs.

Holy smoke.

"Isn't she pretty?"

"What?" He glanced at Peri, trying to order his thoughts. With effort, he looked at Alyssa again, thanking God she couldn't read his mind. "Yeah. You look..." He swallowed, trying to get moisture into his mouth, to make his brain function again. "You look...really nice."

Those words didn't even come close. He wasn't sure there were words.

Her cheeks suffused with color. "Thank you. It's Brooklynn's." After a moment, she added, "Obviously." Her blush deepened. "Anyway, we need to go."

"Right. Yeah." He cleared his throat and turned his attention to Brooklynn, who was pretty, very pretty. But she didn't make it hard for him to remember how to inhale. "I'll drive. You're riding with us, right?"

Brooklynn agreed, and the four of them piled into the Mustang for the short ride up the coast to the country club, his daughter talking the entire way.

He turned at an unobtrusive sign and stopped at a guard shack, rolling down his window.

The older man inside the small building wore a stern expression and a crisp black uniform. "Good afternoon, sir. How can I—?"

"Hey, Dirk." Alyssa leaned across Callan.

"Oh, Ms. Wright. I didn't see you. Here for the big shindig?"

"We are, and I have two guests."

"Very good." The guard opened the gate, and Callan drove through.

"Good security," he noted.

"It's one of Dad's non-negotiables."

Callan maneuvered down the long, manicured driveway toward the clubhouse, marveling at the explosion of flowering trees and blooming bushes set off against the emerald green golf course that stretched along both sides of the narrow way.

This place dripped with wealth and influence. He should've chosen to buy a new suit the day before instead of his on-sale, budget slacks and sports coat.

At a posh place like this, he'd be pegged for a plebeian the moment he walked in the door.

His cell rang, loud over the speakers in the small car. He pulled it from his pocket, glanced at the screen, then answered, "I'll call you in two."

"Got it." The line went dead.

He shot a smile in the rearview to his daughter, tipping his phone toward Alyssa so she could see that it had been her cousin finally getting back to him.

Their destination was a sprawling building big enough to accommodate the entire population of his hometown. White siding sparkled against the bright blue sky and lush grass spread out before it. At one end, a circular room lined with windows reflected the perfect gardens. Behind the building, the Atlantic was a deep blue-gray, white-topped waves crashing against rocks on a jetty, where a few people hopped from rock to rock.

"Can we go out there, Daddy?"

"Maybe, after the party. We'll have to see."

The drive circled in front of overlarge double doors that opened beneath a cupola in the center of the structure. A weathervane on top turned lazily in the breeze. The wide porch was decorated with planters overflowing with flowers and greenery.

It hadn't occurred to him that they'd be coming to *this* club, designed by an old golfing great, written up in architecture magazines. The fact that Callan had heard of it said a lot about the place's prestige.

It was the kind of place that almost made him want to take up golf.

"Wow," Peri said. "It's so pretty."

"Eh, it's okay. Not as pretty as Gigi and Papi's house, though." He grinned at his daughter in the rearview.

She looked out the window, then at him. "You're right, Daddy. Their house is prettier."

Alyssa twisted to face her. "I agree. It's much nicer."

"If it's that pretty," Brooklynn said, "maybe I need to take pictures of it. Will you show me someday?"

"Can I, Daddy?"

"Sure." Not that there'd ever be occasion for Brooklynn to go to his family's house, but he couldn't exactly say no. He stopped in front of the stairs leading to the entrance, and a uniformed attendant opened Alyssa's door. Callan didn't have an angle to see his face. "I'll be back in..."

His own door opened, and another uniformed attendant said, "Welcome, sir."

Alyssa leaned in a whispered, "Valet parking."

Oh. Right. He wasn't used to the rich-and-pampered lifestyle.

"I'd rather park it myself." He lifted his phone. "I have to return a call anyway." And he wasn't going to hand over his keys. Who knew if they'd need to make a quick getaway.

The valet looked confused. "Oh, then I guess, uh..."

The other man came around the front. He didn't wear the valet's uniform but a light gray suit with a name tag pinned to the breast pocket that read *Robert*. He was older with deeply tanned skin and salt-and-pepper hair. A manager of some sort?

Callan's senses prickled. Was this one of Ghazi's men? He directed Callan to where he should park.

Ghazi had unlimited resources. For all Callan knew, he'd had people in place at Gavin Wright's club for months.

Though he hated to leave Peri and Alyssa alone even for a second, he drove away. If Ghazi's men were watching the entrance—assuming Robert hadn't been one of them—they wouldn't see Callan enter with Peri. Even if they were watching, they had no reason to believe Peri was related to him. They'd assume Peri was with Brooklynn, maybe an extended family member.

He dialed Michael and had a short but very informative conversation, which he was still mulling when he jogged up the steps of the county club.

Stopping just inside the door, he wasn't sure what he'd expected. Grand and pretentious, probably. Michelangelo on the ceilings and Mozart playing over hidden speakers.

This wasn't that.

The circular foyer, tiled in white marble, mirrored the shape of the cupola rising overhead, its windows letting in natural light. A round table in the center held a flower arrangement that rose to at least a foot above his head.

Paintings of the golf course and the Maine coastline were displayed in simple gold frames between the doors leading off the space.

It was elegant and understated and tasteful.

Though he was pretty sure that *was* Mozart playing on hidden speakers, so he hadn't been completely wrong.

A door on the right led to the pro shop and, beyond that, a restaurant in the circular room he'd seen on the ride in. A door on the left led to a hallway lined with more doors.

"There he is!"

Peri's voice drew his attention toward the other side of the obtrusive flower arrangement, where his daughter stood with Alyssa and Brooklynn.

"She insisted we wait for you," Alyssa said.

He plastered on a smile as he approached. "Great. Lead the way."

They walked down a hall to a glass doorway that led out the back side of the building. He got a glimpse of the gathering, but not much more than that before Brooklynn pushed through the door, Peri following.

Alyssa gave him a slightly panicked look, and he slipped his hand into hers, giving it a little *we've got this* squeeze.

They'd better have it. They had no choice.

She took a breath, and they stepped into the party.

IF CALLAN HAD BEEN IMPRESSED with the building, now he felt blown away.

The patio extended out from the back of the building, giving patrons a view of the golf course on the sides, the rocky shoreline straight ahead.

White tablecloths covered round tables, each adorned with fresh tulips and hyacinths, which added sweetness to the briny scent of the ocean carried on the breeze.

Around the perimeter, long rectangular tables held appetizers, salads, desserts. There was even a carving station, where a white-apron-clad waiter stood at the ready.

Probably not Ghazi's man. He looked a good fifty pounds overweight with graying hair sticking out from beneath his chef's hat.

There had to be a hundred people, the vast majority of them invited guests. But a few men hovered around the edges, and these had the look of guards.

But could they be Ghazi's men?

Callan didn't know Gavin Wright at all, but surely the man was smart enough not to allow random thugs into his party. No, these guys had to be his security. Why, though? Did the Wright patriarch expect trouble, or did he always travel with them?

Probably the second. He had amassed considerable wealth, and he had a whole lot of secrets in his brain.

Where were Ghazi's people? Robert, the unlikely valet, wasn't out here.

Servers mingled, offering appetizers. Mostly young and attractive women.

The bartender looked like he could handle himself, barely smiling as he prepared and poured drinks. When he looked up to give them to the waiting guest, his gaze roamed the space, then stopped briefly on Callan, who quickly averted his eyes, hoping the man hadn't noticed him noticing watching.

So, maybe the bartender. Or maybe the guy was an ex-cop or ex-military, the kind of guy who'd been trained to expect trouble.

More scanning. Lots of employees, all clad in black pants and white button-downs. Any of them could be with Ghazi, either his people or people he paid for information.

How could Callan do this? How could he let this group of people know that he was Peri's father?

He needed to be very, very careful.

He hadn't expected so many guests, all standing in clusters, sipping cocktails and nibbling appetizers.

He'd known Alyssa had a big family, between her four sisters and her six cousins, most of whom were married or paired up, at least. But this was...this was more people than he even knew, much less knew well enough to invite to a party.

"Oh, there's my family." Alyssa tugged him through the throng, greeting guests along the way to a cluster of people standing together, chatting comfortably.

Not only did Callan feel like he'd been transported into a world of wealth he'd barely known—and had certainly never been a part of—but as they reached her family, he thought, were all rich people so attractive?

Or had they accidentally stumbled into a modeling shoot?

Her cousins were as tall as he was, dark-haired and fit. Their wives were gorgeous. Even the oldest among them, Camilla, was lovely with mahogany-colored hair and bright blue eyes. The only Wrights missing from that branch of the family was Michael, who was still on his honeymoon in Indonesia.

Grant, the fourth oldest, asked the question Callan had been waiting for. "You're with my cousin?" The words came out as a threat. Of all the men, this one was the most powerful. And the most suspicious.

Callan returned his iron grip with one of his own. "I am. Nice to meet you."

"Let me guess. I should see the other guy?"

"Something like that." Callan's lip was no longer swollen, but the bruise on his cheek hadn't faded enough. This guy didn't miss a thing, and his squint-eyed gaze spoke volumes. *You hurt her, I'll kill you.*

Somehow, Callan didn't doubt it.

Grant grunted, then crouched to Peri's level. "Hey there, little bit. What's your name?"

His daughter, utterly unafraid of the warrior, grinned. "I'm Peri, but my real name is Persephone."

"That's a pretty name for a pretty girl." He tapped her on the nose. "Make sure you try the double-chocolate cookies. I hear they're the best."

Alyssa, Callan, and Peri finally made it through the mass of that branch of the family, and Alyssa pulled Callan toward another group of model-gorgeous people who stood off to one side beside an older couple, who were the only people sitting down.

"Caleb," she said, "I'd like you to meet my grandparents, Tom and Susie Wright."

When the man stood, the resemblance to his grandchildren became obvious. He was tall and slender and held himself like a soldier despite his advanced age. His eyes were brown, his hair gray, but Callan imagined it'd once been the same color as all those Wright men.

"It's a pleasure, Mr. Wright." He shook his hand, then bent to the woman, who'd remained sitting. "Mrs. Wright. Congratulations. How many years are you celebrating today?"

Her smile was welcoming. "Sixty-five." Her eyes sparkled as they flicked from Alyssa to him. Rather than shake his hand when he extended it toward her, she gripped it in both of hers, her fingers strong and cool. "It's unusual for Alyssa to bring a gentlemen friend to family gatherings. I look forward to getting to know you."

"Thank you, ma'am. It's an honor to be here."

She continued to hold his hand in one of hers, gesturing to the party going on all around them. "I hope we'll have time to talk when all of this is over."

"Me, too." Despite the flash of guilt for their deception, he kept his smile in place.

Cici was the middle sister. She had hair so bright red that it couldn't possibly be natural, though it looked good against her pale skin and the freckles dotting her nose. She wore no makeup and had opted for a pair of slacks and a blouse instead of a dress. She wasn't polished like her sisters, more natural, down-to-earth.

Delaney had dark blond hair and blue eyes. She seemed quieter than the others, shy even, and more interested in chatting with Peri than getting to know him.

And then there was Kenzie. She was the youngest, probably in her early twenties, with long chestnut hair and eyes the same golden brown as Alyssa's. He thought he saw freckles, like her older sister Cici, though Kenzie had tried to hide them with makeup. Her hair and been pulled up in a messy bun, and she wore a sundress that looked comfortable and casual. When he stuck out his hand to her, she eyed it, amused, before she shook it. "I can't wait to hear this story."

He let out a nervous laugh that was more than just for show. What would Alyssa tell her sisters about him later, when the whole story came out?

The answer that presented itself was not at all pleasant.

"Caleb, this way." She slipped her fingers into the crook of his elbow, and he beckoned Peri, who'd been following along, greeting people with *how-do-you-do's* like a perfect like gentlewoman.

Had Megan taught her that? Or his parents?

He was ashamed that it hadn't been him. Before today, he'd only ever introduced her to his family and Alyssa.

"Caleb." Alyssa stopped in front of an older couple surrounded by people about their same age.

A woman broke away from a conversation and, seeing Alyssa, pulled her into a quick hug. "Beautiful girl, I'm so glad you're here."

"Me too." Alyssa turned to Callan. "Caleb, I'd like you to meet my mother, Evelyn Wright."

He could've picked Alyssa's mother out without the introduction. She was as tall as Alyssa, maybe five-seven or five-eight, with the same silverly blond hair, though hers was a little more silver, a little less blond. Alyssa had inherited her mother's high cheekbones, honey-brown eyes, and warm smile.

Evelyn Wright was sophisticated and elegant and might have been intimidating if not for her kind welcome as she shook his hand. "I'm so glad you're here, Caleb. I hope everyone's treating you well."

"They are, mostly." He caught sight of Grant across the patio giving him the evil eye and gave the warrior-cousin a pointed look as he leaned in conspiratorially. "Though I'm a little worried that one's going to kill me."

Following his gaze, Evelyn laughed, the sound as relaxed as if they were old friends. "Just don't get on his bad side, and you should be fine." She shifted her attention to Peri. "And who is this beauty?"

"This is...Peri." He didn't add *my daughter,* just in case the server walking by was an enemy.

"How do you do." Peri shook her hand, then pressed against Callan shyly, seeming almost awed. He could understand that. Evelyn was not only beautiful, she was regal. She didn't wear a tiara, but she was one of the few women in the world who could get away with it.

It struck Callan that this was Alyssa's life. This woman represented the future Alyssa would have. Beauty and power and wealth and strength, all wrapped up in one perfect package.

If this woman sat on the throne, Alyssa was the princess, next in line.

Which made him...

The pauper? Yeah. That felt right.

Alyssa's hand was still tucked in his elbow. He squelched the temptation to distance himself, knowing she shouldn't be with him, not even if it was all pretend.

It was irrational and unnerving how much that bothered him. He'd never felt inferior to anyone in his life. All this money and beauty and influence was messing with his mind.

A gray-haired man broke away from his conversation and turned toward them, pinning Callan with a piercing look.

Alyssa stiffened, her hand tightening on his biceps. "Hi, Dad." She leaned in and kissed his cheek before turning to Callan. "Caleb Thompson, my father, Gavin Wright."

Callan had spotted Gavin already, of course, having seen his photograph many times over the years. He wasn't as tall as his brother, Roger, whom Callan had met earlier. At maybe five-eleven, Gavin Wright didn't need height to be powerful. He had broad shoulders and a thick chest. His power radiated like an aura. His skin was tanned, wrinkles fanning out around sharp eyes.

When he shook Callan's hand, his grip wasn't as firm as Grant's had been, but it didn't need to be. The threat was implied anyway, somehow. "Caleb, is it?" The way he asked the question told Callan he knew that wasn't his name at all.

That was curious. And worrisome.

Remembering Malcolm's warnings, he wondered... Was Gavin an enemy? Not of Alyssa, but of Callan?

If so, then the security around the patio couldn't be trusted.

If so, they were tiptoeing through a viper's nest.

He hoped it wasn't true, but he couldn't assume.

"It's a pleasure to meet you, sir. Thank you for inviting me."

"Not sure I did." He backed away, his close-mouthed smile doing nothing to soften his features. He gave Callan a long, assessing look.

Callan put up with it, silently, but he didn't like it. If Gavin thought he'd bristle or babble, he had another think coming.

Alyssa, on the other hand, put a little distance between them.

Great. Did she sense a drone-strike coming?

When Gavin noticed Peri, his expression shifted so markedly that he looked like a different man altogether. His hard features softened, his lips slipped into a genuine smile. "Who do we have here? You're not with this guy, are you?"

"He's my daddy."

Callan stifled the groan. He couldn't exactly warn Peri not to tell people that. But danger signs flashed across his mind.

"You're kidding." Gavin shook his head. "How does an ugly ogre like him get a beautiful daughter like you?"

Evelyn's laugh was lighthearted as she gripped her husband's forearm. "You should talk, Mr. Ogre-Man. You've got *five* beautiful daughters."

Gavin clutched his chest as if she'd shot him. "I'm wounded."

Peri giggled at the man's antics.

Callan tried to ignore a sharp jab of jealousy.

"You have five little girls?" Peri sounded awed by the prospect. "Can I meet them?"

"They're not so little anymore." He lowered to his haunches. "You've already met Alyssa. She's my oldest."

Peri glanced up at Alyssa, who smiled at her fondly.

"You've met them all." Alyssa pointed to her sisters, who were standing and chatting nearby. "Brooklynn, Cici, Delaney, and Kenzie."

"Oh. You're all big now."

Gavin chuckled, low and deep. "They are so big. Have you eaten?"

"Huh-uh."

"We should fix that. Little girls need to eat so they grow up tall and strong, like Alyssa here." He held out his hand, not bothering to check with Callan first. "Should we start with the cookies?"

Alyssa said, "Dad—"

"—Gavin." Evelyn spoke at the same time.

They were both suitably shocked, giving Callan the freedom to chuckle and say, "How about a little protein first?"

Gavin shook his head. "Fathers take the fun out of everything."

Peri grinned at Callan, then slipped her hand into the older man's and walked away.

"Don't worry," Evelyn said. "He'll take good care of her."

He hated to think about the expression that must've been on his face to elicit that remark.

"Oh, I'm sure he will." Even so, he'd be sticking close. "I could eat."

"You can always eat." But Alyssa was teasing as she gripped his elbow again. "Lead the way."

Step one: meet the family. Check. Step two: tell them about the engagement.

The hard part was still to come.

# CHAPTER THIRTY-ONE

Alyssa led the way to the food tables, and she and Callan filled their plates. She was thankful to be past the bulk of the introductions.

This was harder than she'd imagined, and her imagination hadn't been kind.

Passing off Callan as her boyfriend wasn't the only problem. Like Brooklynn, Kenzie had been hurt that Alyssa hadn't told her about him. Cici had hugged her and demanded more details. Delaney had seemed genuinely happy, though she wasn't exactly exuberant.

Alyssa never had any idea what Delaney was thinking.

What struck her most was the obvious—none of them questioned it. None of them doubted that Alyssa had started dating a man—a man she must be serious about—and hadn't told anyone.

They believed it.

That was the kind of sister Alyssa had become. So distant from her family that they accepted this giant lie without question.

No doubt they'd believe the even bigger one when she and Callan announced their fake-engagement.

It was...unacceptable. She didn't have the mental space to process what it meant right now, why she'd become so distant from them, why she'd avoided them. But she knew, whatever her reasons, they were not good enough.

*Help me fix it, Lord. Please, don't let what happens in the next hour destroy these relationships.*

Her plate filled with prime rib, mashed potatoes, roasted Brussels sprouts, and a roll, she sat beside Callan at the table where Dad and Peri were already eating. Well, Dad was eating. Peri was talking his ear off, though he didn't seem to mind, listening intently, responding at the proper times.

She tamped down a sharp stab of jealousy. She would have given anything to have his undivided attention when she was eight.

It didn't surprise Alyssa when other guests started filling their plates. Once Dad did something, others naturally followed. That was the kind of man he was, the kind who didn't need to say a word to get people to fall in line.

Mom joined them, settling in next to Dad, and then Brooklynn, Kenzie, Cici, and Delaney. Normally, her sisters would sit with friends or cousins. It seemed everyone wanted a front-row seat to the Alyssa-Callan show.

Alyssa had worried most about Dad's reaction. She'd dated a few guys here and there, but she'd never brought any of them home to meet her family, much less to a function like this. Dad wasn't a person who put a high value on kindness. Truth, justice, and integrity, definitely. But kindness wasn't his strong suit.

So she'd been worried, but Dad had taken Callan's presence in stride, almost as if he was in on the secret. Which he couldn't possibly be, but...

But Dad always knew more than he should, so maybe, somehow.

Mom was far too kind to grill a guest at dinner. She was probably curious, but she wouldn't want to make Callan uncomfortable.

Unfortunately, Alyssa's sisters had no such qualms, peppering him with questions about his life and his past. Even Delaney lobbed a few his way.

Callan had transformed into his *Caleb Thompson* alias easily and talked about a past life close to reality, but just different enough from the truth.

"How did you two meet?" Brooklynn asked.

"We met years ago at a tech exhibit in DC. The details are fuzzy." He wore a self-deprecating smile. "That's what happens when you're dazzled by a beautiful woman and trying to work up the nerve to ask her out."

Alyssa laughed. "He's exaggerating. It wasn't like that at all."

"Not for her." Callan grinned, bumping her shoulder, playing it up. "When I saw her again a few months ago, I decided I was not going to let the opportunity get away a second time. I asked her out. She must've been drunk because she said yes."

Dad had been talking to Peri, but he was listening. He gave Alyssa a dark look—chin lowered, eyebrows hiked.

"He's joking, Dad."

She expected her father to press Callan on the details, but Dad focused on Peri again.

She'd finished her lunch and three cookies—like father, like daughter—so Dad had called over a waiter to bring them coloring books and crayons. Now, they were both coloring, exclaiming over each other's designs.

Had Dad ever colored with Alyssa?

How pathetic was it that she jealous?

Callan continued spinning stories, and Alyssa jumped in when she needed to.

And then Eliza, Sam's wife, approached the table. Her baby bump was obvious, but she wasn't so big she looked uncomfortable. She was followed by her son, Levi, with his adorable curly blond hair, and another young woman who must be the babysitter Brooklynn had mentioned.

Eliza stopped beside Peri's chair. "That's a beautiful picture you have there."

Peri grinned. "Thanks. It's a kitten."

"It's very good, even better than Mr. Wright's."

Gavin scowled at her.

Peri placed her tiny hand on his thick arm. "Yours is good, too, Mr. Wright."

"Thank you. You're very kind." And then he stuck out his tongue at Eliza.

Dad.

Stuck out his tongue.

Had Alyssa been transported to another universe?

Or...or was this the kind of grandfather he'd be? Playful, lighthearted.

The question had her yearning for children. Not that she was going to have kids just to earn Dad's approval. She'd done enough to know the futility of that.

"I wanted to introduce you to Levi." Eliza ushered the boy forward. "Levi, this is Peri."

He was practically bouncing. "We're gonna go look for crabs and sharks. You wanna come?"

Peri's eyes widened, and she looked at Callan. "Sharks?"

"I'm sure he's joking." He turned to the boy. "You are joking, right?"

"Huh-uh. They might be out there, so we're gonna stay on the rocks where they can't get us."

"Very smart. That way you'll be safe." His gaze rose to Eliza, "Where exactly?"

The younger woman who'd followed them answered, "I'm just going to walk them down the jetty." She pointed at the rocky structure he'd noticed on his drive in. "I'm Laine Webb, by the way."

He rose and shook her hand. "Nice to meet you."

"Laine's family owns Webb's Harborside," Dad said. "Their family goes back generations in Shadow Cove." Dad gestured to someone out of Alyssa's line of sight.

One of his guards came around the table. Alyssa had gotten so used to them at public events over the years that she'd neglected to mention them to Callan.

He must've figured out who they were.

This one was named Jock. He'd been with Dad for years. Bald head, small gray eyes, meaty muscles, and wrinkles proving that he'd lived his share of life. "Sir?"

"Accompany our guests, please." He winked at Peri. "Make sure you protect them from sharks."

The guard lifted his lips in a smile, but from the intensity in his eyes, he caught the double-meaning.

Not all sharks kept to the water.

To Callan, Gavin said, "Does that suit you?"

By the way his lips pressed together, it didn't suit him at all. But he said, "Stay with Laine," giving his daughter a *do as you're told* look. "And be careful on those rocks. They might be slippery, and those aren't the best shoes for climbing."

"Okay, Daddy!"

Alyssa watched their progress out the wrought iron gate circling the patio, down a short set of stairs, and along the sand toward the jetty.

The babysitter, Laine, held both children's hands, and the guard followed about ten feet back.

Peri should be safe. And now she she was gone, it was time.

Beneath the table, she gripped Callan's hand and squeezed.

He took a deep breath, quickly scanning the crowd. Would he get everyone's attention?

She leaned in and whispered, "Just announce it to this table. We don't need to make it a huge deal."

His nod was brisk.

Most of the guests were still eating. Uncle Roger's family was much larger than hers, especially with all the new brides and fiancées they'd collected in the past year. They, along with Gram and Pops, filled most of the three tables closest to them.

Every member of the Wright family was about to be lied to.

Her stomach twisted. How could she do this to the people she loved most in the whole world?

But the waiters and waitresses would overhear, along with the bartender she'd never seen before, who looked like he was ready for a fight. Robert, the club manager, was on the patio now. If Ghazi had men here, they'd know what was going on. And that was the point.

Callan cleared his throat. "We have an announcement to make."

Mom and Alyssa's sisters homed in on him instantly.

Dad's eyes narrowed to dangerous slits.

And somehow the other Wrights must've heard, because amid a chorus of *shhhs* and *quiets,* they turned, some actually shifting their chairs to get a better view.

At the nearest table, Summer, Grant's wife, watched with a combination of curiosity and concern. Michael had called Grant for a favor and had probably shared at least the short version of what was going on. No doubt, Grant had told Summer.

Grant had slipped Alyssa a package right after she'd introduced Callan to him, whispering in her ear, "We're here if you need us."

Fortunately, the package was small enough to fit into the tiny lavender purse Brooklynn had insisted she carry.

Callan stood and pulled Alyssa to her feet, though she'd have preferred to remain sitting. Or to escape to the bathroom.

"First, what I'm about to tell you is a secret. I haven't told"—he faltered, swallowed—"Peri, which is a long story, but I'd like it to remain a secret from her, for now."

A few nodded, some tilted their heads in curiosity.

Beyond the Wright family, others were cluing in on the fact that something was going on. People stood to get better views.

Kenzie, Cici, and Delaney leaned in.

Brooklynn took out her camera.

But Dad angled back and crossed his arms. "Go on." The words sounded like a dare.

"I know it's brand new," Callan said, focusing on the women, "and I know you all probably think it's too soon. But when you know, you know."

Mom gasped, her gaze flicking between them.

Dad looked murderous.

Callan lifted their joined hands and kissed her knuckles. "I asked this beautiful, amazing woman to be my bride. And she said yes."

The table exploded in shouts and exclamations.

Mom and all her sisters jumped from their seats, along with most of the Wrights.

Within seconds, Alyssa and Callan were surrounded.

He was receiving hugs and slaps on the back.

Alyssa was passed from family member to family member, their surprise and congratulations coming too fast for her to process.

Callan stayed close, proving much more capable of handling

the mass of questions being hurled at them, answering with quickness and kindness.

And then, her sisters and cousins shifted out of the way, and Dad pushed through the throng.

He stopped in front of Callan, a little too close. "Why haven't you told your daughter?"

Callan stiffened, glaring—actually *glaring*—at Dad.

Nobody stood up to him like that.

She jumped in. "His father had a heart attack, so—"

"That's my business, sir." Callan squeezed her hand but didn't look away from Dad.

Who stepped closer—far too close for a social situation. "Too cheap to buy her a ring?"

"Dad, we're waiting until—"

"Of course not." Callan slipped his hand into his sports coat and pulled out a box.

What in the world?

He turned his back on Dad—another thing most people didn't dare to do—and faced Alyssa.

What was happening?

He opened the box and...

Her hand flew to her mouth, covering her gasp.

Three diamonds. She didn't know carats from carrots, but the center stone was big, and the two at its side were only marginally smaller. Baguettes adorned the band. The silver-colored metal was probably platinum.

It was the most beautiful ring she'd ever seen.

"When did you...?"

"It was my great-grandmother's. If you don't like it, we can get you a new one, but—"

"No, it's perfect." Tears stung her eyes, as if this was real. As if it could ever be.

He slipped it onto her finger. It fit perfectly, which wasn't a sign. Of course it wasn't.

But in that moment, the smallest hint of truth slipped past her defenses.

She wished it were a sign. Wished it were real.

Mom and her sisters bent closer to look.

"It's dazzling." Mom's eyes were swimming when she lifted her gaze to Alyssa. "Just like you." She squeezed Alyssa's arm, then pulled Callan into a hug, whispering something into his ear.

Meanwhile, Brooklynn was snapping pictures, capturing their lies for all eternity.

"Come on," her cousin Derrick yelled. "That deserves a kiss."

Alyssa's cheeks pinked, and she looked up at Callan, unsure what to do.

His quick peck on her lips was met with boos.

"You can do better than that!" That came from the second-youngest cousin, Bryan. Weren't they supposed to be grown men now? Derrick had a kid, for crying out loud.

Callan's eyebrows hiked.

In for a penny, in for a pound, as they said.

He slid his hands along her hips and around to her back, pulling her against his chest.

Her heart nearly exploded with anticipation and desire and all the things she should definitely not be feeling.

But that reminder flitted away when he dove in.

This kiss shouldn't have meant anything. Unlike their kiss in his kitchen the night before, this one was all for show.

But it did mean something. To her, it meant something.

Callan dipped her low, putting on a believable display for her family, earning catcalls and applause.

But the ruckus was drowned out by the feelings, all the conflicting feelings, scrolling across her heart.

*All for show. It's all for show.*

*But did it have to be?*

*Why couldn't it be real?*

Never, never in her life had she wanted someone the way she wanted this man. It wasn't just physical desire, it was a heart-deep yearning for what he offered. Intelligence, kindness, gentleness. Connection.

Did he feel it? Or was it all one-sided?

He raised her to her feet again, then held her just far enough away to see her face. For the briefest moment, he looked tortured as he leaned in and whispered, "I'm sorry."

The same words he'd said to her after their last kiss, moments before he'd rejected her.

The wound was sharp and deep and would certainly leave a scar.

Alyssa backed away, took off the ring, and handed it back. "I'll wear it after we tell Peri."

He nodded, returning it to the box, and then the box to his pocket.

Dad clamped a hand on Callan's upper arm "Come with me. Now."

"Dad." Worry had Alyssa's volume rising. "What are you doing?"

Callan didn't move except to step closer to her father. He leaned in, lowering his voice, but she was near enough to hear. "Take your hand off me, sir, or we're going to have a problem."

Whoa.

She'd never seen anybody talk to Dad like that.

They stared at each other.

Alyssa wanted to do something to lessen the tension, but Callan wouldn't thank her, and her father didn't need her help.

The people close enough to witness the interaction quieted, watching. Fortunately, most of the guests were oblivious.

Finally, Dad loosened his grip. He swiveled and marched away, expecting Callan to follow.

Callan moved in as if to kiss Alyssa's cheek, whispering, "Keep an eye on Peri, please."

"I'll go join them."

"No, you need to—"

"I'll take my sisters. It'll be fine."

His expression look...tortured. "Please, take care of yourself too."

At her nod, he followed the route her father had taken through the throng of guests and into the building.

She wanted to follow, to know what was going on, but Callan trusted her to make sure Peri was safe. She wasn't going to let him down.

# CHAPTER THIRTY-TWO

Callan found Gavin in the hallway near the expansive foyer, speaking to Robert.

"Your preferred room is available," the club employee said.

Callan didn't know how much Gavin knew, but the time for pretenses was past. "A different room, please."

Gavin gave him a squint-eyed glare, but Callan ignored it.

Robert waited until Gavin gave a quick nod.

"The library, then."

The library lived up to its name with books stacked floor to a fifteen-foot ceiling on dark mahogany shelves, complete with rolling ladders. Deep, plush armchairs and sofas were arranged around coffee tables.

All it needed were men in smoking jackets, puffing on pipes.

The place was empty except for a woman wearing yoga pants and a T-shirt reclined in a reading nook. A nice, normal-looking woman, clearly welcome in this very masculine space.

Robert, the manager/valet led them to a door at the back that opened to a tiny room housing a partners' desk with rolling leather chairs on each side. A large window gave Callan a view of the ocean and jetty.

He spotted his daughter outside kneeling on one of the rocks, her tiny hand reaching for something.

Levi was with her. They seemed to have made fast friends as the babysitter looked on. The guard was a few feet back, head on a swivel as if threats could come from any direction.

Alyssa and her sisters meandered along a narrow stretch of sand separating the building from the rocky shore. Talking. Laughing. Perfectly at ease.

Callan saw nobody else. No terrorists moving in. No boats getting too close. They were safe. For now.

"I trust this will work?" Robert asked.

"Yes, thank you." Gavin closed the door behind him, then got in Callan's face. "What are you playing at?"

"I don't know what you mean, sir. Unless you expected me to ask you for Alyssa's hand, but she's—"

"Cut the act, *Caleb*."

No doubt the man knew that wasn't his name, but how? And, more importantly, how much more did he know?

Rather than ask, Callan sealed his lips and waited.

Another standoff, while Peri was out there, surrounded by danger. He didn't like it, but an idea had been niggling at the back of his mind since the first moment he'd met Gavin Wright.

Callan had to know, but he couldn't risk asking.

"It's one thing for you to pretend to be *dating* my daughter, but to pretend you're engaged? That kiss was out of bounds. You'd better watch yourself. You'll have me to answer to."

Callan crossed his arms, lifted his eyebrows.

They were closing in on the truth now.

"Who do you think got you involved in all of this?"

And there it was. The phone call Callan had received, the

odd tip sending him to that restaurant the other night. The person who'd worked so hard to disguise his voice.

Alyssa's father.

"Up until we got here, I didn't have a clue. Why me?"

"Because you and she went to college together. Because I thought you were smart and quick on your feet. I thought you'd protect her."

"That's what I've done. That's what I'm still trying to do."

"Let me rephrase." Gavin hadn't so much as leaned away. "Protect *all* of her. From evil. From terrorists. That's what I expected. Not for you to take advantage of her."

"I didn't." He worked hard to keep his voice from rising. "I wouldn't. And considering *you're* the one who got us into this—"

"Not me. I'm the one trying to get you out of it. Without getting my daughter's heart trampled to pieces in the process."

"It's all for show."

Now, it was Gavin's turn to press his lips closed.

And okay, fine. It hadn't *all* been for show. He didn't know about Alyssa, but his heart was definitely involved.

"Inasmuch as I'm enjoying our little showdown, *sir,* a woman and a child are out there—my daughter and yours—and they need protection." Callan settled in the leather chair where he could keep one eye on Alyssa and Peri, nodding to the chair on the opposite side of the desk. "It's time for you to tell me everything."

The man glared a few more seconds, then plopped himself down. "You first."

"Uh-uh. You started this circus. I want to know how you knew Alyssa was meeting with Ghazi. I want to know why you sucked me into it. I want to know everything you know." He made a show of looking at his watch—a fairly decent brand that looked cheap compared to the one on the other man's wrist. "And try to make it quick."

He was pushing it, but he couldn't let Gavin intimidate him. *Start how you mean to go on*. That was what Dad always told him. If he backed down now, he'd be cowering forever.

Not that it mattered. It wasn't as if Gavin was going to be his father-in-law. But he needed the man's respect.

He expected Gavin's face to flush with anger, so the smile surprised him. "I'm trying to like you, Callan. I didn't know about the kid. She's your daughter?"

"She is. My parents were taking care of her, but my father really did have a heart attack. I was in a bind. I'd have done anything to protect her from this, but we didn't have time to make arrangements. I ran out of options."

"If you'd called me, I'd have found a suitable babysitter."

"If I'd known who you were when you got me involved, I might have considered it. Why didn't you identify yourself?"

Gavin lowered his elbows to the desk and tented his fingers. "Dariush Ghazi is a very dangerous man. I needed to make sure Alyssa was safe."

Not an answer, but Callan didn't push it. "How did you know they were meeting?"

"I got a tip from an old friend at another agency gathering intel on Ghazi. She told me Alyssa's name had come up in a conversation and related the date and time of their meeting."

"Why not just call Alyssa and tell her not to go?"

"I wasn't supposed to know about it."

"She's your daughter. You think she'd turn you in?"

"I heard you were a decent agent, Templeton. If you were Ghazi, working with the daughter of a spy—and make no mistake, he targeted her for a reason—don't you think he'd found a way to tap her phone? I had exactly one hour before the meeting, not enough time to get to the city and protect her myself.

Not another way to reach her without trusting someone else, and I had no idea who I could trust."

"So you sent me."

"I sent an old friend of hers who I *thought* would protect her."

Callan didn't defend himself. Alyssa was alive and well, thanks to him, and Gavin knew that. "Tell me everything your NSA contact told you about what Ghazi is up to."

He'd guessed the agency and was rewarded when the man's lips hardened at the corners. He was good, keeping his eyes from widening, but surprise was nearly impossible to mask completely.

"Not much." Gavin laced his fingers, tapping the pointers together. "I know he's been in the country since at least March. I know he rented a place in Brookline, where a number of questionable people work and reside. I know the Agency has tried to listen in using long-range listening devices, but nothing actionable has come of it. They hear everyday conversations, but nothing helpful."

"They work in the basement," Callan said.

Now, Gavin didn't bother hiding his surprise, the wrinkles in her forehead deepening. "Explain how you know that."

"When you're finished."

"That's all I know." Gavin must've read his skepticism because he added, "We're on the same side, Templeton."

"It sure doesn't feel like it."

Gavin sat back. "What does Ghazi want from Alyssa?"

This was where it got dicey. Malcolm had explicitly told Callan that Gavin might not be trustworthy. But Malcolm hadn't been able to dig up squat about the bombing in Kirkuk—information that should have been easy to get via military records.

Callan had been too busy to gather the intel himself, what

with Dad's heart attack and Peri, but Malcolm had been around longer and had a lot more sources than he did. If the information was out there, he should have been able to find it.

Meaning someone had gone to a lot of trouble to hide something.

There was a reason the Wright family had been targeted. Callan knew this man was the reason, and maybe that bombing was the connection.

Maybe not, but it was worth a shot.

He took a leap and prayed it wasn't a mistake. But first...

"How long has Robert worked here?"

The question startled him. "Years. Why?"

"You trust him?"

"As much as I trust anybody. You don't, though. That's why you didn't want to use my regular room."

"If this is about you, then Ghazi could have people watching you. Robert stood out to me. He doesn't fit the part. And at the party—"

"The bartender."

A man didn't become an *old* spy without knowing a thing or two.

"I've got security," Gavin said. "Nobody's going to touch your daughter or Alyssa."

"But how much did they hear? How much did they know? I assume Ghazi has people here, which is why we did the whole engagement-and-ring show. This party was our excuse for getting out of the city. We're trying to keep Ghazi from suspecting that she's turned against him."

Gavin took the information in. "I figured. That's why I entertained your daughter. I assumed you didn't want them to know about her. But then, when you announced your engagement—"

"I couldn't see another way to protect her from our lie."

He'd asked the guests not to tell Peri, and in doing so, revealed his connection to her. "Thank you for trying."

Gavin lifted a shoulder and let it fall. "I did get you into this." The moment of kindness passed. "Now, explain what Ghazi wants from Alyssa."

It occurred to Callan that Gavin could've just asked Alyssa. Odd that he hadn't. Odd that he'd kept his part in this secret—and continued to keep it secret from Alyssa.

Another puzzle piece that needed to be placed somewhere.

"She's done other jobs for him in the past. She's turned over everything he hired her to do before—nothing worrisome. But on Wednesday night, he hired her to find the name of a Russian. He only had an IP address and a vague idea of the man's recent travel. Even without her tools..." Which reminded Callan. "Did you know her apartment was broken into?"

A frown. "I haven't talked to her."

"If it was Ghazi, then he's a very good liar."

"Who do you suspect?"

"Either rivals of his or an agency trying to make it look like a burglary."

"I'll find out if it was us. Go on."

"Even without her high-tech equipment, she uncovered the Russian's name that night."

"Did she give it to Ghazi?"

"She told him she's still looking, and he seems satisfied with that answer."

"The name?"

"Yefim Lavrentiy."

If Callan hadn't been watching very closely, he might've missed the slight widening of Gavin's eyes, a micro-second of his mouth opening.

"Who is he?" Gavin asked.

Callan sat back, resting his elbows on the armrests. "You tell me."

Gavin has schooled his features. After a moment, he smiled. "Sputnik."

"The satellite?"

"It was his codename."

Callan thought it through. "Because he's always watching?"

That earned a quick grin. "Precisely. Sputnik was a low-level SVR agent in Iraq, tasked with discovering and relating the locations of American personnel to his higher-ups, who passed them on to enemy forces. But while he was serving his country, his wife got pneumonia. Easily cured, but the doctors near their country house where she was staying missed it. By the time he learned about it, it was too late. She was dead. I'd heard rumblings that he was furious, believing his country should've taken better care of her. It's a long story, as these things tend to be, but we turned him."

By *we,* Callan guessed Gavin meant *I*.

Impressive.

"Sputnik has remained with the SVR all these years, moving up in the ranks, passing intel to us. Good intel, mostly."

"Mostly?"

He wagged his head. "A few times, he's given us faulty intel, but he had to do it to throw off suspicion."

"Any chance one of those times led to a bombing in Kirkuk?"

Gavin straightened. "How do you know about that?"

"That bombing killed Dariush Ghazi's girlfriend."

Gavin took that information in. Callan imagined the man flipping through file folders in his head, filling in blanks. Making connections.

Callan had heard a lot of stories about Gavin Wright. What he knew, and what he saw now, was that the man was very, very good at what he did. Hopefully, he was also trustworthy.

"How do you know?" Gavin asked.

"What else can you tell me about Lavrentiy?"

"Sputnik." The reminder of the codename was a subtle chastisement. "I heard the SVR suspects him. There was a botched mission in Germany he was involved in. I was out of the loop, so I don't know what happened, but I guess his higher-ups suspected he'd tipped somebody off."

"Munich? Last fall?"

Eyes narrowed, Gavin nodded. "Sounds right."

"A cache of weapons had been hidden in Bavaria." Weapons of mass destruction. Biological, he'd heard. "Your friend Sputnik had nothing to do with the mission falling apart. Your nephew, Bryan, and his fiancée, Sophie, thwarted it. Well, and Michael and his team."

That had Gavin straightening. "What are you saying? How did that—?"

"Doesn't matter. Michael filled me in. They confirmed that the Russian who'd been sent to buy the weapons was your former asset."

Apparently, Michael had had the one man they'd taken into custody questioned. Mahmoud had confirmed that Lavrentiy—Sputnik—had been the buyer.

Maybe Sputnik had never planned to pass the WMDs along to Putin's government. Callan hoped that was the case. Either way, he'd never had the chance. Michael's team had secured the weapons and whisked them out of Germany.

"Why didn't I know about that?" Gavin asked. "Why wouldn't Michael fill me in himself? I can't believe my nephews were involved. Is that who attacked Roger's house last winter? Why didn't they tell me? Michael knows I could've helped."

Callan shrugged.

"Tell me, son."

Son? Nice touch.

"Some at the Agency question your loyalty."

"Why? Because I left?" For the first time, Callan heard anger—or maybe betrayal in Gavin's voice. "Because I'd had it with being away from my family, with lying to people all the time? Because I'd put in my time and wanted out?"

"I think it's more about the wealth you've amassed in such a short period of time."

"I'm good at what I do." When Callan didn't react, he added, "I'm loyal to my country."

"Okay."

He squinted. "You're not sure."

"I'm telling you what I was told. I was directed not to share any of this with you. I'm putting my career on the line with this conversation."

Gavin rubbed his lips together, looking out the window.

Callan followed his gaze.

Alyssa and her sisters were on the jetty now. Alyssa was crouched beside Peri, who pointed at something in the water.

Brooklynn was snapping pictures. It seemed she always had that camera in her hand. Based on the photos displayed in her apartment, she was very talented.

"They're safe." Was Gavin trying to reassure Callan, or himself?

"Why would Ghazi want Sputnik's name?" Callan asked. "And what does it have to do with the bombing that killed his girlfriend?"

Gavin leaned forward and tented his fingers again. "Sputnik gave us—gave *me*—faulty information. I should've known…" He looked down, shaking his head. "He was the first person I'd ever turned. I didn't have the experience yet to pick up the signs. Everything he'd told me before that had been spot-on, so I took his intel at face value. We'd heard there were Iraqi troops hiding in Kirkuk, and he confirmed with coordinates. We targeted the buildings. We were wrong. They were filled with..." He fell silent, then heaved a sigh. "This is why I got out. Because there's only so much you can take knowing what your mistakes cost people. Nearly a hundred students, dead, because I'd trusted him."

Gavin gazed out the window again. "I almost killed him. I wanted to, but..." Finally meeting Callan's eyes, he shrugged. "It's the job. He was trying to prove his loyalty to his higher-ups. If he'd passed on the Iraqi's actual troop locations, he'd have been discovered. Over the years, he's saved ten times the number of lives lost that day. He justified it—they hadn't been American lives, after all." Gavin scoffed. "As if that would help me sleep at night."

"I'm sorry that happened."

Gavin bristled. "I don't need your sympathy. I'm just telling you what happened."

"Are you still in contact with him?"

"Not in years. Not since I got out."

"Any idea what he's up to?" At the man's quick head-shake, Callan asked, "Could you find out? And let me know."

"I'll make some calls. Now, it's your turn. Tell me everything that's happened."

Callan did, starting with Alyssa's meeting with Ghazi at the restaurant four days ago. Felt like a lifetime.

He gave Gavin the short version while the man studied him with an unwavering gaze.

At the mention of drones, his jaw tightened.

When he learned Callan and Alyssa had been taken to the Brookline house, his stoic facade disappeared. "How could you let that happen?"

"Please, tell me what I should've done differently."

"Gotten her to a safe place, far away."

"And left you and your family vulnerable?"

His mouth opened, then snapped shut.

"As you know, things aren't always so cut-and-dried. I got her out of there."

"You might not've."

As if Callan hadn't figured that out all by himself. As if Callan hadn't experienced that race through the woods, nearly sacrificing his own life to ensure her escape.

"Our excuse for leaving was this party, so we had to come."

"For leaving, but you went out the window."

"She told Ghazi that it was my idea, that I got a bad feeling and insisted we sneak away, not alert the guards."

"He bought that?"

"Alyssa is very, very good. I have no idea what kept her out of the CIA, but..."

His words trailed at the quick wince on Gavin's face, not hidden quickly enough.

"It was you. You blocked her."

"You know what this business is like. You think I want my daughter involved? I've given enough for this country. No way was I going to sacrifice my firstborn."

"And you never told her?"

"She'd have been furious."

"You might've trusted her with the truth. You might've told her exactly what you just told me. You might've indicated to her that you believed she was capable but loved her too much to let her risk her life."

"I don't see how it's any of your business, *Caleb*, how I talk to my daughter."

"Just saying, *Gavin*. It might help her to know you think she's competent. That you're proud of her."

"Of course I am."

Callan didn't bother pressing his point. The man had heard, whether he cared or not.

"What happens now?" Gavin asked.

"We need a safe place so I can put the rest of these puzzle pieces together and Alyssa can create the false zero-day exploit to send to Ghazi, if it comes to that."

"When he figures it out, he'll kill her."

"Which is why we have to stop him. But we need to know the target. We need to know what he's attempting to do, and for whom."

"Okay." Gavin stood. "I'll shake some branches, see what falls out. Meanwhile, you and Alyssa go somewhere away from here. Peri will come home with us."

"I'm not comfortable with that."

"My house has more security than you can offer. Plus, it lends credence to the idea that she's a part of our family, not yours—assuming Ghazi didn't pick up on the part of your announcement. I'll ask Brooklynn to come home with us, too, since you arrived together. I promise, I'll keep her safe."

Callan didn't like it, not one bit. But it was a good solution. If Ghazi tired of waiting and decided to send his goons after Alyssa, Callan didn't want Peri anywhere close by.

He stood and reached across the table to grip the man's hand. "I might not be your future son-in-law, but I've put everything on the line for Alyssa. I expect you to do the same for Peri."

"Trust me, son. I won't let anything happen to her."

Trust him. There was the rub.

# CHAPTER THIRTY-THREE

Alyssa bent to Peri's level. "You'll have a blast at our house with Brooklynn. Your daddy and I will see you soon."

They were in the country club foyer. The guests had left, and Uncle Roger and Aunt Peggy had taken Gram and Pops, so only Alyssa's immediate family remained.

The little girl held on tightly. "You promise?"

Alyssa kissed her forehead. "I promise." She backed away, and Callan swooped Peri into his arms and walked away with her.

Alyssa hugged her sisters and Mom goodbye.

Dad stood a few feet away, watching with a guarded expression. She hadn't learned what he and Callan had talked about, but she had a feeling Dad knew everything now.

Fear had her approaching slowly. He must be furious with her. And so disappointed. But she didn't see either of those emotions on his face, only worry.

"Great party, Dad."

He grunted and pulled her into a tight embrace. "Call me if you need anything."

Yes, Callan had told him. But...but he wasn't angry with her.

"I'm sorry you're involved in this." He held her tight, so tight, as if he feared letting her go. "You be careful." His whisper was so low that she had to strain to hear him. "Take care of yourself." And then, even lower, "You're important...to me. To our family. I tried to protect you, and...I failed."

Oh.

Tears filled her eyes, embarrassing tears that he saw when he held her away from himself.

"None of this is your fault, Dad."

"All of it is my fault."

What? How?

But he didn't explain, just pressed a kiss to her forehead. "I love you."

He was scared. For her.

Her anxiety spiked.

"I love you, too, Dad." She wanted to ask him to explain, but Callan was waiting at the door, eager to leave.

She joined him for the walk along the pretty grounds to his Mustang.

They were far outside of earshot when she said, "What did Dad say?"

Callan smiled at her but shook his head.

In the car, he talked about the people he'd met, the event, the news they'd shared.

"Your dad grilled me good." Callan's laugh sounded authentic. "He was ticked I didn't talk to him before I proposed. And I think he's worried it's too soon, but you can't blame him for that. It probably feels sudden."

Callan think the car was bugged.

She didn't ask where they were going but was certainly

curious what he was thinking when they reached the Portland Headlight, an iconic lighthouse just down the coast.

He parked and then took her hand and led her away from the Mustang, but not inside the keepers' quarters-turned-museum, instead wandering around the side of the building. When they were near the shore, the crashing of waves breaking against the rocks below, he told her everything he'd shared with her father, and everything he'd learned.

She struggled to take it all in.

Lavrentiy was a double-agent called Sputnik. He'd fed Dad bad intel that led to the bombing that killed Ghazi's girlfriend.

Ghazi was still seeking revenge, twenty years later. Somehow, he'd put together the connection between Alyssa's father and the Russian double-agent.

"Talk about playing the long game," she said.

Callan faced the churning Atlantic.

Now they knew Ghazi's motivation, but how could the information help? What should they do with it?

Why now? Why the deadline? Just to keep her from talking? To keep her moving fast, or was there something going on?

"The meeting," she said. "Monday."

Callan's gaze snapped to hers. "What meeting?"

"Dad has to be in DC for something on Monday. That's why we had the anniversary party today instead of on Gram and Pop's actual anniversary. Well, that and Dad wanted to do the whole big party. But I remember them talking about it at Michael's wedding, how my grandparents would've preferred a more intimate gathering, but Dad had insisted. He got defensive and finally admitted that he was going to be out of town on their anniversary." She shrugged. "It's probably not related, but Ghazi told me he needed the zero-day exploit working by tomorrow, which would give him him plenty of time to ensure he knew what he was doing. And since Dad was Sputnik's handler—"

"It could be something. We'll ask your dad about it." Callan's expression softened. "I am sorry about the kiss. I wasn't sure—"

"No need to apologize."

He looked away. She tried to read his thoughts in his profile. His jaw was tight, his lips pressed closed. Had the kiss meant more to him than he'd said?

It'd meant way too much to her.

Even if her body survived whatever happened next, her heart was in serious jeopardy.

"Out of curiosity," she said to change the subject, "why are we here?"

"Leaving the car unattended was a risk."

"The club is very well guarded," she said. "I doubt somebody could've snuck out to the lot."

He gave her a look—chin down, eyebrows up. "Always assume your enemy is one step ahead." He turned his attention to the sea again. "Even if they didn't bug it, it's likely they put a tracker on it. I assume they did since I didn't pick up a tail. I rented a car under another alias, which will be delivered to a hotel. We'll take an Uber there, and we'll get a room so you can build the zero-day exploit."

"The *false* zero-day."

"Right. I just wanted to stop here and make sure we weren't followed. While you're working on that, I'll try to put all these pieces together and figure out what happens next."

Amazing what a strategic thinker Callan was. Alyssa was good at the tech side of things, but her mind didn't work the way his did, seeing the entire chess board and all the possible moves in advance.

She prayed Callan wouldn't miss anything. And prayed she could do her part, little as it might be, to keep them all safe.

That thought was still resonating inside her when her phone rang. She showed Callan the screen, then put it on speaker so he could hear. "Hey, Dad."

"You need to get back here, now."

Alyssa was used to her father issuing commands. But she'd never heard that tone. He sounded...afraid.

Her stomach clenched.

Callan snatched the phone. "What happened?"

"Their car was ambushed on the way out of the club. With Evelyn and Brooklynn and...and Peri. Jock is dead. Your daughter... Peri was taken."

ALYSSA DROVE MUCH FASTER than was wise on the winding roads.

Beside her, Callan was on the phone. "Now. Take him now!"

Issuing orders to his boss.

Malcolm's voice was clear and calm over the car's speakers. "I've already contacted law enforcement—"

"You're giving him time to prepare!" His shout bounced off the windows and metal in the small car. "Get in there. Get the information."

"I know what I'm—"

"This is my daughter!" His voice cracked. "My child. Find her. You have to find her. Do whatever you have to do. Or I'll do it. He has to tell us where she is."

Callan was banking on the idea that Ghazi was still in the Brookline house. Malcolm had agents watching the gated entrance. According to them, Ghazi hadn't left the property.

Malcolm had confirmed that they'd picked up the typical noises from within—the grinding of beans, the steaming of the coffee maker, the ding of the microwave. People's voices, always talking about nothing important. As if they knew they were being surveilled.

It was that last part that worried her. If Ghazi knew, then would he sit there and wait to be taken into custody?

Alyssa doubted it, but she wasn't about to say so to Callan, who was already out of his mind with worry. Instead, she drove and prayed hard. She couldn't stand the thought of sweet little Peri in the hands of those evil, evil men.

It seemed hours had passed since they'd left the country club by the time she whipped the Mustang to the gate. Normally, Dirk would wave her through. This time, he came out of his guard shack, peered into the backseat, then directed her to open the trunk.

He was taking security very seriously, just a little too late.

"We need to get in there." Callan vibrated with fury and fear. When he reached for the door handle, she slipped her hand around his arm.

"It's because of Peri. They're ensuring no other enemies get inside."

Callan pierced her with a look of murder, with the eyes of a lion whose cub was threatened. Anybody who got between Callan and Peri would not survive.

"I know you're scared." She kept her voice low so Dirk wouldn't hear through the open windows. "But you need to think. Your daughter needs you to think."

He pulled his lips in, closed his eyes. He shifted to take her hand, gripping it like it was his only hold on sanity.

"You're all set, Ms. Wright."

She thanked Dirk and accelerated through the gate and down the long driveway, not letting Callan go. Up ahead, police cars lined the circle drive. They were about to walk into total pandemonium.

She stopped a hundred yards from the entrance.

"What are you doing? We have to—"

"Callan." She used her left hand to shift into Park. "Look at me."

He did, and the torture in his expression had her own heart ripping in two.

She closed her eyes. "Father, we need You now. Be a shadow over Peri. Wherever she is, let her rest beneath Your divine wings. Direct Your angels to guard her. Be a hedge surrounding her, not just her body, but her heart, her mind, her spirit. Let no harm come to her. You are Peri's refuge and fortress, even now. Even in this." Emotion cracked her words. "Lord, You are our only hope. Use our gifts and talents, the information we've gathered, the expertise You've given us, to guide us to her. Let nothing, nothing prevent us from finding Peri. Shine a spotlight on her, and take us right there. You are able, Father. We trust..." She swallowed a rise of emotion. "We will trust in You. In Jesus's name, amen."

When she opened her eyes, Callan was bent beside her, still gripping her hand. "Amen." He looked up, blinking back moisture.

"You need to focus. I know it's unthinkable, but you need—"

"I know. You're right." He took a breath, blew it out. And his face transformed from tortured father to something else. Something powerful and beautiful and terrifying. "Let's go."

She pulled around the circle drive. There were no waiting valets now, just cops, everywhere.

Dad jogged down the front steps toward them.

Callan opened the door, and she slammed the brakes to keep him from jumping out of the still-moving car.

He charged her father. "You promised me you'd protect her."

Dad lifted his hands. "I sent them with Jock—"

"*You* were supposed to protect her!" Callan's shout was loud enough that golfers on the seventh hole probably heard.

Alyssa pocketed the keys and hurried around the car. "Callan, Dad's not your enemy."

By the pressed-together lips, he wasn't convinced, but he stormed past her father and into the building.

She flashed Dad a look, expecting to see anger. But Dad surprised her.

He looked nearly as tortured as Callan.

She couldn't process that as she followed Callan into the foyer.

Her mother was there, and her sisters. Grant and Summer.

Callan marched straight past them to...Robert?

The club manager's eyes widened, and he stepped back.

Callan gripped him by the neck, shoved him across the floor and against the wall. "Where is she?"

"I don't... I didn't..." The man's words were choked—literally. Callan lifted him so that his feet barely touched the floor. His face turned a deep shade of red.

"Son." Dad's voice was surprisingly gentle. "I trust Robert. Let him go."

If Callan heard, he made no indication.

Alyssa started to move to Callan's other side, to try to coax him down, but Grant gripped her arm and shook his head.

What was happening?

Had Callan lost his mind?

Had everyone?

"I won't kill you," Callan said. "But you'll wish you were dead. You have three seconds to decide."

"Agent Templeton." Dad had shifted from kind to authoritative. "Let him go."

Callan moved closer to Robert. "Three. Two. On—"

"I didn't know!" The manager's rough whisper was desperate. "I didn't know what he was going to do."

Alyssa gasped, and she wasn't the only one.

Dad uttered an epithet.

Callan's knuckles whitened, squeezing harder.

Robert's eyes widened, the eyes of a man who realized he was about to take his final breath. "I swear." He had no volume, nothing but scant air.

Grant gripped Callan's arm. "We need him alive. For now."

Maybe it was the implied promise, but Callan let up his hold.

Robert crumpled to the floor, sucking lungfuls of air.

Nobody moved to help him.

The marble foyer, the overlarge flower arrangement, the ornate moldings. The foyer was just as it'd been when they'd left an hour earlier.

But everything had changed.

Mom and Alyssa's sisters must know everything now. They must know Alyssa and Callan had lied. That it'd all been an elaborate—and useless—ruse.

Summer stood beside them, tall and powerful. Alyssa had secretly admired the tough warrior-woman ever since she'd married Grant. Summer was pregnant, due in a couple of months, but that didn't make her look vulnerable.

This woman was no less fierce than her husband and Callan.

Callan was breathing hard.

Dad wore a look of utter shock.

Robert was curled in the fetal position.

Nobody spoke, all frozen, waiting to see where the next bomb would land.

And then the bartender from the party stepped into the room on the far side, and Callan's wild eyes were back. He marched that direction.

The guy looked like he could handle himself, but he lifted his hands. "I'm with you."

Dad stepped in front of the man. "He's FBI. Counterterrorism."

Callan blinked. "Why? Why are you—?"

"We're being investigated." His gaze flicked to Alyssa. "Both you and me."

Oh. *Oh.*

Of course she was. But Dad?

The FBI distrusted them so much that they'd planted an agent at an anniversary party.

Two hours before, that information would have sent Alyssa into a tailspin of terror.

Right now, she was just grateful the FBI was already there. It didn't matter what happened to her. If she was prosecuted for working with Ghazi... Well, she deserved nothing better.

As long as Peri was rescued, that was all that mattered.

Everyone seemed to wait for her to react, so she said, "Any chance it was you guys who stole my equipment?"

The agent/bartender paused a long moment, then nodded.

"I assume you haven't gotten into it yet."

His lips quirked in an almost-smile. "We've had a team working on it for days."

"Security is sort of my thing. I'll write down the passwords, but what you really need is a thumb drive." She pulled the tiny thing out of the lavender purse Brooklynn had loaned her and held it out. "Next time, just ask."

The man pocketed it.

Dad focused on Mom and Alyssa's sisters. "Can you wait in the library? I don't want anyone leaving here. The club is safe right now, but out there...?" His gaze flicked to the glass doors, the police cars lined along the drive. "I know it's inconvenient, but please, just stay here where it's safe."

"We will, of course." Mom kissed his cheek, then spoke to Callan. "I am so, so sorry. We tried to protect her but..."

"It wasn't your fault." He glared at Dad but didn't say what he was thinking.

Mom squeezed Alyssa's hand. Alyssa saw no judgment, no anger, just love and concern.

Her mother, who'd witnessed an ambush, who'd probably seen a man shot, was worried about Alyssa. She turned to her other daughters. "Come on, girls."

Mom and Alyssa's sisters walked out.

"You too." Grant turned to his wife. "Just in case."

"Are you worried about their safety," Summer asked, "or mine?"

"Can it be both?"

She smirked, then squeezed his hand and followed Mom.

"You, too, sweetheart." Dad spoke to Alyssa.

"Sure. Okay." Not a chance, but Alyssa saw no point in arguing. The country club was crawling with police, one of whom was standing guard at the massive front doors.

She made to follow her mom and sisters but waited around a corner until Callan, Grant, and Dad had taken Robert the other direction.

Then she returned to the foyer and asked one of the police officers to accompany her to the Mustang, just in case Robert wasn't the only person at the club on Ghazi's payroll.

She grabbed her bag and then went to the locker room to change back into her jeans, T-shirt, and cardigan, then spent a few minutes dealing with the package Grant had given her earlier, thankful she'd thought to pilfer needle and thread from Callan's mother's sewing room. She was no seamstress, but she could make this work.

A few minutes with a knife she'd pocketed during lunch and her shoe-polish-black tennis shoes, and she was ready.

She desperately wanted to find out what was going on with Callan and Dad. Instead, she carried the dress, purse, and shoes she'd borrowed from her sister, along with her bag and Callan's —with a second thumb drive in his jeans' pocket—to the library.

She needed to face the music.

The members who'd been at the club that day had all been dealt with and sent home, so Alyssa's family were the only people there, seated on sofas and in wingback chairs.

They'd been talking, but when the door opened, they silenced and turned her way.

Mom stood. "Any news?"

Shaking her head, Alyssa dropped the bags inside the door, approaching her mother. Her sweet, kind, generous mother. "I'm sorry I lied to you." She scanned her sisters, eyes filling with tears for the first time since they'd gotten that terrible call. "I didn't want to do it. We hoped... It's such a long story, but I would never have..."

"Precious daughter." Mom crossed the room and pulled her close.

Alyssa was a few inches taller than her mom, but in that moment, she felt like a little girl again. And wished, so wished, her mother could make everything better.

"I don't know what this is all about," Mom said, "but I know your heart." She gripped Alyssa's shoulders and met her eyes. "You have a beautiful heart. I'm certain that when we hear the story, we'll understand why you did what you did." Her smile was tentative. "That was a lovely ring, though."

Alyssa barked a surprised laugh. "It was." She shifted her

gaze to her sisters, who'd all moved closer. None of them glared at her. None of them seemed angry or upset. Just concerned.

She hugged them, repeated her apology four more times. And each of them, in her own special way, offered forgiveness and grace.

How had she forgotten this? How had she forgotten what it meant to be a sister? A daughter? How had she drifted so far away?

There was no time to analyze her decisions now. If she had the chance, she would fix things going forward.

"I have to go check on Callan."

"Of course. You let us know—"

"I'm sorry," Brooklynn said, "but if nobody else going to say it, I will."

Delaney's eyes widened with worry.

Cici crossed her arms, flashing to the stubborn child she'd once been.

Kenzie grinned.

"Sweetheart," Mom said, "maybe now isn't the time."

But Brooklynn wasn't having it as she scanned the room, turning to include Summer, who'd remained seated on a chair.

The fierce warrior shrugged and smiled.

"What?" Alyssa asked.

"I'm not the only one who saw it, right? How perfect they are together? Her and Caleb. Or...Callan, you said? Wait." Brooklynn straightened. "Callan, as in—?"

"It's nothing." But Alyssa's cheeks were warming. She might've mentioned her college rival a few times to her sister back then.

"*That's* Callan?" Brooklynn's eyebrows hiked. "*The* Callan?"

"It's pretend. It was only..." Was she really going to lie to them again?

No. No, she wasn't. "Fine. Maybe it's not completely... It started out as pretend, but maybe—"

"I knew it!" Brooklynn pumped her hand in triumph. "I told you guys they're prefect together."

"It's not like that." Unfortunately, Alyssa wasn't lying now. "He's made it very clear he's not interested."

"So he's a liar too?" Cici asked.

"Be nice, Ci," Delaney said. "They didn't mean to hurt us." Her head tilted to the side. "It's because of Peri, right? He doesn't know how to love both of you."

Wow. How did her little sister do that? It was as if people's motivations were stamped on their foreheads. "That's what he said, yes. He has to focus on Peri."

Brooklynn said, "But he could—"

"Who's been kidnapped," Alyssa added. "I need to go find out what's going on. Thank you for understanding." She squeezed her mother's hand. "I love you." Shifting to take in the rest of them, she added, "I love you all, and I'm sorry for..."

"Go, sweetheart," Mom said. "We'll be here, praying."

ALYSSA CLOSED THE LIBRARY DOOR, then leaned against it.

Something, something deep inside told her she would never see them again.

*Lord, please, please...*

*Just save Peri. Whatever it takes.*

She pulled in a deep breath, blew it out, and set out to find Callan and her father. Whatever they were doing, she needed to know.

She was halfway across the foyer when her phone vibrated in her pocket. She glanced at the number.

*Unknown.*

But...

She knew who it was. And she knew what he was going to say.

Because there was only one reason for Ghazi to kidnap Peri, and that was to get Alyssa to finish the job he'd hired her to do.

She shifted, moving toward the back hallway, then out onto the patio that'd been the scene of a celebration a not long before.

Her phone vibrated again.

She was afraid to answer.

But this was the price for all her foolishness. And she wasn't about to let an innocent eight-year-old pay it.

She swiped to answer and lifted the phone to her ear. "What do you want me to do?"

# CHAPTER THIRTY-FOUR

Callan itched to wrap his hands around the traitor's throat again, only this time, he wouldn't let up. He longed to see this gray-haired man breathe his last.

But he didn't. Not because of any moral qualms but because he needed to focus.

Alyssa was right about that.

She'd gone with her mother and sisters, and he was glad she was safe and separate from all this craziness. But he wished she were here.

He needed her.

They were in a small, private dining room as lavish as the rest of the club. They'd pushed the table and most of the chairs to one side, then shoved Robert into a chair in the center of the space.

Callan was seated in front of him, inches away.

Grant loomed behind him, making just enough noise to remind the older man he was there. A solid intimidation tactic.

Callan and Grant hadn't had to do much to start Robert talking. They'd threatened him, and when he'd looked at Gavin for help, Alyssa's father had focused on Callan, "Do whatever you have to do. I'll make sure nobody interrupts." And then he stepped out, closing the door behind him.

The man had spilled everything, talking so fast his words tripped over each other on their way out of his mouth.

A man who'd called himself Abraham had paid Robert to put a listening device in the small office where Gavin often conducted business.

Abraham. Very similar to Ebrahimi. As in Fatemeh Ebrahemi, the name of the woman Ghazi had loved.

It all made so much sense.

"When was that?" Callan asked.

"January, I think." He must've seen something in Callan's expression because he hurried to say, "Definitely January."

"How do you remember?"

"It was after that big blizzard. We had to hire extra people to clear the road."

Specific enough memory that Callan believed him.

Robert went on to explain that in February, *Abraham* had paid Robert to pass along information about Gavin.

"What kind of information?"

"He didn't say. Just asked for anything I heard, anything I knew. When he was at the club, when he was going to be gone, who he met with. I didn't think it mattered." His voice was pleading. "Anyone watching the entrance could see when he was here. I thought...I thought..."

Ghazi was a master manipulator. He'd started small, drawing Robert in. A hundred thousand here, another hundred thousand there. Easy money, especially considering, as far as Robert could tell, nothing was being done with the information.

"I didn't plan to pass along anything important," Robert said. "And nothing bad happened to Mr. Wright. I thought, what did it matter? If this fool wanted to pay me, then why not? And I could pay off debts and—"

"Why not?" Callan got in his face. "How about the fact that Gavin Wright is a former intelligence officer with the CIA? How about the fact that your *Abraham* is a terrorist?"

That had color draining from Robert's face. "I didn't know."

"Irrelevant," Callan snapped

Alyssa hadn't known, either, when she'd started working for the man known as Charles.

Grant clamped a hand on Robert's shoulder, and he jumped like a skittish cat.

"For future reference," Grant said, "most terrorists won't tell you up front what they're up to."

"Yes, yes. I..." He seemed unsure what to say. "I was stupid."

"What happened next?"

"This morning, Abraham asked me to add a name to the guest list for the party."

Robert must've told Ghazi all about the party, long before Alyssa had mentioned it.

"One name." His tone was pleading. "Someone called Benson."

The big blond guard had Peri.

Callan's Peri.

"I thought it wouldn't matter," Robert said. "Mr. Wright always has security. I thought—"

"You thought you'd get paid. A man is dead." He'd barely let himself think about the silent guard who'd given his life. "And my daughter is gone. But the devil with whoever got hurt."

Robert's face crumpled, and he dropped his head. "I didn't know. I just...I didn't know."

Yeah.

When Callan's phone rang, he let Grant take over questioning and answered. "Is he in custody?"

"He wasn't there." Malcolm's words were dark as a grave. "The place was empty."

Ghazi had escaped.

Of course he'd escaped. Callan had expected it. Even so, he couldn't help his fury. "You *lost* him?" Callan's raised voice had both Grant and Robert looking at him. He turned his back. "How could you let that happen?"

"Ghazi and his men must've gone through the backyard, like you and Alyssa did."

"That didn't cross your mind?"

"Of course it did." Malcolm seemed to be working for a civil tone. "I don't know what happened, but I'll find out."

"That's going to do me a lot of good. I thought you said they heard people inside."

"They must've recorded days of sounds. It was playing. They fooled us."

Ghazi was ten moves ahead, and Callan was still studying the stupid game board.

"What have you learned?" Malcolm asked.

He filled his boss in, then ended the call and conferred with Grant. They'd gotten all the information they were going to get from Robert.

As much as Callan would like to take out his frustration on the old man's face, nothing mattered except getting Peri back. Not vengeance. Not answers, not unless they led somewhere. And what Robert had to say didn't help. At all.

He summoned two police officers who were waiting just outside the door. Somehow, Gavin had kept them at bay.

The man had some serious pull.

The cops took the club manager, and then Gavin stepped into the smaller room. "Tell me what—"

"You told me you were going to keep her safe," Callan said, "and then you sent her off with—"

"My wife and daughter, and my most trusted guard. Do you think I'd have put any of them in danger?"

"You *did* put them in danger."

"I didn't know, Templeton. I trusted the wrong man. My contact called me as we were leaving. I thought it would be better to get the information right away." His gaze flicked to Grant, as if not wanting to say more in front of his own nephew.

At this point, Callan trusted Grant, whom he'd never heard of before that day, far more than he trusted Alyssa's father. He'd learned Grant had been a Green Beret and then a bodyguard before becoming a detective.

Callan didn't know Grant's story, but he seemed like a soldier who understood. A man who'd fight to save the innocent.

To save Peri.

Callan wasn't so sure about Gavin Wright, but he trusted Grant.

Grant's gaze flicked from one to another, but he said nothing.

"He's fine." Callan sat again, giving Grant a quick update on what they knew about Ghazi, the zero-day exploit, and the spy they assumed was the terrorist's target. He focused on Gavin, asking, "What did you learn?"

Before he could answer, a soft knock sounded on the door, and then Alyssa stepped inside. She'd changed her clothes and pulled her hair back into a ponytail. "Hey." She scanned the room and then approached him, lowering to her knees at his feet. "How are you?"

Stupid emotion clogged his throat. He didn't answer.

Gavin and Grant both stepped away, giving them privacy. Which Callan appreciated because, suddenly, he felt overwhelmed. Overwrought.

"Any news?"

He shook his head. "Nothing important. I think your dad learned something, but I don't know what yet." He expected Alyssa to grab a chair and listen in.

But she didn't move. "I am so sorry this is happening."

"It's not your fault. I shouldn't have left her. I shouldn't have brought her here."

"Don't do that." She settled her cool palms on his face. "You are a good father. And we're going to get your daughter back. I promise."

More than anything, he wanted to believe her. He just didn't know how.

She wrapped her arms around him, holding him, and for the briefest moment, he allowed it. Allowed himself to be weak and honest, trusting Alyssa with this deep, vulnerable part of himself.

"I'm sorry." Her words were barely a whisper as she backed away and stood. "I'm going back to the library to work on the zero-day. We might need it for leverage. You let me know if I can help."

She started to walk away, but he caught her hand.

She turned back to him.

*I love you.*

*I need you.*

But he couldn't say the words.

He couldn't think past the fear clogging his throat.

Alyssa held his eye contact, and he saw everything in her eyes. His own love returned.

His future.

But there was nothing, nothing beyond this moment. There was no future. And if Peri didn't come home, there never would be.

Alyssa let him go and walked away.

Gavin closed the door behind her. "Sputnik is in the States."

Callan had suspected that.

"After the kerfuffle in Munich last fall." He glanced at

Grant. "The one involving Bryan and his fiancé..." He waited, maybe to see if Grant would question him.

The man just nodded for him to continue. If the *kerfuffle* was news to him, he hid it well. Callan guessed that he knew all about what his brothers had been up to.

"Sputnik's higher-ups decided he'd been turned," Gavin said. "They came after him, but he escaped. He's been in hiding and working his way west ever since. He flew to Montreal by way of Paris and made it across the border into Vermont a month ago."

Callan needed this information, but in the short term, how would it help find Peri?

"Monday night." Callan had just remembered what Alyssa said earlier. "You're supposed to be in DC, right?"

The older man's head lowered and rose. "I wasn't sure exactly what it was, only that my presence was requested. The call I got confirmed that there's a private dinner for a handful of people who've been involved with Sputnik over the years, a way to acknowledge the sacrifices he's made."

"How does Ghazi know?"

"He's got a source."

Which meant they needed to keep this circle very small. "Where is this dinner supposed to take place?"

Gavin named a DC hotel. A giant hotel with hundreds of rooms, potentially thousands of guests at any given time.

Callan thought of the zero-day exploit.

He thought of the attack drones that could be commandeered if the exploit were turned over.

He imagined Sputnik, Gavin, and everyone who'd ever supported the double-agent's activities, sitting at tables and sharing stories.

"That's the target," Grant said. "A drone strike could take out the entire hotel and everyone inside."

All in the name of vengeance. But none of it could happen without the zero-day. Which meant...

"Alyssa." Callan launched to his feet.

He should've anticipated...

When she'd come in just now, it wasn't just to check on him. It was to say goodbye.

Gavin's eyes were wide. "What about her?"

Callan shoved out the door, through the deserted dining room.

He was running across the foyer when something outside the glass doors caught his eye.

He skidded, angled that way, and spoke to a uniformed cop standing guard there. "Where's my car?" He pointed to the empty space in the circle drive. "What happened to the red Mustang?"

"Ms. Wright took it," the cop said. "She said you wanted her to..." The man's words faded, clearly reading Callan's expression.

Callan spun to Gavin, who'd followed.

The man's face had paled to paste.

"He called her. He...he must've..." Callan didn't want to face what he already knew.

Ghazi had called Alyssa and demanded she come.

And Alyssa had gone. To save Peri, she'd gone to meet the terrorist.

## CHAPTER THIRTY-FIVE

Alyssa had known it would come to this.

She'd changed out of the dress because she'd known.

She'd taken the package Grant brought for her because she'd known.

She'd agreed when, the previous afternoon, Michael had insisted she be prepared, because she'd known.

Knowing didn't make it any easier.

The phone call from Ghazi had been short but to the point. "A simple trade. Peri for the information I need to take over the drone system."

He was no longer pretending he owned the company he'd hired her to hack. Everything was on the table now.

"The exploit isn't ready, but I can create it."

"Good. You will leave right now. Alone. Tell no one. Get in the car and drive away." He gave her specific instructions, naming roads she'd driven all her life. "I am watching everything, so do not try to alert anyone. Do not try to get help. Do not try to wear a listening device or a tracker. You understand?"

"I understand."

"We will see you leaving the property in five minutes or the girl will be harmed."

"Ten minutes," she said. "I'll have to tell my mother one story and Caleb and my father another. Otherwise, they'll realize I've gone. I can't let them stop me."

Her request was followed by a long stretch of silence.

Alyssa had stared out at the churning Atlantic. The dark blue water reflected a clear sky. In the distance, all seemed calm, but the waves crashing against the jetty told a more violent story.

"Seven minutes."

"It'll take what it'll take, Charles." She congratulated herself on remembering to use his fake name. "Trust me when I tell you, I'll do everything in my power to save Peri."

"Let's stop pretending that *Caleb* is your fiancé, his daughter your future stepchild."

"Irrelevant." She didn't temper her anger. "Peri is a *child*. She deserves protection. I'll be there as soon as I can."

She'd ended the call, praying as she'd hurried to the library to leave her things, that she hadn't pushed the man too far.

Maybe, deep down, she'd hoped Callan would realize what was happening and stop her.

How foolish. How selfish and cowardly.

But she'd played her part. She'd said what she wanted to say and hopefully, he'd read the words she hadn't said.

That she loved him. That no matter what happened, she loved him.

And then she'd driven away, beating Ghazi's deadline by two minutes.

As soon as she hit the main road, she sent the text she'd typed right after she'd hung up with the terrorist.

*It's on. If it doesn't work, tell Callan I'm sorry.*

Grant responded with two words.

*Got you.*

The tracker was working. God willing, Grant and Callan would get her out of this mess. If nothing else, Alyssa would be with Peri. If she could give her life to protect the child's, then that would suffice.

Or, if all she could do was offer the little girl comfort at the end, be with her until she joined her mother for eternity...

*Please, Father. Please...*

Alyssa shook off her fears.

*Focus.*

She drove a mile past the turn she was meant to take, rolled down her window, and tossed her phone into a gully. Then, she did a U-turn and drove back to where she'd been directed to turn.

The two-lane road was narrow and deserted, flanked by thick forest on either side. A few houses sat at the end of long driveways, but nobody was out this afternoon.

The deeper she drove, the higher her anxiety spiked.

Four minutes later, she spotted a parked silver SUV parked ahead. A man stepped out.

It was Benson.

He pointed to the spot in front of the SUV, and Alyssa parked the Mustang and got out, leaving the keys in the ignition for Callan.

He might not get his daughter back, but his car would be found.

What a ridiculous thought.

Benson approached, a gun pointed at her. "You're alone?"

"Yes."

He checked anyway, then nodded toward the SUV.

The passenger door opened, and Ghazi stepped out.

He looked just as he had a few days earlier, but his veneer

had been scraped away. To her, he no longer resembled the polished British entrepreneur he'd pretended to be.

This man was a terrorist. A killer. And he wasn't bothering to hide it anymore.

"Where's Peri?" she asked.

"You didn't think I would bring her with me. I had to ensure you weren't followed by police. Or CIA agents."

Did he mean Dad? Or Callan? Or both?

She tried to keep her face impassive. "You told me to come alone. I came alone."

"I will take you to the child as soon as you've been thoroughly searched." He gave Benson a go-ahead nod.

Alyssa fought the urge to fight as the meaty man pawed at her clothes, her hair, her body. She closed her eyes and took deep breaths and prayed, prayed, prayed.

When he took her shoes off, she knew.

She'd cut a slit into the sole and shoved the narrow disk inside.

But he saw it, pulled it out, and held it up for Ghazi to see.

"A worthy try." The man actually smiled as he took the tracker and flipped it into the woods. "You are good, Alyssa Wright. But I am better."

She hoped she looked suitably horrified at the man's arrogance.

Arrogance that, God willing, would bring him down.

## CHAPTER THIRTY-SIX

"They'll find it!" Callan was pacing. Furious. Horrified. "They'll find it, and when they do, they'll kill her and Peri both."

Grant said nothing.

On the phone, Michael said, "Think it through, man."

*Think.*

Exactly what Alyssa had said to him. *Your daughter needs you to think.*

And now she did too.

He paused his circuit across the makeshift command center.

Gavin loved his daughter, even if he was terrible at showing it.

He'd learned in the last few minutes how much Grant and Michael loved their cousin. That Alyssa had helped Michael more than once. That her work had saved lives.

She'd located the little curly-haired Levi when he was kidnapped.

She'd aided Michael in escaping from Iraq with Leila and Jasmine, who'd eventually married into the Wright family.

Even Gavin seemed surprised by that information.

These men loved Alyssa, and they didn't feel that for Peri, but she was a child.

It went against everything inside him, but he needed to trust these people to help him find and save Peri and Alyssa.

"She saved my life more than once." Michael's voice on the phone was strangely gentle. "I promise you, we will do everything in our power to protect her."

Protect her. Right. They'd practically sent her to Ghazi, who could kill her.

But Callan thought it through.

Ghazi needed her alive.

And he wasn't going to kill Peri, his only leverage to get Alyssa to do his bidding.

So...

"What's the plan?" He directed the words at the phone.

He'd been shocked when he'd learned what these two brothers had cooked up. Without telling him, or her father.

Gavin had been apoplectic. For a few moments there, right after they'd confirmed that Alyssa had really and truly left, Callan had worried her father might have a heart attack. As if they had time for that.

Now, Gavin looked about like Callan figured he'd looked a few minutes before. White as the frosting on the anniversary cake.

"I gave her a decoy tracker," Grant said.

"Explain."

"One of those cheap tags you can get at the drugstore, the kind you stick on your car keys or your dog's collar."

"He'll find it."

"Thus, the term *decoy*." Michael's words were heavy with sarcasm.

If he were here in person, Callan would punch him in the face.

Grant had barely looked up from his phone during the conversation. "She stopped. Both signals are still strong."

Hands clenched so tightly that they ached, Callan crossed to look over the guy's shoulder.

Grant tapped his screen, which showed a blinking orange dot on some skinny road a few miles away. "That's one." He switched to another app. This one showed a steady blue dot in roughly the same spot. "That's the other."

"Ghazi could find them both." Gavin was looking over Grant's other shoulder.

The soldier was tolerating them both in silence, though Callan figured it was taking effort.

"We can't just sit here," Gavin said. "We need to go."

For the first time, Callan agreed with the old spy.

It was all he could do not to steal a car and go on his own. Trusting these guys—and flimsy technology—to save Peri and Alyssa...

It was killing him.

He wanted to go after them on his own. It might even work.

But it might not. It could just as easily destroy everything.

He needed to work as a team with these men he barely knew. He needed to relinquish control.

He opened his hands, stretched them out. Letting it go.

*Whatever it takes to save them, Lord. I'll do whatever You ask.*

"You three can sit here and stare at that stupid phone screen all you want," Gavin said. "I'm going."

Callan gripped his arm, tight. He knew exactly how Alyssa's father felt. But Michael and Grant had done something ingenious. "They're a step ahead of us," Callan said. "We need to be smart about this. We need to work together."

Grant shot Callan a look over his shoulder, clearly surprised.

Callan was a little surprised himself.

If Alyssa had told him what her cousins had planned, he might've eschewed their help. He might've let his pride and his own desperate need to stay in control get in the way.

But his pride was gone.

His need to stay in control? MIA.

Callan didn't care how Alyssa and Peri were rescued. He didn't care that Alyssa's cousins had thought of something that had never occurred to him.

Not because it wasn't an option, but because he'd believed, foolishly, that he had it all under control.

Stupid, stupid pride.

"We're going to work together, Gavin," Callan said, "to bring both our daughters home."

"She's good," Grant said.

Callan looked at the orange dot moving on the phone screen.

The blue one stayed in place.

"They found the decoy." Grant sounded triumphant as he focused on the phone. "Good job, bro. They think they're in the clear." He looked up at Callan, and smiled.

"We've got them." For the first time since this whole thing started, Callan—thanks to these Wright brothers—was a step ahead.

# CHAPTER THIRTY-SEVEN

Alyssa shivered in the cold wind. Why hadn't she brought her jacket?

Ghazi and Benson had loaded her onto a speedboat. Another man was driving. All three of them wore thick, padded winter parkas. The driver had a hood pulled up over his head, so she'd barely gotten a look at his face.

Ghazi sat on one side of her, Benson the other. As if they feared Alyssa might jump into the freezing North Atlantic waters and try to swim for it.

Leaving Peri to her fate.

Poor Peri. She imagined the child, wearing her sweet little flowered dress, taking this same ride. She must've been so afraid.

Alyssa was an adult. She knew Callan, Dad, and Grant were following her progress. And even so, she was terrified.

She tried not to worry about the tracker.

It was working. Grant had confirmed that in his text as she'd driven away.

She'd sewn the tiny thing—no larger than her thumbnail—beneath the hooks in her bra. The fabric there was naturally stiff, and men didn't know bras. Nobody would notice if it was a smidge stiffer in one spot than the rest.

It'd worked. Benson hadn't found it.

Unlike the cheap tracker he *had* found, the one still with her was connected to a satellite. No need for Wi-Fi or phones. Even out here, bouncing across the rough water, it would work.

She watched the shoreline as the sun dipped behind the trees. The forest had always seemed a magical place to her, filled with treasures and mysteries.

Unlike the ocean—vast and cold and cruel.

The Portland Headlight rose in the distance, the white column gold in the setting sun.

She and Callan had been there, together, just a few hours before. Not for any romantic reasons, though she should've told him how she felt. Who cared if he rejected her—again? At least he'd know.

Alyssa had seen the old lighthouse a thousand times, but the familiarity didn't take away from its beauty. Not just because of its old-school Maine charm but because of its purpose.

A beacon to usher sailors home. A sentinel to protect the innocent from the danger lurking beneath the dark waters.

The lighthouse was a protector. In that sense, Callan was the same. A protector.

But if the lighthouse failed, if a sailor went under and never came back up, the light kept on shining, doing its job. Undeterred. Unperturbed.

Unlike Callan, who would never be the same if Peri were lost. Or if Alyssa were. Even if he didn't love her, he cared. He'd risked everything to protect her.

They reached an island within sight of the mainland and unloaded onto a dock. Even on the shore, the wind whipped off the frigid water, and she hugged herself, ignoring the looming presence of the blond-haired Benson, who stayed too close while the driver and Ghazi secured the boat.

Other boats bobbed in the marina, but most were covered with canvas or stored in a shed. There were no street lights, no building lights. No lights at all.

In the fading darkness, Alyssa saw low structures, side by side, lining the opposite edge of a narrow strip of sand.

Beach houses. Tourist rentals. If the sun were up, she might catch sight of a shack that offered lobster rolls in the summertime—hotdog buns slathered with mayo and filled with buttery white shellfish. They'd sell steamed clams, corn-on-the-cob, and cold beer.

There might be an ice cream parlor—or maybe just an ice cream truck.

A couple of souvenir shops, an overpriced grocery store.

But if those places existed, they were closed today. It was too early, too cold, too far from civilization.

The complete lack of lights told her nobody inhabited this island in the off-season.

Alyssa felt completely alone.

They trudged on the packed sand near the shore, then angled across the beach toward the houses. They all looked identical, nothing to distinguish one from another.

The sand squished beneath her sneakers. At least Ghazi had allowed her to put them back on after the tracker was found. She imagined she'd be hypothermic if he hadn't.

They reached a dark bungalow, but now that she was close, she saw slivers of light peeking around the edges.

They climbed the porch steps. A dark number eleven was displayed on the white clapboard beside the black doorway.

Ahead of her, Ghazi pushed the door open, and light spilled out. "After you."

She stepped into glorious warmth.

She wasn't sure what she'd expected, but this place looked exactly like a beach house should. Worn light-colored floors, whitewashed walls, kitschy blue and green knickknacks. A ceiling fan hung in the living room, a white shell dangling from the pull-cord. The kitchen was small but utilitarian. The backsplash was painted with fish, starfish, and seahorses in various shades of blue

On the far wall, a sign made from old fenceposts read *Beach Rules: Relax, Unwind, Enjoy.*

Plywood was nailed over the windows. A space heater pumped warm air into the small common area.

Two men had stood from the denim sectional as soon as Ghazi walked in. She guessed they'd been playing a video game —looked like some kind of flying simulator—on the TV.

Peri sat in the corner of the sofa, knees pulled to her chest, arms wrapped around them. Eyes wide, flicking from Alyssa to the men who'd accompanied her.

"Sweetheart." Alyssa ignored the guards and rushed to the little girl.

One of the guards stepped out of the way, and Alyssa sat beside Peri, gathered her into her arms, and held her close.

Peri sobbed. Her little nose was cold, pressed against Alyssa's collarbone. She trembled in her arms.

"It's okay, sweetheart. Your daddy sent me to be with you, to take care of you." She glared at Ghazi. "You couldn't spare a blanket?"

"My apologies." He seemed not a bit concerned as he flicked a gaze to one of his men. "Take care of it."

"She couldda asked," the skinnier of the guards grumbled. He sat at the end of the sofa, focus on the screen again.

The other man disappeared down a back hallway. He returned a moment later with a comforter he'd probably pulled off a bed. He draped it over them.

She hadn't realized how cold she was until the that moment. She snuggled Peri closer and ground out a "Thank you" to the guard. Her life was in these men's hands now. She needed to be very careful.

She whispered, "Are you hurt?"

Peri didn't speak, but she shook her head.

"Are you sure? You can tell me."

The child looked up with wide eyes and shook her head again.

"Good. It's going to be okay." She rocked Callan's daughter, holding her close, wanting to tell her that her daddy was on his way. That he'd rescue them.

But she couldn't risk it.

Ghazi had chosen this island, this house—just one of many lining the shore—for a reason.

The driver of the boat hadn't come inside with them. Yet his plan couldn't have been to leave the island, considering he'd made the trek all the way to the beach house. Which meant he was elsewhere. With other men?

Probably.

But how many? And where were they?

Even though Callan had their location, there was no guarantee he'd be able to get to them.

Ghazi was a step ahead, as always.

Alyssa and Peri might be on their own.

# CHAPTER THIRTY-EIGHT

Callan had been going a little crazy, watching Alyssa's location skim across the ocean.

Since no planning could be done until they knew where she was headed, he'd forced himself to leave Grant and Gavin to track her.

Callan needed to walk away for a few minutes, to think. And pray.

He headed for the library. When he pushed on the door, Summer stopped it from opening all the way. She saw who it was and then stepped aside.

Apparently, the tall, pregnant blond was playing the part of bodyguard today.

Alyssa's mother and sisters stood when they saw him, their expressions begging for good news.

But fearing the worst.

"She's still on the move," he said. "No news."

Evelyn stepped around her chair toward him. "We're praying. I'm so sorry about Peri." Tears hovered in her eyes. "I didn't know what to do."

She'd already apologized once.

"There was nothing you could do. I'm sorry I put you in danger. I didn't anticipate..."

"They'll find them, Mom." Brooklynn gripped her hand, and the other sisters hovered as well. All as afraid, as terrified, as he was. "What can we do?"

"Just keep praying. There's nothing more important than that. I was hoping..." He looked around, and his gaze snagged on his bag, lying on the floor a few feet away. He snatched it up. "Good. She left this for me."

He hated to walk away from Alyssa's family, standing there, looking terrified. But he had to get back. Robert said he'd only bugged the room Gavin usually used as an office when he was at the club, so this one shouldn't be wired. And Summer was keeping everyone out.

Even so, he moved close and lowered his voice. "Keep this to yourselves, in case there's another spy among us." Alyssa's mom and sisters wore wide eyes and hopeful expressions. "Alyssa's wearing a tracker. We know exactly where she is. When they stop, we'll make a plan."

Evelyn sagged with relief.

Delaney said, "Come on, Mom. Let's sit down."

But she gripped Callan's hand and met his eyes. In hers, he saw his own terror and hope reflected.

"I know," he said. "I know."

He left them to keep up their prayers, knowing that what they were doing was as important, more important, than what he and the guys were doing.

Callan found the men's locker room and changed his clothes.

He was shoving the pockets of his jeans inside when he felt something unexpected.

A thumb drive.

Alyssa had given the bartender/FBI agent the one containing the files she'd downloaded from her cloud server, which meant this was the zero-day exploit she'd been working on.

It should be a way for him to get access to SJSS's systems. Alyssa had left it for him, which meant she'd have to recreate it for Ghazi.

She was buying time.

And, and he realized, a way to communicate.

Heart thumping, he shoved his feet into his shoes and raced back to the small room that had become their staging area.

When he burst through the door, Gavin straightened from his perch against a windowsill. Beyond him, night had fallen. "What is it?"

Grant had a phone pressed to his ear. "Hold on." He gave Callan his attention.

"I think she might be able to communicate with us." Maybe. If she could do it. If nobody who understood code was watching.

A lot of ifs, but it was worth a try.

Grant stepped closer, lowering the phone. "How?"

"She left me the program with the steps to hack into SJSS's computer system."

"How does that help?" Gavin asked.

"She'll have to recreate it. Which means she'll be *in* the code."

Neither man displayed the *aha* look he was expecting.

"If I'm in there, too, I can see what she's typing. She can type anything, don't you see? And I can watch."

"She can leave you a message?" Grant asked. "Can you reply, tell her—?"

"No, no. Too risky. And she can only do it if nobody's watching or if she finds a way to leave it in code. Even so—"

"Good thinking." Gavin shifted a tablet so Callan could see the map displayed on the screen. "They stopped." He tapped a tiny dot. "They're on this island."

Grant returned to his phone call. Before Callan had left, he'd said he was going to see if he could gather some men to help.

"Should we start heading that way?" Callan asked. "At least get to a port, or—"

"There's a dock on the property we can use once we have a plan," Gavin said. "I've already got a boat en route. And the state police are on standby."

"How far away is she?"

"As the crow flies, about four miles."

"What do you know about the island?"

"Nothing. I'm guessing it's a tourist spot. I sent someone to..."

The door opened, and a police officer stepped in. "Got in touch with the local PD. They told me the island's abandoned during the off-season. Far as he knows, none of the buildings are winterized."

Gavin nodded, gazing at the screen again as if looking away might put his daughter in danger. As if watching helped.

"How long has she been there?" Callan asked.

He didn't look up. "Ten minutes."

Callan set up his laptop on the dining table and plugged in the thumb drive. He let it do its thing, landing on a page of code, which he scanned quickly. This had nothing to do with drones. This page was related to a personnel database.

Hopefully, nobody Ghazi had watching would realize that.

Callan stared at the black screen, the multicolored text, willing something to happen. Some code to pop up. He was tempted to type something, just to nudge her, let her know he was there.

He sat on his hands, literally, to keep from doing something stupid.

They needed to make a plan.

But for now, they waited and gathered intel and...prayed.

While time moved like sludge through a funnel.

## CHAPTER THIRTY-NINE

"Have you eaten anything, sweetheart?"

Alyssa had only been at the beach house for a few minutes, soothing little Peri and praying silently. As they'd snuggled beneath the comforter, a man had emerged from the hallway. Unlike the others, who were Americans, this one might be Iraqi, or at least Arabic, considering the swarthy skin and dark hair. He'd said something to Ghazi, though the words were too low to make out.

With a glare aimed at Alyssa, Ghazi followed him down the hallway and out of sight.

The video game was muted, the room too quiet with no sounds but the whistle of the wind outside and the ticking of a clock, a whimsical, beachy thing with colorful seashells where the numbers should be.

It was after eight on the longest day in Alyssa's life. A day that had begun at a secluded house on a lake. What she wouldn't give to be back at Callan's childhood home right now. Or pretty much anywhere else in the world.

Peri was still nestled in her arms, and Alyssa reveled in her warmth, in the very *aliveness* of her, praying silently, begging God for help.

The child hadn't responded to Alyssa's question, so she tried again. "Are you hungry?"

Alyssa worked to keep her voice level despite the tension in the room, which seemed to thicken with every tick of the secondhand.

Peri nodded.

Alyssa met the eyes of the man sitting closest, the one who'd brought the blanket. He was thick-chested with curly brown hair and surprisingly blue eyes. She'd call them kind eyes, under different circumstances. "Can we have something to eat, please?"

"I offered her a sandwich." His tone was defensive. He was a hulking man with broad shoulders and a barrel chest. Balding, though he didn't look much older than she was.

"I'm sure she was too scared to accept it." Alyssa worked to keep her tone even. "But she needs to eat."

He grumbled, pushing to his feet.

The thinner man had greasy, stringing brown hair. He'd barely looked up from his video game.

Though, now that Alyssa watched, she realized...

It wasn't a video game at all. The infrared video on the screen showed beach houses and a deserted coastline.

He was flying a drone.

Watching the island and the water all around.

Her stomach dropped.

There'd be no sneaking up. There'd be no surprise attack.

She swallowed and looked away, catching sight of Benson staring at her from the small kitchen on the other side of the room. He was sipping from a mug. Now that she noticed the scent of coffee, she longed for a cup.

Not that she'd ask.

He caught her eyes and smiled, the smug expression tempered by the black eye Callan must've given him.

The hulking guard brought a peanut butter sandwich and a handful of chips on a dinner plate, which he plopped on the sofa beside Alyssa, dropping a bottle of water next to it.

"Let's have some food, sweetheart." She tried to shift her to the sofa beside her, but Peri held onto Alyssa's neck.

"Okay. That's okay. You can stay on my lap." Alyssa said. "Just turn to the side so you can eat. Do you like peanut butter?"

Peri still hadn't spoken, but she ate a few bites and took a few sips of water before curling back up, pressing her face into Alyssa's chest.

Ghazi emerged from the hallway. In the few minutes he'd been gone, he must've learned something that he didn't like because his dark eyes flashed with fury. "Come. Now."

She managed to push herself off the cushy sofa with the child in her arms.

"Leave her."

"She stays with me."

If anything, the anger in his eyes blazed brighter. "You will do what I say."

"You have all the control, Charles." She worked very hard to keep her voice steady. "But if she's not with me, I'll spend half my time worrying about her. If you want me to do something for you—"

"You *will* do as I say."

"—then I'll work faster and more efficiently if I know she's safe."

He glared at her, but she didn't budge.

After a moment, he issued a curt nod.

The bedroom had probably been cute before Ghazi and his band of thugs arrived. Pale blue walls over beadboard wainscoting with a thick rope lining the top of the molding between them. Sailboat lamp, sailboat artwork. Round mirrors like you'd find on the lower deck of a yacht.

A desk held two monitors and to a laptop. Beyond it, the one window was boarded up.

"Sit," Ghazi said.

With Peri in her arms, it was going to be impossible to work.

"Put her on the bed." Ghazi's raised voice indicated he was losing his patience.

She swallowed a retort that wouldn't help at all, gentling her voice. "Sweetheart, you're going to have to get off my lap so I can work. The faster I work, the sooner Mr. Sanders will let us go. Isn't that right, Charles?"

"You know who I am. I know who you are. I tire of pretending."

"She's afraid enough...Ghazi."

He displayed no reaction to the use of his real name. "Perhaps. But *you* are not nearly afraid enough." He stepped within inches of her. "That's because you think I don't know everything. But I do. Thanks to your talkative little friend there, I know who her father is. Not Caleb Thompson, hardware salesman."

Acid filled Alyssa's stomach as she realized the source of Ghazi's fury. He knew she'd lied to him. He knew she'd been playing him all along. More importantly, he knew who Callan really was.

Finding his family would be easy.

It was bad enough all of *her* family was in danger, bad enough little Peri was in the middle of this, but now his parents and Hannah were at risk too.

Ghazi had to be stopped. Here and now and permanently, or none of them would ever be safe again.

"He's a CIA agent named Callan Templeton." Ghazi leaned so close that she could smell cinnamon on his breath.

"You thought you could fool me. Trap me. But who's trapped now, Alyssa Wright?"

She swallowed the fear crawling up her throat.

"If you think I care about *any* spawn of the CIA, you have misjudged me." He flicked his gaze behind her.

Benson stepped close and yanked Peri from her arms.

The child screamed, "No." The sound was so pitiable, so helpless.

Alyssa reached for her, but Ghazi grabbed her throat and manhandled her against the wall, moving so close that she couldn't get her hand between them, couldn't even try to fight him off.

"The name of the Russian traitor."

She fought for breath.

She couldn't tell. Now that she knew who the man was, a man who'd given so much to America at such great risk to himself, she couldn't betray him.

If she betrayed this information, it would forever prove she wasn't enough. Wasn't good enough.

"Cut off her hand," Ghazi said.

Alyssa gasped. When she realized whose hand Ghazi had meant, her horror intensified.

Ghazi yanked Alyssa out from the wall, spun her around, and held her against the back his chest, her arms pressed to her sides. Useless.

Benson shifted his jacket aside and unsheathed a hunting knife from his hip. There was no pleasure on his face. He looked emotionless, but she guessed this might be a bridge too far, even for him.

Maybe so, but he didn't argue, just laid Peri on the bed and leaned his body over her to hold her in place.

Ignoring the child's screams that tore Alyssa's heart wide open.

He held her arm down with one meaty arm hand and positioned the knife against her wrist.

"Don't!" Alyssa shouted. "Please, just—"

"The name."

"Don't hurt her." Her gaze flicked from Ghazi to Benson. "If you promise..."

As if she could trust anything these men said. But was she really going to let them harm a helpless little girl to save a Russian man's life?

To keep from disappointing her father?

No. She was not.

"Lavrentiy. Yefim Lavrentiy."

When Benson looked to Ghazi, there was definite relief in his expression. There was a human in there after all.

Ghazi released his hold on Alyssa. "There now. Was that so hard?"

Benson lifted the child and plopped her into Alyssa's arms.

Sobbing, Peri snaked her arms and legs around Alyssa and clamped on.

Ghazi smiled. "If you'll just do as I say, nobody has to get hurt."

Alyssa didn't respond to the obvious lie. Because, when this was over, he would kill them both. Both Peri and Alyssa were, after all, *spawn of the CIA*.

"You still need to put her down in order to work."

She turned her back to the thugs and sat at the desk. "Sweet girl, I'm going to need my hands. Can you crawl under the desk by my feet?"

Peri shook her head.

"Take her," Ghazi said.

"No!" Alyssa lowered her voice. "Peri, you need to crawl down by my feet or that man is going to take you away. I won't be able to stop him."

A few seconds passed, and then Peri slid off Alyssa's lap and beneath the desk. With banks of drawers on each side and the wall behind, it probably felt like a safe space.

"Access to SJSS's navigation system," Ghazi said. "Now."

"Could you grab her a blanket, please?" She directed the question at Benson.

The living area had been warm, but it was cold back here. A space heater in the corner wasn't kicking out nearly enough heat.

He didn't seek permission, just yanked one off the twin bed, along with a pillow.

Peri made herself a little nest and curled up.

Maybe she would fall asleep. Maybe she would find some peace.

Alyssa jiggled the mouse to bring the screen to life and found the computer was already on the company's website.

She set to work, praying for guidance and help and rescue.

Because she'd turned over the Russian's name at the first threat of harm to Peri, and when it came down to it, she feared she'd give Ghazi access to attack drones too.

Was that the right decision, or the wrong one? Was it right to sacrifice one child to save hundreds, potentially thousands of lives?

Logically, yes.

But her God wasn't a God of logic. Or more to the point, He transcended logic.

Jesus would leave ninety-nine sheep to save the one that was lost.

And as much as Alyssa wanted to please her earthly father, her Heavenly Father's pleasure should be much more important to her.

Had she lived to please God? Or Dad?

The answer shamed her.

Hacking into private databases was illegal. A line she'd crossed to prove she could make her business a success. To prove she was competent, capable, and worthy of her father's love.

A million seemingly small decisions, many *wrong* decisions, had led her right here. In danger, and putting those she loved in danger as well.

*Forgive me, Lord. Guide me now. Every single step of the way, I need Your help.*

Keeping up a steady stream of prayers, she hacked into SJSS's system.

# CHAPTER FORTY

Callan was trying to feel optimistic.

Grant was not only a former Green Beret and a current police detective, he and his wife were part owners of a private security company. His wife, the model-beautiful blonde in the library playing the part of bodyguard, had actually *been* a bodyguard.

That would teach Callan to judge a book by its cover.

Grant had called on their other bodyguard buddies, who were on their way up from Boston. He was seated at the table, staring at a screen containing a map of the island, and talking on the phone to a man named Bartlett, another owner of the security company. They were strategizing.

Gavin had been in touch with Agency contacts. One offered to send resources, but the operatives were too far away to be of any use tonight.

The old spy had reached out to the management team at SJSS, hoping they could disable the drones even if Alyssa got access to the command system. He was waiting for a call back, pacing the small dining-room-turned-command-center.

Callan stared at the screen, waiting for something to

happen. Why wasn't Alyssa in the code? Had something gone wrong?

Was she dead? Was Peri?

*Type something.*

*Come on, Alyssa. Give me a—*

He blinked. Had he imagined it, or did the screen shift?

He must've gasped because Gavin moved close. "What?"

Callan didn't answer, just stared, and then...

A line of code appeared.

Random letters and numbers. He tried to decipher it. It didn't make sense as code, which meant...

He wrote the line down.

"What does it mean?" Gavin's tone was commanding, but Callan ignored him.

*COMMAND>HQP1LDKJE2UIR3HQI4LD-KJS1UIA2HQF3LDKJE4*

"That makes no sense." Gavin sounded furious. "What are we supposed too—?"

"Quiet." Callan issued the command as he circled the numbers.

The letters after the numbers were *LUHL...*

That meant nothing. But the letters before the numbers...

*PERISAFE.*

Peri. Safe.

Hot tears stung his eyes.

*Thank God. Thank You, God.*

Gavin squeezed his shoulder. "Looks like they both are." The *for now* was implied.

The line disappeared.

Another replaced it.

*COMMAND>HQM1LDKJA2UIN3HQY4LD-KJM1UIE2HQN3*

The numbers corresponded with the letter placement, so he

knew this was a four-letter word, followed by a three-letter word. "She says many men."

Grant had moved closer. "How many?"

"If she knew, she'd tell us," Callan snapped. "She's doing her best." He copied the next line of code and deciphered it.

"Cabin number eleven, south side of the island." The next line of code was more concerning. Callan turned to Gavin. "She gave him Sputnik's name."

"I'll take care of it." Gavin pulled out his phone to make a call.

Gavin would make sure the Russian double-agent was secured. That didn't concern Callan so much as what Ghazi had done or threatened to do to get Alyssa to give him the name.

A knock sounded on the door, and then Summer and Brooklynn stepped inside. "You wanted our help?" Summer asked.

Grant must've texted her because he answered. "Brooklynn, take Callan's spot." To Callan, he said, "So we can work out a plan."

Brooklyn pulled up a chair.

"Watch the code. If you see a line appear, write it down fast." He explained how to decipher it, and then left her to it.

Grant, Summer, Gavin, and Callan gathered at the table, conferencing with Bartlett and Michael. Together, they worked out a plan.

"She wrote something." Brooklynn bent over the notepad. When she looked up, her face was pale. "They have drones."

Drones.

Of course there were drones providing overwatch.

Their plan relied on the element of surprise.

Which they wouldn't have. So...

How was this going to work?

# CHAPTER FORTY-ONE

"You had me convinced."

Though Ghazi's words had been spoken softly and without malice, the acid in Alyssa's stomach churned. She turned to where he reclined on the twin bed, relaxed as could be. Flicking his antique lighter open, lighting it, then closing it again. Over and over.

Benson stood with his back to the door, arms crossed. A silent prison guard.

Hacking into SJSS's server had been simple, but extra security surrounded the drone control system, which was proving much more difficult to penetrate.

She hadn't actually tried before. She'd never intended to let Ghazi get that far. She didn't begrudge the time it took, only worried he would lose patience and use his leverage.

The eight-year-old girl sound asleep at Alyssa's feet.

"My man at the country club took a video of the engagement announcement." Flick, flame, extinguish.

She hadn't noticed the club manager-turned-traitor recording anything, but she'd been focused on Callan.

"Did you see how your family was moved to tears as you

lied to them? I wonder... Does your fake boyfriend know how you really feel? Because we both know *you* weren't pretending. You might not actually be engaged, but you're in love with Callan Templeton. It must hurt to know he was just using you."

This evil terrorist knew nothing about Callan or his feelings for her. He knew nothing about love. Even if the engagement had been fake, Callan felt something for her. More than just friendship. The only thing keeping him from exploring those feelings with the little girl at Alyssa's feet.

He wasn't a great father yet, but he would be. He knew what his daughter needed, and he intended to provide it. Not just money but love and time and care. That he understood Peri needed to be his priority right now only made Alyssa love him more.

"He's paid to lie," Ghazi said. "He faked it well. And we both know you're an exceptional liar. I am a difficult man to fool, yet you managed it."

She turned back to the computer, ignoring him, scanning the code, trying to find an opening. There must be...

"That must've been some ring," Ghazi said. "That part you hadn't planned in advance. Your tears were authentic. You want it, don't you? Those diamonds. Because of the value? Or because you want the man?" He paused as if waiting for an answer. "Both, probably. You're more of a fool to believe him than I was to believe you. You knew he was lying and still bought it."

Alyssa had been scrolling through the code but not really seeing it. She scrolled back and started again, her fingers like ice in the chilly room.

"How far did he take it? Did he coax you into his bed the way he coaxed you into his heart? How much does that betrayal hurt?"

Callan hadn't *coaxed* her into his bed, and as to his heart...

she'd handed hers over all by herself. "I need to concentrate. If you want me to do this, you should stop talking."

"You can walk and chew gum at the same time."

"I can't focus on this and listen to you at the same time."

"Aren't you curious about how I found out it was all a lie?"

She was, but again, she wasn't about to say so. Whomever had messed with the code to allow her to hack in—and she was convinced someone on the inside had left that door open—must've left a window cracked into the drone security system. She just had to locate it and slip through.

And pray that, on the other end, Dad and Callan were securing those weapons.

"It was when your father and the CIA agent left the party to talk privately. They were going to the room your father always uses—which, of course, had been bugged. But your boyfriend insisted on using a different room. Why would a fiancé do that? A man with nothing to hide?" He paused again, and again Alyssa pretended she wasn't listening. "He wouldn't, but a spy would. We still didn't know his real name, of course. But his little girl provided that information."

Alyssa found it.

The window was barely cracked. One word in one line of code. One key.

She made note of where she was, then navigated away.

It was too soon.

She needed to stall.

"Don't worry," Ghazi said. "We didn't hurt her. We just asked for her father's name. Children are so trusting of adults, even adults who plan to slaughter them."

Alyssa cringed, feeling the sting of his words. She turned in her chair to face him. "Gosh, I feel so much better now."

He nodded to the system behind her. "You need to keep working."

"I can't concentrate with your talking. Go ahead and finish what you want to say, and then I'll get back to it."

A flicker of anger crossed his features, but he tried to hide it with a smile. "You're much braver than I expected."

Brave? She felt anything but.

"Not many women would give themselves up for someone else's child."

"Maybe not where you come from, but I don't know a single woman who wouldn't." Her mother, her sisters, her cousins' wives and girlfriends. All of them would sacrifice themselves to protect the innocent.

"Single women are desperate for a man, so perhaps that's why."

She hadn't meant *single* as in *unmarried,* but she saw no reason to explain herself.

"I have one question," he said. "And then you can continue. When did you find out who I really am? Or have you been playing me all along?"

"I had no idea who you really were until the night we met. When Callan claimed to be my fiancé, that was the first time I'd seen him in years. He told about you."

Ghazi studied her, seemed to be searching for the lie. After a moment, he gave a curt nod. "I am glad to know that. Have you given the authorities information about other things you've found for me since we've been working together?"

"I discovered today, after the party, that the FBI has been surveilling me. They're the ones who stole my computer system the night after we met."

They hadn't gotten past her security yet, but she didn't think it wise to tell Ghazi she'd given them her passwords.

"Your own government doesn't trust you?"

"I'm not the only one being watched, Ghazi."

He took that in, nodding. "Ah, but they have good reason

not to trust me. And at the restaurant that night, did Templeton just happen to be there, or was he sent?"

"He got a tip that somebody was in danger. When he saw me, he made up the lie on the spot."

"You played it well. Though I was suspicious, I believed you were annoyed that he'd interrupted your business meeting."

"Believe me, I was."

That garnered a smile, though on the terrorist, it looked sinister.

"Can I ask you a question?" At his nod, she said, "What was your plan?"

"The Russian is to be honored Monday night in Washington DC. I plan to hit the restaurant."

"And kill all those innocent people?"

The last trace of his smile vanished. "There are no *innocents* in America. You are all guilty. It is only a matter of degree."

She contemplated his words. "I don't disagree. 'All have sinned and fall short of the glory of God.'"

"What is that?"

"Scripture. It's in Romans, though Paul was quoting Isaiah 53, I think. We are all guilty. We are all in need of a savior."

"You'll have no savior today, Alyssa."

They'd see about that. "And now that they're on to you? What will you do?"

"I will have to settle for less strategic strikes."

Strikes. Plural.

As if hitting a hotel that could potentially have a thousand people inside could be considered *strategic*.

"Langley, the Pentagon, and I think"—he tapped his chin—"your father's country club. Your mother and sisters are still there. If your father leaves, then he'll have the rest of his life to grieve, to know their deaths are on his head."

Horror and dread warred for first place in Alyssa's mind. If she gave him what he wanted, everyone she loved would be at risk.

If she didn't, Peri would pay the price.

Ghazi tsked. "Maybe if you'd kept your heart out of it, you guys could've figured a way to bring me down. When love gets involved, one loses the ability to think straight. Love is for fools."

"You've never been a fool? Never been in love?" Her only answer was the flick-flame-extinguish of his lighter. "Not even with Fatemeh?"

He sat up on the bed, his dark brows lowered.

In her peripheral vision, she saw Benson straighten.

"How do you know that name?" Ghazi's words vibrated with anger.

She smiled. "That's the problem, isn't it? When you hire people to dig stuff up, you never know what they might find. I'm curious. Was the lighter a gift from her?"

He curled his fist around it. Though he gave no answer, the flash of surprise in his gaze confirmed her guess.

"You must've been heartbroken," Alyssa said, "considering the lengths you're taking to avenge her death. That sounds a lot like love to me."

Or some misguided, perverted version of it, anyway.

"My father was acting on the intelligence he'd been given. He didn't know the intel was bad."

"You think that excuses it?" Ghazi opened his palm and lit the lighter again. "You think I care what the spy says?"

"You're right about the Russian, though." Alyssa chose to ignore Ghazi's aggressive tone. "He passed on bad intel to protect his position in the SVR."

"He will die. Your father will die. Return to your work, or you will die as well. You have"—Ghazi pocketed the lighter and checked his watch—"thirty minutes to give me access to the control system. And then, for every fifteen minutes you make me wait, your little friend will lose a finger."

She spun back to the computer.

*What now, Lord?*

She navigated to the personnel system, thankful that, though on the front-end, the interfaces would look completely different, their code looked identical.

She typed a quick message in the same line she'd been using before.

*DRONS 30 M. STOP THEM.*

And then...

CNTRY CLB + DC TRGTS.

The Pentagon and Langley would have the security necessary to shoot them down, especially if they were forewarned.

Would Alyssa have the strength to sit by while Benson chopped off Peri's fingers?

She couldn't allow that.

But once Ghazi had access to the system, he wouldn't need to keep the child or herself alive.

What should she do?

She didn't know. *She didn't know.*

## CHAPTER FORTY-TWO

Callan peered through binoculars at the small island, a smudge of black breaking up the moonlight reflecting off the Atlantic.

If not for the moon, the strip of land would be hidden completely.

A boat, lit up like downtown during the holidays, slipped around the south side of the island and disappeared.

When it was gone, there wasn't a single light ahead. Thank God for the tracker that indicated Alyssa's location. Without it, they would never have found her.

That the tracker worked, and that Ghazi hadn't found it, were the first miracles of the operation. For Alyssa and Peri to survive, they would need many more miracles before this was over.

Brooklynn had relayed Alyssa's most recent message. Thirty minutes. And the county club was a target, along with DC, though what in DC was anybody's guess.

Not the hotel, since the Russian wouldn't be there yet.

But there were plenty to choose from.

They needed to be careful not to let on that they knew the

club was a target, so they evacuated the Wright women on police boats. Then, with Robert in custody, the club had closed down, all employees ordered off the property, though they'd leave a few at time so it wasn't obvious.

Just in case.

There was no way to warn the entire city of DC, though, not without alerting Ghazi that they knew his plan.

They would just have to stop him before the drones could be deployed.

The driver of the borrowed fishing boat Callan rode—a state cop named Coulter—had cut the lights a few minutes before and then, about a half mile from shore, cut the engine. Now, they bobbed on the choppy water, waiting for word.

Callan returned belowdecks, scanning the crowd. Grant was standing on the far end, back to a closed door. At a small table were guards he used to work with at the security agency. Bartlett, the one who'd helped with the plan, was there, along with a bunch of other people whose names had escaped Callan.

They were different colors and shapes and sizes, a couple of women but mostly men, all wearing similar intense expressions. Grant had told him most of them were former special forces, and Callan didn't doubt it.

These were people who could handle themselves. Some sat on the floor, others at the table. Most wore scuba gear.

Grant's pregnant wife, Summer, had grudgingly stayed to protect the rest of the Wright family. And her and Grant's unborn child.

Gavin stood with one hand on a counter to keep upright despite the boat pitching this way and that. Too restless to sit.

Grant caught Callan's eye. "We good to go?"

"No activity on shore. No indication they know we're here."

The men in wetsuits made their way past Callan and up to the deck.

Callan followed and watched as they jumped into the frigid water and disappeared.

Grant had followed him and now made his way to the front of the boat. He was their leader. His job was to watch and direct.

Callan returned belowdecks to wait with Gavin and Bartlett.

Gavin and Callan were focused on saving their daughters.

Bartlett had made himself familiar with the SJSS system. His job was to secure the drones, ASAP.

"They know what they're doing," Bartlett directed the words at Gavin, who had a good poker face, but he couldn't hide the fear in his eyes.

Gavin nodded once.

Callan had never been great at being part of a team. He preferred to go it alone.

Right now, the lives of the two most important people in his world depended on the team that'd just slipped into the frigid water, and a lot more peoplee to get it right.

They'd decided, since a sneak attack wasn't going to work, they needed a decoy.

The state police would idle off shore long enough to make sure all eyes were on them.

And give the scuba team time to reach land and move across the narrow island to approach the beach houses from the back.

When they were in place, the cops would disembark at the dock Alyssa's captors had used. There were six of them, who would follow footprints—or at least look like they were following footprints—to the house where Alyssa was being held. They would separate into teams of two, but not hide. One team would approach number eleven and knock.

God willing, Ghazi and his people would answer, not start shooting.

Their story: That an owner of one of the properties had seen the boat and, knowing nobody was meant to be on the island, had called the police, fearing squatters or looters. They'd tell Ghazi and his band of thugs that those owners were disembarking to do some maintenance work on their properties.

The other two teams would be on the lookout for more men and report back to Grant and his team.

Meanwhile, the boat Callan was on would dock on the north side. The driver would wait while Callan, Gavin, Grant, and Bartlett strolled off in full view of everybody.

All wrapped up in winter gear. Their faces hidden.

More decoys, meant to confuse Ghazi and his people. Convince them all was well. No need to panic.

No need kill anybody.

Callan figured another ten, fifteen miracles, and this just might work.

*Please, God. Please, let it work.*

"They're on land," Grant said through the earpiece in Callan's ear.

He was itching to go. To get Alyssa and Peri in his arms.

But still, they waited.

And then, just as the engine rumbled to life, Grant said, "It's time."

Meaning the state police had docked and were headed to the house.

Whatever happened now, it would be over soon enough.

*Please, protect them, Father. The soldiers, the cops.*

*The ones I love.*

# CHAPTER FORTY-THREE

"Time's up." Ghazi clamped a hand on Alyssa's shoulder and squeezed. "Benson, grab the girl."

"No, don't," Alyssa said. "I think I've got it."

He squeezed harder. "How long have you had it?"

She didn't answer, just typed. Slipping through the window the SJSS programmer had left cracked.

On the second screen, the interface opened. Giving Ghazi access to every attack drone the government contractor had ever built.

"Out of the way." To Benson, he said, "Get Spencer in here, and have Eckel take over for him."

Benson slipped out.

"Move onto the bed," Ghazi said.

Alyssa reached down and pulled the child out from beneath the desk, ignoring the strain in her back from the awkward angle. She reclined on the bed, back against the wall, with Peri in her arms.

The child barely reacted, never opening her eyes. Was she such a sound sleeper, or was the Lord keeping her asleep? Either way, Alyssa thanked Him.

The young, skinny guy who must be Spencer stepped into the bedroom and settled at the desk.

Ghazi watched over his shoulder. "Well?"

He was tapping, tapping. "She got us in. I need a minute to get familiar with it."

Ghazi turned to Alyssa, smiling. "You've saved yourself and your little friend some pain. I hope that eases your conscience, knowing that thousands will die because of you." He pulled out a handgun.

She gasped.

She'd known, of course, that he planned to kill her. But already? Just like that?

*I'm sorry, Callan. Dad. I'm so sorry.*

She shouldn't have given him access. But should she have let him harm Peri?

Surely Dad and Callan had disabled the drones by now. Nobody else would die.

*Think!*

"You might still need me." She didn't try to hide the fear and pleading in her voice. "You might run into trouble."

Ghazi didn't look at the man behind him when he asked, "Are we going to run into trouble, Spencer?"

"Too soon to tell. Give me a minute."

Ghazi smirked, then leaned against the wall beside the computer. "I suppose I can wait *one* minute."

Time slowed. Alyssa took deep breaths of cold air.

Was this where she was going to die? In this beach house, surrounded by these men?

Not that she deserved better, but Peri had never harmed a soul. She was innocent, a victim of vengeful terrorists and Alyssa's foolishness.

Spencer looked up at Ghazi. "I have full access."

Ghazi raised the weapon.

The door opened, and Benson poked his head in. "Someone's here. Looks like cops."

Ghazi didn't lower the gun, just held it there, aimed.

Indecision played across his face.

Murderous desire.

And then, slowly, he holstered it.

"How?"

"I don't know, but they're almost to the—"

Banging startled her.

"Police," a woman yelled. "Open up."

The police were here? Surely, Dad and Callan hadn't trusted the cops to rescue them.

No, this must be part of a larger plan.

To Spencer, Ghazi said, "Keep working. No matter what happens, I want those drones in the air." He looked at Benson. "If anyone besides me tries to come in here, stop them." He nodded to Alyssa and Peri. "If you hear shooting, don't wait for me. Kill them both." He walked out, closing the door behind him.

Benson's Adam's apple bobbed, the only indication he'd heard as he stood in front of the door, handgun at the ready.

Spencer continued tapping on the keyboard.

But the police were here. Rescue must be close.

Alyssa had no idea what would happen next, but she'd be ready.

# CHAPTER FORTY-FOUR

It was a tiny island, not even a mile across at the widest point.

Callan strode at a brisk pace down a deserted street toward the south side. He, Bartlett, and Gavin all carried flashlights, making a point to not look like they were trying to hide.

The moment they'd hopped from the deck to a sidewalk, Grant peeled away. Within seconds, Callan had lost him in the wild grasses among the dunes.

He, Gavin, and Bartlett had passed a line of beach houses, crossed a cobblestone street, and now wove among businesses in the center of the island. There were no cars, here, the roads built wide enough to accommodate passing golf carts.

A convenience store. A restaurant. A souvenir shop. All more shacks than buildings, built to withstand the weather but not necessarily protect anyone from it.

Bartlett was in the lead. Gavin walked beside Callan, who carried a tool box that had been emptied of tools and filled with weapons and ammo.

Gavin carried a duffel bag, also filled with munitions. They were meant to look like handymen, Bartlett an owner come to guide them to the property and explain the job.

The timing was bizarre—who would start a repair project after dark on a Saturday night? It didn't make sense, but they hadn't been able to come up with a better plan. They were banking on this going down too fast for Ghazi to think it through.

Ghazi was a fast thinker, but with the cops at his door, he might not know in time to stop them.

*More miracles, Lord.*

None of them held guns, knowing the drone that they couldn't see would detect weapons if they showed them.

Callan was careful not to pat the pocket of his jacket, which hid not only his bulletproof vest but the Glock Malcolm had provided, which he'd stowed in the pocket.

The wind was cold, a good excuse to move quickly. Not fast enough. He wanted to sprint. He wanted to barge in and start shooting enemies, starting with Ghazi.

It was killing him, knowing Peri and Alyssa were so close.

Which was why Bennett was setting the pace.

"Slow and steady," the man muttered as if he could feel Callan's impatience. "The closer we get before they know, the better."

Yeah, yeah. He understood.

Didn't make it easier.

In his ear, the lead on the scuba team said, "Cops are at the door."

This was it. They'd get the men surrounded, get them to surrender.

Ghazi would agree, or bullets would fly.

It was imperative that the good guys disable and disarm the bad guy. Take out the enemy before they could take out the innocent.

That was the goal.

"Door's open," the scuba team leader said. "Cops are inside. We're moving."

Still, Bartlett didn't pick up speed.

"Shouldn't we—?"

"Slow and steady," the annoying man said. Then he nodded ahead. "There're the beach houses. Almost there."

Callan saw the line of shacks.

Flashlights moving among them. That would be the police, the decoys they hoped would keep the terrorists' attention until they and the scuba team could get into position.

"It's that one," Bartlett said. "Where the light's shining."

A tiny sliver of light came from the edge of one of the windows.

Bartlett angled away from it. They'd go into another cabin, turn on all the lights as if they weren't afraid of anybody knowing they were there

And wait. Hopefully, the cops and the SEALs would rescue Alyssa and Peri.

It went against everything in Callan to sit back and let others take the lead, but these men had more experience than he did.

Trust didn't come easily. But he'd do whatever it took.

So far, the plan was working. The cops were inside. The scuba team was creeping close. They were nearly in place. All was quiet.

A gunshot ripped through the silence.

## CHAPTER FORTY-FIVE

Five minutes before the gunshot, Alyssa had shifted Peri onto the bed beside her.

Peri's eyes opened briefly.

"You're okay, sweetheart." Alyssa leaned down and whispered, "If anything bad happens, anything scary at all, go under the bed and stay there." There was enough space between the bed and the wall that Peri should be able to slide right down and take cover, hopefully without being seen.

Alyssa had shifted her own feet to the edge of her side, preparing to move She kissed the top of Peri's head and kept her voice the barest whisper. "Don't go back to sleep. Listen and be ready." She covered the child's body completely with the blanket.

It was the best she could do to protect her. She prayed it wouldn't be necessary. That the police would just start taking people into custody. That she and Peri would be rescued.

Four minutes before the gunshot, she considered her options. She didn't think Spencer was armed. He didn't seem the gun-toting type. Killing people with drones probably felt no different than killing people in a first-person-shooter video game. But in real life, with actual blood...

No, she didn't think Spencer was a threat. If anything, he might be on her side if she could convince him that helping her would help him.

Besides, his attention hadn't shifted for even a second from the drone system.

She watched in horror as he got them flying. They hadn't been disabled.

He had a different view on each screen, and though all she saw was treetops, one showed considerably more lights breaking up the darkness. The forests near Washington DC would be much more densely populated than those on the Maine coast.

*Stop him, Lord. Stop this. Please!*

Benson, the man who'd seemed willing to cut off the hand of an eight-year-old girl, continued to stand vigil in front of the door, his face impassive.

But she'd seen relief there. He didn't want to hurt Peri. Alyssa, maybe, but not Peri.

Three minutes before the gunshot, she devised a plan. There was zero chance it would work, but...

Two minutes before the gunshot, she started praying. Not that she hadn't been all along, but these were specific prayers. Not that God needed instructions, but... Well, if you don't ask, you don't get. That was what it said in James.

One minute before the gunshot, a sense of peace overwhelmed her. It was all going to be okay. God had it in hand.

She was so sure that she thought, any minute, the door would burst open and a police officer would step in. He'd cuff Benson and Spencer, shut down the SJSS drone system, and ensure that Alyssa and Peri were all right. He'd give them water and coffee and blankets.

He'd take them to Callan.

It would all be okay.

She was wrong. About everything.

WHEN THE FIRST BULLET FLEW, Alyssa didn't think about any of that.

She shoved at the child.

Her feet hit the floor. She launched herself toward the opposite side of the tiny room. Away from Peri.

Benson fired.

The bullet hit the bed. The bed where still Peri huddled beneath the blankets.

*Peri!*

Alyssa couldn't think about that.

She dove at the hulking guard, expecting a bullet to tear through her body.

But he was slow. Much slower than he should've been. As if God had answered Alyssa's prayer that he be flummoxed. Confused. Unable to adapt.

And weak.

And that Spencer would be useless in a fight.

She didn't think about that, either.

She barreled into Benson, aiming both of her hands toward the gun.

She knocked him off balance. And managed to wrench the weapon out of his hand.

She didn't manage to hang onto it, though.

It skittered away.

Benson flipped her onto her back and pinned her down. "Now what are you going to do?" His face was red, his eyes not filled with fury, as she'd have expected, but something else. Fear? "You should've just let me shoot you. Then it would be over."

"You looking forward to beating a woman to death? Is that how your mother raised you?"

He winced.

Yes, there was a human in there.

"Did she raise you to kill children? Ghazi's going to kill thousands of people. Thousands and thousands of Americans. *Your* countrymen. You're going to let that happen, and for what? Money? You think you're going to enjoy spending it, knowing all the graves you're responsible for?"

The fear in his eyes disappeared.

Dead Benson was back. "I made my bed. And so did you." He punched her in the head. Again. And again.

And the world was gray and fuzzy and part of her, a tiny part of her, thought maybe he was right.

She should've just let him shoot her.

Then, it would be over.

# CHAPTER FORTY-SIX

The gunshot was still echoing when Callan swiveled and bolted toward the cabin.

He didn't care what anybody else was doing.

He was going to rescue Peri and Alyssa if it killed him. Which it just might.

"Drop the bag," Grant said in his ear.

Right. The guns and ammo he'd brought, just in case.

He did, in stride, pulling out his own handgun.

"Down! On your right!"

The word was huffed by Bartlett.

Callan hit the ground, feeling the whoosh of a bullet too close. He saw the gunman running for cover and aimed. Before he fired, the guy went down.

Bartlett crouched beside him. "You hit?"

"No. Did you—?"

"Yup."

"Thanks." He started to get up, but Bartlett gripped his arm.

"You can't help them if you're dead. Move slowly and keep cover."

Right. He was right, of course.

Together they continued toward cabin number eleven, keeping out of the moonlight.

Enemies were streaming out of nearby beach houses.

And going down, one at a time, though neither Bartlett nor Callan ever had a chance to take a shot.

Grant, Gavin, and the scuba team were picking off enemies one by one.

No doubt the terrorists were going to lose this battle.

But would Alyssa and Peri survive?

*More miracles, Lord. Please.*

They were creeping behind the neighboring beach house when the tiny sliver of light coming from the window widened a second before the lamp inside went off.

A man leaned out the window. Saw them. Aimed.

Callan took the shot.

The man disappeared inside. Hit?

Callan didn't know.

Either way, they'd been seen. They were out of time.

"Going around front." Callan made his way toward the space between the beach houses. The ground was sandy and made the movement slow. But muffled his footsteps.

He spoke low. "Emerging from the west of the house." He needed to alert allies that he wasn't an enemy.

"You're covered," Grant said. Then, as Callan stepped out, "Got you. Shooters inside."

Yeah, well. He knew that. But so were Alyssa and Peri. Someone had to breach the door.

"No activity at the first window," Grant said.

From here, he had a view of the beach-side of the little house.

A person lay in front of the door. Facedown. Dead.

She wore a uniform. A state cop who'd also served in combat.

She'd taken the first bullet.

They'd decided to send her to the door because they figured Ghazi and his people wouldn't fear a woman. They wouldn't consider her a threat.

The sight of her corpse made it all feel very real.

She was dead.

A woman who'd worked with them, plotted with them, helped plan this whole thing.

Dead.

*Don't think about it.*

Because though it was definitely the cop's body lying there, Callan saw Peri. And Alyssa. And both of them.

Lifeless.

*Not helping.*

Forcing himself to focus, he crouch-walked to the space beneath the window.. When he pushed up on the glass, it rose easily. The question was, how hard would it be to get past the plywood that'd been nailed to the inside?

He was about to find out.

Grant said, "He's in position."

Talking to Bartlett, since Callan couldn't exactly speak. No idea who was on the other side.

A gasp came from inside, then a thump that had his stomach flipping.

Like a fist against flesh.

Then a door. A curse word.

"I told you to kill her."

Ghazi.

"She knocked the gun away." That was Benson.

"I'll do it. Move out of the... Hey... Whoa."

A door closed.

Callan was out of time.

He shoved on the plywood, and it gave, not enough for him to push all the way through. He squeezed into the gap.

The scene flashed like an image from a horror movie.

A man at a computer, focus on the screen as if nothing was going on behind him.

Benson had straddled Alyssa, who wasn't fighting at all. The man was looking at something out of Callan's line of sight.

He pushed on the board more. And saw… Peri.

His little girl was holding a gun, aimed at Benson. Eyes wide, terror-filled.

Benson caught movement and shifted, catching Callan in the window.

He should've raised his hands. He should've backed away from Alyssa.

But he didn't. He gripped her neck and squeezed.

Callan fired.

Benson collapsed on top of her.

She didn't move.

Peri screamed.

The guy at the computer turned, took in the situation.

And launched himself not toward the door, but toward Peri. Maybe thinking to hide behind her. Or use her as a hostage.

Same thing.

Callan fired again.

The man fell.

Callan pushed on the board so he could get in. "I got them. Two down. Ghazi's in the house!"

Somewhere. Callan had definitely heard his voice. He must've left when he saw Peri with the gun. The coward.

Peri was still screaming.

"It's me, Peri. It's Daddy." Callan shoved his handgun into his pocket and shoved against the plywood with all his strength.

It gave, and he shoved his head in the gap between the wood and the window jamb.

Peri was still holding the weapon.

Fear and adrenaline thumped through his veins. An enemy was in the house somewhere. He needed to get inside, find Ghazi and take him out. But first...

"Put the gun down. It's Daddy."

She blinked.

The wood budged.

He shoved it aside and levered into the room, landing on the end of a twin bed.

His daughter was staring at him. The gun dangled from her hand. She looked shellshocked. Terrified. As if she didn't know who he was. Or what was happening.

"It's me, sweetheart. It's Daddy." She still didn't move, so he pushed off the bed and scooped her into his arms, sliding the gun out of her little hand. "You're safe now. You're safe."

She melted against him, sobbing. "He killed her, Daddy. She's dead. She's dead."

He spun to face Alyssa.

Benson's lifeless body lay atop hers. He couldn't see her face, but he didn't need to.

She still hadn't moved. Wasn't even trying to get out from under him.

Outside the window, Gavin man screamed, the sound visceral, nearly inhuman.

But it *was* human.

It was the sound of a father who knew he'd failed to do the most important job he'd ever be given.

To protect his child.

Alyssa. Beautiful, talented, brilliant Alyssa. She'd given her life to protect Callan's child.

A debt he could never, ever repay.

~

THINK.

That was what Alyssa had told him. That he had to think.

Bartlett entered through the window and sat. "I'm at the control. Weapons activated. I think I can disable."

"Do it," Grant said, his voice demanding in Callan's ear. Then, "Callan, there're enemies shooting from the door and windows. You gotta gotta flank 'em."

"Right." He kissed his daughter on the forehead and, going against every fatherly instinct, set her on the bed. "My friend will protect you. Trust me."

She gripped his hand. "Don't leave."

It killed him to walk away. It *killed* him.

Bartlett swiveled. "I got her." To Peri, he said, "We're the good guys. Just stay there." He was already back at the system.

Callan let her go. Praying he wouldn't leave her an orphan.

But if Ghazi got away, his whole family would pay the price.

He crept to the door and was about to open it when one of Grant's men slipped through the window, face painted black, armed and ready.

Peri gasped, but the soldier smiled at her and gave her a thumbs-up.

"Also a good guy," Bennett said.

Callan exhaled a little of his fear, happy that he wouldn't have to do this alone.

He opened the door, staying out of the gap.

No gunshots.

He got low and peeked.

Nobody was there.

"Door across the hall is closed."

"I'll clear it," the soldier behind him said. "Head to the front. Stay low."

They moved into the hallway.

Callan crept toward the main rooms of the house. There were no lights, and with the windows boarded up, it was dark as pitch.

Behind, a gunshot told him the soldier had taken out the enemy.

In front of him, a shout in Arabic. *They're here.*

"Do not move from your post." That was Ghazi.

A shadow shifted in the darkness ahead.

Callan fired.

The shadow went down.

As the blast of the gunshot faded, the silence was stifling. Nothing but the sound of his breath and that of the soldier behind him.

They reached an open doorway. Callan should clear the room, but all he cared about was stopping Ghazi. Nothing else mattered. Nobody else mattered.

He bent low and bolted forward.

A bullet whizzed over his head.

The soldier behind him took out the enemy.

Callan moved to the threshold of the main room.

Two enemies, backs to him, guns aimed outside. Callan took out one.

The soldier took out the other shooter.

Ghazi was in the kitchen. His eyes met Callan's.

Callan backed out of sight and leaned against the hallway wall. "It's over, Ghazi," Callan said. "You lost."

"Wright's daughter is dead."

Callan winced, shook it off.

"Your child will never be the same. The drone strike cannot be stopped. I win."

He didn't know if that was true and prayed Bartlett would figure it out.

"You're finished."

"She is avenged."

The girlfriend. "I wonder what Fatemeh would think of all you've done. Would she proud of you for the innocents you killed? Or horrified. Not that you'll ever find out. There's a special place in hell for people like you, a place I assume your girlfriend will never have to see. But if she could speak to you now, what would she say?" He let the question hang there.

"It doesn't matter."

"Ah, but it does. Because I think...I think she'd hate you. Put the gun down."

Callan squatted very low and peeked around the corner.

Ghazi fired, but the shot was high and a little late as Callan retreated behind the wall again.

Callan hadn't expected him to surrender, nor did he want him to.

The front door creaked open. A figure moved into the gap.

Callan peeked and watched as Ghazi swung the gun toward whoever was coming inside.

Callan took aim at the man who'd tried to kill Peri—and thousands of other souls.

Who'd tracked the Wrights and a single double-agent across continents on his quest for revenge.

Who'd ordered Alyssa's murder.

Who was, after all, just flesh and blood.

Callan fired.

And that flesh-and-blood enemy went down.

## CHAPTER FORTY-SEVEN

The world was dark and heavy and painful.

From far away, someone said, "He killed her, Daddy. She's dead. She's dead."

Who was dead?

Had she heard right? The sounds were strangely muffled.

A howl, long and tortured, twisted something inside her.

All was not well. She didn't know what had happened, but somehow, it was her fault.

She'd failed. Again.

With that thought, she drifted away.

Hammering.

Someone was hammering, and each bang pounded in her head.

*Wake up.*

She had to figure out what was going on.

Where was she? What was she supposed to do?

Something, something vital. Something...

Scraping sounds. Voices.

"Daddy." A little girl. She sounded like she was crying.

"I got you, I got you. It's over." The man's voice was kind.

She loved that voice. A few moments later, he said, "I'll be right here, okay? I want to check on Alyssa."

"I gotcha, little bit."

Grant?

Then, the heaviness was gone.

Cold, precious air filled her lungs. She sucked in.

"She's breathing!"

More weight lifted.

Then, warmth against her face.

"Alyssa." It was Callan. He sounded tortured. "Open your eyes. Open your eyes, darling. Please."

She did, and it all came back to her. The beach house. The guns.

Benson.

He'd hit her, over and over.

Everything had gone dark.

Callan was here. But he'd said someone was dead. "Who is it? Peri?" No, that didn't make sense. She'd heard Peri's voice, hadn't she?

"It's me." Callan crouched over her. "Thank God. Thank God. She's alive, Gavin. She's alive."

"Is it Peri? I'm so sorry. I tried."

"Is what...? Peri's fine." He shifted, giving her a view of Grant holding Peri, who was watching her with wide eyes.

Wide, beautiful, life-filled eyes.

"I don't..." She pushed herself up. "You said someone was dead."

"You. She thought... We thought..." Callan wrapped his arms around her, and she realized...

It'd been her. They'd thought she was dead.

The howl she'd heard...

Her father. Because he'd thought she was dead.

"Thank you. I'll never... I can't even..." Callan's words

trailed as he buried his head in her hair and held her. "Thank you."

"I don't even know... I didn't do anything. This is all my fault."

He leaned away to meet her eyes. "Alyssa. You're alive. Peri's alive." His gaze flicked beyond her. "The drones?"

"Landing them now," a man said.

That wasn't a voice she knew, but it didn't matter.

All was well. Somehow...

Somehow, they'd survived.

Callan pulled her close again, and she melted against him. It was over.

*Thank You, God.*

OUTSIDE THE TINY bedroom that had been her prison, a whirlwind of activity. Men shouting, a helicopter landing.

Alyssa could do nothing but sit on the bed, back to the wall, and fight to stay conscious.

Callan had left to help with...whatever it was they were doing, his daughter clamped to him.

The door opened, and she expected him step inside. But it wasn't Callan. It was Dad.

She'd known he was there, then forgotten. Whatever was wrong with her brain, she prayed it wouldn't be permanent.

Dad crossed the room and sat on the bed beside her.

"I'm sorry, Dad. I shouldn't have—"

"Thank God you're all right." He crushed her to his chest. "You saved that child's life. And your life."

His embrace made her head pound, but she didn't tell him. She didn't back away. She craved that embrace, had craved it since she was twelve years old.

He let her go and leaned back.

Her vision was a little blurry, but she thought she saw tears streaming from his eyes as he pressed his hands to her cheeks. "Alyssa. Are you with me?"

She must've looked horrible for him to ask. She worked very hard to focus. "I'm all right."

His gaze flicked from one of her eyes to the other. "Hear me. I love you. I adore you. I'm so proud of you, of everything you've done. You're brilliant. You're kind and generous. You're so, so brave." His voice cracked. "I'm sorry I've done a lousy job of telling you that. I almost...I could've... If you'd died not knowing..." He pulled her against his chest again. "I'm sorry. I'm sorry."

She didn't know what to say, couldn't form a response. There was no response to express what his words meant to her. She settled with the simple truth, the only truth that really mattered. "I love you, Daddy."

"I love you, sweetheart. I always have."

She rested in those words. Rested knowing she'd pleased her earthly father.

And her Heavenly Father, who'd saved her life.

## CHAPTER FORTY-EIGHT

Callan paced in the waiting room of the Portland hospital, his daughter in his arms.

Peri had barely let him go since he'd taken her back from Grant the night before.

She'd fallen asleep on the boat ride back to shore. He might have been able to lay her down across the padded bench seat, but he hadn't wanted to let her go.

If not for Peri, he might've fought Gavin for the empty seat on the helicopter that carried Alyssa straight to the hospital. But her father had the right to be with her.

Somehow, both of their daughters had survived.

There'd been hours of questions from the local police and the FBI. He'd told the police what he knew, then listened while Peri told the story from her perspective. How Alyssa had shown up, taken care of her, protected her.

How she'd told Peri to hide, then pushed her when the a gun fired. How Peri had dropped in the crack between the edge of the bed and the wall.

How she'd watched from under the bed as Alyssa had charged Benson.

How the gun had slid across the wood, right to her.

"I wasn't gonna shoot anyone, Daddy." Her little eyes were filled with tears. "But I didn't want that man to hurt Alyssa. I was scared. I didn't know what to do."

"You did exactly the right thing, my darling girl." He'd held her tiny face and met her eyes, ignoring the police officer waiting in the empty hospital room where they'd set up shop. "You were brave and amazing, and I am so, so proud of you. I love you more than..." He'd choked up. "Sorry. I can't..."

Peri had wiped his tears with her small fingers. "It's okay to cry. I cried a lot."

He held her close. And he'd keep holding her close. He'd never forget what could've happened.

One of Grant's friends had been shot, but the bullet hit his vest. He was being treated for bruised ribs.

Only the courageous police woman had been killed. His heart ached for her family and selfishly thanked God he wasn't the only grieving right now.

Peri had been examined, though it'd taken some coaxing to let the doctor have a look at her.

"Physically, she's fine," the doctor had said. The implication was clear. His daughter would need trauma therapy.

Callan would make sure she got it. Whatever she needed, he'd be here for her.

If not for her, he wouldn't have left the hospital. But the doctors had assured him that Alyssa was fine and needed rest more than anything. He'd seen her, but she'd been sound asleep.

Evelyn and all of Alyssa's sisters had shown up at the hospital. Each one had hugged him and Peri as if they were part of the Wright family.

Maybe, someday, they would be family. If he could figure out how to make it work.

The thought that he'd almost lost Alyssa made him realize how very, very much he wanted to keep her.

One thing at a time.

Last night, he'd left Gavin and Evelyn at Alyssa's bedside and taken his little girl to a hotel to get some sleep.

She had slept, in his arms. When she'd had nightmares, he'd been there, whispering in her ear.

"Daddy's here, sweet girl. You're safe. You're safe."

And she'd fall back asleep.

When he woke up, the sun was bright outside. He called Gavin. "How is she?"

"Awake. A little fuzzy, but the doctor's pleased."

"Thank God. Can I talk to her?"

"Her mother's helping her get cleaned up right now. Just get here when you can."

Callan showered, cleaned up, changed into the clothes Alyssa's sisters left with the front desk, along with some clothes they'd picked up for Peri.

He'd taken his daughter to breakfast, and he'd listened to her story again.

She kept repeating what'd happened, and even though he wanted her to put it out of her mind, trauma didn't work like that. One didn't just forget it. It had to be worked through, examined from every angle. It had to be brought to the forefront. Trauma, like bacteria, thrived in darkness. It reproduced and spread, infecting everything it touched.

The only cure for trauma was bringing it to the light.

The more Peri exposed her experience to the light, the weaker it became. So he'd listen, and listen again, and listen a thousand times if that was what it took for his daughter to be healthy.

And that she told him, didn't wait for Mom or Dad or Hannah, but trusted Callan?

That meant everything to him.

It was after nine by the time he pushed into the hospital, carrying Peri, who didn't seem to want out of his arms at all. They made their way to Alyssa's room. He knocked on the door, and Gavin met him there, looking like he'd aged two decades since the anniversary party the day before. He still wore the jeans and sweatshirt he'd donned before they bordered the boat the night before. "Glad you're here. I have an update for you, but you should see her first. She's asking for you."

Inside the room, Evelyn saw him, then moved out of his line of sight toward the head of Alyssa's bed.

"What update?" Callan asked.

"I think they've figured out the inside man at SJSS."

"Ghazi had to have a contact at the CIA. Someone told him about that meeting."

"We're working on that. We'll find him, or her." Hardness settled in his eyes. "Whoever it was, they'll..." He swallowed, looking at Peri. His tone shifted to the grandfatherly one he'd used the day before. "We're all safe now. You want to go for a walk?"

She gripped Callan tighter. "I wanna see Alyssa."

"You can see her," Callan said. "Then I need to talk to Alyssa alone for a couple of minutes. Is that okay?"

Peri seemed to mull the question.

Gavin said, "There's a play room on the next floor down. I hear it's got coloring books."

"Okay."

"I'll wait for you out here," Gavin said.

Callan started to pass him, but Gavin grabbed his arm. "Son."

He paused. "Yeah?"

He pulled Callan into a hug, awkward with Peri between

them. "Thank you. I heard all the stories, and...you saved her life. Things could've turned out much worse."

Callan stepped back, nodding. "God was on our side."

Still holding Callan's arms, Gavin squeezed. "You're not wrong. Just saying, I'm glad you were on our side too."

Unsure how to respond, he carried Peri into the hospital room.

Evelyn saw him, hugged him tight, and slipped out.

Alyssa lay on the gurney. Face bruised. Hair mussed.

The most beautiful creature in the world.

She smiled and pressed the button to raise her head. "Hey, you two." Her voice was strong.

It was a moment before he could speak past emotion clogging his throat.

"Hi, Alyssa." Peri sounded tentative. "Daddy said you were okay, but I wanted to see."

"Well, come on in."

He moved to the head of the bed, wanting more than anything to lean down and kiss her. But he didn't. Not yet.

"Just a little headache. But the doctor said I'm gonna be just fine."

"You don't look very good."

He wasn't sure if he should reprimand his daughter, but Alyssa's grin only widened. "I figure it must be bad because I asked for a mirror, and the nurse told me she's afraid I'm so ugly that I'll break it."

Peri giggled. "Nuh-uh. She didn't say that."

"Maybe that's not *exactly* what she said."

"You're not ugly, just a little..." She lifted a shoulder and let it drop.

"Battle worn," Callan said. "Like a warrior princess."

Alyssa started to shake her head but stopped, squinting. He'd bet that hurt. "Your dad's a weirdo."

"Heroes get hurt. Right, Daddy?"

"That's right." He forced himself to look at his daughter, though it took considerable effort. "And Alyssa isn't just a hero, she's a superhero."

Peri liked that.

A slight knock, and Gavin stepped in. "The nurse just told me there's a soda machine in the playroom." He waggled his eyebrows. "You ever tried all the flavors mixed together?"

Her eyes widened. "Huh-uh."

"Wanna?"

She gave Callan a *Can I?* look.

"Just don't overdo it."

She slid from his arms and took Gavin's hand, and headed for the door.

Before she she stepped out, she turned to him.

He waved. "I'll be right here."

Satisfied, she walked away with Alyssa's dad.

Callan returned to Alyssa, took her hand, and pressed a gentle kiss to the corner of her lips, the only spot that wasn't swollen.

He backed away enough to see her face. "Are you okay? Really?"

"It's just a concussion."

He pulled a doctor's rolling stool close and sat.

"Did anybody get hurt? Dad wouldn't tell me anything, just kept saying I was fine, and that was all that mattered."

"Your father didn't hang around to find out what happened. I don't think he could focus knowing you were hurt."

"Yeah. He was..." Her eyes filled.

"When he thought you were dead..." Callan could still hear the keening. The grieved howl. "He adores you."

"Yeah. He said..." Her eyes narrowed. "Did you say something to him? About me?"

"Nothing I said affected how he feels about you, Alyssa. Those feelings didn't just suddenly show up last night."

"That's true." The admission seemed hesitant, as if she didn't trust it.

The same way Peri's faith in Callan still wavered. But he was going to fix it.

His daughter was not going to grow up hoping her father loved her. Wondering if he loved her enough. He'd prove it, and he'd keep proving it, every single day, if it took the rest of his life. He'd prove to her that he could be her dad. More than just the man who'd fathered her but the man who adored her.

"So what happened?"

He gave her a rundown on the attack, what they'd planned, and how it'd gone wrong.

"A brave state cop was killed, a woman, and another was shot, but it hit his vest. He's got some bruised ribs."

"Ghazi?"

"Dead. So is Benson. All Ghazi's men were killed or injured."

"The drones?"

"The pilot—"

"Spencer."

He hadn't heard the guy's name. "He'd programmed the targets, but Bartlett managed to undo it. None of the missiles were fired."

"Thank God. I can't believe it all worked out."

"Miracles. I kept asking God for miracles."

She smiled. "Me too. I'm sorry for that police woman."

"Yeah. It's tragic."

Now that he knew Alyssa was all right, and Peri was all right, and it was all over... He was exhausted. Despite the few hours of sleep, felt like he could pass out for a week.

He said, "I wanted to say—"

"—I'm sorry it..."

They'd both spoken at the same time.

Callan nodded to her. "Ladies first."

"I'm sorry it all happened." Her words came out on a flood. "If I hadn't started working for Ghazi in the first place—"

"You wouldn't have if you'd known who he was. You're allowed to have a business."

"Not a business where I break the law. Bend the rules to get what I want. If I hadn't, Ghazi might've moved on to someone else, someone more amenable. But I showed him my morals were iffy, where hacking was concerned, anyway."

He wasn't about to let Alyssa carry the burden for this. "As soon as you understood what was going on, you did the right thing. Hacking into a private database is one thing. Hacking into a defense contractor is something else."

"But the Russian—"

"Don't do that. You risked your life to save my daughter. You protected her. As far as I'm concerned, you redeemed yourself times a thousand. I'll never stop owing you for that."

"This isn't a transaction, Callan. If you forgive me, I'll take that. You don't owe me a thing. What were you going to say?"

He took a breath and dove in. "I love you."

Her eyes popped wide.

"I know it was supposed to be pretend, the engagement and the kissing, and... I know it was supposed to be for show. But it stopped being that for me somewhere between the dancing and Dad's heart attack, when you showed up. Or maybe... I don't know." He took her hand in both of his, praying she felt at least a hint of the depth of emotion he did. "What I felt for you in college never went away. And since I saw you again Wednesday night, my feelings have grown and... And I love you."

He forced himself to shut up. Let her talk.

"I love you too."

"Oh."

She smiled.

He didn't. "It's just... I'm going to quit my job. I mean, I have to. I have to be with Peri, and if I want to be a good father... I will be a good father."

"You *are* a good father."

Not really. Not yet. "That has to come first. So I don't know... I mean, I'm gonna be unemployed, and probably live at home. Hopefully, my parents won't make me live in the basement, but they might as well." He took a breath, blew it out. "I'm saying I'm not exactly a catch. I have nothing to offer you."

"Wow. You're really selling it."

"I'm sorry. I just..."

"Callan?"

He sealed his lips.

"I'm going to be out of work too. And the only reason I have an apartment is because Dad pays for it. I'm not exactly a catch, either. Does that change how you feel about me?"

"It's not like you'll be destitute, Paris."

"You think I won't love you if you have less money than I do? Or, let me rephrase. Than my father does? How could you love a woman who would do that?"

"I don't... That's not what I'm saying."

"Should we not act on our feelings because of short-term joblessness and short-term living arrangements?"

When she put it that way... "I hear what you're saying, but still, I have Peri."

"I get it."

"I don't know how long it'll take me to convince her she can trust me. It might be months. It might be years. Until I do that—"

"I'm in no hurry."

"That's not fair to you."

"I love you. And I love your daughter. I want what's best for you—and for her."

Callan took the words in, hope coming to life inside him as it hadn't since…since Peri had turned up in his life.

His beautiful. Perfect daughter.

He was coming to understand that maybe there wasn't a right way and a wrong way to be a father. There was just doing his best. Maybe doing well sometimes. Maybe messing up royally other times.

Loving her, through it all.

Alyssa wasn't finished. "I want you and Peri to have a strong bond. I'm no expert on this stuff, but I think that's what love is supposed to be, right? Wanting what's best? Sacrificial? Patient?"

"Yeah, that's…" He swallowed a lump. "That sounds…right."

"Then let's not worry about what it's going to look like. Let's just…wing it."

He grinned. "I thought you weren't a *wing it* kind of woman."

"I've been practicing."

That she had, and she'd done it beautifully.

He lifted her hand and kissed her knuckles. "We'll put our trust in the God who got us this far."

"There's a good idea. I mean, if He can do this…" She gestured toward the door. Toward the little girl who'd just walked out, and the men who'd risked their lives to rescue them. Toward the people who still breathed because Ghazi had been stopped.

Callan's family was safe. Her family was safe.

"He can do anything." Callan leaned in and pressed his lips to hers. Sealing their future with a kiss.

The End…

For now, but you won't want to miss the bonus epilogue. Check it out here. [INSERT LINK]

if you liked Alyssa and Callan's story, you're going to love Brooklynn's. On the quest for the perfect landscape photograph, Brooklynn witnesses a crime and runs...

Landing in the arms of a handsome stranger, who helps her escape.

Or...takes her captive.

You're going to love *Capturing You,* book 6 in the Wright heroes of Maine series. It releases spring, 2024.

DON'T WANT TO WAIT? Check out *Glimmer in the Darkness,* book one in the Coventry Saga. This story has a kidnapped little girl, an unsolved mystery, and a second-chance romance. With 2,500 reviews and ratings on Amazon—and 4.6-stars!—readers are loving it.

ALSO, check out *Escaping with You*, a Wright Heroes of Maine prequel. When Darcy and her aunt are shot at, Logan steps in to save their lives. They escape into the Maine woods to elude the shooter and reach safety.

NOW, enjoy the (unedited and very rough) first chapter of *Capturing You*.

SHE WAS FINALLY GOING to get the perfect shot.

In the gray light of pre-dawn, Brooklynn Wright shifted on the jagged outcropping of rocks, scraping her belly through her long-sleeved T-shirt. At least it was low tide. Otherwise, she'd be not just cold, but wet.

She peered at the screen of her Nikon, then at her watch, adjusted the small tripod, and snapped a few photos.

Yes. This was right.

Excitement bubbled inside of her, and she peeked at her watch.

The sun would peek over the Atlantic in four minutes.

The storm that'd moved east overnight left clear skies but turbulent waters.

She could see it, in her mind's eye. The rising sun shining through a wave as it crested and rolled.

Catching it in action, though. That was the problem.

Like too many other mornings in the last month, she'd

woken an hour before sunrise and checked the weather, then the tide. Too many of those days had had her setting up her camera on the beach at the end of the Shadow Cove's downtown.

She'd never caught the shot, no matter how she angled her camera.

It'd taken too long to find a place with the right background, the right vantage point. Finally, she'd found this secluded cove that must've once been used for something, considering the dilapidated dock in an inlet right around the rocky outcropping behind her. The adjacent property had been empty as long as Brooklynn could remember. Sad, considering the house that rose above the ocean, a gorgeous old Victorian.

Growing up, she'd heard it was haunted.

That morning, after she'd parked and before she'd trekked down the steep, rocky slope to just above the waterline, she'd gazed at the place. It was creepy, no question. She could see why people made up stories about it. But it had good bones.

She'd heard the property had sold and prayed the new owners planned to restore it. All that beauty had been wasted for too long.

One more minute to sunrise.

She snapped photos as the eastern sky turned from midnight blue to indigo.

Clouds she hadn't seen in the darkness added richness to the view as light shone around them in deep red and orange.

She adjusted the shutter speed and aperture, picking up seagulls zooming and diving, their caws adding melody to the rhythm of the surf.

Her focus shifted to the high waves crashing against the rocky cliff to her right. High enough, though? That remained to be seen.

Finally, finally, the sun climbed, clawing back darkness with its perfect light.

The birds quieted as if to mark the moment.

Beautiful.

Brooklynn snapped, snapped. Catching waves and sunlight.

Sunlight and waves.

But sunlight *through* waves? She didn't know, didn't stop to see. Just kept snapping photographs.

A low hum rumbled beneath the sound of the incoming tide, but she couldn't focus on that. She had a minute, maybe less, to get this.

Her father thought she was flighty, and...whatever. It didn't matter. But he didn't know this part of her. None of her family understood the singleminded focus it took to catch nature's fleeting moments of beauty.

If this photograph came out the way she thought it would, even if it won the prestigious [name of institution] award, her sisters would congratulate her, her mother would sing her praises. And her father would pat her on the head—metaphorically, if not physically—like a cute little puppy.

Didn't matter.

She'd given up trying to impress her father.

The hum intensified.

*Ignore it. Focus.*

When the sun was above the horizon, bathing Brooklynn and the entire Maine coast in its warm light, Brooklyn removed her camera from the tripod and flipped through the photos.

Decent. Good. Maybe great, but...

She gasped. Enlarged the tiny image.

Yes! She'd done it. Finally.

This image was everything the judges would be looking for. And even if she didn't win, it would sell.

Maybe her gallery would survive past the heavy tourist season.

A shout carried on the breeze.

What in the world?

Brooklynn stood, brushed sand off herself, and then shoved her camera and tripod into her bag before slinging it onto her back.

The shout had come from the inlet behind her. Now that she thought about it, had that hum been a boat engine?

She realized now that it'd cut off.

If Brooklynn were smart, she'd hightail it out of there before she got caught. Who knew how the new owners would feel about trespassers?

But she couldn't resist.

She climbed to the top of the rocky cliff, slipped between the few trees separating this edge of the outcropping from the other, and peeked down at the old dock.

Sure enough, a boat bumped against the rotting wood. Men—she counted five—carried boxes off the boat and stacked them on the edge of a dirt path...

*CAPTURING YOU* RELEASES THIS SPRING. Preorder your copy today.

# ALSO BY ROBIN PATCHEN

## The Wright Heroes of Maine

Running to You

Rescuing You

Finding You

Sheltering You

Protecting You

Capturing You

## The Coventry Saga

Glimmer in the Darkness

Tides of Duplicity

Betrayal of Genius

Traces of Virtue

Touch of Innocence

Inheritance of Secrets

Lineage of Corruption

Wreathed in Disgrace

Courage in the Shadows

Vengeance in the Mist

A Mountain Too Steep

## The Nutfield Saga

Convenient Lies

Twisted Lies

Generous Lies

Innocent Lies

Beautiful Lies

Legacy Rejected

Legacy Restored

Legacy Reclaimed

Legacy Redeemed

Christmas in Nutfield

## Amanda Series

Chasing Amanda

Finding Amanda

# ABOUT ROBIN PATCHEN

Robin Patchen is a *USA Today* bestselling and award-winning author of Christian romantic suspense. She grew up in a small town in New Hampshire, the setting of her Coventry Saga books, and then headed to Boston to earn a journalism degree. After college, working in marketing and public relations, she discovered how much she loathed the nine-to-five ball and chain. She started writing her first novel while she homeschooled her three children. The novel was dreadful, but her passion for storytelling didn't wane. Thankfully, as her children grew, so did her skill. Now that her kids are adults, she has more time to play with the lives of fictional heroes and heroines, wreaking havoc and working magic to give her characters happy endings. When she's not writing, she's editing or reading, proving that most of her life revolves around the twenty-six letters of the alphabet.